ACCLAIM FOR
JANE STANTON HITCHCOCK'S
NOVELS

ONE DANGEROUS LADY

"Jane Stanton Hitchcock is back and better than ever! ONE DANGEROUS LADY is full of haute crimes and glamorous social climbers—a deadly combination that will keep you turning the pages. With riveting twists and turns, and the wittiest dialogue this side of Park Avenue—high society has never been nailed with such chilling accuracy. This Hitchcock is a killer."
—LINDA FAIRSTEIN

"A delicious dark truffle to devour in one bite . . . a witty, elegant fiction about the lowdown behavior of high society. If it is fiction."
—BARBARA GOLDSMITH

"A sleek and villainous tale."
—DOMINICK DUNNE

"One terrific book . . . Jane Stanton Hitchcock makes me smile as I (quickly) turn the pages."
—Christopher Buckley

more...

"An artful romp among the rich and criminal, as well as laugh-out-loud funny. This is Hitchcock's best book yet."
—**MARIA BRENNER, author of *Great Dames***

SOCIAL CRIMES

"A killer read . . . this deliciously dark novel sneaks a knowing glimpse at a gilded world."
—*People*

"A smashing job . . . clever and funny. An amusing and highly readable x-ray of Manhattan's smart set."
—*Newsday*

"Deliciously dark and witty . . . a bubbly cocktail."
—*Library Journal*

"Sophisticated entertainment for readers with a taste for luxury and a peeping-Tom urge to spy on high society."
—*New York Observer*

"A good, sizzling novel."
—**MATT LAUER, *The Today Show***

"The most entertaining look at a small but powerful section of American society since Dominick Dunne's engaging *The Two Mrs. Carrolls*. Were Truman Capote alive, he would probably try to take credit for it . . . And if Glenn Close is shopping around for a good movie, she can start by purchasing the film rights to this novel."
—*Bay Area Reporter*

more...

"Ruth Rendell meets Dominick Dunne . . . strongly recommended."
—*Library Journal*

"Hitchcock sets out to bring New York's high society low, in a witty little book that taxes only the rich."
—*New York Daily News*

"[A] rags-to-riches story [that] generates undeniable charm and will leave readers rooting for a magical Cinderella ending."
—*Booklist*

"A riveting tale of obsession and revenge . . . It kept me up very late at night."
—Dominick Dunne

"Thrums with wicked wit and an insider's view of court life in the Manhattan and Southampton of the twenty-first century. Hitchcock has seen it and lived it and shares it all. She has a keen eye and a perfect ear."
—Marie Brenner, author of *Great Dames*

Also by Jane Stanton Hitchcock

*Social Crimes
Trick of the Eye
The Witches' Hammer

*Published by Warner Books

One Dangerous Lady

JANE STANTON HITCHCOCK

WARNER BOOKS

NEW YORK   BOSTON

This Warner Books edition is published in arrangement with Miramax Books.

Warner Books and the "W" logo are trademarks of Time Warner Inc. or an affiliated company. Used under license by Hachette Book Group USA, which is not affiliated with Time Warner Inc.

Cover design by Diane Luger
Cover photo-illustration by Shasti-O'Leary Soudant

Warner Books
Hachette Book Group USA
237 Park Avenue
New York, NY 10169
Visit our Web site at www.HachetteBookGroupUSA.com

Printed in the United States of America

First Paperback Edition: June 2007

10 9 8 7 6 5 4 3 2 1

For Jim

The social ramble ain't restful.

—Satchel Paige

One

I T IS A TRUTH UNIVERSALLY ACKNOWLEDGED
that a widow in possession of a good fortune
must be in want of a husband. Or so all my
friends constantly tell me. Being such a widow, however,
I'm a little more skeptical. Just as I'm skeptical of those
who say that doing something once makes it easier to do
a second time. That may be true of such things as sky-
diving or buying a couture dress. It is not true of murder.
Believe me, I know. But let me begin where it all began
again for me.

My name is Jo Slater and I am happy to be back on top
of the tiny, privileged world known as New York society—a hallowed, some say hollow place—from which I
had been cast out for several years because of the treachery of my late husband (may he rot in hell). I doubt I will
ever remarry, despite my friends' constant hopes and
meddling. How could I ever trust a man again? But just
because I don't want to tie a legal knot doesn't mean I've
entered a convent. I'm open to trying my luck on the

romance market once more, paltry though the pickings are in New York. That is especially true for women like myself, who are what my friend Betty Waterman calls "of an uncertain age."

Romance was not the main reason I accepted Betty and Gil Waterman's kind invitation to stay with them in Barbados for the wedding of their only daughter, Missy. Betty was, after all, one of my very closest friends, and I had known Missy her entire life. Still, the possibility of romance was definitely alluring, and Betty had made a point of letting me know that among those she had invited to join the wedding party was Lord Max Vermilion, whom she termed an international catch. Known as "the Lord of the Rings" because he had been married so many times, Max was available once more, having just been divorced from his sixth or seventh wife—no one could ever keep track, not even Max. Betty thought he would be perfect for me, if not as a husband, then at least as "a juicy walker," which was how she put it.

At a little past ten in the morning of the day before the wedding, Betty and I were having breakfast out on the terrace of the lovely, old coralstone villa on the beach the Watermans had rented for the weeklong festivities. We barely said a word to each other because the two of us were so miserably hungover from the night before. Wearing a bathing suit and one of the fluffy white terry cloth robes Betty had thoughtfully provided for me in my guest room, I poured myself a cup of strong, black coffee and gazed out over the pale aquamarine sea. Though fun, the trip so far had not turned out as I'd expected. I'd been to Barbados years ago with my late husband, Lucius Slater, and I was sure that the soft, tropical air and the leisurely rhythm of island life would provide a welcome change of pace from the hectic New York social life. How wrong I was. We hadn't stopped since I'd arrived. The constant round of lunches and dinners and excursions thus far made Manhattan seem monastic by comparison. Last night's dinner in a local restaurant had ended somewhere around two in the morning.

"I may not survive this wedding," Betty said at last. Taking a sip of her vodka-laced papaya juice, she lapsed into silence.

"So what's on the schedule for today?" I asked her.

"Well, there's a tour of Cockleshell. I suppose you'll want to go on that," she said with a dismal air.

Cockleshell was the sprawling seaside villa owned by Freddy and Mina Brill, the parents of Woody Brill, Missy Waterman's fiancé. Missy was getting married there. Mina Brill, an American married to a Brit, was an expert on gardens, and the gardens of Cockleshell were featured in a classic book entitled *Paradise Found, Splendors of the Tropical Garden*. Betty couldn't be bothered with gardens, but she knew of my passion for horticulture.

"I'd love to see them," I said.

"Fine. I'll take you. Call it an errand of mercy. But I warn you, if you and Mina start schmoozing about herbaceous borders, I'm going to deadhead the pair of you."

"Don't worry, I'm too hungover to have any kind of conversation, even about flowers."

"Max just arrived. He'll probably be there. Then tonight's the bridal dinner on the Cole yacht," she said with a glimmer of brightness. "And tomorrow, of course, is the wedding. Frankly, I can't wait for it to be over. Why Missy couldn't get married in New York and have a party at the Plaza or the St. Regis roof like everyone else is beyond me!"

With that, Betty got up from her chair and staggered over to one of the blue-and-white–striped chaises facing the ocean, where she lay down and dozed off. Alone, I sat at the table thinking about Max and about romance in general. I wasn't exactly past my prime; and it would be nice to have a steady companion, someone with whom I could travel and share common interests. In truth, though, I have to say I had less hope for myself and Max than Betty did.

Max, the eighth Earl Vermilion, was reputedly one of the richest, brightest, and most elegant men in England. The sun had never set on his personal British Empire—nor was it ever going to, if Max had anything to say about it. Taunton Hall, his ancestral home, was famous not only for its priceless Old Master paintings, including two Titians and a disputed Vermeer, but for having the largest collection of Chinese bronzes in the world. Scholars and collectors from around the globe came to sit under the vaulted arches of its sixteenth-century wing and pore over the famous collection assembled by Max's great-grandfather when he lived in China in the nineteenth century. The "Working Vermilion," as the fifth earl was called, had replenished the family fortune in the very unaristocratic way of earning money by trade. Having made millions importing tea and silk, the Vermilion family had gone on to distinguish itself as a major social and philanthropic force in England.

I had actually met Max in London years ago when I was married to Lucius, but I doubted if he would remember me. We'd all been guests at a large party. I remembered Max as a tall, handsome man with a long, thin face, bright blue eyes, thinning gray hair, and the lanky physique of an athlete. He spoke in a deep, drawly voice, which ladies found sexy. Everyone agreed that when Max turned his charm on you, he was very difficult to resist. He was polite to a fault, and brilliant, but he had a streak of mischief in him that made those who knew him wary of his charm. All his wives and mistresses said his naughtiness was both what seduced them at first and alienated them eventually. No, in so many ways he wasn't my type, and his marital record didn't bode well, either.

It was common knowledge that he was a great philanderer. In fact, the speculation was that his second-to-last wife, Henrietta, was actually driven to her grave by Max's infidelities. Still, in a world where rich, single, heterosexual men are scarcer than ninety-carat diamonds, I knew that there were literally hundreds of women, both married and single and on both sides of the Atlantic, who were now atwitter with the idea that they might become the next Lady Vermilion—especially those with whom Max already had had affairs. Unrealistic though some of those middle-aged hopes undoubtedly were, the contest had begun, and it would be interesting to see who would nab him. Betty was sure that if I stuck my foot in the ring I would get the glass slipper, because Max always married rich, socially prominent women—with one grand exception. It was rumored that Max once had a very brief marriage to a much younger woman no one knew. She was known as "the shady Lady Vermilion."

Despite all my misgivings, I had to admit that Max held a certain allure. Most of the men my age were interested in women half my age, as my last walk out with a Chicago billionaire had ultimately proved. After he suggested a threesome with our twenty-year-old female ski instructor in Aspen, I packed my bags, thinking how chivalry was not only dead but dismembered. And since

I'd always preferred older men, my horizons were narrowing. My friends were constantly trying to fix me up with that tattered crew of "eligibles" around town. I resisted their efforts because, frankly, I hated wasting even a single evening making polite conversation with some careless Casanova who was only interested in me for my social access or a free ticket to some coveted event. Better to stay home and read or watch a movie. Drawbacks aside, therefore, Max was indeed a possibility. And I confess, I was rather excited about seeing him again.

Betty finally awoke from her hungover stupor and glanced at her watch.

"If you want to see those gardens, we'd better get going," she said, hauling herself up from her chaise. "I've just been dreaming that you would marry Max and become the mistress of Taunton Hall."

" 'The Mistress of Taunton Hall' sounds like a gothic novel in which a New York socialite garners the title only to be attacked and torn to pieces on the property by a wild pack of English debutantes," I said.

"Or by Max," Betty said, as she loped into the house.

We arrived at Cockleshell at around noon. The Brills' sprawling pink stucco villa with two tennis courts, a huge swimming pool, and separate staff quarters was dramatically set under towering palm trees on six acres of prime oceanfront property. It was so big, it looked more like a hotel than a private residence. As we walked through the luscious grounds rife with exotic flowers, plants, and fragrant trees, a high-pitched, stylized laugh rang out over the air, trumping the chirping birds and rustling palms.

"That's Mina!" Betty said with irritation. "She's from Hagerstown, Maryland, but now she even *laughs* like the

Queen of England." Betty was none too fond of her only daughter's future mother-in-law.

We changed direction to follow the rippling sound. Betty led the way through an alley of towering banana palms into a little forest surrounding a man-made pond nestled among large, mossy rocks. Low-slung tree trunks curled out over this miniature lagoon like thick, black snakes. Murky rays of sunlight filtered through the thick foliage gilding patches of the dark water. Mina Brill, a tall, wild-haired woman who was dressed in a pair of khaki safari shorts, which accentuated her skinny legs, and a white T-shirt, which accentuated her large bosom, stood at the edge of the pond. Surrounded by the familiar crowd of well-heeled wedding guests we had seen throughout the week's events, she was pointing up at the trees. Everyone's gaze was intently focused on something high above in the tangle of branches.

"Uh-oh, not that fucking monkey *again*," Betty moaned as we approached. She apparently knew the drill.

When Mina spotted Betty and me out of the corner of her eye, she waved us over to join the group, signaling us with forefinger to lips to be very quiet. The air of expectancy was palpable. Betty and I trod cautiously across the lawn. No one dared move.

"The green monkey," Mina said softly as we drew close. "Be very quiet or you'll scare him away."

"With any luck," Betty muttered under her breath.

The vigil resumed. Betty scanned the group.

"I don't see Max," she whispered. "Oh, wait! There he is! Right over there!"

She pointed discreetly—or discreetly for Betty, at any rate—at a tall, attractive man standing off to one side with his arms crossed in front of him, peering up at the

trees with a slightly bemused expression on his face. Max
had the kind of looks that appear mature in youth and
young in maturity. At sixty, he was even more attractive
than I remembered him. There was a grand air of detachment about him that I suspect rather appealed to sophisticated women possessed with a slight streak of
masochism. I'm not sure why, but in observing him I
sensed immediately that he was one of those men who are
emotionally unattainable. His aloofness had a soft sheen
to it, rather like a well-worn suit of armor.

"He looks pretty good for an old codger, doesn't he?"
Betty said, nudging me.

"Betts, if he's an old codger, what does that make us?"
I asked.

"Old bats," she replied, and walked on.

I have to say that the prolonged and earnest viewing of
monkeys, however rare and exotic, is not my thing, and it
certainly isn't Betty's. For the sake of politeness, however, I stared up at the trees like everyone else, although
after a while my attention wandered, as I was more interested in looking over the crowd. I saw mainly the same
faces I'd seen all week, including Missy, the bride-to-be,
who resembled an Afghan hound with her long face and
long hair; Woody Brill, her fiancé, a clean-cut stockbroker in his late twenties; and my old pals, Ethan Monk,
now the curator of Old Master paintings at the Municipal
Museum, and Miranda Somers, the beautiful and ageless
chronicler of New York society. Miranda writes the
"Daisy" column for *Nous* magazine, and her presence at
any event signals that it is the right place to be. Miranda,
Ethan, and I had all sat at the same table the night before,
and like myself, they both seemed a little the worse for
wear. In fact, seeing their haggard faces made me wish I

was meeting Max in light slightly more forgiving than bright, tropical sunshine.

There were also some new additions to the crowd today, a few more pals, some people I didn't recognize at all, and one couple whom I hadn't seen in ages, Russell and Carla Cole. Russell Cole was Missy Waterman's billionaire godfather, and he and his wife were giving Missy her bridal dinner that night aboard their spectacular two-hundred-and-twenty-five-foot yacht called *The Lady C.* Carla Cole was Russell's controversial second wife. I didn't know her well, but I had always liked her. Theirs had been a famously celebrated and stormy union.

Anyone familiar with the history of costly breakups in New York knows that Russell Cole paid almost as dearly to get out of his first marriage as did Henry the Eighth. In a road-company version of that historic split, the Cole divorce some years ago caused a major rift in our social circle. Lulu—the first Mrs. Cole—did not only not go gently into the divorcée night, she went raging into it with the fury of a thousand women scorned. I remember Betty joking at the time, "If Russell had known Lulu was capable of that much passion, he might not have left her."

I watched the Coles as they stood next to each other, attired in color-coordinated outfits. With their fixed smiles and slightly vacant demeanors, they subtly proclaimed a pampered and privileged existence, a life lived far above the fray. They were both uncannily well groomed, neat and immaculate in chic, razor-pressed linen with shiny, unwilted hair. Their manicured appearance was miraculously immune to the humidity. It was as if their presentation was in some inexplicable way a great measure of their life together. The accoutrements of wealth—the custom-made resort clothes, the most expensive watches, the latest sunglasses, etc.—were on view, but they were understated, not flashy or obvious, meant only for those who understood them.

Russell Cole, in his late fifties, was not a prepossessing man. He had a slim build and was only slightly taller than his much younger wife. His boyish face harbored a pair of melancholy gray eyes. He had sand-colored hair, perfectly parted to one side, and the rigid stance of someone who either had once been to military school or had served in the armed forces. He was wearing a pale blue voile shirt, and in a chic, offbeat touch, he had threaded a blue necktie through the loops of the waistband of his cream linen trousers and tied it in a loose knot off to one side. Very Fred Astaire.

Carla, a striking woman in her late thirties, had asymmetrical features and an exotic aura. She was truly what the French call a *jolie laide*—a "beautiful ugly." Her nose was slightly too long, her eyes were set too close together, and her lips were thin, like two slashes. Yet all together, they formed a fascinating face, enhanced by her inner vivacity and the allure of a throaty foreign accent. She had luminous skin, which, despite the fact that she spent most of her time on a boat, was creamy white, as if she never saw the sun.

"Oh, look! There's Russell and Carla," Betty said. "I've gotta talk to Carla about tonight. Come with me."

As we quietly edged our way closer to the Coles, there was a sudden, faint swishing noise in the branches above. Mina went on high alert.

"There!" she said, pointing up. *"He's there!"*

Betty and I paused to look. I saw the glint of what could conceivably have been a simian face—or, more likely, the knot of a tree exposed when a gust of wind parted the surrounding leaves. I couldn't tell which, and I seriously doubted if anyone else could, either. Nor, I might add, did we care.

"*See him there! There!*" Mina cried out.

Betty and I kept our eyes peeled, straining to see what some of the others apparently saw, until finally young Woody Brill threw his hands up in exasperation and stormed off, saying, "Forget it, Mother! That bloody monkey's a figment of your imagination!"

The spell effectively broken, everyone began chattering away, obviously filled with relief. Betty and I continued heading over to the Coles and to Max, who was standing nearby.

"Carla, darling!" Betty shrieked. "You're here!"

"Well, of course, we are, darling," she said in her husky Italian accent. "We could not let you have the bridal dinner in the water, after all."

Forced laughter all around.

"And, of course, you both know Jo Slater," Betty said.

"Jo!" Carla cried. "So nice to see you again! We were very excited when Betty told us you were coming."

Carla and I air kissed on both cheeks. I had always preferred the younger woman to Russell's first wife, Lulu, who had dropped me the second I lost all my money and, indeed, had befriended my late husband's mistress. But that's another story.

"Hello, Carla, it's so nice to see you again. And Russell. How are you?"

"Hi, Jo," Russell said with his usual reserve.

"We never see you guys around New York," Betty said. "You're both so busy gallivanting around the world in that big, beautiful tub of yours."

Russell gave her a thin smile. It was well known that Russell adored his yacht *The Lady C.*

Betty leaned in and whispered conspiratorially to Carla, "Do you know Max Vermilion?"

"Well, we have met, of course," Carla said. "But I cannot say we *know* him, no."

I noticed how Carla referred to herself as "we," as though she and Russell were one person. Then Betty said something that made me want to kill her.

"I want to fix Jo up with Max. He's such a fabulous eligible, and we all know how much he loves attractive, rich, and cultivated women!"

My teeth clenched as I cringed with embarrassment. "*Betteeee* . . ." I said softly.

Betty was someone who thought that the love life of all single women was fair game for general conversation—even among relative strangers. It was one of her most annoying traits.

"Oh, come on, Jo, now don't be shy," she went on, irritatingly oblivious to my discomfort. "I'm going to take you over and introduce you to Max this minute."

She grabbed my arm, but I demurred.

"Not just now," I said, shrugging her off. I couldn't think of anything worse than having Betty drag me over to Max like some sort of prom wallflower who had asked to meet the most popular boy in senior class.

It was not long, however, before Max approached us with a mischievous twinkle in his eye. He tapped Betty on the shoulder and said in his very laid-back, upper-crust English accent, "I say, is that the bride or the mother?"

Betty whirled around.

"*Max!*" she exclaimed, throwing her arms around him. "How're ya, kiddo?"

"It's the mother! I could hardly tell the difference. Betty, dear, how lovely to see you. Don't you look marvelous!"

"You look pretty swell yourself. Divorce obviously agrees with you."

"No, but settlements do," he said dryly.

"Do you know everyone here? Russell and Carla Cole? My best friend, Jo Slater?"

Max bowed slightly to the Coles. "We have already greeted one another," he said. "But I haven't seen this charming lady in a very long time." He mock kissed my hand. "I wonder if you remember me, Jo. We met years ago on a private tour of the Tate."

"I remember it well, Max. You love Louis the Sixteenth furniture as much as I do, as I recall."

"Indeed. How lovely to see you again after all this time." His bright blue eyes met mine. Even in a crowd, he made me feel as if I were the only one he was really interested in talking to.

Max was still an able flirt. What would have seemed rather oily in another man, merely added to Max's veneer of charm. I think that's because he had a slightly mocking air about him, as if he didn't take anything seriously, least of all himself. It was obvious why he was catnip to women.

"And where is my good friend Gil? Scouring the island for hidden treasure?" Max said, referring to Betty's art dealer husband.

"On the golf course, where else? Christ, if you think I could get Gil over to look at gardens and invisible monkeys, you're crazy."

Max smiled somewhat tolerantly at Betty's brashness. He looked like he was going to say something dismissive like, "You Americans . . ." but he resisted.

Mina then stalked over and looped her arm through Max's arm and dragged him off to the next point of interest, her orchids. He looked back at me rather soulfully, I thought, as if he'd rather have stayed behind. Betty and Carla followed suit, walking away together, deep in conversation about the upcoming bridal dinner that night. I lagged behind with Russell Cole. I didn't want to look as if I were chasing after Max. Also, Russell hung back from the crowd, and I sensed he wanted to talk to me.

"It's so nice to see you again, Jo," he said. "A friendly face from the old days."

By "the old days," he meant premillennium New York when Russell was married to Lulu and I was married to my first and only husband, that rat, the late Lucius Slater—a time that now seemed to me as distant and uncomplicated as the Stone Age. We chitchatted about this and that, how time flies, how people change—or don't, as the case may be. I asked Russell if he was enjoying the peripatetic existence of the perennial yachtsman. He said he "rather liked" traveling the world, "deciding where to go, as we go." He then described a life of endless options.

Picking up anchor whenever one felt like it and sailing anywhere in the world on a moment's notice may sound idyllic, but I knew from observation that that sort of eternal aimlessness can easily wear thin, and eventually lead to only one real destination, boredom. And, indeed, as Russell and I strolled together and he aimlessly brushed some leaves with his hand, I sensed that the old, deep-seated weariness had returned. He had lost his exuberance and seemed a bit the way he was during his final years with Lulu—polite but distant, slightly distracted, a touch melancholy, and shy of crowds.

"That was an awful thing that Lucius did to you," he suddenly said to me.

"Yes, it was," I said softly, as we continued to stroll.

"And you had absolutely no idea? No sense that he was betraying you?"

"Not a clue. I can tell you, it was a quite a shock. But all's well that ends well, as they say. And here I am."

That episode of my life now seemed like a bad dream. Russell was, of course, referring to the fact that my late husband, who had been carrying on an affair for a year behind my back, compounded the outrage of his infidelity by leaving all his money to his mistress when he died. I figured that was the reason Russell had hung back to talk to me, to let me know he empathized with what I'd gone through. But it was over now and I saw no point in dwelling on it.

"Do you think it's possible to ever really know another human being?" Russell asked me.

"Well, based on experience, I'd have to say no," I replied, half joking, thinking of how profoundly my husband had deceived me.

"No, I don't think so, either. Because so few of us really know ourselves, you see. And if we don't know ourselves, how can we possibly expect someone else to know us?"

"That's very true," I responded, although when I looked at Russell I realized that he was talking more to himself than to me.

Then he said, "How well do you know yourself, Jo?"

Rather a heavy question for a casual afternoon stroll, I thought.

Flashing back on all I'd gone through, I replied, "Well, I believe I'm better acquainted with myself than I once was. How about you?"

"Me?" He seemed surprised by the question. He thought for a long moment, a pensive look on his face, and finally said, "I'm kind of like that monkey in the tree."

His intriguing answer made me smile. "How so?"

"Well, sometimes I think I get a glimpse of myself. But I can't be sure if it's really me or not. And then . . ." He stopped suddenly, as if deep in thought.

"And then . . .?"

"Then I disappear," he said with a little shrug.

Two

"SO WHADDYA THINK OF MAX?" BETTY SAID excitedly on the way back home from the Brills'.

"From the little I saw of him, I thought he was pretty attractive."

"He likes you. I can tell."

"How on earth can you tell that? We hardly said two words to each other."

"Oh, don't be so coy, Jo. He couldn't take his eyes off you."

"Let's not exaggerate, Betts. I think that's more a reflex than true love."

"Yeah, well, I'm seating you next to him at the wedding. And I told Carla to be sure and put him next to you tonight at the bridal dinner."

"Betty, overkill. Hello!"

"Listen, sweetie, you know as well as I do that you gotta grab 'em while they're available! Exposure, that's the key. Just imagine Max as a stag with a pack of couture dogs on his trail. You've gotta be fast and strong and ready to pounce. I remember when Gil and I were courting and I invited him up to see *my* etchings. Literally. I kid you not. Faint heart ne'er won rich eligible."

"Whatever happened to the idea of men pursuing women?" I asked her.

"Whatever happened to quill pens?!" she said in exasperation. "Listen to me, Jo, just getting these guys to sit still long enough to really get to know you is almost an impossibility nowadays. Here you have not one, but *two* great shots at one of the world's most desirable bachelors. I say go for it."

Betty had a point. I liked Max, or at least I liked my impression of him, and as I dressed for the bridal dinner that night, I took special care with my appearance as one does when the scent of romance is in the air. The humidity of the tropics is not exactly conducive to good grooming, however, and my short blonde hair was not cooperating as well as it might have. It looked less like a sleek helmet and more like a straw hat. However, after I applied my makeup and put on a form-fitting cream-colored silk sheath and some colorful vintage costume jewelry, I looked in the mirror and thought, Well, not too bad.

I'd fared pretty well over the years. I'm about five foot, six inches tall and not what you would call a beauty, by any means, but my blue eyes are set far apart and I have small, regular features that seem to complement one another well enough. In my youth I was considered quite pretty. And while age has taken its toll somewhat, I still have a good sense of style, which in the long haul is more important than looks. I favor a simple cut in clothes, and I'm back in shape now, doing exercises with a trainer four times a week and usually sticking to my diet. I occasionally toy with having a face-lift, but I'm holding out for the time when they invent a form of Krazy Glue where you can just go home, hike your face up to where you want it, and cement it in place.

I think Betty was more nervous about me and Max getting together than she was about her own daughter getting married the next day. When I walked out onto the terrace, she looked me over with a critical eye.

"Couldn't you have worn something a little sexier? I mean, you look great, but you look like a column," she said.

She was a fine one to talk. Betty, who was famous for her truly terrible taste in clothes, would disappoint none of her detractors that night. She looked like an enormous trellis of bougainvillea, dressed as she was in a long dress studded with tiny fuchsia chiffon flowers. Not only did the color clash with her red hair, the effect of the dress made her look a lot heftier than she actually was.

"Well, I think Jo looks divine. In fact, I think you both look divine," Gil said, ever the chivalrous husband.

"You look pretty spiffy there yourself," I said to Gil, as he handed me one of his lethal rum punches.

Gil Waterman was a tall, athletic man in his fifties, with craggy good looks and a jutting jaw. He always wore thick-framed, black glasses and an earnest expression. On this eve of his only daughter's wedding, he looked particularly dapper in his custom-made tuxedo and black needlepoint pumps embroidered in red with his initials.

"Well, there she is," Gil said, pointing out at the sea. "I can't believe I'm finally going to get to see her."

A large white yacht was anchored in the distance, shimmering on the dusky water.

"Wow," I said admiringly. "That's a big boat."

"Not that big by today's standards, but très luxurious. Russell built it for Carla," Betty said. "It's their real home."

"Don't they have an apartment in New York?" I inquired.

"Not in years. Russell hates New York," Gil said. "He goes there as little as possible."

"That's because Lulu's there," Betty said. "The town ain't big enough for the three of them. The whole continent isn't."

"No," Gil said thoughtfully. "I think Russell just hates the city. He's not a big one for social life, you know."

"I know, but I don't see how Carla stands it all the time on that tub. I don't care how nice it is. Can you imagine spending your life on a boat? I'd go completely nuts," Betty said.

I seconded her. "Who was it who said, 'Boats are prisons on which you can drown'?"

"Me!" Betty cried.

Just then, Missy Waterman walked out onto the terrace. The twenty-seven-year-old bride-to-be had eschewed her trademark shaggy grooming and funky clothes for neat hair, an elegant blue silk evening dress, and the heirloom sapphire-and-diamond necklace Betty and Gil had given their beloved only child as a wedding present. A self-styled "video artist," Missy had lived at home like a teenager for years, keeping odd hours and odder friends, going through the rugged patch of experimenting with drugs and alcohol, which her art dealer father tactfully referred to as Missy's Blue Period. Gil and Betty were understandably thrilled that their unconventional daughter was finally settling down, and that she had chosen a husband not from the ranks of the tortured, tatooed, body-pierced boyfriends she had favored in the past, but Woodson "Woody" Brill, who was a nice, clean-cut young man and from an eminently respectable family.

Gil, obviously moved by the sight of his daughter, gave Missy a little hug. His eyes grew moist and then he said, "Well, I guess we'd better get going."

"Now have fun tonight, sweetie," Betty said. "Enjoy your freedom, because tomorrow you'll be hauling an old ball and chain around like the rest of us."

Betty had a tough time with sentimental moments.

"I can't wait to see the Cole collection," Gil said to me as we walked down to the dock.

"Oh, Gil, all you ever think about is art," Betty said dismissively.

"That's not true. I think about golf . . . anyway, you're all in for a treat."

Gil explained to us all that the Cole collection had been started by Russell's father in the days when some of the greatest Impressionist and post-Impressionist pictures were still on the market. Russell, who loved art, had added significantly to his father's legacy after his father died. He expanded the collection to include twentieth-century masters like Pollock, Rothko, Jasper Johns, de Kooning, and Lucian Freud, to name but a few. Unlike some collections that are simply a catalog of famous signatures on mediocre works, the Cole collection was truly remarkable for the superb quality of each and every one of its paintings.

"Russell Cole has the three things an important collector needs, a great eye, a great fortune, and a great dealer—me!" Gil said with a wink.

Missy, who referred to her godfather as "uncle," said, "You sold Uncle Russell a lot of his paintings, didn't you, Dad?"

"I most certainly did," Gil said proudly. "*The Lady C* is a floating museum. I'm hoping Russell will take us on a private tour before dinner. Can you believe I've never seen this boat?"

"That's because you're such an old stick in the mud, honey. God knows they've invited us to cruise with them. But you won't go. You won't go anywhere but Southampton," Betty said.

"I go to Lyford," Gil said defensively.

"The only way you could get Dad on a boat for any length of time is if they had a golf course on board. Right, Dad?" Missy laughed and gently nudged her father.

"I see nothing wrong with liking golf," Gil said.

"Most boring game *ever* created, with the possible exception of curling!" Betty groaned. "Plus, there's gotta be something deeply Freudian about wanting to get a tiny ball in a tiny hole over and over and over again. Don'tchya think?"

"Frankly, it's the same thing as wanting to get a little ball across a net all the time," Gil countered. "I mean, I used to like tennis all right. But then one day I had this overwhelming feeling of futility about the game. I saw the ball coming at me and I thought, 'Wait a minute, didn't I just hit that little sucker?' I put down my racket and I never picked it up again."

"Oh, that's such a big, fat lie!" Betty said irritably. "I played with you twice last summer and I beat you both times."

Betty and Gil were like the proverbial Bickersons, but beneath their bantering was real affection.

We finally reached the dock. A large tender was there, ready to take us out to the yacht. We were helped on board the motorboat one at a time by two crew members wearing white T-shirts on which THE LADY C was discreetly embroidered in red, along with a little crest. The motor revved up and we glided over the darkening water toward the huge, white boat, aglow with a kind of ethereal light. Alone on the sea, set against a purple sky, the massive craft looked like a surreal apartment building. As we approached, the bouncy Latin rhythms of a famous salsa band, flown in from New York just for the occasion, wafted through the air, getting everyone in the mood for an evening of fun and sentiment. Missy squeezed her father's hand and put her head affectionately on his shoulder as we skimmed along the water.

There was limited space on *The Lady C*, which meant that only a hundred guests could be accommodated for the dinner. Once on board, we all trooped up a flight of steps to the main deck where Carla Cole, blazing with turquoise and diamonds, greeted us effusively.

"Welcome! Welcome to our little home, everyone!" she said.

"She means her little house on the water prairie," Betty whispered to me, making fun of Carla's overly humble description of the magnificent yacht.

Some of the other guests were already there, including Ethan Monk and Miranda Somers. Ethan sidled up to me and said, "You think we can get a look at the collection?"

"I don't know. Ask Gil. He's dying to see it."

Carla was a good hostess, introducing everyone to everyone, and making us all feel welcome. I looked around for Max, but didn't see him. Stewards wearing the more formal white-and-gold uniform of the yacht passed around silver trays loaded with a sublime concoction made of champagne and fresh mango juice and some other unidentifiable liquor, which Betty and I later figured out must have been absinthe because it was so strong. I had two sips and my head started spinning. Betty was working on her second glass before I could warn her to watch her step.

"These things are lethal," I said.

"Good, I need something lethal to get me through this evening. Where the fuck is Max?" she said.

More and more guests arrived, ferried out to the yacht in groups of ten. Soon there was a large crowd, including several new faces—lots of young people, who were friends of Missy and Woody's, plus friends of the Watermans and the Brills who had flown in just for the wedding. Most of the guests were from New York, but several were from England, Europe, and South America, and every so often the hum of the festive atmophere was pierced by cries of delight from friends who hadn't clapped eyes on one another in some time.

I said hello to Russell, who was standing off in a corner by himself. He seemed to be very distant and distracted. He was holding a drink and at one point he raised his glass to me and said, "To green monkeys—human and otherwise."

I had no idea what he meant and I thought he might have been a bit drunk.

Gil came over to us with Carla, who said, "Russell, darling, Gil is dying to see the collection. Can we give him a little tour?"

Russell looked at her dourly. "I guess."

"We will sneak away for a few moments. . . . No one will miss us," Carla said.

Gil was beside himself with excitement. He particularly wanted us to see Russell's latest acquisition, a Cézanne portrait of a woman in a red hat, which he had obtained for the Coles from a private collection in France. Believed to have been lost in the war, it was considered to be one of the artist's greatest pictures. Ethan, Miranda, and I all accompanied the Coles and the Watermans on the speedy private tour. We went inside and walked through the hallways, suites, and cabins of the yacht, marveling at the compact gracefulness of the boat, and at the great pictures. First-rate examples of artists like Monet, Renoir, Matisse, Picasso, plus a scattering of slightly lesser luminaries like Vlaminck, Van Dongen, and Sisley, hung in immovable frames, all of which, we were quickly told, had alarms attached. Lit by unseen lights, the paintings shone like jewels against the dark mahogany paneling, gracing the interiors with a profound and unexpected beauty. Russell, a shy man who clearly didn't like showing off his wealth or even the collection of which he was so proud, hurried us along without any commentary, forcing Gil to surreptitiously point out various works, whispering, "I sold them that," or, "They got that from me."

Carla and Russell each had their own unconnected living quarters, large, lavishly appointed suites with walk-in closets, huge marble bathrooms with gold fixtures, and separate dressing and sitting rooms. In order to get from one cabin complex to the other, you had to walk out into a private corridor.

Russell's suite was sleekly furnished in shades of beige and gray. Curiously enough, there was almost no art in his cabin—just one picture, a stark gray-and-black Rothko above the bed, which I found depressing, and a miniscule Giacometti bronze sculpture, the skeletal figure of man with a tormented face. Despite its luxury, the cabin had the impersonal feeling of a hotel room.

Carla's quarters were just the opposite. Her suite was decorated like a boudoir in an eighteenth-century *hôtel particulier*. No dark mahogany for her. The walls of her cabin were paneled with pale blue-and-white wood, distressed to make them look antique. In contrast to her husband, Carla preferred to live with watercolors depicting pretty country scenes and detailed interiors of royal rooms. In her dressing room hung a lovely little study of a woman seated on a chair wearing a flowing, white dress and a large straw hat covered with a gauzy veil that partially obscured her face. The picture's initial charm turned macabre on closer inspection, as the viewer realized that the faint outline beneath the veil was not, in fact, a face, but a skull. Carla stopped in front of the little oddity, explaining that it was an anonymous Dutch *vanitas* picture of the eighteenth century she had picked up for a pittance in a flea market in Paris.

"I think it is most amusing, no?" Carla said as we passed it.

"*No*," Betty blurted out. "I mean *yes*," she quickly corrected herself, rolling her eyes at me. If Carla heard the slip, she ignored it.

The tour concluded, we all trooped up to the main deck. There was still no sign of Max. Betty, who was fearless and at this point rather tipsy, said to Carla, "So where the hell is Lord Vermilion?"

Carla smiled sweetly. "I am afraid that Max could not come tonight."

"*What*?" Betty screeched. "Why the hell not? We talked about the seating this morning! You were supposed to put him next to Jo, remember?"

"I do not know," Carla said with a shrug. "He canceled at the last moment."

Betty and I looked at each other. I have to admit, I felt somewhat of a letdown. Betty pressed Carla, asking her if Max had given any reason for the cancellation, but Carla was oddly evasive. She walked off saying she had to attend to her other guests. Later on, Miranda Somers, who knew the scoop on everybody, and who had in fact been the one who broke the story that Russell had left his wife of twenty-some years and had run off with Carla, told us the real reason that Max Vermilion wasn't there that night.

"The reason Max isn't here is because Russell disinvited him," Miranda said. "Russell practically had a conniption fit when he found out Max was coming."

"*Why*?" Betty asked.

Miranda paused for effect. "Because Max has been dating *Lulu*," she said with a knowing air.

Lulu Cole, of course, was Russell Cole's vindictive ex-wife.

Betty's jaw dropped. "You are fucking kidding me! He's dating the Chiffon Bulldozer? I don't fucking well believe it. How did she get her claws into him so fast?"

Betty always referred to Lulu as "the Chiffon Bulldozer" because of Lulu's airy determination to control whatever environment she was in. Lulu Cole was just the opposite of her ex-husband. A taut, resolute woman with a strict sense of style, Lulu threw herself into everything she did and at everyone she met—particularly when it was in her best interests. This quality was both her strength and her weakness. Lulu got a lot done, but made many enemies in the process. She had a knack of stepping on other people's toes and not saying "excuse me."

However, even her detractors—of which there were many—said she was a "capable" woman, brimming with generosity, energy, and organizational talents.

As Betty and Miranda discussed this new development, my mind drifted back to the days when the billionaire Coles first moved to Manhattan in the early nineties. Russell was then married to Marylou Cole, or Lulu, as she was called. Primed in the ways of social climbing, they bought an expensive apartment in one of the best buildings on Fifth Avenue, hired a chic decorator, donated ostentatiously to "fashionable" charities, and, most importantly, gave grand parties to which everyone yearned to go, if only to see Van Gogh's *Irises*, for which Russell Cole had paid a record sixty-five million dollars at auction. Lulu discovered Paris couture and became a great supporter of the Metropolitan Museum's Costume Institute. She bought signed vintage jewelry from Pearce, the glittery shop on Madison Avenue which was then in its heyday, and she arrived on the Best Dressed List in short order.

Photographed at chic opening nights and benefit galas, the Coles quickly became stars in *Nous* magazine, society's scrapbook. In her "Daisy" column for the magazine, Miranda herself had recoined the phrase "a Lulu of a party," paying homage to Lulu Cole's formal dinners. In short, the Coles made all the right moves and soon reached the highest-level social life in the city, in a position to judge newcomers with the same catty eye by which they themselves had once been judged.

But as anyone who has ever endured the charity ball circuit will tell you, the smiles of social life are often masks for deep unhappiness. And Russell Cole was not happy. His rugged, midwestern good looks were bruised by melancholy. In conversation, his considerable charm was tainted by detachment.

As Lulu's interest in social life increased, Russell's interest waned. It seemed the more he marched, the more he tired of the parade. People who saw the Coles together often remarked on the lack of intimacy between them, and on the fact that Russell looked terminally bored. Betty said to me way back when, "You'd be bored, too, if you were treated like an accessory."

Then, six years ago, Russell Cole bolted, with no warning. He left his chic and proper wife to marry Carla, who was then Carla Hernandez, an exotic widow with a murky past, more than twenty years his junior. Rumor had it Russell fell for Carla at a gala benefit when she flirtatiously started a bread fight with him from across the dinner table. He had asked her to dance and that apparently was that.

But Lulu was a fighter with a lot to fight for. She'd been married to Russell for over twenty-five years and she was the mother of his only child, a daughter named Courtney. When it became clear that Carla was not a passing fancy, Lulu hired a bomber lawyer who sicced a pack of private detectives on the flagrant couple. Lulu's hatred of Carla, already in full bloom, was fertilized by what she found out about Carla's background. The divorce dragged on for two gruelling years. Lulu eventually settled out of court for a rumored two-hundred-and-fifty million dollars, plus real estate, plus artwork, on the strict condition she would never speak about the case, the settlement, or the past of the future Mrs. Cole.

The exact nature of the dirt she'd uncovered on Carla remained a topic of gossip in the social world for years, although people assumed that Carla was simply one more in that long line of courtesans and call girls who quickly launder their pasts once they marry rich men. And no one much cared whether Carla had been a call girl or not— no one except my other best friend, June Kahn, that is, who remained steadfastly loyal to Lulu and who always referred to Carla as "the hookerina."

Carla's wedding to Russell famously divided New York. "To go or not to go——" that was the question. Obviously, those who went would incur Lulu's wrath. And those who did not go had little hope of joining the charmed circle of the notorious newlyweds. June Kahn had no problem. She boycotted the wedding. June was a foul-weather friend who loved taking up lost causes. She became an even greater friend of Lulu after Russell left her. Betty was in a trickier situation because not only was Russell Cole the godfather of her child, he was one of her husband's biggest clients. Betty and Gil went to the wedding. Lulu never forgave them.

As for myself, I was invited and I very much appreciated the invitation—particularly because at that period in my life I was down on my luck and invitations to anything other than clearance sales were in short supply. I would have liked to have gone, but it was a period when I was just too depressed to attend social functions. I heard from Betty that it had been quite a shindig. She said that Russell Cole looked years younger, and his entire toast to his bride was a single whoop of joy.

"Hey, that's what happens when you finally get laid," Betty had said at the time.

And now Lord Max Vermilion was dating the first Mrs. Cole, which supposedly was why Russell was in a bad mood. But why? I wondered. Why would he give a damn?

*   *   *

The bridal dinner took place two flights up on the sun deck, amidst a little topiary forest, the theme of which was Wonderland because *Alice in Wonderland* was Missy's favorite childhood book. There were boxwood bushes cut in the shapes of the characters from the Lewis Carroll classic—the White Rabbit, the Cheshire Cat, the Red Queen, the Mad Hatter, Tweedledum and Tweedledee, the Dormouse, the Caterpillar, and Alice herself. It was cozy and spectacular at the same time. A real tour de force.

Ten round tables seating ten guests each were elegantly set with votive candles, antique silver, cut crystal glasses, and blue-and-white Chinese export vases brimming with fresh tropical flowers. At the place of each guest was a telltale red box tied prettily with white ribbon. One eager person at our table immediately opened the gift, inspiring the rest of us to do likewise. The boxes contained small gold Cartier desk clocks with diamond hands, each one individually engraved with the date of the wedding-to-be.

Later on, Betty and I figured out the little favors had to have cost a few hundred thousand dollars, probably more, prompting Betty to remark, "I always say there's nothing like a Cartier clock to count the minutes until the revolution."

I was seated across the table from Russell Cole, who was flanked by Betty and Mina Brill. He looked morose throughout the dinner, and when the time came, he gave a tepid toast. He and Carla didn't look at each other all evening. Something had happened between the two of them, and Betty and I figured it must have had something to do with Max, although I still found it a little hard to believe that Russell would care who was going out with his ex-wife, especially after all these years.

"They should have told me they didn't want him in the first place," Betty said. "Poor old Maxy—all alone at the Sandy Lane Hotel. Although, if I know Max, he's probably found ample companionship."

Visible in the distance, across an expanse of black sea, was King's Fort, the rented villa where the Watermans and I were staying. The sky was sprinkled with stars. A pale moon hovered just above the horizon. I thought how nice it would have been to get to know Max better under those circumstances, but fate had obviously had other plans for us.

In any case, no one had any idea what was in store the next day, nor that what happened after that bridal dinner was to become the stuff of legend, as well as one of the great mysteries of the social world of New York.

Three

A T NINE THE NEXT MORNING — THE WEDDING day — Betty and I staggered out onto the terrace for breakfast. Betty was wearing a loud, flower-print caftan, a thatched roof masquerading as a hat, and a pair of extremely large, extremely dark sunglasses. I was once again in my beloved terry cloth robe. I looked out over the ocean where the Coles' big white yacht gleamed like an evil smile on the horizon — a floating reminder of where I got my headache. Betty walked very slowly toward one of the chaises and eased herself down onto the long, striped cushion with great care. She kept the upper half of her body very still as she moved, as if she were trying to balance her head on her shoulders to keep it from falling off. Dermott, the tall, reed-thin, coffee-colored majordomo, was standing by with her usual — vodka and papaya juice — Betty's own "homeopathic" remedy for a hangover. She took a long sip, then let out the most enormous groan.

"Don't worry, Betts. It'll all be over soon," I said.

"What? Me or the wedding? Just bury me here, okay? Under a palm tree. Because I'm dead. Why I said I'd give this lunch today is beyond me. . . . Oh well, I have to go over the seating for the wedding dinner with Mina anyway. Tonight you are *definitely* getting a crack at Max. I wonder where the old bugger went last night. Probably to find 'a bit of strange.' "

"What's that?" I asked.

"Oh, that's that wonderful expression the English have for extracurricular sexual activity."

" 'A bit of strange.' I like that."

"So does Max, from what I hear."

With that, Betty turned her face up to the sun and lay still. I sat motionless in my chair, staring out at the sun-spangled water. Hazy memories of the previous alcohol-drenched evening were tumbling through my mind in slow motion when my eyes gradually focused on a motorboat hurtling toward us. At first I dismissed it as just another pleasure craft out for a jaunt on a Saturday morning. Then I realized it was aiming straight for our little dock. As it neared, I recognized it as one of the tenders from *The Lady C*.

Jasper Jenks, the handsome, young Australian captain of the yacht, was standing up in the bow, stiff and alert in his spiffy white-with-gold-trim uniform and matching cap. Behind him sat two crewmen, gripping the sides of the boat as it bumped along the waves. In the stern sat Carla Cole, dressed in white, wearing sunglasses, a white scarf tied tightly around her head. Loose strands of her rust-colored hair blew in the wind. The helmsman slowed the motor and cut the power, expertly steering the boat alongside the small jetty. The two crewmen immediately jumped out and secured the craft. The captain gave his hand to Carla as he guided her up out of the boat and onto the sturdy wood planks of the dock.

"Well, well, well, look who's here," I said, too tired to point at the little boat.

Betty cracked open an eye. "*Oh, Gawd!*" she groaned. "Don't *tell* me that's Carla! I invited them for lunch, not *breakfast*, for Chrissakes. What the fuck time is it?" She glanced at her watch. "Not even nine. *Shit.*"

Betty managed to rise from her chair and muster a wave and a smile at Carla, who was trotting up the beach toward the villa with the muscular young captain at her side. I, too, waved hello to our hostess of the night before, although my greeting was somewhat compromised by the pain of a nuclear headache. As Carla hurried across the lawn toward the steps of the flagstone veranda, Betty called out, "Carla, darling! That was the *most* divine party last night! Missy was thrilled. Thank you so much!"

The closer Carla got, the more apparent it became that she was in great distress. When she and the captain finally reached us on the patio, she stopped to recover her breath. Removing her sunglasses, her eyes darted anxiously between the two of us.

"Have either of you seen Russell?" she said, still panting.

Betty and I glanced at each other.

"Not since last night," Betty replied.

Carla touched her hand to her forehead and reeled slightly, as if she were going to faint. The captain steadied her. Betty and I then ushered her to a chair. Betty offered her something to drink, but she declined with a shake of her head.

The captain said in his chipper Australian accent, "Captain Jenks, at your service, ladies. Mind if me and my lads have a look 'round the property?"

Betty, who was more concerned about Carla, waved him off, "Yeah, sure, go ahead."

He trotted away. Betty and I pulled up chairs and sat down beside Carla, who stared into space as if she were in shock.

"Carla, honey, what's wrong? What happened?" Betty said.

No response.

Betty took off her sunglasses to make eye contact with me, but she quickly put them back on again because the light was too intense for her eyes. Betty knew from long years of experience that the hungover body had to be "eased into sobriety" the morning after, and I could see she dreaded coping with this drama. She braced herself with several sips of her spiked papaya juice, then said more firmly and with a hint of irritation, "Please, Carla . . . you *have* to tell us what's going on." Betty had no patience for coyness before noon.

Carla flicked her eyes up at Betty.

"Russell is gone. We found his scull floating in the water."

"His *skull*?" Betty ripped off her glasses and flung me a horrified look.

Carla's head bobbed up and down. "Yes, he takes it out in the mornings for exercise when the sea is calm. He loves to row."

"Oh, *that* kind of scull," Betty said, relieved. "Look, sweetie, I know you're upset, but try to tell us *exactly* what happened."

Carla laid her sunglasses down on the table and took off her scarf. She spoke slowly and deliberately, staring into the distance as if she were reliving each moment in her mind.

"Russell and I got to bed quite late on account of the party," she began.

"Thank you again, by the way. It was an absolutely marvelous evening," Betty exclaimed. I found her polite interjection a little macabre at this point, what with a potential body floating around in the water. But Betty was oblivious.

"Thank you, darling, you are sweet," Carla said, acknowledging her. "Anyway, the last launch left just after three o'clock. Russell had had a great deal to drink . . ."

"Join the club," Betty said.

"He was a bit unsteady," Carla went on, "so I helped him to his room. We said good night and I went to my room as usual. Russell often gets up in the middle of the night or very early in the morning to go work on his computer. He does not like to disturb me. He's such a considerate man . . . a wonderful man . . ." she said, her voice cracking with sentiment. She recovered and went on, "Sometimes he knocks on my door to see if I am awake. He loves to tell me the news . . . He Googles everyone, you know, to find out all about them. . . . Anyway, this morning, I heard the tapping on my door at a very early hour, and of course, I thought it was Russ. But it was not. It was the captain. He apologized for waking me up. He said that they had found the scull floating nearby in the sea and it was empty. Naturally, they immediately checked to see if Russell was in his cabin. He was not. So now they were checking to see if he was with me. Well! You can imagine how I felt. I was frantic. *Frantic*! So I got up immediately and put on a dressing gown and we all searched the yacht. But he was nowhere. I thought that perhaps he had swam ashore. So I got dressed and came here and . . ." Her voice trailed off. "*Oh, God. He's gone,"* she cried, as if the idea were dawning on her for the very first time.

As I looked at the distraught younger woman, I couldn't help thinking that if Russell Cole had indeed drowned, what a bizarre and tragic twist it was to one of New York's most notorious love affairs.

Carla managed to get a grip on herself. She talked on, going over the events she had just described in more detail. I felt sorry for her. However, I remember thinking even then that there was something slightly studied about her distress, some note that didn't quite ring true. It was as though she were watching herself from afar, rather than really living in the moment. At the time, I chalked it up to shock.

"Russell loves rowing," she went on. "He was a champion in college and he does not understand that he must be very careful in these waters. When he gets into that scull, he thinks he is young again, and immortal. I have warned him over and over not to take that thing out when there is no one watching. *Oh, why he did not listen to me?!"* she cried in broken English.

"He's a man, honey," Betty said, as if that were the obvious answer to her question.

Betty and I moved in closer around Carla, who twisted her scarf obsessively in her hands, hovering on the verge of tears. We encouraged her to be optimistic; meanwhile, we were exchanging despairing glances behind her back. Things didn't look good, to say the least.

"Russell is a very vigorous man, Carla, dear," Betty said. "Even if his little boat did capsize, he could easily swim to shore. He's probably off sunning himself on the beach somewhere as we speak, never dreaming he's causing this much concern. He'll show up. You watch."

Carla looked at her hopefully. "You think so? Really?"

"Yes, I do," Betty said, sounding unconvinced. "Has the captain notified the Coast Guard?"

Carla shook her head. "I do not think so. We were so certain we would find him here."

"Well, then, for caution's sake, I think we do need to get the professionals involved as soon as possible. I'll go find the captain and get things moving," Betty said, rising wearily. "Jo will stay with you."

As the mother of the bride, Betty was already nervous, coping with the inevitable problems which arise during the staging of any large wedding—particularly one on unfamiliar turf. The very last thing she needed was a full-blown crisis, but it seemed that's exactly what she now had on her hands. She hurried off in search of the captain, leaving me alone with Carla.

Further words of consolation seemed futile. I reached out and put a gentle hand on her arm to communicate my sympathy. Something about that human contact triggered a deep response. Carla clasped my hand and, in a dramatic, if somewhat awkward, gesture, she literally threw her arms around me and hugged me close, weeping like a little girl. I had no idea what to do except hold her and say the platitudinous, "There, there, it's going to be all right," as she sobbed.

Ordinarily, a histrionic liberty coming from someone I didn't know all that well would have put me off, but in this case, I was extremely moved. Such a raw display of emotion is a rare occurrence, implying great trust. I felt a swell of sisterly affection for this younger woman who had turned to me so spontaneously. Her grief spent, she pulled away and kept her eyes lowered, as if she felt embarrassed by her outburst.

"I am so sorry, Jo," she murmured, patting her eyes dry with her scarf. Her black mascara marred the white silk.

"Oh, don't be silly, Carla, dear. It's only natural to be upset. But I'm sure he's all right."

I wasn't, of course. But what else can you say at a moment like that?

Carla looked up at me with a hopeful little smile, her eyes glowing with tears. Sorrow made her look childlike.

"Thank you for being so kind to me, *cara* Jo."

The two of us sat in silence, both of us staring out at *The Lady C*, always referred to as "The Love Yacht" by the wags in New York. After a time, still gazing at the craft, floating majestically on the horizon, Carla turned to me and said in an unexpectedly cold voice, "I always hated that boat."

Four

THE HANDSOME YOUNG CAPTAIN OF *THE LADY C* finally informed the Coast Guard. At Betty's insistence, Carla Cole personally telephoned the governor general, who had been a guest at the bridal dinner the night before, to apprise him of the situation.

"Honey, this ain't the moment to be shy about using your connections," Betty assured her.

Almost immediately following that call, two officers from the Barbadian Port Authority were dispatched to the villa. The Coast Guard searched the yacht and patrolled the area. Carla told everyone she was anxious to keep news of her husband's disappearance under wraps for as long as possible. She argued that in the event he'd been kidnapped—a distinct, if remote, possibility—the utmost secrecy was imperative. Carla took the officers and some members of the Coast Guard out to the yacht so they could all look around. Both Betty and I offered to go with her, but Carla assured us she would be all right on her own. It was close to noon by the time everyone left.

"If my daughter's wedding turns into a funeral, I'm going to kill somebody," Betty said. She took a deep, disgruntled breath and added, "Well, I don't know about you, Jo, but I'm going swimming!"

Betty went inside the pool cabana and changed into the black "neck-to-knee" bathing suit she had ordered from an online swimwear catalogue. Designed for women who are self-conscious about their figures, the suit achieved the opposite of its purpose, drawing maximum attention to the areas she wished to hide. It covered her thighs to just above her knees and with a bouffant bathing cap on her head, she looked like a hi-tech, middle-aged Bloomer girl.

"Pray I don't bump into Russell," she said just before plunging in.

I was watching Betty swim when I suddenly remembered the moment in Mina's garden yesterday when Russell had compared himself to the green monkey. I recalled his exact words, "Sometimes I think I get a glimpse of myself . . . and then I disappear."

Then I disappear.

I'd laughed politely at his macabre little joke, not thinking much of it at the time. But now it seemed prophetic.

As I watched Betty swim back and forth, completing her daily ritual, I wondered if Russell had been trying to tell me something, or if he'd perhaps had some sort of premonition. Did he know he was going to vanish?

Finally, Betty slogged up out of the water, dried herself off with a towel, and said, "I've been thinking, do you think we should set a place for Russell at the wedding dinner or not? I mean, in case he does show up?" She looked at her large, red waterproof watch. "Christ, look at the time! People will be coming in twenty minutes! I've got to go put on my face!"

"Social life goes on," as the saying goes, so Betty didn't cancel the lunch—although she would have had a perfect right under the circumstances. The party was mercifully small, however, compared to previous festivities, being pretty much a family affair, just Betty and me and the Brills and Miranda and Ethan. Gil Waterman would not be there. He was aboard *The Lady C*, helping Carla cope. Betty planned to tell everyone he'd gone to play golf. Missy and Woody were off having lunch at a local restaurant with their friends.

Betty changed into a stiff beige-and-white caftan with a brick design that made her look like the Great Pyramid. I put on a pair of white pants and a T-shirt. She and I waited anxiously for the guests to arrive, slurping down a couple of rum punches in the process, reiterating over and over how vital it was to keep our mouths shut about Russell.

"If anyone finds out, it will ruin the wedding," Betty said.

"Right. It's crucial we tell no one," I concurred.

"Plus the fact, Carla's afraid he might have been kidnapped, so if we tell anyone, it could put his life in danger."

"Right."

We were both trying hard to convince each other not to spill these golden beans, however tempting it was.

"So we're agreed, right?" Betty said. "Not a word. Not one single word."

"Not even a hint. My lips are sealed," I said, running my fingers over my mouth as if to zipper it.

Miranda and Ethan were the first to arrive. They were staying just down the road at the Sandy Lane Hotel. Miranda was wearing a yellow muumuu, a rather chic gold turban, and sunglasses. Her pale skin appeared even paler in the harsh sunshine. Ethan, a scholar and a very professorial type, looked surprisingly fit in a pair of khaki shorts and a T-shirt. He had great legs, buff arms, and he obviously worked out. Betty and I steeled ourselves as they walked in.

"Remember—not a word," Betty whispered.

We all air kissed each other hello as Dermott passed around a trayful of his wicked rum punches.

Miranda raised her glass to us and said, "Well, here's hoping they find poor old Russell Cole!"

Betty's jaw dropped. She looked at me, then at Miranda, and said, "How the hell did *you* hear about it?"

"Oh, darling," Miranda said with a dismissive wave of her hand, "I hear *everything*! Remember, I was the one who first broke the news that Carla and Russell had run off together, for Chrissakes. You think I'm not going to hear about it when he vanishes off the face of the earth?"

"Tell me how you found out about it!" Betty demanded.

"Now, Betts, you know I'm never going to tell you, so why ask?"

Miranda never revealed her sources. People had begged her for years to write a book about all the dirt she knew, to which her double-edged reply was always, "Oh, honey, I want to live a little longer." No one was ever quite sure if that meant she wasn't yet ready to hunker down and write her memoirs, or if she thought such a revealing exercise would surely get her killed. One thing was clear. If any person knew where all the bodies in

New York society were buried, it was Miranda Somers, who had been reporting on the parties, pastimes, and peccadilloes of the rich for close to four decades. And part of the reason she knew as much as she did was because she was discreet—at least in print.

We all knew of Miranda's long and complicated history with Russell Cole and his two wives. When Russell Cole first arrived in New York married to Lulu, Miranda had elevated the couple to the social pantheon in *Nous* magazine. But it was also Miranda who broke the story when Russell ran off with Carla and the two of them holed up in the Hassler Hotel in Rome. In fact, word was that Lulu actually learned of her husband's affair by reading Miranda's column, the headline of which was "Cole Comfort."

Miranda had steadfastly refused to tell a soul who had tipped her off about the fugitive couple, and many suspected that the informant was, in fact, Carla herself, who may have cannily calculated that bringing the affair out into the open would force Russell's hand. Whoever told Miranda, the strategy worked. Lulu was so upset over the public humiliation, she behaved extremely badly, thus ruining any chance she might have had at a reconciliation. This was all old news, of course, but of considerable current interest in view of recent developments.

"You've *got* to tell us," Betty pleaded with her. "I mean, if Russell's been kidnapped, it could be a matter of life and death."

Miranda hesitated for a moment. "Well," she said, obviously dying to tell us. "Just this once. Larry Locket called me."

Larry Locket, a lanky southerner whose books about low crime in high places had all become international bestsellers, was a great friend of all of ours. He had made a brilliant career hunting down rich reprobates and turning their stories into long magazine articles or else thinly disguised works of fiction.

"And how the hell did *Larry* find out?" Betty asked.

"Who knows? Larry always knows things practically before they happen. He's already on the story," Miranda said. "He called me to find out what I knew. Of course, I hadn't heard a word until he told me. I do know one thing for sure, though. Lulu won't be a bit surprised. She always said Carla would kill Russell one day."

"Oh, Lulu's obsessed," Betty said. "Hell hath no fury . . ."

"Still," Miranda went on, "Carla seems to have rather bad luck with husbands. Remember poor old Mr. Hernandez."

"Oh, that's right," Ethan recalled. "He committed suicide, didn't he?"

"If you call shooting yourself *twice* suicide," Miranda said. She nonchalantly examined her manicured red fingernails with the air of one who is no longer impressed by the horror of such stories.

Ethan said, "How could it possibly have been a suicide if he was shot twice? *Bang!*" he joked, pointing his index finger at his head as if it were a gun. "Oops, I'm not quite dead yet! Bang again? I don't think so."

"I think that's the point, Sweets," I said, amused at how dense my brilliant friend could be at times.

"Oh. Wait. Do we think Carla *killed* him?" Ethan said, wide-eyed.

"Or had him killed," Miranda said. "I don't know for sure, of course, but the rumors were certainly flying around at the time. Of course, there was no proof. The body was cremated and there wasn't an autopsy, so we'll never know what really happened. You know how it is—people will believe what they want to believe, depending on whom they like or dislike. It's just social life."

"God, you sound exactly like June," Betty said.

Betty was referring to our close friend June Kahn, who dismissed almost all interaction between people, from minor spats to armed conflict, as being "just social life," as she put it.

Betty shuddered. "Jesus, what if Russell washes up on the beach during the wedding?"

"The wedding's at night. No one will see," Miranda said dryly.

Since the cat was out of the bag, Betty and I told Miranda and Ethan all about Carla showing up earlier that morning, and how Gil was on the boat as we spoke, helping her coordinate the search.

"I'm telling everyone—including Missy—that Gil is playing golf," Betty said.

"They'll certainly believe that," Miranda said.

"Under *no* circumstances can we tell Missy or Woody or the Brills," Betty said firmly. "In fact, I'd appreciate it if you wouldn't mention this to another soul. I really don't want my daughter's wedding to be remembered as a missing person's case."

At that precise moment, the Brills arrived. Betty plastered a smile on her face and sailed over to greet the arriving party.

"Mina! Freddy! Welcome! Let's all have another rum punch!"

"Greetings, everyone," Freddy Brill said, waving a hairy arm. "I remember when Michael Duncan used to own this villa," he said.

Freddy, a beefy English stockbroker who had inherited Cockleshell from his father and who had vacationed in Barbados as a child, was always full of island trivia.

"Yes, dear Michael Duncan!" Miranda exclaimed. "I knew him quite well. He was such a ladies' man. And, of course, you know he was 'excused shorts' in the British army because his schlong was so long, it dangled down to the middle of his inner thigh."

Betty and I laughed out loud, but Freddy and Mina Brill both looked completely mystified, and I really did wonder what on earth these clean-cut, shiny-faced people were thinking. I was well aware of just how insulated and wrapped up in ourselves our little social set was. Like sixteenth-century Paduans, the New Yorkers in my rarified group believe and behave as though we are the center of the universe. But the truth is, despite the fact that we live like kings and queens and our real estate is a thousand times more expensive than most anywhere else in the world, we're quite a provincial bunch. So it's always fascinating for me to see people from the outside world reacting to us.

"Did you all know that this villa was designed by Oliver Messel?" Ethan asked, obviously hoping to break the slight tension. Oliver Messel was the late, great English set designer who had settled in Barbados in the 1950s and been responsible for creating some of the most famous houses on the island.

"Oh, yes," Mina Brill said. "Messel green. Such a lovely, soft color. The color of sage . . ."

During all this polite banter, I could feel Betty rumbling with consternation, like a volcano ready to explode.

"Well, listen, everyone, we have a big day ahead, so let's eat!" she said.

As they all headed for lunch, I made an excuse and sneaked back to my room to call Larry Locket. Larry and I were great friends. We loved dishing the latest gossip with each other and I wanted to tell him I was on the scene. There was no answer, though, so I left a message on his answering machine.

"Larry, Jo Slater. Guess where I am? Barbados, staying with Betty and Gil Waterman. I'll be your stringer!"

I left a number where he could call me.

Lunch was served in the lattice gazebo a short walk from the main house. A large, round table was set with flowered linens, green-and-white china, green-tinted glasses, and in the center, a shallow glass bowl filled with tropical flowers. It was a cool spot in the middle of the day.

"Wasn't last night simply divine? And by the way, where *are* Russell and Carla?" Mina Brill asked as the six of us sat down.

"Yes, Russell and Carla," echoed Freddy Brill in his huffingly British voice. "And Gil. Where's Gil?"

"And Gil, of course!" Mina said. "Where are they all?"

Miranda, Ethan, and I all exchanged surreptitious looks. I knew that Betty was champing at the bit to tell the Brills that Russell was missing, but she wisely refrained, answering Mina's question nonchalantly.

"Oh, Gil's playing golf and Russell and Carla are resting on the boat. They said they wanted to conserve their energy for tonight."

"I am just so thrilled that Missy wanted to get married at Cockleshell—endless trouble though it is. That flower man you sent me knows nothing about flowers," Mina

Brill said. "And we really do need to go over the seating again, Betty."

"No problem," Betty said with clenched teeth. "The only thing I insist on is that we seat Jo next to Max Vermilion."

Mina Brill got a beatific look in her eye. "Oh, Lord Vermilion! Isn't he the most charming and handsome man in the whole, wide world?"

"I thought *I* was the most charming and handsome man in the world, darling!" Freddy Brill said with a cartoon wink.

Mina, who related everything to horticulture, responded, "Yes, but there's something so . . . so rare and elegant about Lord Vermilion. He's like a black tulip."

"More like a Venus flytrap," Betty muttered under her breath.

During lunch, I noticed that the air, so cool and pleasant in the morning, was growing humid and heavier by the minute. Betty obviously felt it, too, for she casually remarked, "Christ, I hope it's not gonna rain."

"*You* hope!" Mina Brill cried. "Good Lord, if it rains, we're *ruined! Ruined!*"

"Now, now, ladies, don't fret. It's not going to rain," Freddy Brill assured us all, raising his hands as if he were pushing back our fears.

"No? What are those, then, Freddy?" Betty pointed out to sea at the pile of lead ingot clouds stacked up on the horizon.

"Nothing to be concerned about, Betty, dear," Freddy Brill said. "Just a slight afternoon buildup. Happens all the time down here. They'll all clear away by evening. You watch."

"They look pretty dark," Ethan observed.

"Trust me, Mr. Monk, this old Bajan here knows his Barbados weather. Been coming down here since I was a lad. It's going to be a splendid evening . . . *splendid*. Bet you a hundred American dollars."

Freddy put his arm around Betty to give her a reassuring little hug. Miranda leaned into me and whispered, "Honey, I'll take that bet."

Five

LATER ON THAT AFTERNOON, THE SKY TURNED to slate. Intermittent gusts of wind ruffled the still air as an ominous restlessness pervaded the atmosphere. Thunder growled in the distance. I was getting dressed when Larry Locket called me back.

"Jo! Larry!" he said in his southern-accented voice. "I can't believe you're right there in the eye of the storm!" He didn't mean the weather.

"God, Larry, isn't it just incredible what's happened? How did you find out?"

"Oh, I have my sources," he said evasively.

"Are you coming down here?" I asked him.

"I can't right now. I'm working on two other stories. But as soon as I get through, I'm on this one. Any news?"

"No, but I'm staying with the Watermans, and Carla arrived here at nine this morning looking for Russell."

"Jo, we've got to talk the minute you get back. I want you to take notes. Wear a videocam and tape recorder!" he said, only half-jokingly.

Though Larry Locket and I saw each other only intermittently, we had one of those close, enduring friendships that always takes up where it left off. Our conversation was brief because I had to finish getting dressed for the wedding, but I promised to call him the minute I returned to New York. Larry was the mystery lover's Santa Claus who, each year, brought his fans the present of a book on a tantalizing new case. And there was no case that promised to be more tantalizing than this one.

I walked out on the veranda, dressed for the wedding in a brand-new long, strapless yellow chiffon gown. I knew it was becoming, and I confess I was looking forward to seeing Max. Gil Waterman, just back from the boat, was at the bar fixing himself a drink. He looked dapper, as usual, in his custom-made tuxedo.

"Any word?" I asked him.

"Nothing. Want one?" he said, offering me a scotch.

"No, thanks." I thought I detected a slight air of exasperation about him.

Gil took a long swig of scotch. "Why in hell they hired a kid captain who knows fuck all about procedure to run that luxurious tub is beyond me."

"He's cute," I said, recalling the fresh good looks of Captain Jenks.

"With all that money, couldn't they have afforded a captain who was cute *and* competent? The kid's a joke. 'Captain Jenks at your service, sir!' " he said, mimicking the young man's stance and Australian voice. "*I* know more about boats than he does, for Pete's sakes! They used to have a great captain. Mike Rankin was his name, I think. An American. Russell used to sing his praises all the time. I wonder what happened to him."

"Jenks does seem a little out of his depth, pardon the

pun," I said. "You know, Betty was the one who suggested calling the Coast Guard."

Gil rolled his eyes. "Doesn't surprise me. You can't believe how disorganized it is out there." Gil drained his glass and poured himself another drink.

"How's Carla holding up?" I asked him.

"Fine, under the circumstances. Oh, she sends her love to you, by the way. She said you were wonderful to her this morning. She's coming to the wedding."

"You're kidding. I'm surprised."

He paused for a moment. "Why? You think she shouldn't? I was kind of wondering about that myself."

I thought for a moment. Unfortunately, no etiquette book covers what to do if you're invited to a wedding when your husband has just vanished off the face of the earth.

"When people find out Russell's disappeared, and then they realize that she went to the party. . . . Well, let's just say, it won't look great."

"I know," Gil said. "But sitting out there all alone on the boat waiting for news is too depressing. I told her she should come if she felt like it."

"I certainly wouldn't feel like going to a party if *you* were missing, darling!" cried a voice behind us. "Jo's right. It looks like shit!"

Betty burst onto the terrace in a long, pale green caftan hand painted with red tropical flowers that looked like little penises. Her voluminous red hair has frizzed up in the humidity and her makeup was too heavy. There was a hint of Bozo the Clown about her.

"Oh, don't you look pretty, sweetheart," Gil said right away. It was hard to tell whether Gil's reaction was stunned or serious. He certainly was a courtly husband.

"Fix me a drink, will you, Gil? I need one. . . . Actually, fix me three. Might as well get a head start. I can't tell if I'm homicidal or suicidal. Missy can't get into her wedding dress. She refuses to let me help her. And will you please just *look* at the weather!"

"Freddy Brill may lose his bet," I said.

"*May* lose his bet? *A fucking monsoon's coming!*" Betty cried, looking up at the sky. "And Freddy's the one who persuaded us *not* to put in any walkways, even though Trebor kept insisting. That man is a complete idiot. I hope Woody hasn't inherited his brain."

Though the wedding was at Cockleshell, the Brill villa, Betty had imported Trebor Bellini from New York to handle the décor. Bellini, an alchemist of the visual, was one of the best in the business for designing opulent parties. He was a genius at transforming pedestrian spaces into palaces, but his fees were as imperial as his vision and I was impressed that Betty was using him. Betty was quite the tightwad when it came to decoration. In her own art-laden house, she never had any fresh flowers around, saying, "What would you rather look at? A bunch of blooms on the table, or my Monet *Water Lilies* on the wall?" Still, this was the wedding of their only child, and Betty and Gil wanted nothing but the best for Missy. Also, as Betty pointed out, it was good business for Gil, who had invited all of his best clients down for the occasion.

"Oh, Jo, you're gorgeous!" Betty said.

"You, too, sweetie. I hope Max likes this color," I said, glancing down at my pale yellow dress.

"Max likes skin color," Betty said.

We were still waiting for Missy when Dermott came in to announce that I had a telephone call. "It's Mrs. Kahn from New York City," he said in his basso voice.

"Jo, for God's sakes, don't breathe a *word* to June about Russell!" Betty said.

I rolled my eyes at Betty in disbelief that she would even have to mention such a thing, considering that everyone knew June Kahn was a human Internet when it came to dispensing information. Picking up the phone in the living room, I heard June's terminally chirpy voice at the other end say, "So Jo, sweetie, have they found poor Russell yet?"

There's an old saying in New York that if you don't want a secret to get out, you can't repeat it—not even to yourself.

I cupped my hand over the receiver and called out to Betty, "She knows!"

Betty skittered across the terrace in her high-heeled sandals and grabbed the phone away from me.

"*June, Betty. Who the fuck told you about it?*" Betty listened for a minute and then cried, "*You're not serious!*" Betty put her hand over the mouthpiece and whispered to me, "*Lulu* told her."

"How does *Lulu* know?" I said.

Catching Betty's eye, Gil pointed to his watch, indicating that we were now seriously late.

"Listen, Junie, I gotta go," Betty said. "I'll call you later . . . I promise I will . . . no, look . . . I promise . . . listen, Junie, you know more than we do, for heaven sakes! I'll call you the minute I hear anything! I *will*. I gotta go!" Betty said, hanging up. The promise of future gossip was the only way to get June off the phone.

Betty looked at Gil and said, "How the hell did *Lulu* find out? Do you think Larry told her? Or did she tell Larry?"

"Who knows? And what does it matter?" Gil said, unimpressed.

"Gil, it *matters!* They knew practically before we did! And we're *here!*" Betty said. "It's just incredible."

"I'll tell you what's incredible—the time," Gil said, pointing to his watch again. "Now let's get a move on. Where *is* Missy?"

"Well, that's it, then. It's out," Betty said. "Lulu had a choice between calling a live press conference or telling June. And she knew June would get it out there faster."

Just then, Missy swept through the arch of the veranda, looking like an exotic flower in her sleek white satin wedding dress and the same diamond-and-sapphire necklace she had worn to the bridal dinner the previous night. She stood for a long moment as both Betty and Gil stared at her in sentimental awe.

"Sweetheart, you're gorgeous," Gil said with a crack of emotion in his voice.

Betty was at an uncharacteristic loss for words. She and Gil walked over and hugged their daughter. It was a sweet moment that brought tears to everyone's eyes, including my own. But it was short-lived. After Missy thanked her parents and told them she loved them—"You guys are just the best!"—we all hurried out the door to the awaiting limousine and into the arms of disaster.

Six

TWO MONTHS AFTER THE FACT, IN HER COLUMN in the large, glossy pages of *Nous* magazine, Miranda Somers would describe Missy Waterman's wedding at Cockleshell as "a tropical dream . . . An orchid-filled paradise . . . A luscious occasion. . . . The highlight of the social season." Miranda's gracious account notwithstanding, I think I speak for everyone who was actually *there* when I say that in the annals of social fiascos, that wedding took the five-tiered cake. "The wedding from hell," "a tropical nightmare," and "misadventure in paradise" were some of the milder of the disparaging comments I heard expressed during the course of a long, stormy evening. If not the absolute worst, expensive wedding ever endured, it was certainly the wettest.

Almost immediately following the private ceremony, there was a brief but brutal thunderstorm, which Freddy Brill, in his infinite knowledge of Barbados weather, predicted would "clear the air." After that, rain poured down in buckets. The enormous tent, which had been set up in the garden for dinner and dancing, decorated from floor to ceiling with orchids, was located at least twenty yards away from the main house and there was no walkway covering the flooded grounds.

Gil Waterman and Freddy Brill made the rounds, apologizing to everyone for the ghastly weather, while Mina and Betty and I scurried around frantically searching for extra umbrellas. There were only five of any decent size, all belonging to the valet parkers, two of whom were enlisted to help shepherd guests from the house to the tent—an interminably slow process. In desperation over the long wait, some people made a dash for the tent. They arrived in sopping wet clothes and shoes, looking as bedraggled as shipwreck survivors.

I heard one woman exclaim rhapsodically upon entering the tent, "My God, a sea of orchids!" To which her husband snapped back, "Screw the orchids, where's the ark?"

The tent was damp and chilly. The storm had cut the power so that none of the crucial spotlights hidden in the columns were lit. Low votive candles amidst the orchids on each table provided the only light, and while their soft glow made everyone look slightly less awful, it was difficult to actually see anything. People tripped over the flower garlands festooning the long tablecloths as they tried to locate their seats. The initial camaraderie naturally engendered by adverse conditions gradually curdled into irritation, then anger, then grim resignation, as it dawned on people that this was an evening to be endured, not enjoyed.

In the midst of the mayhem, I spotted Carla standing by herself in a far corner of the tent. She was chicly dressed in a long coral sheath and dazzling coral-and-diamond jewelry, clutching a bag that looked like a gold brick. Unlike the rest of us, she was surprisingly unwilted from the rain. Though Gil warned me she was coming, I still wondered what in hell she was doing there, why she wasn't out on the boat waiting for word of her husband. She seemed pleased to see me and flashed me a warm smile as I approached her.

"You are surprised to see me here, are you not, Jo?" she said intuitively.

"Well, kind of."

"I must admit I feel a bit strange being at a party. But I knew that if I stayed on that boat another minute waiting for news, I would go mad, so I have come. No one here knows about Russell so, hopefully, they will not think too badly of me."

"How about later on when they find out?"

"I am not worried. I have never been worried about what people think of me. They always think the wrong thing anyway."

"Well, that's a good attitude, I guess." Under the circumstances, her toughness amazed me.

"But you know, Jo," she began in a gentler voice, "I do care what *you* think of me. So I am going to tell you a big secret. But you must swear to me on your life you will not breathe a word of this to anyone else."

"I swear," I said warily.

She leaned in and whispered, "Russell is alive."

I pulled back. "Where is he?"

"Shhh! Not so loud."

"But where is he?"

"I don't know exactly. But I do know that he is alive. I know it inside, *here*." She put her hand on her heart. Her eyes burned with conviction.

"But you haven't actually heard anything?"

"No."

I mustered a halfhearted smile, thinking this was merely wishful thinking on her part. My assumption was that if they hadn't found Russell Cole by now, he'd most likely drowned. But I didn't want to dash her hopes.

"Okay, well, let's pray he is then."

"Do not look so skeptical, Jo. You do not understand. Russell *is* alive," she said emphatically. "This has happened before."

"What do you mean?"

"You swear you will keep this in confidence?"

"I swear."

She gave me a single, solemn nod. "Russell has disappeared before, Jo. And not just once."

"You're kidding. How? *When*?"

"I can not go into it. But I will tell you that my darling husband is not a well man. He has a terrible psychological affliction. We will find him sooner or later. We always do."

"What kind of affliction?"

She raised her palm like a traffic cop. "That is all I can tell you, I am afraid. But I have been through this before and I know it will all turn out well in the end."

I was dying to ask more questions, but she clearly wasn't going to talk, and the steady stream of wet, cranky guests filing into the tent started to intrude on our space. Suddenly, I felt a tap on my shoulder. I turned around. It was Max, looking amazingly dry and handsome in an old-style double-breasted tuxedo.

"I believe you're my dinner partner," he said.

I confess that I felt a little frisson of real attraction.

"You know Carla Cole, don't you?" I said, trying not to forget my manners.

Max mock kissed Carla's hand, as was his wont. "We have indeed met," he said. "Terribly sorry to have missed your party last evening."

"Yes, I am so sorry, too," Carla said. "You were supposed to be sitting next to Jo, but you will make up for it tonight."

With that, a gong sounded and harried waiters made pleas for all of us to be seated.

"Come, dear lady," Max said, taking my hand. "I believe they want us to sit down before the tent falls in on us."

As we were walking to our table, Carla said to me, "I know you are going to be my great friend and mentor in New York, Jo, because we are sisters under the skin."

It was an odd thing to say. Was Carla going to be spending more time in New York? I wondered. When I glanced back, Carla was staring at Max and me with a strange look on her face. When she saw me, she smiled as if she were embarrassed I'd caught her, and turned away.

At dinner, I was seated between Max and Sir Arthur Tilden, the governor general of Barbados, a lean, bespectacled black man with wiry, salt-and-pepper hair and a grave countenance. Sir Arthur had performed the marriage ceremony. He, of course, knew that Russell Cole was missing, because it was he who Carla had called for help, at Betty's insistence. He'd helped get things mobililized. He didn't say a word to me about Russell, however. Sir Arthur was very discreet—an admirable if dull trait. I wondered if Max knew, because if he was going out with Lulu, perhaps she'd phoned him, as well as Miranda. In any case, I wasn't going to be the one to bring it up with either man. I kept thinking about what Carla had said about Russell and wondered what kind of "psychological affliction" she could have been talking about.

The woman on Max's other side, some European countess of no account I didn't know, monopolized him from the moment we sat down—which was just as well. I didn't want to appear anxious. Max was very laid-back and polite, but he did assume an almost cartoonishly defensive posture, tilted way back away from her with his arms crossed in front of him. The more she leaned in toward him, the more he tilted backward. Still, it didn't stop her from trying to make an impression.

Sir Arthur and I talked during the appetizer. We had a nice conversation about Barbados and his career (he had started out as a lawyer, then became a magistrate). There was no mention of Russell Cole. As drenched waiters served lukewarm entrees, Max managed to extract himself from the overattentive woman on his right. He turned to me and said, "Well, dear lady, finally we get to sit together. How was the dinner last night?"

"It was really extraordinary. I'm so sorry you weren't there."

"Not as sorry as I am," he said with a flirtatious air.

Since he seemed to be somewhat interested in me, I then asked him a question to which I thought I knew the answer, just to see what he would say.

"Why weren't you there, if I may ask?"

Max sighed. "Well, apparently Russell thinks I'm a rather good friend of his ex-wife, whom I'm sure you know."

"Lulu. Yes, I know her," I said coldly.

"You don't sound as if you like her."

"I can't say I'm her greatest fan, no."

"Oh?" He cocked his handsome head to one side. "Why not?"

"Well, let's just say that when I was down on my luck, Lulu wasn't exactly supportive. I have a little motto in life, which is, I may not remember, but I *never* forget."

Max chuckled. "That's rather good. I'm going to remember that one."

"So are you and Lulu an 'item,' as they say?"

"An item? What does *that* mean?"

I couldn't figure out whether Max was genuinely perplexed or whether he just wanted me to elaborate because he was mischievous.

"Uh . . . are you dating Lulu?"

He leaned in, put his hand under his chin, and gazed at me intently. There was a twinkle in his cool eyes. "What are you *really* asking me, Jo?" he said, with a sly nuance to his voice.

I got a little flustered. My little ruse had backfired.

"I don't know. I was just wondering if you two were involved."

"Involved?"

"You know . . . romantically."

"I see. And why were you wondering that?" he pressed me.

"I guess because New York is a very small town. I know Lulu. I sort of know you. It's a point of interest, that's all."

"A point of interest," he said, and nodded. "Like a stop on a sightseeing tour . . . no other reason?"

"What other reason would there be?" I asked him.

He considered a moment. "Oh, I don't know. I could probably think of a more congenial one if I put my mind to it." He gave me a warm smile. I couldn't figure out whether he was flirting with me or just being coy. "Lulu and I are merely good friends," he went on. "But it seems that in New York, if one is seen with a person more than once, people think you're engaged. The fact is, I happen to be footloose and fancy-free at the moment. A fairly rare occurrence in my life, I must say."

In other words, he was available—or so he seemed to be indicating.

I decided to change the subject and we talked a little about Taunton Hall, his ancestral home. He obviously adored the place and took great pride in it.

"It's a Herculean task to keep the thing up and running," he said. "Something's always falling down. This year, it's my roof." There was a pause. Max looked around the room, then said, "Pity about Russell Cole. I wonder if he'll turn up."

"So you *know*," I said, marveling at his coolness. "How did you find out?"

"Lulu called me this afternoon, actually."

Lulu—with whom he wasn't involved.

"The whole town seems to know. Larry Locket called us this afternoon. I wonder if Lulu told him."

"Larry Locket, the writer . . ." Max shrugged. "Possibly."

"Well, June Kahn knows, which is like posting it on the Internet."

"June Kahn, yes. And her husband—that funny little man who always wears the matching cummerbunds and ties . . . what's his name?"

"Charlie."

"Charlie Kahn. That's right. I've met them. They came to my house one year for the ball."

"How do you think Lulu found out?" I asked him.

"No idea. But I suspect she keeps rather close tabs on the two of them—Russell and Carla. She's a bit obsessed with her successor, you know. . . . Tell me, what do people in New York think of Carla Cole?"

"She's not around New York much," I demurred.

"No, but you know what I mean. What's the *scoop* on her, as you say? I'm curious because Lulu goes on and on about how Carla Cole used to be some sort of lady of the night. Do we think that's true?"

"Well, I've heard that, yes. I mean, it was a huge scandal when they ran off together."

"I remember. I didn't know them at the time, but I heard all about it. Of course, most people in Europe thought that Russell was rather foolish to run off and get divorced the way he did. Particularly with a woman who wasn't anybody, *what*? English and European men simply don't get divorced. They get mistresses. 'Cept me, of course. But I'm considered a bit bonkers," he said with a laugh. "I just don't see why one shouldn't move on if one feels like it. You know what Louis the Fifteenth said when he was asked what the greatest aphrodisiac in the world was . . . ?"

I did know, but I pretended not to. "No, what?"

"Change," Max said with a grin. I smiled appreciatively. "I think people should do exactly as they please in life, don't you? Provided they can, of course," he quickly added.

"I guess that depends on what pleases them," I answered.

"Well, what would please me is to call you when I come to New York. May I?"

"Yes. You may indeed."

I had no idea what to make of Max. His antithetical

combination of aloofness and flirtatiousness was slightly disconcerting. I didn't know whether he liked me or—more to the point—whether I liked him. But there was something very intriguing about him, and I definitely wanted to see him again.

For the rest of the dinner, we talked more about Russell, speculating on what might have happened. Max said he hardly knew Russell at all. He just knew Lulu. I got the feeling that he and Lulu might once have been involved, but that they weren't now. Several times during our conversation, I glanced over at Carla. Every single time I looked at her, she was already looking at me, staring at me with a knowing little smile. I couldn't figure out if she was smiling because of what she'd told me about Russell, or because of some other reason. Her observation earlier that we were "sisters under the skin" echoed in my brain. It was almost as if she knew something confidential about me.

Suddenly, a woman from another table got up and approached a man at the opposite side of our table. She leaned down and whispered something into his ear. The man's face registered shock and he immediately craned his neck to peer around one of the orchid-plastered columns. The object of his gaze was Carla Cole, who was seated at a neighboring table in my direct line of sight. That man took a good look at Carla and then whispered something to his dinner partner. The woman who had whispered something to him moved on to another table. Pretty soon I felt the whole room simmering with curiosity as people whispered to one another and shifted in their seats in order to get a glimpse of Carla. I knew that word about Russell Cole was out, prowling the tent like a hungry dog. It was no surprise. A secret that big has the life span of a mayfly.

Despite the infusion of gossip, the dinner quickly deteriorated, and long before the dessert plates were cleared away, everyone had just basically given up. Instead of dancing or lingering around to talk, people got up in droves, desperate to get back to their hotels, houses, private planes—wherever they could get some rest. No one stayed for coffee. Max kissed my hand, looked deep into my eyes, and said, "Dear lady, I hate to leave you after all we've been through together. I will call you very soon." He left. I couldn't help wondering where he was going.

On the way out, several people stopped to ask me if I'd heard the "news" about Russell Cole. I just nodded, knowing that by this time tomorrow the whole western world would know. Carla had disappeared. I had no idea where she went.

While waiting for Betty and Gil, I stood at the door with Miranda, who looked a true fright with her ruined gold sandals slung over her right shoulder, her strawberry hair a frizzy halo, her undereyes blackened with mascara, and her red caftan streaked with mud. God only knows what I looked like. We just stared at each other.

When her car, driven by Ethan, finally pulled up, she gazed at it for a moment as though it were the Holy Grail. Before getting in, she air kissed me good-bye and said in a weary voice, "Well, at least now we all know how it felt trying to get out of Saigon."

I just smiled, wondering how she was going to muster the energy to give this wedding a positive spin in her column.

Missy and Woody spent the night in the honeymoon suite of the Sandy Lane Hotel. It was past three when Betty, Gil, and I got back to King's Fort. Gil looked as if he'd drowned. So did Betty. I knew how utterly exhausted she was when she didn't even ask me about Max. We all just stared at one another in utter defeat. Finally, Betty said, "Russell Cole had a choice between attending that wedding or disappearing. And, honey, he made the right decision!"

With that, we all slogged off to bed.

Seven

RUSSELL COLE NEVER DID TURN UP. THE MEDIA soon got hold of the story and the tabloids had a field day. The world was eager for news, and, as is usual in such cases, a torrent of rumors swept through the factual wasteland. Theories as to what had actually happened to the Oklahoma billionaire flooded international social circles. The Coles were already well-known figures in that miniscule province of privilege, which made this ongoing mystery just too tantalizing for its inhabitants to ignore.

Everyone had an opinion about the case. Was Russell really dead? And if so, was Carla involved? Was it a kidnapping, a Mob hit, a terrorist act, suicide, murder, or just a plain, old, boring accident? Wild stories were rampant, but there was no hard evidence to support any of the speculation. Just about all the wedding guests left the island the next day. Carla remained in decorous seclusion aboard *The Lady C*, which became a floating target for enterprising paparazzi until Carla again used her influence with Sir Arthur. He ordered the Coast Guard to keep leering lensmen at bay.

Everyone who was at the wedding dined out on the story as soon as they returned home. It was one of those moments in social life when close proximity to a scandal made even the dullest of souls sought-after dinner guests. People who didn't even know Carla Cole were now claiming to have had heart-to-heart conversations with her in Barbados. As a result, many ridiculous falsehoods emerged, such as the conflicting rumors that Carla had actually seen Russell fall overboard and jumped in to try and save him, or that Carla had actually seen Russell fall overboard and *didn't* jump in to try and save him. As Betty said, "If everybody claiming to have spoken to Carla had *actually* spoken to her, she'd still be talking."

I arrived back in New York on a steely, cold January day. The slushy streets were dotted with dirty snowdrifts. I was thrilled to be home again. I could hardly wait to get back inside my cozy apartment which overlooked Fifth Avenue and Central Park. Caspar, my chauffeur, picked me up at the airport. Few chauffeurs were either as dependable as Caspar, or as dull-witted—which meant I could rely on him without having to talk to him.

I was met at the door by Cyril, my English butler, a gray-haired older man with a military bearing and a thick English accent. He had worked for enough royalty and rich people in his time to understand the value of silence both inside and outside his place of employment. Cyril had excellent references and had even offered to sign one of those ludicrously self-important "non-disclosure" agreements before coming to work for me (I told him that would not be necessary).

I thought of my apartment as a little oasis in the hurly-burly of modern life. It was on a lower floor than my old apartment just down the street. I had sold that one because among a host of glorious memories, there was one glaringly unpleasant one of which I didn't care to be reminded. But that's another story. The new apartment was larger, but much less fussy than the old one. Some said it was more stylish in its way. In addition, I wasn't so wedded to eighteenth-century France in my choice of décor as I'd once been. Grand furniture requires a lot of upkeep, and I got rid of a lot of stuff simply because I couldn't be bothered with the maintenance. I was at the point in life where I didn't want the things I owned to own me. I wanted to be freer. The ups and downs of life had changed me, and I wanted my surroundings to be more relaxed.

I branched out and even acquired some interesting contemporary paintings—like the Francis Bacon portrait of a screaming cleric, for example. Gil Waterman had sold it to me to go above the fireplace in the library. However, people found it so disturbing that I moved it to an out-of-the-way corridor where only I could see it from time to time, to remind myself that the universe is not the well-ordered old master triangle I once envisioned, but an insane, godless place that will drive us mad if we are unlucky, or if we fail to take care.

A pile of mail and a long list of messages were waiting for me. I scanned the names quickly to see if Lord Vermilion had called. He hadn't. I was frankly a bit disappointed, but I decided there was no point in dwelling on it. *Qué sera, sera*, I thought to myself.

I saw that Larry Locket had called and I immediately called him back. He picked up the phone on the first ring, sounding distracted.

"Larry? Jo . . . I'm back."

"And I'm going," he said. "I'm just on the phone with the airline. Hold on. . . . No, wait, listen . . . Jo, can I come over for a drink? I have to talk to you about Barbados. And besides, I haven't seen you in ages."

"Sure. I'm right here. Come when you want."

About an hour later, Cyril showed Larry Locket into the library.

"Jo," he said, beaming at me through his trademark tortoiseshell glasses. "Don't you look great!"

"You look pretty swell yourself there, my friend!"

The image of Larry seated at his desk, holding a pipe, his thick silver hair swept back from a kind, comfortable face, staring at the camera with an aloof little smile, was familiar to readers throughout the world. In person, he was much more intense. His bushy eyebrows hung over his brown eyes like little black canopies. He had the impish charm of a leprechaun. I loved his company, his humor, and the interest that he took in everything. His fierce intelligence was amplified by intuition. In the twenty-odd years since his first book had appeared, Larry Locket had become more than a celebrity, he was a force to be reckoned with, loved and respected by his friends, feared by his enemies.

There was a time when I had been afraid Larry might level his sharp, investigative gaze at me, and the prospect made me very worried, I can tell you. But that time passed and since then we had enjoyed many a jolly meal together, discussing the vicissitudes of New York—how it had changed over the years, the threat of terrorism, social and otherwise, how so many people had come and gone, reigned for a time, then gone broke or been indicted, and the fact that the new ante to play the game of social life in Manhattan had steadily increased to national deficit proportions.

I fixed Larry his usual drink, a Diet Coke, and poured myself a white wine. We sat down and chitchatted about the wedding for a few moments. Of course, Larry already knew all about it from a variety of sources.

"I hear it was rather moist," he said.

"It was a monsoon. Poor Betty, I felt so sorry for her. She didn't want to have it in Barbados in the first place. She wanted to have it in New York. But Missy insisted."

"Well, I want to hear about the bridal dinner on the Cole yacht and the morning Russell went missing. I'm going down there tomorrow for a couple of weeks. Tell me *everything*. Tell me who I should see. I've already lined up the head of the Coast Guard and the governor general."

I gave Larry a brief recap. He was particularly fascinated by the green monkey story. I debated whether or not to tell him what Carla had told me, namely, that Russell had disappeared before. Carla had sworn me to secrecy, but Larry was an old and dear friend, and we often told each other things we'd been sworn not to tell. Then he said, "Carla's agreed to talk to me."

"Do you know her?"

"Not well, no. But we've met a few times over the years. I've seen her in a few of her various incarnations. She's made quite a transformation from the first time I ever laid eyes on her."

"Oh, *tell* me, Larry," I said.

Larry leaned back in the burgundy velvet chair and lit his pipe. The aroma of sweet tobacco filled the room.

"Let's see," he said, puffing away. "I first ran across Carla years ago when my wife and I were living in London. Carla was called Carla Corelli or Corallo—or something like that. Some Italian name. She was one of those jolly good-time, girls-about-town on the London party circuit. She was living with another woman, actually."

"Living with, as in having an *affair* with?"

"No, I don't think so. Maybe. Who knows? They were roommates. I remember she had long, blonde hair then and quite a voluptuous figure. She laughed a lot."

"Long, blonde hair? I can't picture it."

"*Bright* blonde hair," he said, raising his eyebrows. "Nearly to her waist. Very sexy. My wife called her a 'three-bottle blonde.' She made no bones about wanting to marry money. Everyone knew she was looking for a good catch. Then, of course, she struck gold. She married Antonio Hernandez, as you know, and they went to live in Mexico. Now she's thin and chic and very—*propah*," he said with a wry smile. "Last time I saw her, I hardly recognized her."

"Did you know Hernandez?"

"I met him once at an an amazing party they gave in Acapulco. Hernandez had this huge villa down there and I was staying with a friend who had the villa next door and she took me. 'This is not to be missed,' she said. And, honey, she wasn't kidding."

"What was it like?"

"Oh, my dear. Well, for starters, as you came in you had to pass by this huge tower with turrets at the top and there were about a dozen men with machine guns peering down at you, ready to open fire if you so much as sneezed the wrong way. Then you walked through this kind of mazey tropical garden and suddenly, there was Yankee Stadium—the biggest, most vulgar house you've ever seen in your life! It had two Olympic-size swimming pools on two different levels, and a terrace the size of a football field, studded with life-size plaster camels."

"No!"

"And that was the tasteful part. That's where we had cocktails. The place had its own disco with a big, blue dolphin in the center, spouting rainbow-colored water. Worst-looking thing you've ever seen. No expense had been spared except, I gather, in the guest rooms, which everybody complained were cramped and dark. Hernandez spent the money where it showed and not for the comfort of others."

"So what was Hernandez like?" I was fascinated.

"A shy, exceedingly uncomfortable man. Hardly spoke to anyone. Just lurked in a corner, looking furtive and miserable the whole entire time."

"Maybe he hated parties."

Larry shook his head. "No, I think it was much more than that. He was a very strange man. A famous depressive. I made an effort to talk to him because I felt sort of sorry for him and also because I was curious about Mexico's 'pharmaceutical king,' as he was always referred to. Most stilted conversation I've ever had, Jo. Filled with aborted takeoffs. He'd start to talk, then stop dead right in the middle of a sentence. He couldn't focus on anything but Carla. He was obsessed with her. Watched her like a hawk. I remember how those beady little eyes of his darted around after her wherever she went. Of course, she was much younger than he was, and very flirtatious. It was kind of touching in a way."

"So is it true that he committed suicide by shooting himself twice in the chest? Miranda told us that."

Larry laughed. "No, I think he just shot himself once. As I said, he had a history of depression. That was well known."

"Then why do people say he was murdered?"

"People love scandal." He took another puff of his pipe and smiled at me through strings of blue smoke.

"Okay, so is it true that the reason Russell gave Lulu such a big settlement is because Lulu found out that Carla used to be a call girl and they were afraid she would broadcast it to the world?"

Larry shook his head in amusement. "Well, first of all, the world thought Carla *was* a call girl. So if Russell gave Lulu a big settlement to keep her mouth shut about *that*, I'd say he wasted his money, wouldn't you? And besides, who *cares* anymore? That's one scenario we're all quite used to by now among the ranks of rich men's wives . . . I won't name names, of course," he quickly added. "But just think of old Madame Celeste."

Madame Celeste ran a famous French bordello whose international call girls were renowned for their looks, their charm, and their fabled ability to marry or otherwise insinuate themselves into the precincts of power all over the world. Over the years, a few international socialites and wives of powerful men were reputed to be former Madame Celeste girls. But it was one of those associations that is tough to prove—secrecy being as closely guarded a commodity in the courtesan trade as certain exotic sexual techniques.

"Do you think Carla was a Madame Celeste girl?" I asked Larry.

"Not literally. Madame Celeste must be long gone by now. But do I think Carla was once a 'lady of the night'? *Yes*. Do I care? *No*. Would I like to find out the exact reason Russell paid Lulu all that dough? *You bet*. But I know it wasn't simply because Lulu found out his new wife was a pro or a semipro."

"I wonder why, then?"

Turning to me with a mock grin, Larry said sarcastically, "Maybe Russell's just a *really nice guy*."

"So you're definitely going to see Carla when you're down there?"

"It's the main reason I'm going. Though I do want to check out the whole scene."

I was aching to tell him what I knew, but since I'd been sworn to secrecy and he was going to see Carla anyway, I restrained myself. I knew Larry would get it out of her himself. He had that strange power that made people want to tell him things. We talked for a few more minutes, then Larry got up to leave.

"Early plane to catch," he said. "Call you when I get back."

"Keep me posted, will you? Tell me everything Carla says."

I walked him to the door and just before the elevator came, I casually asked, "By the way, Larry, what do you know about Max Vermilion?"

"The Lord of the Rings?" he said with a little laugh. "Just that he likes the low life but only marries the high born. Except for once when he supposedly married the so-called Shady Lady Vermilion. But that's just a rumor no one can prove. Why?"

"What do you mean, he likes the low life?"

"Oh, there have always been rumors about Max and his dark side. But I understand from people who know him—I don't, personally—that he's very conscious of who's who and what's what. And that he's extremely fond of money and ladies who have a lot of it—well born or not. Why are you so interested in Lord Vermilion?"

There was no point in beating around the bush with Larry, who found out everything anyway.

"I sat next to him in Barbados. Betty's trying to fix me up."

"And . . . ?"

"Nothing. He was very charming. But I think he's going out with Lulu Cole."

Larry gave a dismissive little wave of his hand. "From what I hear, he goes out with a lot of people. He's considered a great catch."

"I don't want to catch him, Larry. I just thought he was interesting, that's all. Betty and June are always trying to fix me up. They don't think a woman can be happy without a man."

"People always want to fix me up, too. They never believe you if you tell them you prefer being alone."

There was a kind of sad resignation in his voice. In all the years we'd known each other, I was never aware of Larry being involved with anyone, although he had many women friends whom he escorted here and there. His own story was tragic. A wealthy psychopath had killed his wife years ago. Then, due to fancy legal maneuvering and a team of high-priced lawyers, the man got off with a ridiculously light sentence. Having lost the love of his life, Larry went into a deep depression. He once told me that through that experience he not only saw the dark side of human nature, but of himself. Though he managed to pull himself away from the brink of the abyss just in time, he apparently was left with a psychological wound that would not heal.

The gruesome death of Helena Locket then became

the defining factor of Larry's life—one of those unfore-
seen obstacles in midstream that can change the course of
a person's destiny for better or ill. In Larry's case, the
wrenching loss of his beloved partner turned his journalistic bent into a brilliant writing career and a crusade for
justice. His targets were primarily rich miscreants, who,
like his wife's killer, managed to evade just punishment
because they had plenty of money and a team of smart
lawyers.

The elevator arrived. I gave Larry a hug and kiss good-
bye and wished him a safe journey.

"Wish me luck," he said.

"Say hi to Carla for me," I told him. "Tell her I'm
thinking of her."

And I was, with genuine curiosity.

Eight

THE NEXT MORNING, CASPAR DROVE ME DOWN-
town. It was another cold, gray January day,
and I would have preferred to stay at home
and catch up on my mail, but I had to get some important
business out of the way.

Every four months, like clockwork, I visited David
Millstein, a diamond dealer who operated out of one of
the nondescript buildings on Fifth Avenue and Forty-
eighth Street, right around the corner from the Diamond
District. Security was tight. A uniformed guard sat behind a desk at the entrance, asking people where they
were going and directing them to sign in. I added my
name to a lengthy list and rode up with two Hassidic
Jews dressed in their black suits and hats, and a delivery
boy from a local deli carrying an order that reeked of
garlic. I got off at the seventh floor, walked down the
long, gray corridor to suite 720, and pressed the button
to the side of the door. As I waited, I glanced up at the
security camera poised overhead. After a few seconds, I

was buzzed in and greeted by Mr. Millstein himself, a stocky, middle-aged man with a jowly face that reminded me of a beagle. Loosely pinned to the back of his curly salt-and-pepper hair was a yarmulke. He was wearing baggy black pants and a white shirt with the sleeves rolled up just below the elbow—no tie or jacket. His left hand was burrowed deep into his pants pocket, his right hand suspended in midair ready to greet me.

"Mrs. Slater," he said in his usual forthright and friendly manner, shaking my hand. "Good to see you."

The plain-looking, young blonde secretary sitting behind a desk in the front room gave me a brief nod as Millstein led me back into his office, a small space with white walls, fluorescent overhead lights, a desk, and a large safe crouched like a big, black bear in the far corner of the room. Two grimy-paned windows faced north with a view of Rockefeller Center. Millstein walked over to the safe, the heavy door of which was ajar. He pulled out two small, thin, white paper packets from a stack of identical packets secured with a rubber band. Replacing the stack in the safe, he brought the two packets over to his desk, sat down, and motioned me to do likewise.

Carefully unfolding the first packet, he revealed a sparkly little diamond, which he secured with a pair of tweezers and placed on the digital diamond scale in front of him to weigh it.

"Four-point-eight-six carats," he said, picking up the diamond again with the tweezers. He stopped for an instant, holding it up to the light for a critical look. "Nice goods," he said before dropping it back into its little paper envelope.

He wrote the weight of the stone with a ballpoint pen on one corner of the wrapper.

"Your diamond and your GIA certificate," he said, handing me the first packet across the desk along with a laminated card from the Gemological Institute documenting the diamond's particular specifications, including weight, color, cut, clarity, inclusions, etc.

He repeated the entire process with the same precision on another stone with similar characteristics.

"Thank you, Mr. Millstein," I said, slipping both packets into my purse.

Old mine diamonds in original antique settings were more my thing, of course, but I wasn't there to indulge my passion for beautiful jewelry. I was there to get this meeting over with as fast as possible.

"Always a pleasure doing business with you, Mrs. Slater."

My dealings with Mr. Millstein were routine by now. Every four months I trekked down to his office to buy two diamonds worth about fifty thousand dollars each, having prearranged a wire transfer from my bank into his account. These transactions were brief and businesslike. I'd come to Millstein originally explaining that I wanted to buy D-flawless diamonds for "investment purposes." He understood perfectly, telling me he had several clients who were doing precisely the same thing. "A little hedge against inflation," he said.

However, I was not being entirely honest with Mr. Millstein. I didn't actually keep the diamonds I bought from him. I wrapped them and sent them along in an unmarked envelope to a post office box in Las Vegas. The investment I was actually making had nothing to do with a hedge against inflation or anything of a prudent economic nature. I was investing in my own future, making sure that a blackmailer I hadn't seen in a very long time kept her mouth shut.

I went directly from Mr. Millstein's establishment to Pug's for a lunch with Betty and June. Pug's is a clubby little bistro in the East Seventies, which basically serves gourmet school food, and where one is always bound to run into someone one knows. Betty was sitting at the table when I arrived. She was wearing a bright red wool suit that clashed with her red hair, which, though neatly coiffed, looked a little brittle and dried out from the sun. Her skin, however, was a healthy bronze color, making her look more robust than the washed-out, winter-weary faces around her. June was uncharacteristically late, so Betty and I each ordered a glass of white wine and settled in. Betty was still smarting over the disastrous wedding.

"When we got home I said to Gil that we should have just flushed the four hundred thousand dollars down the toilet. God knows it would have been less painful—and less wet."

"How are the honeymooners?" I said, trying to be upbeat.

"In Paris. No word. A good sign," she said.

"Have you heard from Carla?"

"Gil spoke to her. She's still down there cruising around. She's offering a million-dollar reward to anyone with any information."

"If that doesn't work, nothing will."

It was all I could do not to tell Betty what Carla had told me about Russell having disappeared before. But I was determined to respect my promise to Carla not to say anything about that. The last thing I wanted was to get a reputation like our friend June Kahn.

"So, any word from Lord Viagra?" Betty said, referring to Max Vermilion.

"Nope."

"I thought you two had hit it off," she said, disappointed.

"We kind of did. It's difficult to tell with Max. Besides, I think he's sort of involved with Lulu, even if he says he's not."

"That's never stopped him before, believe me. Junie's close to Lulu. We'll ask her when she comes."

"No we *won't*. I don't want it broadcast to the world that I'm even vaguely interested in Max Vermilion, thank you very much."

"*Are* you interested in him, Jo?"

I thought for a moment. "I'm not sure, actually. There's something odd about him that I can't quite put my finger on."

"Listen, I've known Max for twenty years, okay?" Betty said. "He's a law unto himself. Max loves women and women love Max. He's marvelous company. Very cultivated. And he likes grand ladies. I just know you two would have fun together. You and he have so much in common."

"Like what?"

"Well, you both love art. You both love to travel. You know a lot of the same people. And wouldn't it be nice to be with a man whose ticket you didn't have to pay for? Someone who might actually give you a good night kiss? Or more? Frankly, I don't understand what's holding you back, Jo."

"Holding me back from *what*, may I ask?"

"Calling him. You should just call him up and invite him to something. Or, better yet, give a party for him. Someone's always giving a party for Max and he loves them. Trust me, Jo, he's the type who needs that little extra push."

"Absolutely not! I realize we live in an age where the rules of courtship have been burned at the stake, but I'm too old to pursue a man in every sense of that statement. You start off on that foot and it never changes, believe me. He's got to make the first move."

"Oh, that's ridiculous. Jesus, if I'd waited for Gil to call me, we never would have hooked up." She paused to reflect. "Of course, then we never would have gotten married, Missy never would have been born, and we never would have given that ghastly wedding. So on second thought, maybe you're right." She gulped down the rest of her white wine and signaled the waiter for another.

Just then, June Kahn, aided by a waiter, hobbled through the front door on crutches. A dark-haired, bird-like woman in her early fifties, June was obviously still maintaining the fiction that a sprained ankle had prevented her from going to Missy's wedding. However, Betty and I both strongly suspected the real reason June had stayed away from Barbados was because she hadn't been invited to the glamorous bridal dinner aboard the Cole yacht. June hated to miss a party—especially one to which she was not invited. But being one of Lulu Cole's best friends, there was no way Carla would have included her. And, as everyone knew, for June Kahn to be excluded from a festivity was an oblivion worse than death. It was better to feign an injury.

June was so agitated that when she saw us, she practically threw her crutches at the waiter and strode over to the table, forgetting all about her ankle.

"Welcome to Lourdes," Betty said under her breath.

We both loved June. She never changed.

"You'll never guess what's happened!" she announced, plunking herself down on one of the wooden chairs. "God, I need a drink. *Waiter!*"

June ordered a martini—an impressive drink for lunch and very uncharacteristic of our friend, who usually had iced tea even when the two of us had wine. Betty and I just looked at each other, wondering what on earth was up.

"I've just heard the most ghastly thing," June said. "I can't believe it. I cannot *believe* it! *And* I'm going to fight it. You just watch. If she thinks she's going to get away with this, she has another think coming. I won't let this happen and that's that!"

"*What?*" Betty and I cried in unison.

June took a deep breath and leveled the two of us with one of her parakeet-impersonating-a-hawk gazes. "Carla Cole has bid the asking price on the Wilman apartment in *my* building."

Betty and I looked at each other.

"What about the yacht?" I said.

"Oh, she's selling the yacht," June said dismissively.

"How do you know?" Betty asked.

"I just know," June said.

Betty, who knew how easy it was to pry information out of our gossipy friend, said in a threatening tone, "*Juuune*, how do you know?"

June leaned in. "Well, this is to the grave, right?"

"Right," we both said. After years and years of hearing secrets June was sworn to keep, this was just a formality.

"Lulu told me," she said.

"And how does Lulu know?" Betty inquired.

"Oh, Lulu knows everything about those two," June said with an offhand air, as if it were the most natural thing in the world for an ex-wife to keep tabs on her ex-husband and the wife for whom he had left her.

"Well, Carla told me she always hated that boat," I said, recalling her chilling comment on the day Russell had disappeared. "And she mentioned something to me about coming to New York at the wedding."

"Is she giving up the search for Russell?" Betty asked.

"Apparently," June said. "Of course, Lulu's positive she killed him, so why would she hang around searching for someone she already knows is dead? Lulu warned Russell about Carla way before he married her. What they do to one, they'll do to another. She killed her first husband, after all."

Like all June's friends, Betty and I had long ago come to the realization that the world according to June Kahn was about as reliable as an alien sighting.

Betty sighed in exasperation. "You know, June, we've all heard that rumor about Hernandez shooting himself twice. But there's absolutely no proof that Hernandez was murdered. He committed suicide."

"I talked to Larry Locket, who says it isn't true, either," I said.

"Well, Lulu knows it for a *fact*," June insisted.

I could see Betty getting irritated.

"Has Lulu seen the autopsy report?" Betty asked.

June hesitated, as she always did before she told a lie. "Yes."

"Oh, June, Hernandez never *had* an autopsy!" Betty said. "That was the whole point. If you ask me, that entire story is a myth, probably concocted by Lulu. It's just one of those facts that's too good to check." Betty leaned back in her chair and thought for a second. "But if she really is selling the boat . . . now that's pretty interesting."

"And pretty quick, don't you think?" I said. "What do you think it means?"

"I think it means she knows he's not coming back," Betty said.

"Of course he's not! I'm telling you. He's *dead*," June said. "But that doesn't matter. What matters is that Carla wants to move into *my* building."

June always said "my building" when referring to 831 Fifth Avenue, despite the fact that there were many other tenants. Having been president of the cooperative's board for twelve years, she considered it her own personal fiefdom. June Kahn was the iron fist in that white-glove building and everyone knew it. We both waited for her to elaborate, but her thunderous silence indicated that this maneuver by Carla was the entire basis of her fury.

Finally Betty said, "So what?"

"*So what?*" June cried, throwing up her hands in indignation. "How you can even *ask* that question is beyond me! You think I want to run into a *murderess* in the lobby?"

831 Fifth was one of the most fashionable co-ops in the city—a building so notoriously difficult to get into it was dubbed "Versailles" by savvy real estate agents. Indeed, the politics and snobberies of the entire cooperative apartment market in New York made life at the ancient French court seem sunny and simplistic by comparison. It was almost impossible to get into certain buildings—particularly a luxurious prewar like 831 Fifth. Its famously tough board of directors had a mandate to keep "undesirables" out. Even having pots of

money didn't automatically guarantee admittance. Movie stars, newly minted billionaires, and all show business types were told by real estate agents that they need not even bother to apply there because they had no hope of getting in. In order to be numbered among the very rich and very social tenants, one needed hefty amounts of both cash and cachet.

The Wilman apartment was once owned by Clara Wilman, my dear late friend and mentor, who was a great philanthropist and patron of the arts and the reigning grande dame of New York until her death some years ago at the ripe age of eighty-seven. Not only was her apartment considered to be one of the most beautiful in New York, it had enormous prestige simply because it had once belonged to Clara. It is a curious fact of New York life that apartments that have been owned by great socialites are forever identified by the names of those figures. Hence, though occupied by at least two successive owners, Clara's apartment was still referred to as "the Wilman Apartment," and, like the goods at a celebrity auction, its purchase price was inflated on account of its distinguished provenance. It was as if possessing such an abode somehow automatically conferred the style of its most distinguished occupant upon the next owner. Style is something for which people in New York are always willing to pay dearly, despite the conclusive evidence that it can't be bought.

The most recent owner of the Wilman apartment, Marcy Conifer Ludinghausen, a multidivorced heiress whose latest husband had cost her yet another bundle of cash, had put the apartment on the market two years ago for a whopping twenty-eight million dollars. During that time, two separate individuals—one a clothing manufacturer from California, and the other a hotel owner from Colorado—had stepped forward to bid the hefty asking price. Lacking the necessary social credentials and personal connections, however, both parties were summarily turned down by 831's famously stuffy board.

June clearly viewed Carla's attempt to purchase the Wilman apartment as nothing short of a terrorist act. The apartment, with its grand layout and grander history, was widely considered to be a major weapon in any serious social climber's arsenal. June didn't want any competition in that area, particularly not from Carla Cole, who had stolen away the husband of one of her best friends. June was as loyal as she was indiscreet—which was really saying something. She went on:

"The awful thing is that Hadley Grimes, that old fart, who's also on the board, used to be Russell's stockbroker. He likes Carla and he wants her to get in. We have to vote, of course, and it's dangerously close. There's a good chance she'll get in. I'm a complete wreck. This is all I needed. I have so many other things to do. I don't know how I'm going to deal with this. The trouble is, I'm responsible for too many things. I'm on too many committees. I have too many commitments. You girls know me. I never stop working for the benefit of others. Do I?" June looked at us with pleading eyes.

For June, Carla's move into her building was the New York equivalent of Hitler's annexation of the Sudetenland, or the Soviet occupation of Czechoslovakia.

"I don't know what it is about this town that inspires the tsarina in rich ladies. Entertain and let entertain, that's my motto," Betty said.

"*Oh my God!*" June exclaimed. "You're not going to *see* her if she moves here, are you?"

"Honey, just call me Switzerland," Betty replied.

"Betty Waterman, you have no standards at all!" June said.

Betty grew serious. "Look, Junie, she may be an enemy of yours. She's *not*—I repeat, *not*—an enemy of mine. In fact, I rather like her. She's married to my daughter's godfather and she's been very nice to me. 'Nice is nice to me.' It's on my family crest."

June pursed her lips and said sanctimoniously, "There is a proverb which says, The enemy of my enemy is my enemy."

After a moment's reflection, Betty said, "I think that one goes, The enemy of my *friend* is my enemy, Junie."

"Whatever! It's the same thing!" June huffed. "You shouldn't talk to her because I hate her! And you're my best friend!"

Betty just shook her head in exasperation. I tried to diffuse the situation.

"Junie, you're the head of the board. Can't you veto her?"

"I *wish!* No. Unfortunately, we have to *vote.* I hate democracy. Well, it could be worse. I *was* going to resign this year. I've served that building for twelve long years and I thought it might be time to abdicate. *Thank God I didn't!* You never know what's going to go wrong. Let that be a lesson to Queen Elizabeth!"

When June finally paused to draw breath, Betty said, "Okay, let's stop talking about this and order."

During lunch, June went on, "The only ray of hope is that Carla needs a very good personal reference. Russell's not the problem, but she definitely is. And with him missing or dead or whatever he is, if she doesn't get some great letters of support, well, I don't think the other board members are going to vote with Hadley. They'll have to vote with me."

"She has lots of friends," Betty said. "They entertained a lot on the yacht."

"The international white trash set?" June said dismissively, flinging her hand in the air. "That Eurotrash she hangs out with has no weight here, believe me. No one of any standing in New York will write a letter for her. I'm sure of that. . . . Anyway, enough of all that. How was the wedding? I hear it was a disaster."

"Thank you for sharing that, June," Betty said.

"Well, I hear it *was*," June said defensively. "I mean, it's not your fault there was a typhoon that night."

"It wasn't a typhoon. It was a storm," Betty said.

"That's not what I heard. Anyway, I really wish we could have been there though. But this damn ankle." Betty looked at me and raised her eyebrows. June caught the look. "I know what you're thinking, Betty. You're thinking I made this up because I wasn't invited to the Coles' bridal dinner."

"I wasn't thinking any such thing," Betty said unconvincingly.

"Well, it just so happens that my foot doctor told me I would be permanently crippled if I reinjured the ankle. He absolutely forbade me to travel. Otherwise I wouldn't have missed it for the world. You know how much I adore Missy, and I did want to tell her that although Woody Brill is really boring, he's really, really nice. And that's what's important in life. Niceness."

"Well, we had some fun, despite the moisture," Betty said. "Jo here had a very good seat at the wedding, didn't you, Jo?" Before I could stop her, she said, "She sat between Sir Arthur Tilden, the governor general of Barbados, and Max Vermilion."

Betty was about as subtle as an overzealous face-lift. June took the bait.

"Max was there? I love Max!" June said. "He's going out with Lulu, you know."

"Really?" Betty said. "Is it serious?"

"Oh, yes! Absolutely . . ." June said. She thought for a moment. "Anyway, I think so . . ." She thought for another moment. "Well, I'm actually not sure . . . but I know they're friends!" she said confidently. "Max is *the most* charming man, isn't he? And have you ever been to Taunton Hall? What a *divine* place. The arches, the gardens! Charlie loves the Chinese bronzes. Shang, Tang, Wang—I never can get them straight. They all look like dirty old pots to me. But then, I'm not a scholar. So how is Max? I haven't seen him in ages."

"He's Max," Betty said, as if being Max Vermilion was a world unto itself.

"Don't you just love him, Jo?" June asked me.

"Well, I don't know him that well. I met him once years ago, but that's about it."

June's eyes widened in an almost cartoonish way. I could see the lightbulb going on over her head. "You know, Jo," she said in a low, conspiratorial voice, "I really should find out just how serious Lulu *is* about Max. Because if she isn't interested in him, he would be absolutely perfect for *you!*"

Betty pitched me a satisfied smile. "That's exactly what I've been telling her."

I leaned back in my chair. "I don't know why you girls want to rush me into the arms of a man who's been married umpteen times."

"Only six," June sniffed. "Or maybe seven. Possibly eight, if you count the Shady Lady."

"A multiple marrier, then," I corrected myself. "But at least a man with a rather dicey reputation where women are concerned."

"You don't have to *marry* him, Jo," June said.

"That's what I told her!" Betty interjected. "He'd just be someone fun to pal around with."

"And he'd take you to Taunton Hall and ravage you under the arches!" June said rapturously.

"Well, I have to hear from him before he can ravage me. And I haven't. So I doubt he's interested."

"You never know," Betty said. "Maybe he's shy."

"Please. Shy men don't have so many ex-wives," I said.

"I bet he's not in town," Betty said. "He went straight back to London from the wedding."

"Last I heard, there were phones in London," I said.

"Well, I'm calling Lulu tonight," June assured me. "I have to speak to her anyway. I'll broach the subject tactfully."

Betty rolled her eyes heavenward. Tact was not only not June's strong suit, it wasn't a single card in her deck.

"Please do *not* mention me," I said firmly. "There's no love lost between me and Lulu, as you well know. And if she thinks I'm trying to steal her boyfriend, she'll blow me up or something."

"Yes, if she thinks Jo's after him, even if she isn't interested, she may suddenly *get* interested," Betty said. "You know how it is. Dog in the manger. You don't want them, but you don't want anyone else to have them."

"Leave it to me, girls," June said, getting up from her chair.

June was late for her hairdresser appointment. As she was about to leave, she pointed her finger at the two of us and said, "Now I'm sending you both a list of the people who are on the board of my building. I want you to call the ones you know and tell them that Carla Cole is a murderess, okay? And that she shouldn't be allowed in the building under any cirumstances. That it would be very, very bad for the building's reputation. Okay?"

"Oh, okay, Junie," Betty said in mock earnestness. "Jo and I will get right on that, won't we, Jo?"

"Absolutely, Betts. We'll have a telethon all afternoon," I said.

June smiled with satisfaction and walked straight across the room to the waiter, who was holding her coat. He helped her on with it and then produced her crutches. Glancing back at us, she suddenly remembered she was supposed to be injured and started to limp. As she hobbled out the door, Betty turned to me and said, "Let's face it, Jo, our friend June is insane."

Nine

L ATE THAT AFTERNOON I RECEIVED A PACKAGE at home. Cyril came into my bedroom carrying the large, white box tied with a black ribbon. I recognized the wrapping. It was from Pianissimo, a pricey Italian cashmere boutique on Madison Avenue.

"This just arrived for you, madam." His snooty English voice always sounded fake to me. It was my suspicion that if I woke Cyril up in the middle of the night, he would talk just like I did.

Ever correct and expressionless, he laid the package gingerly on the bench at the foot of my bed and walked out. Cyril knew instinctively when to leave a room. I never had to say anything trite like, "That will be all," a phrase favored by my pal Trish Bromire when she addressed her help.

I untied the black satin ribbon, lifted the lid of the box, and there, on a bed of black tissue paper, was a thick ecru envelope addressed to "Mrs. Slater," written in black ink in a scrawly hand. For a minute I thought it might be from

Max. Wishful thinking. I opened the envelope and pulled out a sheet of Carla Cole's stationery with her intertwined initials "CC" embossed in ornate gold script at the top. They looked like a crest. Written in the same scrawly hand on the envelope, the note read,

> *Dear Jo,*
> *I am back in New York and I wanted to thank you for all your kindness. There is no news and it continues to be a sad time for me. Are you, by any chance, free for luncheon tomorrow? I have something I would very much like to discuss with you. Please call me if you have time.*
>
> > *With fondest regards,*
> > *Carla*
>
> *P.S. Enclosed please find a token of my appreciation, something to keep you warm in this cold winter.*

Back in New York already, eh? I thought that was odd, given the fact that her husband was still missing. I wondered if Larry had managed to get his interview with her.

Digging deep into the folds of tissue paper, I uncovered a fawn-colored cashmere and sheared mink throw, trimmed in matching brown suede, embroidered with my initials in dark brown. I was flabbergasted, particularly as I happened to know exactly how much this little item cost because I'd thought of ordering one, but decided it was too expensive.

The phone rang. It was Betty.

"Jo, you won't *believe* what just arrived," she said breathlessly.

"Let me guess . . . a mink-and-cashmere throw from Pianissimo with your initials on it from Carla Cole."

"*You, too!*" Betty shrieked. "The woman is crazy. Do you have any idea how much these things *cost*? Ten thousand dollars at least!"

"I know. I'm sending it back."

"Why?"

"Because it's much too expensive. I can't accept a present like that from someone I barely know."

Betty sighed. "I admire you, Jo. I really do. You have principles. Fortunately, I gave mine up for Lent in 1975. I wouldn't *dream* of sending this cozy little thing back. I'm sitting here with it wrapped around me as we speak. I love it! And I *adore* Carla! I'd vote her into that building myself if I could."

"Betty Waterman! Don't let June hear you."

"Honey, what can I say? I'm easy. I can be bought. I love generous, rich people. And, God knows, there are precious few of them."

I called Carla and agreed to meet her for lunch the next day, more out of curiosity than compassion. I had the feeling she was up to something and I wanted to find out what it was—fast. She suggested The Forum, a restaurant more associated with high-powered deal makers than lunching ladies. She said she would make the reservation.

I arrived at The Forum a little before one, checked my coat in the cloakroom on the ground floor, and walked up the split flight of marble steps to the second level where the restaurant was located. The vast, airy space, with its polished wood walls and sleek modern design, was a far cry from the intimate atmosphere of Pug's. At the top of the landing, behind a long, wooden station that served as a kind of barricade against intruders, stood Giovanni, the maître d' who had been there since the Civil War. Giovanni was a rather impish man with a keen eye trained to sort out the great from the near-great, and discard the inconsequentials altogether. He served as a stage director whose job it is to keep the stars up front and the powerless out of sight. Tables were therefore divided into three groups, the Good, the Bad, and the Invisible.

In the old days, I used to lunch there occasionally with Lucius, my late husband, who enjoyed the testosterone-scented atmosphere of the place much more than I did. Lucius had been one of the stars, of course, and he ate there frequently with his cronies, either conducting business or trading gossip, while a hush of waiters hovered nearby waiting to serve him. I hadn't been there in years, however, so I was pleasantly surpised when Giovanni recognized me.

"Ah, Mrs. Slater," he said warmly. "How nice to see you again. You deserted us."

I shook his hand. "Hello, Giovanni. It has been a long time."

Without so much as a glance at the reservations roster, he said, "And you are meeting Mrs. Cole, who just this moment telephoned to say she would be a few minutes late. Would you like to be seated at the table or do you prefer to wait here?"

"I'll go to the table, thank you."

Giovanni led me to one of the banquette tables against the wall, an excellent seat with a prime view of all the other notable diners. I ordered a mineral water and looked around the room while I waited for Carla. There was the usual sprinkling of billionaires, top CEO's, politicos, and media moguls. But the surprise for me was the number of women who seemed to be there on their own steam rather than as accessories for powerful men. As I sipped my water, I couldn't help overhearing the two women seated at the next table who were talking about something called "the long bond." I gathered from their conversation that it had nothing whatsoever to do with relationships.

Suddenly, over in the far corner, I spotted Gil Waterman dining with a man whose back was toward me. Even from that angle, the man looked vaguely familiar, and when he turned his head slightly I saw that it was none other than Max Vermilion. I felt an odd combination of elation and disappointment—elation at seeing him again, disappointment at the fact that he was in New York and hadn't called me. I wondered if Betty knew that Gil was lunching with him. I sincerely doubted it, or she definitely would have suggested we come here. I immediately took out my compact and checked myself in the mirror to see if I looked okay, in case Max came over to the table. Unfortunately, it wasn't one of my best days. I had circles under my eyes and I wished I'd chosen my snappy, new red suit instead of the tired old black one I was wearing. I thought of Clara Wilman, who used to say to me, "Always look your best. You never know who you'll bump into."

After a few moments, Carla arrived looking chic and rich, wearing a sable-trimmed suit, light lens sunglasses, and an air of entitlement. Her thick hair was pulled back in a tight chignon. She exuded the quiet confidence of a woman who is used to getting her way without ever having to insist. Her gestures were mannered, as if she were conscious of being watched. Giovanni scooted out from behind his little bulwark to greet her. She extended her hand to the maître d' with the aloofness of royalty and they chatted. Her cool self-possession made his eagerness to please look slightly manic. He reminded me of a jumping jack, bobbing nervously up and and down, unable to keep still. I watched them closely. After a moment or two, I saw Giovanni pick up on the almost imperceptible shift in her body language that indicated she was through talking to him and wanted to be led to the table.

As Carla walked through the room, I felt a certain frisson in the air, as one by one people noticed her. Several prominent diners pitched her fond salutes. Carla graciously acknowledged them, like a great star acknowledging her fans. It wasn't condescension, but more an awareness of her role. She seemed to understand she was at the vortex of an international mystery and, as a result, she projected what I can only describe as a kind of melancholy hauteur which, paradoxically, made her seem both helpless and invulnerable at the same time. I marveled at the number of influential friends she seemed to have for someone who had spent so little time in New York. I was forgetting, of course, that ultrarich players like the Coles occupy a borderless country, the inhabitants of which are all known to one another, if not to the general public.

In addition to her admirers, however, there were other diners who seemed less entranced with Carla. A few of them gave her the once-over, quickly averted their eyes, or else ostentatiously turned away as she walked by their tables. Indeed, this group seemed to view the lady with suspicion.

Gil and Max were so deep in conversation they didn't even notice her, but she noticed them. I saw her eyeing the two of them as she walked. The maître d' pulled out the table so she could sit down.

"Jo! It is wonderful to see you," Carla said, sliding

into the banquette beside me. She took my hand and air kissed me on both cheeks. "I cannot tell you how thrilled I was when you called to accept my invitation." She glanced around the room. "Oh, there's Gil," she said, pretending she had just spotted him. "Who is he with? Is that Max Vermilion?"

"Yes, it is."

"I did not know Max was in New York. Have you seen him?"

"No. I didn't know he was here either."

She peered at me over the tops of her glasses. "Are you sure? A little bird told me that you and Max were seeing each other."

"Well, that little bird is mistaken. I haven't seen Max since the wedding."

"If you do not mind my saying so, Jo, Max would be perfect for you."

I sighed in exasperation. "So everyone keeps telling me. Perhaps someone ought to tell Max."

"So you like him, do you?"

"I don't really know him. Anyway, isn't he involved with Lulu? Isn't that why he was disinvited to the bridal dinner on your boat?"

"Yes, of course, that was the reason. Not that Russell still cares for Lulu. He absolutely loathes her. However, Max's presence there would have reminded him of her, and he did not want to spoil such a glorious night."

"A glorious night" struck me as an odd way to describe the evening that her husband disappeared.

"Have you had any news about Russell?" I asked.

Carla shook her head sadly. "No . . . and the press are really awful. They made my life a nightmare on the boat. I was a prisoner, so I left."

"I know that Larry Locket was going down there to interview you. Did you see him?"

She seemed distressed. "Oh, yes, Larry Locket! I feel so badly about him. I said I would see him and then, well, I just could not. But I will see him here in New York."

"I heard you sold the boat."

Her eyes widened. "Where did you hear that?"

"I forget."

She pinned me with her gaze. "No, you do not. But you are not going to tell me, are you? Never mind. It really doesn't matter. Yes, I sold the boat. There is no point in keeping it now."

"Aren't you afraid that when Russell comes back, he'll be upset?"

"No." She shrugged. "We have been talking about getting rid of it for some time now. We are moving to New York. We have bid on an apartment."

"Really?" I didn't let on that I knew about the Wilman apartment.

"In fact, that is why I asked you to lunch, Jo. I would like very much to talk to you about that."

I wanted to hear what Carla had to say, of course, but first I felt it necessary to get the Pianissimo throw question out of the way. After the waiter took our orders, I approached the subject as delicately as possible.

"Carla, I don't wish to appear ungrateful, but you know that beautiful present you sent me . . . ? I'm afraid I can't accept it."

Her face fell. "Oh, but I thought it was so pretty."

"It's lovely. That's not the point. It's just . . . well . . . unnecessary. It was extremely generous of you, and very sweet, but I feel, well, awkward about it. I don't want to hurt your feelings, but . . . I'm sure you understand."

Taking a sip of water, she reflected for a long moment. Then she put the glass down decisively, looked me square in the eye and said, "You know, Jo, you are exactly right! I see now that it was a bit vulgar. Perhaps a letter expressing my appreciation would have been more elegant. But my handwriting is so bad. You and Betty were so kind to me in Barbados. I just wanted to show you both how much your friendship means to me."

"Yes, but you didn't have to give us anything. Particularly not something so lavish."

She cocked her head to one side. "To be honest, Jo, I did not even ask the price. Is that too terrible? I really didn't think of it. I just saw them in the shop and they were beautiful and I thought of you and Betty. Now I feel badly."

I shook my head. "No, no. I know you meant well, Carla, dear. You're very thoughtful. But I feel it makes the friendship a little off balance, if you know what I mean."

Carla knew our little world well enough to understand what I was really saying: She wasn't a good enough friend to give such an expensive present or for me to accept it. It was one thing if Betty or June or Trish or the late Clara Wilman had given it to me. But Carla's and my friendship needed more time to develop on its own without the catalyst of an overly generous act, or a veiled bribe—however one wanted to interpret her kindness.

I went on, "My initials are on it, so I feel rather rude giving it back."

"Do not give it another thought," she said. "I completely understand. I will have my chauffeur come around and collect it this afternoon. Perhaps one day, when we are better friends, I will give you a present you will not be able to refuse."

We shared a knowing little laugh, which eased the tension somewhat. Our lunch arrived. As we ate The Forum's famous white truffle risotto, Carla said, "On to another subject. Jo, I need your help."

Okay, now we're getting down to it, I thought: the reason for the lunch and the real reason for the present.

She drew a long breath. "As I mentioned to you, I—that is *we*, Russell and I—" she corrected herself, "have bid on an apartment."

"The Wilman apartment," I said.

"So you know about that, too?"

"You'll learn quickly there are no secrets in New York," I said, laughing.

"There are no secrets anywhere, Jo," she shot back like a threat.

"So you've bid on Clara's apartment," I said, ignoring the undertone in her words.

"Your great friend, Clara Wilman," Carla nodded. "It is in the same building as your other great friend, June Kahn."

"June's mentioned it," I said with an uneasy smile.

"I am sure she has. And I am sure you know that she is making my life extremely difficult."

"June's been known to do that on occasion."

"When Russell comes back, he will be furious, of course. But Jo, she is being simply awful about me. I understand she is Lulu's best friend. But she is the head of the board and she is going around telling all these terrible lies about me. Fortunately, I have another friend on the board—Hadley Grimes. But my real estate broker called me and said she doubts very seriously that I can get into the building if June continues her campaign against me. June has enormous power in that building."

"I know. And she's being very unreasonable. Betty and I told her that."

"Even if I were not trying to get into the building, I cannot have her spreading all these ghastly rumors about me, Jo. It's bad enough with Lulu. But at least Lulu has a reason to dislike me. June Kahn is a woman I barely know."

"Look, Carla, June is an extremely loyal person and she's very loyal to Lulu. She loves taking up other people's causes. She's a true foul-weather friend."

Carla scoffed at this. "That is not the reason she has a vendetta against me."

"No?"

"No . . . it really comes from the time when I married Russell."

"What do you mean?"

"June Kahn was *desperate* to be invited to the wedding and Russell didn't want to have her."

Now *this* was news.

"Wait—let me get this straight. June wanted to be invited to *your* wedding to Russell?" I asked in disbelief.

Carla told the story in a light, offhand way: "Yes. Russ and I were very surprised, to say the least. Particularly because she was supposed to be such a great friend of Lulu's and she had taken Lulu's side during the divorce. Russ could not believe it when June called him and asked if she could come."

"Wait a minute. June called Russell and asked if she could come to your wedding? I don't believe it!"

"Jo, I swear to you," Carla said, putting her hand on her heart. "She rang him up and said that since they had once been such great friends and that he was so happy now, she and her husband wanted to come and help him celebrate his marriage to me."

It was hard for me to believe that June, who had been so outspoken against Carla and the wedding, had actually tried to wangle herself an invitation. The only thing more humiliating than not being invited to a party you want to go to is trying to *get* yourself invited to a party you want to go to—without succeeding.

"Are you absolutely sure about this?" I asked her.

"Absolutely! You ask Russell. He was *furrrrious*," Carla went on, her accent sounding like a growl. "Do you know what he said to me? He said, 'June Kahn would rather die than miss a party'—particularly one that all her friends are going to."

I knew that was true. June was a famous and shameless party hound. She had been known to call up people she hardly knew and ask to be invited to things. As far as her friends were concerned, she had no problem calling them to insist she be included in on everything. Betty once told her, "Listen, Junie, everyone can't be invited to everything," to which June responded in a huff, "Well, I'm not *everyone*!"

"In any case," Carla continued, "Russell refused to invite her. Not just because she was so close to Lulu, but because of all the terrible things she had said about me. Russell was always so protective of me. *Is* so protective of me," she corrected herself.

"I'm speechless, Carla, because I remember June telling me at the time she wouldn't go to your wedding even if Russell begged her to. She didn't want to upset Lulu."

Carla sighed. "Well, I really do not know what to say,

Jo. I know she is your dear friend, but that is a complete lie. And what is more, I told Russell to go right ahead and invite her if she wanted to come so badly."

"That was big of you, I must say."

Carla leaned back on the banquette. A dreamy expression softened her face. "You know, at that time, Jo, I was so happy that I would even have asked Lulu, or the devil himself, to my wedding if they had wanted to come."

I smiled to myself, thinking that in Carla's view Lulu and the devil must be pretty much the same person.

"I promise you, it was *Russell* who did not want June," she went on. "But June blamed me. Why is it that women always get the blame for everything? And now, when Russell is not here to defend me, June is trying to get her revenge by blocking me—*us*—from buying that beautiful apartment. I've done nothing to this woman, Jo. *Niente!*"

If the story Carla had told me about the wedding were true, June's behavior was not merely a simple case of overzealous loyalty to Lulu. It was more like, "hell hath no fury like an uninvited guest." I was starting to feel vaguely sympathetic to Carla.

"I agree with you. June's being very unreasonable. But there's nothing I can do to help you, I'm afraid. She's adamant."

Carla shifted in her seat. "Do you know Hadley Grimes?"

"Yes. I've known Hadley and Ellen for years." The Grimeses were fringe people I knew but didn't see much of.

"Hadley was Russell's stockbroker at Ranley Gorman. He is on the board and he is on my side. He will support me."

"Well, that's good, then."

"Hadley told me that if I could find someone very prestigious to write me a letter of recommendation, it would count for a lot with the board."

"Yes, I'm sure that's true."

"Would you write a letter for me, Jo?" She gave me a soulful look.

Bingo. The real reason for the lunch and the present.

I lowered my eyes and moved some risotto around my plate, avoiding Carla's insistent gaze.

"You know I can't do that, Carla."

"Why not?"

"Well, for one thing, when you write a letter of recommendation for someone to get into a building—and I've written several in my time—you really have to know the person quite well. And I don't know you very well. But even aside from that, June is one of my oldest and dearest friends. And you know how she feels about this—irrrational as it may be. I just couldn't do that to her."

"I see," Carla said softly.

"You'll find someone else. You have so many friends."

"There is no one else like you, Jo."

"That's not true." I was embarassed by the flattery.

"But it *is*. You are one of the great grande dames of New York. Everyone knows it. And the very fact that you are so close to June would make your recommendation that much more powerful."

There she had a point.

I shook my head with a sad smile and said, "Carla, dear, I'd like to help you out, but I can't. You understand."

There was an awkward silence as the waiter cleared our places. When he brought us our coffees, Carla said,

"You stupid little man, I ordered a cappucino, not an espresso. Take it back immediately." Her tone was matter-of-fact, which made her words oddly more chilling.

"I'm very sorry," the waiter muttered as he swooped up the offending little cup.

It didn't take Freud to understand that her outburst at the waiter was obliquely directed at me. Still, I was quite appalled, particularly as she seemed to have no idea what she had done. I loathe bad manners and there is nothing more ill-mannered than being rude to people who are not in a position to be rude back. For the first time, I actively disliked Carla.

Aimlessly tapping her well-manicured nails on the tablecloth, she suddenly changed gears.

"Tell me, Jo, have you ever been to Las Vegas?" she said in a perky voice.

A startling question.

"No. Why?"

"But you have friends there, no?"

"No," I said, warily.

"No?" She cocked her head to one side. "Somehow I thought you did."

"Not that I recall."

I wondered, was it *possible* that Carla knew about Oliva, the woman who was blackmailing me? Sending unmarked envelopes with diamonds in them to a post office box number in Las Vegas was as close as I'd ever gotten to that city. It was an odd question for her to ask.

"I've never been to Las Vegas and I don't have any friends there," I said firmly.

"No matter," she said.

She quickly let the subject drop, but I felt a frisson of foreboding. The implication was that she knew something about me—something I didn't want known. Still, I couldn't quite be sure. It was so hard to tell.

Carla put her hand on my sleeve and said earnestly, "Jo, please reconsider. It would be such a great favor to me if you would write that letter to the board. Do this for me, Jo. You won't regret it."

"I'll have to think about it, Carla. June's a very close friend."

"I know, but you are a very fair person, and she is being so unreasonable. I think Betty will write a letter for me."

"Really?"

"Well, Russell is Missy's godfather, after all. And I gave her daughter quite a nice party."

Even though what she said was all true, I thought it a bit tacky of her to bring it up herself, particularly since Betty was well aware of the debt she owed her.

Carla suddenly preened. Gil and Max, finished with their lunch, were heading over to our table to say hello. But by the time I saw them coming, it was too late to freshen up.

"Ah, Gil! And Lord Vermilion," she said, extending her hand. "How lovely to see you both. Of course, you know Jo Slater."

Max and Gil both wore somber expressions. "Carla, dear, any word about Russell?" Gil said.

Carla switched gears again, growing very serious, as if she suddenly remembered her husband was missing. She shook her head and said sadly, "No. No word yet." Then she looked up with a sort of beatific expression on her face, and said, "But I am still very, very optimistic."

"You must continue to be, dear lady," Max said with the utmost earnestness.

"That's right. Never give up hope," Gil echoed.

"I never will," Carla said piously.

I couldn't help noticing how dashing and rather old-fashioned Max looked dressed in one of his old-style Savile Row suits. He looked at me with one of his you're-the-only-woman-in-the-room gazes and said, "Jo, I just got to town. May I call you this evening?"

"Of course."

"Jo and I have been through the war together," he announced with a little chuckle.

"What do you mean?" I asked him.

"The wedding, dear girl . . . a night to remember . . . or forget. No offense, Gil, old boy."

"Please . . ." Gil rolled his eyes. "Don't remind me."

Gil and Max moved on. Carla gazed after them wistfully. "Lord Vermilion is a very attractive man," she said.

"Yes."

"He likes you."

"Really? You could've fooled me."

"I can always tell when a man likes a woman," she said with an assured edge. "You should really make a try for him." She got a sort of faraway look on her face and added, "Being Lady Vermilion is a great thing."

"God knows there have been quite a few of them," I said.

"Have you ever been to Taunton Hall?"

"No, never. I hear it's quite something."

"It is the most beautiful property I have ever seen. There is nothing to compare with it."

It struck me at that moment that Carla herself might be a little interested in Lord Vermilion.

"Carla, remember you told me in Barbados that Russell had disappeared before? What exactly did you mean?"

Carla glanced at her watch. "Oh, I would love to explain it to you, Jo, but unfortunately, I have an appointment and I must go now."

"Fine. Then let's get the check," I said, understanding that this line of inquiry was pointless.

"No, no. It is all taken care of."

Before we both stood up to leave, she took my hand. "*Cara* Jo, you *will* think about writing me that letter, won't you? It would make things so much simpler, and I would so appreciate it. Russell will be so grateful when he comes back."

This sounded to me more like a command than a request. On the other hand, it just could have been my guilty conscience talking. I couldn't be sure.

Ten

CARLA'S LAS VEGAS COMMENT GNAWED AT ME all afternoon. When I got home that evening, I went straight to the library and poured myself a stiff drink. I sank into the burgundy velvet couch flanking the fireplace, thinking what a nuisance this was. Did she or did she not know I was being blackmailed? Just when I had rather cheerfully resigned myself to that unpleasant situation, it was irritating to think I had another threat to contend with.

I stared up at the Vigée-Lebrun portrait above the carved wooden mantelpiece. This sunny depiction of a smiling, dewy-eyed young noblewoman, who looked as though she didn't have a care in the world, wearing a large straw hat with streaming blue taffeta ribbons and with an open book in her lap, was painted in 1788, a year before the French Revolution. Two years later, this same young woman was guillotined. I empathized with her, knowing how quickly things in life can change.

Just then, the phone rang, piercing the gloom and startling me out of my ruminations. I hesitated before picking it up, hoping it might be Max. I wanted to sound calm and upbeat. Finally, I lifted the receiver and said an overly chirpy, "Hello!"

"Mrs. Slater—*Slaytah*—please," said a patrician male voice at the other end of the line.

"Speaking."

"Jooooo!" the voice broke free. "Hadley Grimes here—*heah*."

Hadley Grimes, a charter member of that severely dwindled tribe of patrician WASPs who once ruled New York, spoke with a pronounced mid-Atlantic accent, reflective of his prep school and Ivy League background.

"Oh, Hadley," I said, deflated. "Hello."

"Fine, dear—*deah*—fine," he said, without my having asked how he was. "Listen, I understand you've heard—*heurhed*—about our little situation here with the Coles and the Wilman apartment."

"Yes, Hadley, I certainly have."

"Now, the reason I'm calling," he said, pausing to clear his throat, "is because I just got a call from Carla Cole, who informs me that you've agreed to write a letter to the board on their behalf. Is that correct?"

Not one to waste any time, that Carla.

"No, it's not."

"What do you mean, dear?" *Deah*.

"Uh, well, I was just sitting here thinking about it, as a matter of fact. June is one of my closest and dearest friends, as you know. And I'm sure you can appreciate the fact that if I write a letter for Carla, it will put a great strain on our friendship. On the other hand, I do happen to think June's being very unreasonable about the whole thing."

"She certainly—*seuhtainly*—is! June practically beaned me with her umbrella in the lobby the other day over this thing."

Despite that hilarious image, there was an air of immense seriousness about the conversation. I could just picture Hadley—dessicated, old bird that he was—pursing his lips and shaking his balding head in disapproval.

"Carla is the problem—not Russell, of course. Several people on the board are quite skeptical about her, on account of the scandal and all. That's why your letter would carry so much weight, Jo. Marcy's threatening to sue if we turn down the Coles. We've already turned down two of her other candidates. Marcy's a great friend of my wife's," Hadley went on, boasting of the acquaintance, "and between you and me, she needs the cash. This last divorce from Baron Ludinghausen has cost her quite a bundle. In any case, the Coles are about the only ones who can afford her price. You know, they bid the asking price. Twenty-eight million dollars. Staggering, no? The last thing we need is a lawsuit over this. Very unseemly, lawsuits."

Hadley Grimes was one of the "Tut-tut people," as Betty Waterman nicknamed them. The Tut-tuts were third- or fourth-generation members of the former ruling class of New York whose forebears had treated the city as their own personal fiefdom, and who, as late as the 1980s, took pains to exclude certain "elements" (as anyone who wasn't a white Anglo-Saxon Protestant was called) from their social surroundings, like clubs and apartment buildings. When a new crop of plutocrats upset the old order and stormed the bastions of privilege, the Tut-tuts took refuge in the condemnation of "new money." They also took great offense at any suggestion that their own conduct was less than impeccable.

Hadley was, admittedly, one of the nicer Tut-tuts, free of racial and religious prejudice at least, although Betty swore he was an awful sexist, having heard him refer to his wife as "the little woman" on more than one occasion—and not as a joke. I suspected he recognized that his days as a power broker in any sphere but his coveted apartment building were over, and that's why he was making the most of his position as a member of the board.

"Let me ask you something, Hadley. Can the Coles get into this building without my letter?"

He thought for a moment. "Well, I want them in. And at least two other people on the board want them in. But several are undecided. It's going to be a very close vote. June's the head of the board so she does carry a lot of weight. But she still only has one vote. The honest answer is, I don't know. . . . Look, Jo, if you think June is being unreasonable, you ought to support the Coles. It simply isn't fair—either to them or to Marcy, who's been very patient with us so far. As I said, we've turned down two of her candidates already because June didn't like them. June has blown this whole thing way out of proportion. We're a co-op, not a battleground, after all."

"Strikes me as pretty much the same thing," I said.

He didn't laugh. Not that I expected him to. Hadley, who had precious little humor, was known for having once seriously proposed a WASP Day Parade in honor of New York's newest minority.

"All the other groups have parades," he sniffed. "At least we'd keep the lines down Fifth Avenue white."

When Betty heard about this, she shrieked with laughter, saying that they ought to hold it on April fifteenth—income tax day—"the day that really lives in infamy for the WASPs," she said. "And let Hadley be king of the Trust Fund Float, which starts out big and shrinks to nothing as the day goes on!" Betty added with glee.

I hung up the phone with Hadley, feeling some trepidation. If Carla *did* know about my blackmailer, it was just conceivable that she also knew what I was being blackmailed *for*. That would be an inconvenience, to say the least. However, I didn't want her to think I was writing that letter to the board because I was frightened of her. I'm not one to let myself be pushed around by anyone. That went for Carla, as well as my friend June. I decided to call Betty to ask for her advice, leaving out, of course, the salient detail that Carla Cole might have something unpleasant on me. Betty picked up the phone, sounding agitated. When I told her Hadley Grimes had just called me, she started a tirade.

"Well, I just got off the phone with Marcy Ludinghausen, who's having a conniption fit!" Betty said. "She asked me if I would write a letter on behalf of the Coles and by God, I'm going to do it! I love our friend June, but talk about a brat! Marcy said June threatened her! If you ask me, June is making a big stink over nothing. I know the reason why—and so does Marcy."

"Because she's great friends with Lulu," I said.

"That, too. But if you ask me, that's not it."

"What do you mean?"

"Listen, if I know June, the *real* reason she's doing this is because she's worried about not being invited to Carla's parties—of which there will be *many*, I assure you."

It was true that if June Kahn had ever formed a concrete conception of hell in her mind, it would have been to live in a building where, night after night, all her friends and other glamorous people were going to a lavish party from which she was permanently excluded. I thought back to what Carla had said at lunch about June wanting to come to her wedding and I knew that Betty was right.

"I hate to say it, but you have a point," I said.

"Oh, I *know* that's it! June's loyalty to Lulu is less important than her desire to get to every party there is. She goes to the opening of an envelope, as we all know. Plus, we've got to think of poor old Russell. What if he turns up? He has no boat, no apartment . . . fuck it! I'm writing a letter for them. I don't care. You can do what you want. June is so damn imperious. I just think it's time she was taught a lesson, that's all. She can't have absolutely everything her way *all* the time!"

There was something more in Betty's voice, however, some deeper hurt that seemed to be gnawing at her. She paused for a moment. Then she said, "And I really think that as one of my oldest friends, June could have made the effort to come to Missy's wedding, even if she wasn't invited to the bridal dinner. Instead she fakes that ridiculous injury! She goes to every party in the world except my daughter's wedding? That's nice. And I hear from everyone she's been going all around town saying what a nightmare it was when she wasn't even there! Frankly, Jo, I'm really pissed at her."

We both loved June, despite the fact that she had grown more obsessive about social life over the years. June was one of those friends I cherished primarily on account of a shared history and long acquaintance. Her foolishness was always tempered by my abiding fondness for her, even when she was being her most unreasonable. But I sensed that Betty's irritation with our old pal was about something more profound than simply teaching her a lesson. It always amazes me how both consequential and inconsequential social life is. You never know what will make people take offense. I never imagined that Betty was so hurt that June hadn't come to Missy's wedding. She'd never said a word. But she clearly was. And even if she didn't fully realize it herself, helping Carla was her revenge.

"Be careful, Betts. June'll have a fit if she finds out you're on Carla's side."

"I'm on Russell's side, not Carla's."

"Somehow I doubt June will see it that way."

"I don't care," Betty said. "I'm writing them a letter."

Oddly enough, I hung up the phone feeling more uneasy than ever. If I did write a letter, it might send a signal to Carla that I could be coerced into doing anything she wanted. On the other hand, if I didn't write the letter, June would think *she* could boss me around. I decided to sit down and write the damn thing, stick it in an envelope, and think about it overnight.

It was dark when I finally hauled myself up and walked over to the desk that faced one of the large picture windows overlooking Fifth Avenue and Central Park. I sat down and took out a sheet of stationery and a fountain pen from the top drawer. I gazed down at the darkening cloak of trees aglitter with pinpricks of lamplight stretching to the horizon. I thought I would take a stab at composing the damn letter to Hadley Grimes on Carla's behalf just to see what it felt like. On the thin, pale blue paper embossed with my name in white, I began my letter to the board.

> *Dear Ladies and Gentlemen,*
> *I understand that Carla and Russell Cole wish to purchase an apartment in your building . . .*

Just as I was finishing up the damn thing, the phone rang again. I picked it up without thinking and said a curt, "Hello."

"May I speak with Mrs. Slater, please?"

It was Max.

"Max?"

"Jo . . . am I interrupting you?"

"No, no. I was just, uh, sorting out the mail, that's all."

"Lovely seeing you at lunch today."

"Yes, lovely seeing you, too. Where are you staying?" I asked him.

"The Carlyle."

"And how long are you here for?"

"Just a few days . . . I wonder, what's your view of the opera?"

Opera was not exactly my thing, although I occasionally went with Ethan Monk because he was so knowledgeable.

I decided to hedge my bet: "Well, I'm not the greatest opera fan. But I like it sometimes."

Max laughed. "I applaud your honesty. You wouldn't put aside your prejudice and come with me to the opening of *Tosca* tomorrow night, would you? If we hate it, we'll leave. I promise."

I accepted Max's invitation not because I wanted to

see the opera, but because I wanted to see Max and find out once and for all if there was some spark between us. He said he would pick me up at seven and take me to supper afterward. I hung up the phone feeling cautiously elated.

Eleven

THE FOLLOWING MORNING AT TEN O'CLOCK, Caspar drove me up to the Municipal Museum for a meeting of the acquisitions committee. I sat in the back of my black Mercedes, staring at the letter I had written for the Coles like it was a bomb, thinking that if Carla did get into June's building it would become a social hot spot that made the Middle East look like an oasis of calm by comparison. We pulled up in front of the Muni, a magisterial limestone museum complex on Fifth Avenue, and Caspar got out of the car, trotting around to open the door for me. I was about to hand him the letter to deliver to Hadley Grimes, but I put it back into my purse instead. I wanted to think about it some more.

It was with a conflicted heart that I walked up the wide stone steps to the entrance of the building. Once inside its cool stone precincts, however, I felt better. I loved walking through the vast halls, hearing my footsteps echo on the venerable old marble floors of the institution I had dedicated all my philanthropic efforts to for nearly a quarter of a century. I took the elevator up to the fourth floor where the acquisitions committee met in the large conference room adjoining the patrons' lounge. The meeting was just getting started and everyone was settling in.

I said hello to my fellow committee members, who were, with a couple of exceptions, bright, attractive, philanthropists who shared a passion for collecting and for our great museum. One exception was Robert Mueller, a socially ambitious, titanically rich man who had bailed the museum out of its terrible financial woes in the nineties. He had been so instrumental in helping us that we couldn't very well turn down his request that he be elected to the board. Then he wanted to be on the acquisitions committee, and no one felt they could refuse him that, either. Alas, it was a disaster. Mueller had strong opinions on a variety of subjects, particularly one about which he knew absolutely nothing: art.

I took my usual place next to Edmond Norbeau, the cultivated and attractive director of the Muni. Edmond greeted me warmly. A reserved and extremely correct man by nature, he never actually came out and said he was happy to have me back on the board after that humiliating period in my life where I'd been gently forced to resign, but I sensed he was thrilled.

That day, my darling Ethan Monk, now the head curator of Old Master paintings, was proposing that we acquire a haunting work entitled *Judas and the Thirty Pieces of Silver*, attributed to Etienne de La Tour. However, Ethan strongly believed the picture was actually by Etienne's father, the great seventeenth-century master Georges de La Tour, which, if true, would make it a major find. Robert Mueller disagreed with Ethan's assessment, of course, which only confirmed Ethan's educated hunch in the eyes of the other committee members. The picture was being deaccessioned by the Foster collection, a small museum in Virginia which was closing due to lack of funds. They were asking a million dollars—a real bargain if it did indeed turn out to be by Etienne's more celebrated father. The problem was we didn't have a million to spend on a speculative painting, no matter how convinced Ethan was of its true creator.

As I examined a large color transparency of the work—a study of the arch traitor Judas Iscariot, his tormented face illuminated by the light from a single candle flame as he stares at the silver coins shimmering on the table in front of him—I understood exactly how he felt, being on the brink of betraying my own best friend for a self-serving piece of silence, if not silver.

The committee agreed that the picture would be a fine addition to the museum and it was now just a matter of finding the funds to buy it. I knew that Ethan had his heart set on it, so I pledged half a million dollars specifically toward its purchase. That half million was over and above the two million I gave annually to the museum as a matter of course. However, that still left another five hundred thousand to be raised to buy the painting. There was some discussion about where the remaining funds might be located. But for the moment, the question was left unresolved.

After the meeting, I asked Ethan to ride down with me to the main floor.

"I'm going to the opening of *Tosca* tonight," I said, certain he was, too.

"Me, too. Who are you going with?"

"Max Vermilion."

"Well, well, well," Ethan said with an approving smile. "I'm impressed."

"I told him I wasn't a big opera fan."

"That's putting it mildly. You only like it when I tell you who's sleeping with who in the cast."

Ethan, a rabid opera lover, once confided to me that he forced potential boyfriends to sit through the entire Ring Cycle—all seventeen hours of it—before he would get involved with them. "It's a good way to tell whether or not they're serious about the relationship," Ethan said earnestly, then added. "Of course these days seventeen hours *is* a relationship."

"Anyway, I'll see you there," I said.

"I doubt it. I'm sitting in Lulu Cole's box."

"God, I forgot. Of course, Lulu will be there. She's the chairman. Well, I won't see you, then."

"Maybe at intermission. Listen, Jo, I want you to become Lady Vermilion so I can come and live with you at Taunton Hall. Imagine waking up to all that beauty every morning."

"Just let me get through *Tosca* first, okay?"

Even Ethan was trying to fix me up with Max.

Caspar was waiting for me outside the Muni. I got in the car and we headed down Fifth to the Pierre Hotel, where Trish Bromire was giving a benefit luncheon. Poor Trish needed all the support she could get right now. Her husband, Dick Bromire, was about to go on trial for tax evasion and other money-related crimes. There was a real possibility he might go to jail. It was the job of Trish's girlfriends to support her in her hour of need. Though I didn't much feel like going to the luncheon, I couldn't very well let her down.

Before I took my compact out of my purse to freshen up, I extracted the letter I had written for Carla Cole. As we rolled along the avenue, I stared at it for a long moment. I had considered dropping it off on my way to Trish's luncheon. However, that portrait of Judas Iscariot had hit home. I didn't feel like seeing Judas staring back at me in the compact mirror. Betty could teach June a lesson if she wanted to, but I was not about to betray one of my best friends, whether Carla Cole had something on me or not. I ripped it up.

The luncheon at the Pierre was being held in The Cotillion Room, a large, light, and airy space with three picture windows facing Fifth Avenue. Trish was involved in so many charities, it was difficult to keep track of them all, but this was one of her less fashionable causes, the Bromire Center for the Aged. I applauded Trish for using her social clout to support "people" institutions as opposed to "arts" institutions, which were distinctly more sought after on account of their ability to springboard big supporters to social prominence. It was disconcerting the number of rich people in New York who eagerly shelled out millions of dollars for a seat on the board of the great old institutions like the Municipal Museum or the Metropolitan Opera, but who balked at spending fifty dollars for a more needy but less stellar cause.

Everyone knew that if Trish Bromire's name was on an invitation, the event would be filled with prominent socialites and photo opportunities, if you liked that sort of thing (I don't). Understanding she attracted a chic crowd and flashy coverage in *Nous* magazine, Trish used her power wisely—spreading it around to include minority scholarship programs, small dance and theater companies, cancer hospices, and other obscure but worthy organizations that never got any attention.

A couple of photographers, lying in wait for the lunching ladies, snapped my picture in the lobby. I climbed the long flight of steps to the second floor to the Regency Room, a cocktail area in front of The Cotillion Room, where drinks were being served. I greeted many old pals along the way. As bad luck would have it, June was standing near the entrance in a fussy, pale blue luncheon suit with bows on the sleeves and ruffles at the neck. I imagined what I might have felt like seeing her now had I delivered that letter, and I was happily reaffirmed in my decision to rip it up. She was engrossed in conversation with a woman I didn't know and they didn't look as though they wanted to be interrupted. I tried to sneak by, but June caught sight of me and motioned me over to say hello. She gave me a kiss. So did the other woman, whose warm greeting I returned, pretending to know her, even though I hadn't the slightest idea who she was. The two of them obviously wanted to resume their talk, so I excused myself and walked away.

I grabbed a glass of wine from a waiter carrying a tray with glasses of wine, orange juice, and water. Betty marched up to me wearing a white suit made of some sort of rolled material that made her look like the Michelin Man or a padded cell, depending on the angle. I could tell by her blotchy complexion and watery eyes that the champagne flute she was holding wasn't her first.

"So whaddya think of Marcy Ludinghausen?" Betty asked, slightly sloshed.

"Marcy's here?" I said, looking around the room.

"You just said hello to her. She's over there talking to

June—about the apartment, I'm sure. Wait'll June finds out I wrote a letter for Carla. Oy!"

I whirled around and stared at the stranger who had greeted me at the door, trying to divine any traces of the Marcy Ludinghausen I had once known.

"My God, that's *Marcy?* I didn't recognize her! What the hell happened to her?"

"Aggressive face-lift," Betty said, matter-of-factly. "Youth may be wasted on the young, but it looks ridiculous on the old."

Marcy Ludinghausen was the artistic heiress to a mouthwash fortune whose avocation in life was marrying and divorcing. People had lost count of all her husbands by now, including Marcy. Betty once asked her what her definition of "safe sex" was, to which Marcy blithely replied, "An inner tube zipped all the way above my head." Marcy flitted in and out of New York social life, depending on whom she was married to at the time. Each time she got rid of a husband, she sold the abode in which the two of them had lived together. I'd always liked Marcy because she was quirky and lots of fun.

I stared at the new Marcy, thinking of the old Marcy. The old Marcy had been an exotic beauty with an alluring depth to her striking looks. In contrast, the new Marcy's face was flat and characterless, like an old blouse that had been too zealously starched and ironed.

Thinking what a pity this was, I remarked, "If I have a face-lift—and God knows it's getting to that point—I just want to look refreshed."

"Only *refreshed?* Not me, kiddo!" Betty pointed her index finger at her face like a gun. "Hey, if I'm gonna spend thirty thousand bucks and a lot of downtime overhauling this kisser, I wanna look more than fucking *re-*

freshed. I want to look *sensational!* But there's a big difference between looking fabulous for your age and looking like an episode of *Star Trek.*"

"She must be husband hunting again," I said.

"I hear tell she has her eye on Lord Vermilion. Just think, if they got married, they'd have, like, fifteen spouses between them. They could have reunions in Yankee Stadium."

"Betty," I whispered. "He called me."

"You're kidding! I knew he would!"

"Keep your voice down, please. I'm going to the opera with him tonight."

"I thought you hated the opera, Jo."

"Well, I do, sort of. But he promised we could leave if we were bored."

"I like everything about the opera except the singing. Unfortunately Gil adores it as you *well* know," she said, referring to that bleak period when I was evicted from my apartment and the Watermans had so kindly taken me in for a time. Gil played opera nonstop. It drove me crazy. But that's another story.

June broke away from Marcy and hurried over to us. She was in a state.

"Well!" she announced breathlessly. "I've just had the most unpleasant talk with Marcy Ludinghausen! She's selling that apartment to Carla no matter what. The board meeting's next week and if they vote her into the building I'm going to kill myself—*and* Hadley Grimes. He's behind all this."

Betty looked at me and rolled her eyes heavenward. "Junie, you're obsessed. You realize that?"

June ignored Betty. "That's the thing about this town. People will do *anything* for money. It's just outrageous.

Do you know what Marcy had the nerve to say to me? She said, 'Find me another person who'll pay me twenty-eight million dollars for my apartment and I won't sell it to Carla.' All she's thinking about is the money."

"And who can blame her?" Betty said. "She's been trying to unload that white elephant for two years."

June turned to me for sympathy. "You understand, don't you, Jo?"

"Junie, I have to say I agree with Betty. I think you're being a tad unreasonable, sweetie. It's not as if Carla stole *your* husband."

"Oh, she will if she gets the chance. She's that kind of woman. Although Charlie's not rich enough for her. Don't you see? Having someone like that in the building brings the whole tone of the place down. If Carla gets in, I'm sure the value of all our apartments will suffer."

"Oh, *please!*" Betty said, exasperated. "She's paying a record price for that old behemoth. If anything, the value of your apartment will go *up!*"

"Well, then it's blood money," June sputtered. "I'm ill! I hope you girls have told everyone not to support her, like I asked you."

Betty looked at me sheepishly. "June, I feel I have to tell you something. . . . Russell is Missy's godfather and, well, I talked it over with Gil and he—" she began hesitantly.

Just as Betty was about to confess what she had done, June's eyes casually wandered toward the entrance. Her mouth dropped open in a gasp and she cried, "*Dear God! Tell me that's not who I think it is!*"

It is the Rule of Social Inevitability that the thing one most dreads happening at a party *will* happen. Betty and

I turned to look at the door and there, indeed, was Carla Cole, poised at the entrance, surveying the room.

"Oh, shit," Betty said under her breath.

Carla looked both demure and splendid in a black suit, matching hat, with a dark green crocodile bag slung over her shoulder. Trish walked over to greet her. Other women in the room noticed her, too, and one could just feel the whispering begin. Carla was the object of intense speculation and fascination within our little set. I suddenly realized I had to give some real thought to the deeper consequences of Carla moving permanently to New York. Her appearance at this somewhat cozy lunch of Trish's suddenly hit home the realization that she was going to be a fact of my life from here on out, and possibly a sword of Damocles hanging over my head.

Betty tugged June's sleeve. "Junie, I forbid you to make a scene."

"Please don't, June—" I warned her.

June turned on both of us. She looked like a furious parrot. "You know who you two remind me of? Those people in Germany who thought Goering was a charming houseguest! The woman is evil. She's killed two husbands. Now I don't know about you two, but my standards have not yet lowered to the point where I think it's okay to dine with a murderess—*no matter how much money she has!*"

"*Shhh! Keep your voice down, for Chrissakes!*" Betty said.

Now here was a real first, Betty Waterman urging discretion.

"Think of poor Trish," I urged her.

"Don't worry, I'm leaving," June said in a huff. She was gearing up for a grand exit.

"If you go, it'll be worse," Betty said. "It'll just start a big, huge rift in New York."

"Betty's right. Please don't leave, Junie," I implored her.

"Trish knows exactly how I feel about *that woman*. To think she could have asked her here after she roped me into buying a table for this dreary charity, whatever it is—I forget—it's cruel! She should have warned me Carla was coming. That's the *least* she could have done."

Betty grabbed June's arm and faced her squarely. "*June, get a grip!* Don't make a scene! Can't you just chalk it up to social life?"

June shrugged her away and glanced down at the two pale blue ribbons dangling from her right sleeve, which had come undone. "Now look what you've done to my bow! Don't worry," she said trying unsuccessfully to tie it up again, "I'm just going to slip out quietly. And if Trish should happen to ask you where I am—*not that she will, not that she cares!*—just tell her I remembered I had a funeral to attend."

"What funeral is that?" Betty asked facetiously.

"The funeral for common decency!" June said with prim fury. "Good-bye and good luck, you two. And in the immortal words of Adolf Hitler, 'Have a nice day!' "

Betty and I shook our heads in dismay as we watched June steam toward the entrance, exuding such a bright aura of rage that she looked as if she might spontaneously combust. She purposely brushed past Trish on her way out. Trish looked stunned. Carla remained cool and expressionless.

Betty turned to me and said, "You think June has the makings of a suicide bomber?"

"We'll soon find out, if Carla gets into that building," I replied.

"Thank God I live in a town house," Betty sighed.

"Yes, but, Betts, what's she going to do when she finds out you wrote a letter for Carla?"

"I had to. For Russell. I talked it over with Gil and we both agreed that if Russell ever comes back and finds out we didn't support his wife, that would be the end of the friendship. I thought you were writing her one, too."

"No . . . I decided against it."

"Well, you don't have the history we have with them. If June wants to hold it against me, then she bloody well can. But I doubt she will. You know June. Things blow over with her quickly."

I thought I detected a hint of remorse in Betty's voice, despite her attitude of righteous indignation.

"Somehow, I think this is different," I said.

It escaped no one that June had left the lunch in a rage. Trish ran over to us in a state.

"I can't believe June!" she said in a loud whisper. "Did you *see* that performance? Okay, so I forgot how much she hates Carla. I should never have invited the two of them together. But I can't keep track of everyone's feuds. I can barely keep track of my own! Thank God Lulu couldn't come."

Betty's eyes widened. "Trish, you invited *Lulu* to this lunch? With *Carla*?"

"Well, I just didn't think," Trish said, clearly unnerved. "And besides, if you only invite the people who *like* each other to a lunch, no one will come! Or very few, anyway."

"Calm down, Trish. June was wrong. But she'll get over it," I said.

"You'd think she'd have some compassion for *me!* Dick's about to go on trial. He might have to go to *jail*, for heaven's sakes. And poor Carla, with Russell missing and all! June's behavior is an absolute disgrace. I'm never speaking to her again."

"Let's all calm down, have some lunch, and get drunk—not necessarily in that order," Betty said.

I tried my best to avoid Carla, but no such luck. She glided over and thanked me for writing the letter to Hadley Grimes. I didn't disabuse her of the notion that I had. I figured, with any luck, she would think I'd done her a favor. Why did she need to know I'd chickened out? Maybe I could have my cake and eat it, too. She didn't linger long. She seemed far more interested in talking to Marcy Ludinghausen. The two of them walked off and stayed huddled together in a corner until lunch was announced. Fortunately, Carla and I were seated at separate tables.

All anyone at my table could talk about was Carla. She was an object of intense interest—not just for the obvious reasons, but also because she was rumored to be moving permanently to New York. At first, the women at my table were all quite careful in what they said about her because it was widely assumed that she and I were friendly. Word had leaked out that I was down in Barbados at the famous bridal dinner she hosted and that Betty and I were the first ones she turned to for help after Russell vanished. The group tiptoed around the topic during the crabmeat appetizer, feeling me out on the subject of Carla before firing any direct shots at her.

"Well, of course, Carla's a great friend of Jo's, isn't she, Jo?" one of them said, obviously probing.

My response was purposely tepid. I didn't particularly

want people thinking I was such a great friend of hers, nor did I want it getting back to her that I disliked her in any way. I basically wanted to steer clear of her. When I said I didn't know her all that well, there were glances all around and the verbal tiptoeing ceased. People hunkered down for a good, old-fashioned gabfest.

"You don't think she had anything to do with it, do you, Jo?" another woman whispered across the table.

The "it" in question was, of course, Russell's disappearance. If I'd had to venture a guess at that time, I'd have said that nearly all the women in that room believed Carla guilty of something—whether it was man stealing or manslaughter depended on their own sense of the macabre or how close they were to Lulu, who had been a fixture on the New York social scene for years.

I tried to think about how my great, late friend Clara Wilman would have dealt with this situation, she being the standard by which I measured all impeccable behavior. Clara was a great believer in the art of silence—rarely practiced these days. People always seemed to be aching to tell their sides of any story whether they had any involvement in it or not.

"This may not be the appropriate moment to discuss that particular subject," I said.

Old New York saw: You can lead the girls to discretion, but you can't make them shut up. The subject was just too juicy. Leave it to one of the most badly behaved women in New York to get the criticism of Carla really rolling. Sue-Sue Moran piped up first. Sue-Sue was always having affairs with men—both married and single—hoping to segue from the humdrum investment banker to whom she was married to a richer, more interesting catch. She was of the old school that believed it is always better to find your next husband while you are still married, thus avoiding the indignity of the dicey singles market in New York. According to June, Sue-Sue had made an unsuccessful play for Russell Cole back in the days when he was unhappily married to Lulu. It was Sue-Sue who once proclaimed with a slightly too-intimate certainty, "Russell Cole will never leave his wife." When Carla and Russell ran off together, Sue-Sue was among the first to condemn the fugitive couple. That day at lunch, her venom, stored for years in an old vial of rejection, was lethal.

"Well, I hear that Carla went to a party the very night she knew poor Russell was missing," Sue-Sue said, referring, of course, to the disastrous wedding dinner. "All I can say is that woman must be tough as nails," she went on. "I mean, she obviously doesn't care a thing about her husband. If my husband were missing, I certainly wouldn't go to a party," she said sanctimoniously.

No—you'd *give* one, I thought to myself, marveling at how scandal always seemed to bring out the piety in people, especially the naughtiest ones. Scandals are a tried-and-true way of displacing one's own unhappiness by diverting it to a more impersonal subject. I didn't join in the subsequent conversation, which seemed to invigorate all the women at my table with deliciously malicious energy. I just listened and thought my own thoughts, knowing that no one at that ladies' luncheon could possibly have imagined what they were.

Twelve

A LMOST ANY OPENING NIGHT AT THE METRO-
politan Opera is a glittering occasion, but the
new production of *Tosca*, with lavish sets by
the great Italian set designer Gianfranco Brignetti, and
the incomparable Swedish soprano Nellie Bergsen in the
title role, was an occasion not to be missed. Tickets were
almost impossible to come by. Scalpers commanded upward of a thousand dollars for a pair of second-rate seats.

I took great pains with my appearance that night, not
only because it was an important opening, but because I
was going with Max. I had a professional makeup artist
and a hairdresser come to the house to help me look my
best. I chose the couture burgundy velvet sheath to match
the blood-red rubies of my stunning signature piece of
jewelry—an exact copy of a necklace which had once
belonged to Marie Antoinette. The original had been
smashed to pieces in an unfortunate accident, but I had
salvaged some of the stones and had the copy made.
When the doorman rang up to say that Lord Vermilion

was downstairs, I felt as resilient and confident in couture as any medieval knight in a suit of armor.

Max was outside, standing in front of a run-down taxi. He greeted me warmly, complimenting me on my appearance. As I slid uncomfortably across the ripped vinyl seat in my sable-trimmed opera coat and long gown, carefully avoiding some rubbish on the floor, I must confess I was a little surprised he had not hired a private car for such a gala evening. However, I figured that when you're as grand as Lord Vermilion, you don't have to worry about impressing people with the superficial trappings of life.

As the taxi lurched its way through the thick traffic heading toward Lincoln Center, Max absently stroked the sleeve of his topcoat and talked about *Tosca*.

"Now I know you're not fond of the opera, Jo, but I always think it's a bit more fun when you know something of the players," Max said.

That was certainly true. One of the reasons I didn't mind going to the opera with Ethan Monk was because it was like going to a baseball game with the manager of the Yankees. Ethan knew all of the behind-the-scenes gossip. During any given performance, he might point to some soprano singing her heart out onstage and whisper to me that she was sleeping with so-and-so, or give me some other tidbit of gossip regarding the cast or crew. Max knew other kinds of gossip.

"*Tosca* premiered on January 14th, 1900, in Rome," he went on. "Got rotten reviews. Not as bad as *Madame Butterfly*, but almost. But Puccini was quite a determined young fellow. My grandfather became rather good friends with him actually, right around the time of the scandal."

"What scandal?" I asked.

"Oh, well, Puccini was quite a ladies' man, you know. He once described himself as 'a mighty hunter of wild fowl, operatic librettos, and attractive women.' His wife accused him of having an affair with one of their young maidservants. The girl was so upset she committed suicide. But when they did an autopsy, they discovered she was a virgin, poor thing. So, you see, the one crime Puccini didn't commit was the one he paid for most dearly, both privately and in the press. Typical, *what*?"

Max was full of all sorts of historical trivia like this, and his delivery was wry and oddly self-effacing. He casually peppered his conversation with personal references. In some way or another, one or more of his ancestors had known, financed, or been in contact with all the great and gifted personages of their times. Max wasn't at all boastful about this. It was simply a fact of his life. He never sounded like he was name-dropping, but simply recounting family history—just as I might have told people my father was a chiropractor in Oklahoma. His light touch and knowledge of a wide range of subjects made him wonderful company. And yet, there was something distant about him—as if there were an invisible partition between him and the world, which prevented anyone—including myself—from getting too close.

We arrived at Lincoln Center, which looked like a huge diamond lit from within on this gala opening night. Max paid the cab fare and I noticed the driver grumbled at the meager tip. That, of course, was another sign that Max was rich. He was stingy.

Max and I joined the throng of well-heeled patrons filing into the building. Photographers snapped our picture at the entrance. Max regarded them with a slightly imperious look, as if their attentions were both his due and yet a slight inconvenience at the same time.

"Well, now that we've gotten past all the little Cerberuses, we can breathe easy," he said, readjusting his posture.

"Uh-oh. I hope the opera's not going to be hell," I said with a little laugh.

As with any opening night, the atmosphere was electric and full of expectation. As Max and I wended our way with the crowd up the red carpeted staircase to the boxes on the first level, we ran into June Kahn, who was descending. She was reminiscent of Faberge's Imperial lily-of-the-valley egg in a bright pink dress trimmed with little, white organza flowers and sparkly gold braid. June halted abruptly, causing traffic problems on the steps. When I introduced her to Max, she practically genuflected.

"Oh, yes! Lord Vermilion! I've been to Taunton Hall, to a wonderful ball," she said. "Do you have a lot of balls?"

"Just two, last time I checked." I stifled a giggle. "Oh, you mean at my *house!*" he said facetiously. "One a year. To raise money for the trust."

This all went over June's head, but she persevered.

"And how is dear Lady Vermilion?" she asked.

"Which one?" Max said.

June flushed and laughed nervously. "Oh, I forgot! You're divorced now, aren't you? Sorry!"

"I'm always divorced or divorcing," Max said. "But Mother's fine. She's ninety and going strong. And all my other ex-ladies seem to be thriving quite happily on my money, thank you."

Titles of any sort impressed June, especially English titles—though those of any monarchy, living or defunct, would do in a pinch.

"Anyway," June went on, "do you believe, they *found* Russell Cole?"

Max and I looked at each other, then back at her. "*What?!*" we said, practically in unison.

"Dead or alive?" I asked her.

A look of beatific happiness illuminated June Kahn's thin little face as she spoke the five most treasured words in her vocabulary, "You mean you haven't *heard*?"

When both of us confirmed our ignorance by shaking our heads, June immediately changed direction and accompanied us up the stairs, eagerly telling us the story. She seemed particularly excited to be telling Max, whose grand aloofness only heightened June's eagerness to please.

According to June, two local fishermen had picked up Russell in Bridgetown, Barbados, two days after he disappeared. The fishermen said they noticed him because he was acting strange, "like he was drunk," and he stood out from the largely local crowd on the wharf. They said he asked them if he could work for his passage and they took him on as far as Saint Lucia, where they dropped him off. The reason they hadn't come forward sooner was because they'd been at sea for two weeks and it wasn't until they returned and spotted the photograph of Russell Cole, which the authorities had circulated all over the island, that they understood who their passenger might have been. They claimed to have had no knowledge of the million-dollar reward Carla Cole was offering for the recovery of her husband, which made their story even more credible. They had simply come forward in order to help.

"So anyway, there's a man fitting Russell's description

being held in the jail in Castries. He has amnesia and the police are trying to find out who he is."

"Are they sure it's Russell?" I asked her.

"I think so. I mean, who else could it be?"

Suddenly I smelled June's talent for exaggeration. "Where did you hear this, Junie?" I asked her.

"It's going to be in the papers tomorrow," she said. "Reporters have been calling Lulu all day, asking her to comment. Carla's apparently flown down there, playing the dutiful wife. It's all a big fat act, if you ask me."

June suddenly looked at her watch and cried, "Oh my God, the time! I've *got* to go find Charlie. He's always late. We're in Lulu's box, too. Tell her not to worry. We won't miss the curtain!"

June turned around and pushed her way downstairs through the ascending crowd. I stared at Max.

"Are we in *Lulu's* box?" I asked him, dreading the answer.

"We are indeed," he said in a chipper tone.

"You're kidding."

"No, my dear. Why? Is there a problem?"

I pulled Max over to the side of the corridor. "Max, I think I mentioned to you that Lulu and I don't get along. And besides, didn't you two used to go out together?"

"You asked me that in Barbados," he said with a smile. "And I told you then, Lulu and I are just friends."

I was flustered. I didn't quite know what to think, or to say.

"Won't she think it odd, your bringing me?"

"On the contrary, she was thrilled I was bringing you. Look, I understand that years ago you two had some sort of misunderstanding. But I think that's all water under the bridge now, at least as far as she's concerned."

"Well, it's not as far as I'm concerned."

He tilted his head back and said slyly, "Oh, that's right. I forgot about your motto, You may not remember, but you *never* forget." Then he took my hand, looked deeply into my eyes, and said seriously, "Would you rather not go, my dear? I can easily make our excuses."

I swallowed hard. I didn't want to make a scene. I loathe scenes. I didn't want Max to think I was being difficult. I also remembered that Ethan would be there and I could always turn to him for moral support.

"No, that's all right. I'll be fine, thanks. But if the opera's boring, I'm leaving."

"Frankly, Mrs. Slater, I doubt anything could be boring with you."

I was flattered. Max had a way of making one feel special. As he opened the door to the box, he whispered to me, "Do we really think they've found poor old Russell Cole?"

"With *June Kahn* as the source? Are you kidding? It's probably Osama bin Laden."

"We'll ask Lulu," Max said.

"Won't that be tricky?"

"How so?"

"Well, won't it smack of intrusive concern to assume that Lulu would be interested in the fate of the man who had once so publicly humiliated her?"

Max shrugged. "I don't think it matters a bit."

The presidential box was dead center in the grand horseshoe. With its lofty view of both the stage and the audience below, the seats in this prominent aerie were supposedly the best in the house—although Ethan Monk, a real aficionado, said he much preferred the orchestra for sheer quality of listening. However, the center box was certainly the best place to be seen if not to see, and as we walked in, I could feel all inquisitive eyes upon us. Ethan was there as promised, and didn't seem surprised to see us. Lulu had obviously tipped him off. He said hello to Max and greeted me warmly, giving me a surreptitious wink.

Lulu Cole was standing down front, talking to friends in the neighboring box. She cut her conversation short and swept forward to greet us. Dressed in a honey-colored sheath shimmering with hand-sewn bugle beads, Lulu had changed quite a bit since the days when I first knew her. Thanks to artful plastic surgery, she still held some claim to the wholesome prettiness everyone had remarked upon when she first moved to New York, but her wide-eyed, little girl face was clearly older, harder, and sadder. Her smiles looked like frowns and her laughter often sounded like sobs.

Lulu was one of those women whose perfection of dress makes them oddly less chic than they suppose themselves to be. Everything fit perfectly; everything matched. Consequently, there was nothing unexpected or offbeat to amuse the eye, which is the hallmark of great style. Her place on the Best-Dressed List was due to the vast amount of money she spent in the couture houses, and not because she was truly chic. What she did have, however, was a lean and well-proportioned body with exaggerated good posture. She held her black-haired head very high, with her little nose angled upward. I have to say she always looked to me as if she were sniffing the air, trying to detect the source of an unpleasant aroma, but others thought her regal. In fact, there was a certain innate arrogance about her which may have been beyond her control. Even her cordial welcome to us came across a bit like the benign boredom of a duchess viewing a delegation of tradespeople. She gave Max a kiss on both cheeks. I quickly stepped back to prevent even that perfunctory intimacy. She got the drift.

"Jo, I'm so happy to see you," she said, shaking my hand. "Thank you for coming."

"Thank you for including me," I replied coolly, unable to forget how badly she had once treated me.

"Such an exciting night," she said. "Nellie Bergsen is my favorite opera singer, and *Tosca*, well . . . heaven, no?"

Silence.

Sensing the tension between us, Ethan piped up and said, apropos of nothing, "I used to have a cat name Tosca!"

Max then complimented Lulu on her showstopping antique pin—a stalk of diamond flowers cascading down from the left shoulder of her dress. The petal clusters were *en tremblant* so they moved slightly, sparkling softly as they caught the light. Lulu touched it automatically, without thinking.

"Thanks. I love it, too," she said. "Russell gave it to me for our fifteenth anniversary."

Ethan shot me a sidelong glance. The nostalgia in her voice was evident. For the first time, I saw traces of genuine emotion streak Lulu's hard face. I could see that even after all these years, she was still carrying a torch for the husband who had left her. This didn't seem to bother Max at all. On the contrary, he patted her arm and said, "There, there, my dear, don't worry, they'll find him. What about this man in Castries?"

Lulu was clearly annoyed. "You ran into June! Trust June Kahn to turn a dubious sighting into an absolute certainty. Look, this man hasn't been reliably identified. We don't know for sure it's Russ. The media is grasping at straws because that's what sells papers. But I'll bet you the price of that tacky yacht of theirs it's *not* Russell," she said, angrily confident.

"It would be nice if it were though, wouldn't it?" I said softly.

"Yes," she said. "It would be."

Max excused himself, ostensibly to go say hello to some pals in a neighboring box. Ethan and I were left standing with Lulu.

"The Bromires and the Kahns are joining us," she said. "And my daughter, Courtney."

"Little Courtney. I haven't seen her in ages," Ethan said.

"She's not so little anymore, dear. She's in business school."

"God, time flies, doesn't it?" Ethan said.

Silence.

I didn't trust Lulu as far as I could throw her. She had been downright cruel to me once, and I wasn't going to let her off the hook so easily by being charming and helping make conversation. It was clear that she had no idea what to say to me, and with Max off talking to someone else, Ethan was left holding the ball. Shy by nature, the Monk's discomfort was palpable. I just knew he was going to put his foot in his mouth in an effort to allay his anxiety. In fact, I even saw the lightbulb go on over his head as he suddenly thought of something to break the silence. The Imp of the Perverse was about to take control when Lulu looked at me directly and said, "Listen, Jo, I want to say something to you."

"Yes?" I was wary.

"I know I behaved badly toward you in the past, and I owe you a profound apology. But believe me when I tell you that I didn't do it out of malice. I just wasn't thinking. I don't know, I guess I felt sorry for Monique because everyone was so against her. And she convinced me that she had absolutely no idea that Lucius was going to leave her all his money. But I understand that doesn't excuse the fact that I was disloyal to you. I know I was and I deeply regret it. You ask June. I've wanted to say this to you for years. I apologize to you, Jo, I really do."

"Thank you," I said.

Ethan tugged nervously at the droopy collar of his tuxedo shirt, looking as if he were about to crawl under his seat with embarassment.

"I'm not even hoping you could forgive me, because I'm sure that's too much to ask," she went on. "But I do want you to know how truly terrible I feel. If I could go back and do things differently, I would."

When Lulu said this, I softened slightly toward her. Who among us wouldn't do certain things differently if we could go back in time? I had to admire her courage in apologizing to me after all these years, particularly in front of Ethan.

"And I think at this time, when a certain person is moving to New York, we should all band together and take a stand," she said pointedly.

I knew the person she was referring to was Carla Cole. I felt June Kahn's not-so-subtle hand behind this. June was busy circling the wagons, trying to unite old antagonists against a new enemy. Ethan, obviously unnerved by all this, pulled out the wrinkled, white handkerchief stuffed in his breast pocket and patted the perspiration off his brow.

Thank God for the Bromires!

Trish and Dick's timely entrance into the box broke the tension. Trish gave us all a fluttery wave hello. Lulu went to greet them.

When Lulu was out of earshot, Ethan said, "Now you know why I prefer paintings to people. Paintings can't talk."

Trish seemed all recovered from her lunch. An athletic former beauty queen from Florida, fifteen years younger than her husband, she looked appropriately seasonal in a red-and-green satin evening suit and a parure of big emeralds and rubies to match. Betty affectionately referred to Trish as "the Shabanou of Park Avenue," on account of Trish's penchant for wearing much too much gaudy jewelry at any given time.

Dick Bromire, a beefy man in his mid-sixties with thinning hair and the jowly face of a hound, had put on a good deal more weight since I last saw him, due in part, I imagined, to all the tension he was under as he awaited his trial. Like many husbands, Dick Bromire was dragged to cultural events by a wife who enjoyed them more than he did. He viewed them as a chore, like washing the dishes, only they went on longer. I'd observed Dick nodding off through more ballets, operas, and concerts than I could count. The year that Trish was the chairman of the Municipal Ballet's gala evening, Dick had unwisely confided in a reporter, who had asked him what he thought of the ballet, "I only like it when they jump." The remark had caused a minor uproar, but I suspect many men secretly agreed with him. And though Dick may have dozed off during performances, he always came alive for socializing at the intermissions.

The Bromires had been invited to Missy Waterman's

wedding, of course, as well as to the coveted bridal dinner aboard *The Lady C*. But because Dick was under a court order that prevented him from leaving the country, he couldn't travel to Barbados. There was a moment when Trish toyed with the idea of going without him— just a quick trip, down and back in their private plane— but Betty persuaded her this was not a good idea.

"Stand by your man, kiddo. Otherwise you look like shit," Betty had advised her.

Trish wisely took Betty's advice, and the Bromires had laid low in their house in Southampton over the holidays, inspiring everyone at the now infamous wedding to say how devoted Trish was to Dick and how fortunate they were to have missed the event from hell.

Dick Bromire made a beeline for Max, who was still engrossed in conversation down front. The moment the two men clapped eyes on each other, however, they shook hands warmly. I later learned that Dick and Max were old shooting buddies in England. On several occasions, Dick had rented the shoot of Max's aristocratic neighbor, Sir Edward Wiloughby—pronounced "Wilby." Max was always invited to stroll over and help "the Americanos," as Sir Edward termed the renters, divest the skies of hundreds of fowl. Trish, of course, preferred what she called the "après-shoot," which included all the fancy lunches and dinners that leavened the slaughter and gave her a chance to parade her couture outfits.

Max made a point of telling me that he liked Dick Bromire from the little he knew of him on the field, though he did it in a backhanded way: "Clothes, too new. Aim, too bad. But other than that, he's a rather nice chap, *what*?"

There were air kisses all around and a smattering of polite conversation before June and Charlie finally showed up just as the curtain was about to rise. I braced myself for a scene between Trish and June on account of the now notorious lunch, but they barely said hello and studiously avoided each other for the rest of the night. Carla was already having an effect on our close-knit little set.

"Junie," I whispered as she came to greet me, "I think you owe Trish an apology."

"Well, that's very interesting because I think she owes me one," June said loudly so Trish could hear.

Trish ostentatiously turned her back on June. I was sorry I'd brought it up, but I felt I had to make the effort. I hated to see two of my close friends fighting.

Charlie Kahn, a thin, shy, aristocratic-looking man with grey hair who expressed his individuality by wearing garishly colorful cummerbunds and matching bow ties, gave my hand a timid little squeeze, as was his wont. I was much indebted to Charlie. He'd helped me out once upon a time when I was in dire straits, and I knew him to be a loyal, discreet soul who was much cannier than people thought. He kept silent as his wife nattered on. He adored June despite her flightiness, accepting her unthinking behavior with the tolerant air of a long-suffering vicar who accepts yet another cross to bear—in this case, his wife. But I think he believed she was a little nuts on the subject because he leaned in and said to me, "I don't know what's gotten into June lately. She's obsessed about Carla Cole. I wish she'd let this whole thing drop."

"Can't you try and reason with her, Charlie?" I said.

"Reason with June?" he said as though the very idea

were an oxymoron. "Jo, you know what she's like when she gets a bee in her bonnet . . ." He shrugged.

What I knew was that June Kahn's bonnet was basically the whole hive. Carla Cole was just the latest in a long line of June's obsessions.

As the lights dimmed, Max and I sat down front together. Max enjoyed the opera, I could tell. Leaning back with arms and legs crossed, he focused on the stage, moving his foot up and down in time to the music, occasionally mouthing a word or two of an aria he knew. My own attention for singing intrigue was short, however, and I grew restless. Glancing behind me, I noticed a young woman slipping quietly into a seat at the back of the box. The light from the stage cast a glow on her pale face and glinted off a pair of gold, wire-rimmed glasses. I was right in assuming this was Courtney Cole. During the first intermission, Lulu introduced her daughter to us.

"Everybody, please, your attention! This is my daughter, Courtney. Courtney, darling, this is Mr. and Mrs. Kahn, Mr. and Mrs. Bromire, Mr. Monk, Mrs. Slater, and, of course, Lord Vermilion. . . ."

Courtney Cole took no pains to enhance her looks. In contrast to her famously chic mother, she purposely played down every aspect of her physical appearance, wearing no makeup, granny glasses, and an ill-fitting, high-necked black dress. She could not, however, hide a pair of keen brown eyes which, despite the unflattering spectacles, projected a sharp intelligence.

As the shy, thoughtful young woman went around the box shaking hands with each of us, it was clear from the way she self-consciously looked down, avoiding eye contact, that she could barely tolerate her mother's social enthusiasm. Lulu treated Courtney almost as if she were an obedient pet, patting her after the social ordeal was through. With the introductions over with, everyone filed out of the box to get some refreshments and mingle with friends in the opening-night crowd. Max and I were walking out together when Courtney hesitantly approached me and said, "Excuse me, Mrs. Slater, can I talk to you for a minute?"

"Of course, dear."

"I'll go on ahead and get you a glass of champagne," Max said, tactfully retreating.

Courtney and I sat down in the back of the empty box. Courtney cleared her throat and said, "Mrs. Slater, I'd like to talk to you about my father, if I may."

"How can I help you, dear?"

Like everyone else in New York, I'd heard that Russell Cole and his only daughter, Courtney, had been estranged since her parents' breakup. Word was that Courtney was none too fond of her new stepmother and that her refusal to accept Carla had caused a terrible rift between her and her father. Of course, that was all rumor, and I had no real way of knowing whether it was true or merely another instance of false "inside information" spread around for want of new gossip.

"I know you were down in Barbados when my dad disappeared. I was just wondering if you got a chance to talk to him at all."

I felt real sympathy for this young woman and I decided to be frank with her.

"Courtney, I don't know your father very well. We were social friends years ago when I was married to my late husband. I always liked him. And since you ask me, we did have a conversation that strikes me as odd, particularly in light of what's happened."

Her attention sharpened and she leaned in closer to me. "Oh, please tell me."

I told her the green monkey story, including Russell's haunting line to me: " 'Sometimes I think I get a glimpse of myself, and then I disappear.' "

Courtney let out an inadvertent little gasp. "He *said* that?"

"Yes."

She stared off into the distance for a long moment, then snapped her dark eyes back onto mine.

"Did he say anything to you about my stepmother?"

"No."

"Look, Mrs. Slater, I know my mother's nuts on the subject of Carla. And that's partly because I think she's still in love with Dad." I was dying to ask her about her mother's relationship with Max, but I decided that would be too tacky. She went on. "I took my mother's side in the divorce because, well, she's my mother. But the truth is, I never thought Carla was bad. I actually liked her. I knew how unhappy my parents were together. I'm not stupid. I was probably the only one who wasn't surprised when my father left. Carla always made a huge effort with me. She made my dad very happy. And that made me happy. She was really fun and nice—at least in the beginning."

"But that changed?"

"And how." She nodded emphatically. "See, before they got married, Carla kept telling Dad how much she hated New York and social life and how she really just wanted to be alone with him. That's why he built her the yacht."

"For people who hated social life, they certainly entertained a lot on that boat."

Courtney snickered. "Yeah, well, sure. Carla lied. Now my dad—he truly does hate social life. He hated it when he was married to Mom. He never even wanted to move away from Tulsa. It was all Mom's idea to come to New York. So then he met Carla and she convinced him she wasn't interested in social life—despite all evidence to the contrary, I have to say. But he was in love with her so he believed anything she told him. When they first got the boat they kept to themselves. But then she started entertaining, nonstop. I remember being on the yacht a couple of times when Carla gave these huge parties and Dad would just retreat to his cabin and go on his computer. All he really wanted to do was sail. He just got more and more unhappy as time went on, and he realized that Carla wasn't the person he thought she was when he married her. Far from it."

"So why didn't he leave her?"

"My dad is obsessed with Carla. He'd never leave her. Plus, he was probably afraid the whole world would laugh at him again. People thought he was crazy to divorce Mom and marry her in the first place. Carla has this weird hold on my father. I'm not sure exactly what it is, but it's very strong. You're certain he never said anything about her to you?"

I liked this young woman. I liked her candor and her kindness. "No . . . but Carla said something about him."

She narrowed her eyes. "What?"

"Carla told me she was sure your father wasn't . . ." I was going to say *dead*, but decided that sounded harsh, so I amended it to, "She was sure your father would be found because he's disappeared before."

Courtney's tense posture deflated in a beleaguered sigh. "So she told you, huh?"

"*Has* he disappeared before?"

The young woman nodded. "Yeah . . . my dad's had some real problems."

"What kinds of problems?"

Courtney hesitated. "I guess it'll be all over the papers soon anyway." She took a deep breath. "Years ago, he was diagnosed with something called Dissociative Fugue Disorder. It's this very rare thing where people go away and forget who they are and they take on a whole new identity. Sometimes they come back and then don't remember where they've been. Other times, they just wake up one day, something triggers a memory, and they know who they are but they don't know how they got where they are. They just want to get home—if they remember where home is. It's horrible."

"Like schizophrenia?"

"No. It's its own thing, really."

"Do they know what causes it?"

"There are lots of theories. Some doctors think it could be triggered by a form of epilepsy. Some think it's set off by severe emotional distress. But no one really knows. Anyway, my dad's had some serious episodes in the past, which were hushed up for obvious reasons. But he told Carla about it before they were married. It wouldn't have been fair to her if he hadn't."

I suddenly wondered if the real reason that Russell had paid all that money to Lulu in the divorce settlement was to keep her from divulging his condition. I cocked my head to one side, probing her face. "Well, isn't this good news? Doesn't this mean he could still be alive, like Carla says?"

"Yeah, it does. But that doesn't mean he's not in trouble. One time when it happened, he was living in this horrible dive in Providence, which is where he went to college. He was panhandling and he got mugged. They took him to the hospital. That's how Mom eventually found him. Surviving in this world without an identity or money automatically puts you on the fringes of society and in very unsafe places."

"When was this?"

"Several years ago."

"And how long was he gone?"

"Nine weeks. And that wasn't even the longest of his episodes."

"My God."

"Mom told everyone he was away on business. And when he came back, he went into a sanitorium."

"Well, maybe this man they have in custody really is your father. You never know."

"It's not. We know that for a fact. If it were, my mother wouldn't be here. She'd be down there with him. She still loves him. She'll never love anyone else. . . . And there's another thing. . . ." She hesitated. I could tell this was difficult for her. "Did Dad ever mention anything to you about another woman?"

I was astonished by the question. "No. Why? Do you think your father was having an affair?"

"No . . ." She hesitated again. "I think Carla is."

"With a *woman*?"

"Sure, why not? It happens," she said with a shrug. "I mean, I'm lesbian. I have affairs with women." She announced her sexuality so matter-of-factly it seemed banal.

Of course, I was well aware that one of the best-kept secrets of so-called New York society is that many of the women, married and single, have had affairs with each other at one time or another, which doesn't necessarily mean they're gay—just adventurous. I thought of what Larry Locket had told me about Carla living with a woman in London years ago when she was single.

"What makes you think Carla's having an affair with a woman?"

"I'm not sure it's a woman, okay? But my dad's very jealous of someone in Carla's life. And we think it's a woman because he's, like, so secretive about it."

"But why a woman?"

"Mom thinks it is. During the divorce she dug up all this dirt on Carla. She found out she was living in London with a woman and that she'd had affairs with women in the past. She's not allowed to talk about it, of course. The whole thing was hushed up. Dad claims Carla confessed everything to him. But just think how humiliating it would be for my father if after everything he went through to get her, after everything he gave up, all that money he paid Mom, plus the public scandal, Carla turns around and starts having an affair with a woman! My dad's really old-fashioned, Mrs. Slater. I mean, it's the one thing Mom and I can think of that would drive him absolutely up the wall. He just couldn't take it."

"But it's just a hunch you have. You're not sure. You don't have any proof."

She shook her head. "No . . . look, Mrs. Slater, I could care less if Carla is gay, straight, having an affair, whatever. But I *do* care if she's done anything to hurt my dad."

"And you think she has?"

She leveled me with a hard gaze. "He's missing, isn't he? And Mom definitely thinks she killed him. Or had him killed."

"But what about you? What do you think?"

"I just don't know. She doesn't have that much to gain if he's dead."

"Presumably she'd get a lot of money, no? Half the estate."

"Um, well, actually no. Under the terms of my father's will she only gets ten million dollars. In fact, that's the reason I don't think she killed him. I told Mom, she's much better off with him alive because if he dies all the money goes to me. I know she tried to get my dad to change the will at one point, but he never would—thank God."

"What happens if they get divorced?"

"Same thing. Prenup . . . but I just have this weird feeling she's up to something. And I can't figure out what it is. That's what I'm trying to find out. I thought my dad might have said something to you that would give us a clue as to what's going on."

"Just the green monkey episode. That's all I can think of," I said, glancing down at the huge orchestra section below us. People were beginning to file back in and find their seats for the next act. "Based on what you say, Courtney, and based on your father's comment to me, it really sounds like he could be having an episode."

She nodded. "I think you're right. I just pray he's okay," she said as if she wanted me to reassure her that her father was alive.

"I'm sure he is, dear," I said, without really believing it.

Just then, Max ambled in with champagne flutes for me and Courtney. Courtney declined, but I hoovered mine right down. God knows I needed a drink. Everyone gradually returned to the box, infused with new life from having socialized at intermission. June had clearly found many more people to tell about Russell.

As the lights went down, Max leaned into me and whispered, "Interesting talk?"

"Yes. She's a lovely young lady," I said evasively.

"Does nothing with her looks, though, *what*?"

With that, the lights went down.

I couldn't concentrate on the opera in light of what Courtney Cole had told me. I watched this Swedish Tosca sing her heart out without really hearing her, thinking instead about what Carla had said to me about us being "sisters under the skin." Had Carla been coming on to me in some subtle way? Or had she perhaps had an affair with Oliva, my blackmailer? Was that how she knew about me sending payments to Las Vegas? The last time I saw Oliva she had been dressed in costume as a man. And in my dealings with her, she had always struck me as a sexy sociopath who would go any which way you asked her as long as you paid her enough. I also thought more deeply about my green monkey conversation with Russell Cole. He'd asked me how we could ever really know another person if we didn't really know ourselves. Was it just that he felt one of his episodes coming on? Or was he perhaps talking about Carla and her sexuality? About Carla and a lover?

Of course there was one other, more profound reason that Carla might have called us "sisters under the skin." And that was if she, like myself, had planned a murder.

At the end of the last act, Trish Bromire, who always saw herself as the star of anything she was watching, gasped at the sight of Tosca on the parapet poised to jump. Trish's anguished cry startled me out of my reverie. I'd forgotten that this was an opera about a woman who leaps to her death—an image that for me in particular conjures up some pretty harrowing memories. But that's another story.

Thirteen

RATHER THAN JOIN THE GROUP FOR THE LATE supper Lulu had organized at the Café des Artistes, Max and I said our thanks to our hostess and bid everyone good night. Lulu didn't seem the least bit upset that Max and I were peeling off together. In fact, she gave me what I thought was a little wink. Max took me to Circo, a fashionable, brightly lit trattoria in midtown. The maître d' and several of the waiters seemed to know him, but everyone maintained a rather deferential air around Max. We sat at a corner table of the lively, colorful restaurant and ordered the pasta special. Max was eager to know all about my conversation with Courtney Cole.

"Tell me, Jo," he began, "does the daughter support her mother's contention that Carla has done away with Russell?"

"Not really, because Carla has nothing to gain with Russell dead."

"What do you mean?"

"Courtney told me that the will leaves everything to her. Carla only gets a pittance compared to what there is. But she does think Carla's up to something and she's worried. How well do you know Carla, Max?"

Max leaned back and thought for a moment. "Hardly 'tall. Heard about her for years, of course. When a woman like that marries as well as she did, one tends to hear about them."

"What do you mean, 'a woman like that'?"

"*Poule deluxe. Grande horizontale*. Courtesan . . . whatever you want to call her. She's one of those women who sparks a great deal of controversy. People either love her or hate her. Very little middle ground, *what?*"

"What about you? Do you like her?"

"Oh, I find her quite charming, actually. And you? What do you think of her?"

"I can't quite make up my mind. She's always been nice to me, but, to be honest, something about her makes me uneasy."

"Yes, I can see how women wouldn't care for her. She's much more of a man's woman. She's very interested in my house—which I always appreciate. Knows quite a lot about its history and everything—and the fact that it's always in desperate need of repair," he added with a rueful smile. "I'd love to show you Taunton Hall one day, Jo. I think you'd like it."

"I'd love to see it. Everyone says it's magnificent."

"Oh, well, I s'pose it is," he said dismissively. "But when you grow up in a place, you don't think of it as magnificent. You think of it as a refuge. There are very cozy corners in the Hall. Those are the corners I'd like to show you. . . . Where did you grow up, Jo?"

"Me? I'm just a hick from the sticks, I'm afraid. Born

in Oklahoma City. My father was a chiropractor. My mother worked in a department store and made clothes for rich ladies. But I always knew I was going to get out of there. What do they say about people who know they were born in the wrong cradle? I met my husband while I was working out there and moved here to New York."

Max smiled at me. "I like it that you don't put on airs," he said. "Lots of ladies one meets in New York invent these grand heritages for themselves. It's such a bore. And one can catch them out so easily." He paused. "But you've been rather controversial in your day, I hear."

"Don't I know it!"

"Had rather a bad patch, did you?"

Max had obviously done his homework on me.

"Yes. But I'd rather not talk about that, if you don't mind. I don't like to look back."

"No, I quite agree. Just let me say that I admire people who pick themselves up and get on with life, as it were. Can't stand people who dwell on things that can't be changed."

I couldn't figure Max out. He was an emotional paradox, warm and distant at the same time. Sometimes he reminded me of a lion, surveying life from a lofty lair. Other times, he was as cozy as a pet tabby.

We walked back to my apartment, and just for form's sake, I asked him if he wanted to come up for a drink. I was surprised when he replied, "I'd love to, thanks."

The building attendants were not used to seeing me with a man, no less very late at night. Max and I got a couple of sidelong glances from the doorman and elevator man as we walked through the marble-floored lobby to the elevator in the back. The three of us—myself, Max, and the elevator man—rode up to the ninth floor in silence, with Max and me standing staring face front, trying to keep from looking at each other and cracking up. The elevator man bid me a pointed, "Good night," and once Max and I stepped into the vestibule and the elevator door closed behind us, we burst out laughing.

"You're now the scandal of the building, Mrs. Slater," Max said.

"Oh, I'm sure I always was."

Max had never been to my apartment, so he was eager to take a look around. He said he was a fan of the Slater Gallery, those re-creations of French royal apartments that my late husband and I had donated to the Municipal Museum years ago, the nucleus of which was furniture and paintings from our own collection. Max had great taste in art and antiques, as well as a curatorial knowledge of certain periods—especially the Louis Seize period, which is my own particular favorite, both historically and as an area of collecting. I think he was a little disappointed. As I said, I'd relaxed my decorating standards quite a bit, and my new apartment was a far cry from the old days when nearly all the furniture was period and top quality, made by the great *ebenistes* of the eighteenth century. There were a few remaining pieces, of course, but not many. Max particularly liked the disturbing Francis Bacon that no one else cared for and told me I should move it back to the living room. After perusing what little there was in the way of really first-class stuff, he brought up Taunton Hall again.

"You must promise to let me show you my house one day soon, Jo. I know you'd find it fascinating. Unfortunately so much of it's in disrepair. The maintenance is simply staggering. Old houses are like old mistresses, *what*? They cost a bundle, yet one can't find it in one's heart to abandon them."

It was an unfortunate analogy, I thought, and I began to get the feeling that the real love of Max Vermilion's life was Taunton Hall.

Max and I stood in front of the picture window in the living room looking out over Central Park, which lay before us like a black velvet cloak studded with sequins of lamplight.

"Marvelous view," he said.

"I love living on the park and watching the seasons change."

I was about to go fix us a drink when Max suddenly and somewhat stealthily slipped his hand around my waist. I understood this to be a pass.

"What a jolly girl you are, Jo," he said, tugging me to him. "Great fun being with you, *what*?"

I tilted my head against his shoulder to show that I was not averse to intimacy. With that bit of encouragement, he grabbed my chin with his other hand, pulled my face around, and planted a rather harsh kiss on my mouth. I knew immediately that there was no spark between me and Max. In fact, his kiss felt oddly obligatory, a little like he was closing his eyes and thinking of England—or of his house, more likely. When it was over, he stared down at me and said, "What do you think, Jo? Shall we have a go at it?"

"What do you mean, 'have a go at it'?"

"Go to bed. Might be fun, *what*?"

I was so amused by this rather perfunctory invitation that I burst out laughing. Max looked wounded.

"I'm deflating rapidly," he said dryly.

"I'm sorry, Max," I said, still laughing. "I can't help it.

I don't think we really like each other in that way. Do you? Really?"

He seemed bewildered. "How does one know until one tries?"

"But you can't try if you don't feel any passion, can you?"

"Oh, I don't know. If everyone one slept with had to be the love of one's life . . ."

"I'm not talking about being the love of your life, Max. I'm talking *attraction*. I don't think we're attracted to each other, are we?"

"Speak for yourself, m'dear. I find you *most* attractive."

I smiled. I didn't believe him. "You're very gallant, Max. But I think we're both better off being great friends."

"Can't we be friends after we've gotten this out of the way?"

I laughed again. "Do you think that sex is something that needs to be gotten out of the way?"

He thought for a moment. "Quite candidly, I find it hard to be friends with a woman until we've sorted that out."

"Why?" I was incredulous.

"Well, unless a man's gay, he's bound to have feelings about a woman, if she's halfway attractive. As I said, one wants to sort it out before one abandons the quest."

"Did you *sort it out* with Lulu?" I asked.

He held up his hand, palm outward. "Oh, my dear, I learned long ago never to kiss and tell. I will say this, however: Once one has been intimate with someone, one has a very special feeling about them. Mind you, the intimacy needn't continue. In fact, it's preferable if it doesn't. I find that sex creates all sorts of problems in a relationship eventually, so it's better to get it over with as quickly as possible, as I said. But to me there are no better friends than old lovers. Of course, I'm not counting *wives* in that equation. That's a whole other category of misery."

I literally couldn't stop laughing. Max's convoluted thought processes made me realize just how screwed up he was.

"Max, you are a true original," I said.

He looked at me like a forlorn little boy. "I take it from your ongoing mirth that the answer is no?"

I shook my head. "I don't think so, Max. But thanks anyway. I appreciate the offer."

"I'm devastated." Max had such a wry way about him, I could never tell if he was being serious or not. "Involved with someone else, are you?" he asked.

"No."

"Then what's the difference? Come on, Jo, let's have a go. In the eighteenth century, sex was considered a sport—like hunting or shooting."

"Yes, but we're in the twenty-first century now, Max. And when and if I do get involved with someone, I'm going to have to feel passionate about them. It's just the way I'm built."

"One of *those* women, eh?" He sighed. "Well, perhaps one day you'll feel that way about me, Jo."

"Max, can I tell you something honestly?"

"Better than *dis*honestly, I s'pose," he replied.

"I don't think you really want me to feel that way about you."

"Why on earth not?"

"Because I don't think you feel remotely that way about me."

He cocked his head to one side. "What makes you say that?"

"You haven't been turned down by a lot of ladies, have you?"

He scratched his ear and thought for a moment. "Not really, no. But I do have sense enough to know that most of them are far more interested in Lord Vermilion than they are in little Maxy," he said with charming self-effacement. "The thing about you is that you don't seem to want or need anything from me. To be perfectly honest with you, Jo, I prefer women who are slightly more disadvantaged than you are—and not just in the monetary sense."

"I think you felt obliged to make a pass at me, didn't you? You thought I expected it."

"Don't most ladies expect it?"

"No!"

"Forgive me, Jo, but I think they do."

"Well, this lady doesn't." I took his hand and looked him straight in the eye. "Max, dear, I think it would be a great relief to both of us if we could just *pretend* we'd been to bed together, gotten it out of the way and over with, as you say, so now we can just be pals."

He looked deeply into my eyes and for the first time, I saw some connection there.

"I do *like* you, Jo."

"I like you, too, Max. So let's keep it that way, shall we?"

He leaned down and gave me a platonic kiss on the forehead. "I'm going back to England tomorrow. But I still want you to come stay with me and see my house," he said.

"And I want you to call me whenever you come to New York. Will you do that?"

"Oh, m'dear, it's a promise."

* * *

That night I went to bed alone, thinking what an odd duck Max Vermilion was. I was just as happy to be his friend, although I knew Betty would be sorely disappointed. In fact, she called me at the crack of dawn, launching in without so much as a hello.

"I hear you were at the opera with Max last night and that the two of you went off alone together afterward. So tell all! What happened?!"

I knew right away that June had given her a blow by blow.

"Nothing happened."

"Come on, Jo! Give me a break. Max sleeps with everyone at least once. He's like One Pounce Potter."

"Who's One Pounce Potter?" I asked her.

"Don't you remember Peter Potter from years ago? Bootsie Baines's horrible cousin who always attacked everyone on the first date and then was never to be heard from again?"

"Vaguely," I said.

"Well, Max is supposed to be like One Pounce Potter. Only he likes to stay friends once the thing is over with. That's what happened with Lulu—at least according to June. Lulu told June that Max really doesn't enjoy sex he doesn't have to pay for."

"Really? Well, that would explain it."

"So? What happened?"

"He made a pass at me, but his heart definitely wasn't in it. I turned him down and that was that. We're friends."

"Damn! I was counting on you being the twentieth Lady Vermilion, or whatever number you'd be."

"I get the feeling you don't necessarily have to sleep with Max to become Lady Vermilion. In fact, I think the odds are better if you don't."

"Well, anyway," Betty said with a sigh, "the other reason I'm calling? Take a look at the paper this morning and call me back."

By "the paper," Betty did not mean the *New York Times*, the *Wall Street Journal*, or any other comparably serious publication. She meant very specifically the *New York Post*. Betty called the *Post* "the paper for those who love fiction in the morning." I have to admit I enjoy the tabloids myself because they're always filled with horrible news that's fun to read, as opposed to horrible news that's horrible to read.

The headline on the front page of the *New York Post* read simply, "SURVIVOR?" Underneath was a blurry photograph of the camera-shy Russell Cole taken some years ago when he was still married to Lulu. I read the coverage which in the *Post*, at least, had muscled aside all other news.

The story was about the mystery man being held in custody in Castries. Was he really Russell Cole? Well, I knew from Courtney that he wasn't, but that wasn't what was interesting about the article. What was interesting was that it delved into the missing billionaire's psychiatric history and his bouts with Dissociative Fugue Disorder. A staff psychiatrist at the Payne Whitney Clinic in New York was interviewed. Though she admitted to having no direct knowledge of Russell Cole's particular case, she described the disorder generally.

"Dissociative Fugue, or Psychogenic Fugue, as it was once known, is an unanticipated and sudden departure from one's home with an inability to recall one's past," she was quoted as saying. "It's pretty rare, but we're seeing more cases of it nowadays than we used to. Just recently, in fact, there was a case of a man who walked into his house again after six years with absolutely no recollection where he'd been for all that time. He found his wife living with a whole new family."

Betty phoned me back just as I was finishing the piece.

"So whadya think? Is it Russell?" she asked.

"I doubt it. Courtney Cole was at the opera last night and she says definitely not."

"Well, Trish just called me. I hear you and Lulu made up."

"That's not quite true. She apologized."

"About time. Trish and June are barely speaking, though."

"Don't I know it. They were icy to each other at the opera. I tell you, Betty, this place is turning into a war zone."

"Well, these things happen every so often, just like in the Mafia. Time to dust off the couture flak jackets," she said, then hung up.

Fourteen

THAT AFTERNOON, A SMALL PACKAGE ARRIVED from S. J. Phillip's, the venerable old London shop renowned for its antique jewelry and silver. Enclosed was a card of heavy ecru stock with a gold coronet at the top. A note written in black ink in almost illegible penmanship read, "With love and admiration from your friend, Max." "Friend" was underlined three times. I opened the little burgundy leather box with some excitement. There, on the white satin interior, lay an exquisite little diamond dragonfly pin.

I was so touched by this gesture that I immediately called Betty to tell her. She was sanguine about the whole thing.

"Are you *sure* you didn't sleep with him?" she said.

"Positive."

"Because he gives insect pins to all his mistresses. There's a story about a party in London where several of

Max's former lovers showed up wearing the insect pins he'd given them and Max famously remarked, 'Anyone got the bug spray?' "

"Charming!" I said, repelled.

"And that's how one of his wives supposedly found out he was having an affair. Her best friend came to her house wearing *three* diamond bees and a spider. The best friend later became the next Lady Vermilion."

"Well, I didn't sleep with him, Betty. You know I'd tell you if I had."

"If you wear it, everyone will think you did."

"Maybe that's what he wants them to think," I said. "I should probably send it back. I gave Carla back her throw."

"Oh, keep it, for Chrissakes!" Betty said. "Max won't get the point if you send it back. He won't even notice. I think he orders them by the gross."

As predicted, the man in Castries turned out *not* to be Russell Cole. But I learned from Larry Locket, who called me from Barbados, that Carla had flown down to check him out herself.

"She's backed out of *three* separate interviews with me," he said on the phone, sounding more than irritated. "I come down here, she promises to see me twice, doesn't, and then she leaves almost immediately. Then this man turns up in Castries. I go there and she promises to see me, and about an hour before we're supposed to meet, her lawyer calls and cancels. Either she's the rudest person in the world or she's hiding something. Well, at least my time down here hasn't been wasted, Jo," he said. "I'm putting the jigsaw puzzle together."

I filled Larry in on the whole brouhaha regarding the Wilman apartment. He said he was traveling from Barbados to Florida, where he was going to try and interview Antonio Hernandez's son about his former stepmother.

"He's reluctant to talk to me, but I've convinced him that our conversation will be off the record, so at least he's agreed to see me. Now let's hope *he* doesn't back out."

Larry promised to call me the instant he got back to New York.

Then I spoke to Betty, who said that Carla had called her, wanting to have lunch.

"She's on pins and needles about that fucking apartment," Betty said. "I don't have the heart to tell her my letter won't make a damn bit of difference. The only way she'll ever get into that building is over June's dead body."

Prophetic words.

On the eve of the board's vote a week later, June called and asked if she could stop by on her way to the Winter Wonderland Ball. June, known as "the Iron Organizer," was a philanthropic workhorse, involved with more worthy causes than the Red Cross. June's motto has always been, You go to mine, I'll go to yours. The only trouble is, most people can't stand parties you have to pay for, whereas, according to Betty, June "never met a benefit she didn't like." June was always recruiting her pals to buy tickets to some big, dreary "gala evening," as she put it. But this one was unquestionably the worst of the lot.

The Winter Wonderland Ball, an annual party benefiting the Carnegie Hill Hospital, had been buried by an avalanche of really boring people years ago—the kinds of people who actually *enjoy* dressing up in dirndls and lederhosen and dancing polkas until dawn in a room decorated with Styrofoam sleighs and fake snow. One year I sat next to a man who had the largest beer stein collection in the world. I *ask* you. Rather than be stranded again in this social crevasse, I agreed to lend my name to the committee and send in my money—on the condition that I did not, under *any* circumstances, have to go.

June arrived on the dot of six. I opened the door and she flew in, breezing past me without so much as a howdy-do, throwing her white fur cape on the hall settee along with the matching muff. Barking at poor Cyril to get her a white wine, June headed straight for the living room. Her dark hair was curled in an unflattering style and sprinkled with little diamond snowflakes. Her outfit—a floor-length, faded blue velvet dress with a ratty white fur hemline and matching ratty fur collar and cuffs—was a sight to behold. June, who was clearly pleased with the look, announced in passing that it was "vintage costume." Vintage hideous, I thought. It looked like something the old-time skater, Sonja Henie, might have been buried in. And indeed, the vague smell of mothballs mingled unhappily with June's signature floral scent of Joy perfume.

"*This is it, Jo! I've had it! I've come to the end of a long road of friendship!*" she cried, throwing her hands in the air and facing me.

"What's up?"

"Well!" she huffed, sinking down onto the yellow silk

sofa in front of the coffee table. "I have just received *all* the letters that have been written to the board on the Coles' behalf. The vote is tomorrow, as you know. And who do you think wrote a letter for them?"

"Who?" I braced myself because I knew the answer.

"*Betty!*" she cried.

"Really?"

"*Yes!* Our dear friend Betty!" June defiantly crossed her fur-cuffed arms in front of her. "Betty, it turns out, is a guerilla warrior—just like that awful man Che Godiva."

"You mean Che Guevara? The great revolutionary hero?"

"Yes, him. Whatever. She's a traitor. Now we know why Carla gave her that fur throw, don't we? It was a bribe, pure and simple. She wanted Betty to write a letter for her, and Betty *did*. So much for loyalty!"

I couldn't face the fact that June now wouldn't be speaking to Betty on account of Carla. That she and Trish were on the outs was bad enough. I tried to reason with her.

"Junie, Russell *is* Missy's godfather, after all. I mean, you have to take that into consideration. I'm sure that Betty agonized over this decision."

"Nonsense! The only decision Betty's ever agonized over in her life is whether to start drinking in the morning or the afternoon. She did this to spite me because she's angry we didn't come to Missy's wedding! She thinks I faked my injury because I wasn't invited to that vulgar bridal dinner which, by the way, I wouldn't have gone to anyway—even if we *had* been invited."

"I really think you're wrong," I said, lying, knowing she'd hit the nail on the head.

"I'm not wrong! Gil mentioned something about it to Charlie when they were playing golf last week. She feels hurt. Well, that's no reason for her to ruin my life, for heaven's sakes! Jo, I feel like sending her divine Dr. Newman's report about my foot. I really *did* bang it up and he really did advise me not to travel. . . . Well, anyway, I know Betty thinks I'm willful and imperious. And maybe I am. But it's *my* building, after all. It's not enough that I have to see Carla Cole at social functions. Now I have to share an elevator with her? Not on your life! But never you mind," she said just as Cyril offered her the glass of white wine on a silver tray. "Thank you, Cyril." June chugged down nearly half the glass before resuming. "She's *not* getting in, thank God! I've taken a poll and it's fifty-fifty. Guess who breaks the tie?"

"I can't," I said facetiously.

"*Me!*" she said with the smug air of a minor bureaucrat.

"I figured, Junie. And I think Betty knows that, too. She just did Carla a favor because Carla did so much for her at the wedding. But she knows Carla can't get into your building if you don't want her to."

"That's right! And she's *not* getting in—no matter what that old fart Hadley Grimes says. I have the final say! Take *that*, Marcy Ludinghausen!"

"Okay, but just calm down for a moment and try to think about it another way."

She glared at me. "What are you talking about, Jo?"

I was trying to play Eisenhower here, appeasing the egos of my two best friends.

"Junie, can't you just forget about it and vote for Carla just for the sake of peace in the building, and for Betty, for that matter? Think about it. You'll never run into Carla. I never see *any* of my neighbors."

"Oh, you sound just like Charlie," June said, giving me an irritable flick of her wrist. "He wants me to forget about it, too. But how *can* I? Among other things, Lulu would never forgive me if I let Carla in."

"Why does Lulu have to know? Tell her you were outvoted."

"Oh, don't be absurd. People know everything. Jo, the truth is, I'm just thankful that I'm in a position of great power. I will crush her."

June Kahn, the George S. Patton of New York society.

I could see it was no use arguing with her.

"Where *is* Charlie, by the way?" I asked, thinking that I might be able to talk more rationally to him. Charlie Kahn was sometimes a temperate influence on his socially militant wife.

"In Europe on business," she said. "He doesn't get back until tomorrow."

"What does he say about all this?"

"Oh, he thinks I'm obsessed. He couldn't care less whether she moves in or not."

"Well, maybe he has a point."

"Thanks a lot!"

"Junie, just forget Carla. She's not worth it, believe me. It's a waste of energy. So she *does* get into the building. So what? If we all band together, we can freeze her out of New York. She'll be just another woman in a couture suit looking for a lunch date. Eventually, she'll leave town."

June crossed and uncrossed her arms, then fidgeted with the fur on her cuffs, her birdlike face even more twittery than usual.

"No, Jo, it's just not that simple. I can't back down now. I'm voting against her and that's that. And I'll never forgive Betty for writing that letter. I feel so *betrayed*," she said in a sad little voice. "Betty's supposed to be sitting at my table tonight. I don't know how I'm even going to *look* at her—the snake!" She sighed deeply and rose to her feet. "Well, I'd better go."

I got up, too.

"How did you get here, Junie? You didn't walk here by yourself, did you?"

I knew how cheap June and Charlie were when it came to transportation. They never dreamed of hiring a car for the night, even when June was dressed to the nines in a gown and jewels. A taxi was as close as they got to luxury, and they walked whenever possible. Betty and I were always afraid the two of them would get mugged one day if they weren't careful.

"Of course, I walked. I only live three blocks from here, for heaven's sakes."

"Let me have Caspar take you to the Plaza."

"Thanks. That'd be great."

As I escorted her to the door, she said, "Did I tell you that Marcy Ludinghausen sent me quite a pretty little pin from Pearce to try and butter me up? I returned it, of course." She shook her thin little finger at me. "There are *some* people in this world who still cannot be bought!"

I made one last stab at getting her to drop the cudgel.

"Junie, listen to me. You're already not speaking to Trish. If you stop speaking to Betty, it's going to have a ripple effect. No one's going to be speaking to *anyone* by the time this is over—if it ever is over. Is there no way I can convince you not to make a big issue out of this?"

She thought for a brief moment and then said simply, "No."

She headed for the hall closet, where Cyril had hung her cape. Pulling it off the hanger, she threw it around her, pulled up the hood, and opened the front door. I grabbed her muff and followed her into the vestibule, where I pleaded with her.

"Junie, come on, you're being so unreasonable."

She glared at me. "Don't tell me you're on Carla's side, too, Jo!"

"I most certainly am not! In fact, I refused to write a letter for her." I offered her the muff. "I was supporting you."

"Well, you're not supporting me now!" Grabbing the moth-eaten thing, she turned her back on me and rang for the elevator.

One could never win with June.

I was so exasperated I could hardly see straight. "I *am* supporting you by giving you good advice. I just don't want you to shoot yourself in that wounded foot of yours, that's all. Think of what Clara Wilman always used to say, 'No matter how right you are, bad behavior can make you look wrong.' "

She didn't answer—a first for June.

"Well, take the car," I said, sighing. "I don't want you walking alone at night."

"Screw you *and* your car," she said without turning around.

"Don't tell me you're mad at me now, Junie? What the hell have *I* done?"

June maintained a stoney silence until the elevator arrived. She stepped inside the wood-paneled car and faced front with a glacial expression.

"*Et tu,* Jo?" she said at last.

Her grand display of indignity was severely compromised by the white fur around her face and her 1930s snow queen outfit. The elevator door slid shut. If she hadn't looked quite so ridiculous, I would have felt more sympathetic.

in the middle of all the people, was a very small moment, the whole lit up as her face and her fans'
new questions. The attention her she shall, she
hadn't looked past us there for, they would have felt more
sympathetic.

Fifteen

BETTY CALLED ME EARLY THE NEXT MORNING.
I was dozing in bed, unable to sleep. I knew
exactly why she was calling, of course, and
was rather amazed at her restraint. I'd expected her to
ring me from the party to tell me that June had refused to
speak to her and made a huge scene.

"Jo? I'm sorry to wake you." Her voice sounded very
shaky indeed.

"Are you kidding? I didn't sleep a wink all night. I
take it you've heard."

"Yes. It's too awful. I just can't believe it. I can't believe it. Charlie just called Gil. He's beside himself."

"Betty, I tried to reason with her, I really did. Don't
you think everybody's overreacting just a bit?"

"*Overreacting?!*" Betty cried. "*June's in a coma!
Goddamn right, I'm overreacting!*"

When people say someone is in a coma in New York,
it usually means they've been demoted to the C list. But

this time I had the ghastly feeling that Betty meant coma in the cosmic sense, as in no longer functioning.

"What are you talking about?"

Her tone became conciliatory. "Oh, Jo, you haven't heard, have you? Junie was hit by a car last night. She's in a coma in Carnegie Hill Hospital."

Betty started to cry. I listened to her soft sobbing, thinking this was a bad dream.

"Oh my God, no. That's not possible. I just saw her."

"When?" Betty sniffled.

"Last night, I told you. She came by to see me before the ball. She was upset because of the letter you wrote for Carla."

"Oh, Christ! I was at her table. She tried not to speak to me, but then we got into a fight. And guess who was there? Carla!"

"Oh my God. Who was she with?"

"Bootsie Baines, who else? June threatened to bolt like she did at Trish's lunch. I told her she absolutely couldn't *think* of leaving because she was the chairman. Anyway, Gil and I managed to calm her down. And Carla was at another table pretty far away. We got through the meal, at least—ghastly as it was. God, I loathe knockwurst. Then came time for the door prizes. Because she's the head of the thing, June draws the tickets and gives out the certificates. So she goes up to the microphone, starts the drawing, and the third winner is—guess who?"

"Carla."

"You got it."

"Jesus, Betty. What are the odds of *that*?"

"They're good if you buy *five hundred fucking chances!* Which is apparently what Carla did."

"You're kidding."

"No, I mean, Carla probably thought she was doing it to be nice to June because she wants so desperately to get into that building. I mean, the more chances they sell, the more money the hospital makes, after all. But when June announced the number and then saw Carla coming up to the stage, she lost it. Just turned on her heel and walked off. I thought she'd come back, but she didn't. She up and left the party."

I shook my head in dismay. "Oh, June, June, *June* . . . !"

"Everyone felt sort of sorry for Carla because June had acted so badly. . . . Anyway, when Junie didn't come back, Gil and I figured she'd probably gone home. I called to check on her. No answer. So I thought, okay, she's just not picking up her phone. Jo, I was so pissed off at her for making a scene with me, I didn't care where the hell she was," Betty said, her voice cracking with emotion.

"Did they catch the driver?"

"No . . . hit and run. But you know June. She was so angry, she probably just bolted out into the middle of the street. I'm sure it was nobody's fault. Oh, Jo, now I wish I hadn't written that damn letter!"

Betty broke down, unable to continue. I listened to her sobbing for a few moments. Finally, she went on. "Anyway, this morning Colleen called me. She said the police were there and that June was in the hospital in a coma, hit by a car. Poor Colleen was hysterical. Charlie isn't getting back until this afternoon. Think of Charlie! He has no idea what's happened. Anyway, they wanted Colleen to come down and see her. But Colleen can't cope. Anyway, she has to get the apartment ready for when Charlie comes home. She called me and I'm going there now. Want to come?"

"I'll be dressed in ten minutes. Meet you there."

A New York definition of irony: June had fled a benefit for the very hospital in which she was now fighting for her life. On our way to the special wing of Carnegie Hill, where rich patients supposedly enjoyed medical care along with all the amenities of a first-class hotel, Betty commented, "All I can say is they better treat her like the fucking queen, she's raised so many millions for them." It crossed my mind that had June not been so rash, she might not have been hit by a car, and consequently she might not be lying in a coma now. But history does not disclose its alternatives and it was heartwrenching to see her there, lying in bed with the diamond sparkles still in her hair and bruises on her narrow, pale face, breathing with the aid of a respirator.

Betty and I stayed together in a silent vigil at June's bedside for most of the morning. The bleeping and humming of many machines, plus the antiseptic smell pervading the atmosphere, made the confined room feel a little like a spaceship. For once in our lives, we were both too stricken to speak.

That afternoon, Charlie Kahn arrived back from Europe. Betty and I were waiting for him in his apartment. We broke the news to him gently, trying to put a positive spin on the situation, telling him what the nice, young doctor at the hospital had told us—namely, that June had a good chance of coming out of the coma, that she had sustained no other serious internal injuries, and that only time would tell. Charlie stared at us with almost total incomprehension, fueled by the fatigue of a long flight. He didn't utter a word. He sank down into a chair in slow motion and stared at the ground for a long time. Then he looked up at us and said, "There must be some mistake. It can't be June. Not *my* June," as if there were someone else's June it might be.

We then took him over to the hospital where he stayed, camping out in her room, refusing to leave her side.

"Charlie would die without her," I said to Betty as we left the hospital.

"That's what you think. Rich men all mourn for about a week and then they become merry widowers with every woman in the world calling them."

"I think Charlie's different."

"I doubt it. But let's pray we never find out," Betty said.

Hadley Grimes, old stickler for protocol that he was, refused to postpone the meeting of the co-op board that afternoon, despite the fact that June was in a coma.

"That whole board's been in a coma for years, so how would he know the difference?" Betty said.

According to Betty, who got it from Trish, who got it from Hadley's wife, Ellen, Hadley maintained that as president of the board, June would have wanted things to go on "as usual" in her absence. This was a fiction, if ever there was one. Everyone who knew June knew that she was the kind of person who wanted to be in on everything—even funerals. Betty once observed that June was the only person she knew who wasn't altogether against nuclear war.

"Let's be honest here, Jo, June doesn't want the party

to go on without her—even if it means blowing up the whole world," Betty said.

That night, Betty called to tell me that the Coles had passed the board. Carla was now an official resident of 831 Fifth Avenue. And June was an official resident of the Carnegie Hill Hospital.

A few days later, Page Six in the *New York Post* confirmed the sale in an item that said that Carla and "the missing Russell Cole" had successfully purchased the Wilman apartment—"a sprawling triplex which mouthwash heiress Marcy Ludinghausen has been trying to unload for two years"—for the third-highest price ever paid for an apartment in Manhattan, twenty-eight million dollars. After a brief sketch of the Coles' scandal-ridden marriage and the current mystery involving Russell's disappearance, the article said that the co-op was notoriously difficult to get into, but that the "controversial Coles" had "breezed through the building's stuffy board" because the board's president, June Kahn, was in a coma and had not been there to veto their approval. Page Six really got it right this time.

Betty called me and said, "Come to think of it, Jo, I think June's much safer in a coma because if she comes out of it and finds out Carla's passed the board, she's going to kill herself."

"Or Carla," I added.

"Gil now refers to that building as the Gaza Strip," Betty said.

"With less chance of a peace agreement," I added.

Sixteen

THERE ARE MEMORABLE MOMENTS IN SOCIAL life when a convergence of scandals and bad news cause what Betty Waterman terms, "the perfect shit storm." This was such a moment. Russell Cole was missing, presumed murdered or mentally impaired, depending on your like or dislike of Carla Cole. June Kahn was in a coma. Carla was moving to New York. The wags had it that Max Vermilion had jilted Lulu Cole for me. And now, to top it all off, Dick Bromire was finally going on trial for income tax evasion and other money-related crimes. Expressions of supposed deep concern dominated all conversation. But as Betty said: "You can't cut the Schadenfreude with a chain saw!"

The night before Dick's trial, Trish gave a dinner party at their apartment on Park Avenue. There were those, however, who didn't think that Dick Bromire should be either having parties or going to them, given the disgrace of being indicted. In New York, one is guilty until proven innocent, even if one hasn't been formally charged with anything, not to mention when one has. And even if one is charged and acquitted, the odor of some scandals never entirely fades. It was quickly pointed out by his loyal friends that Dick hadn't killed anyone, like some erstwhile members of New York society. But that didn't seem to mollify those who discover their own piety in the sins of others. There was a lot of talk about the dinner and how inappropriate and shameful it was—particularly among those who hadn't been invited.

Larry Locket called me to tell me he was back in town. He'd heard about June, of course, and about Carla buying the Wilman apartment.

"How's poor June doing?" he asked me.

"The same."

"I'm so sorry, Jo. I know how close you two are," he said.

"Thank you, Larry. It's been awful, I must say."

"Will she pull through?"

"It's impossible to tell. Betty and I go visit her almost every day. We just keep praying. Tell me how *you* are. Did you see Hernandez's son?"

"Did I ever! I had a riveting time with him and I'm dying to tell you about it, Jo. By any chance, will I be seeing you later tonight?" he asked me.

I knew he was being discreet. It's never a good idea to announce where you're going in New York in case the person you're speaking to hasn't been invited to the same party. So you do a little verbal minuet before either of you gives out any specifics.

"I believe so," I said.

"The future felon's house?" he ventured.

"Bite your tongue," I said, laughing. "Are you covering the trial?"

"No. Dick's too good a friend. Besides, I'm working full-time on the Cole case now. But everyone says he's guilty. . . . Honey, we have so much to discuss!"

"I'll ask Trish to put us next to each other at dinner," I told him.

"Great. This is gonna be some party!"

I hung up with a slightly uneasy feeling. In light of recent events, I was now quite worried to learn that Larry was working so hard on the Cole case. Larry was a brilliant reporter who had solved cases that had baffled the police. I knew that if he leveled his gaze at Carla, there was no telling what he might find out about *me*—if, indeed, she knew something about me, which she had certainly hinted she did. I tried to put this feeling out of my mind, but it gnawed at me as I got dressed.

The Bromire dinner that night did not have a festive feel to it, to say the least. Trish had filled their Park Avenue penthouse with so many altar-size bunches of lilies and chrysanthemums it looked like a funeral parlor. The curtains were drawn, thus obscuring the spectacular city views and creating an oddly claustrophobic effect in the huge, boxy white rooms. Trish, usually decked out in sparkling clothes and colorful jewels, was in a long, severe black dress with a high collar that made her look like the abbess in a medieval convent, or an undertaker—I couldn't quite make up my mind which. She stood at the door, greeting her guests with a thin smile, diluted by worry. Dick Bromire was nowhere in sight.

"Thank you so much for coming. Thank you so much for coming," Trish repeated solemnly to each guest, as if we were about to view a body. And in some sense, we were—Dick's. The only real sign of life about the place was a pair of black miniature schnauzer puppies, who barked and jumped around like little castanets until a maid scooped them up and carried them away. Dick had apparently given them to Trish to keep her company in case things "didn't turn out well."

I walked into the living room where a fairly large crowd seemed to be tiptoeing around one another, speaking in hushed tones, in deference to the somber mood of our hostess. I noticed that not only were all the men in dark suits and dark ties, all the women were in black. In my red silk sheath, I felt like a spot of blood. I saw Betty and Gil standing in the far corner underneath the towering Calder mobile that Gil had sold the Bromires years ago. Betty looked like an expensive coffin in a long, shiny black dress embroidered with ropes of gold on each sleeve. I walked over and kissed them both hello.

"Where's Dick?" I said, looking around.

"Holed up in his room having a nervous breakdown," Gil said.

"God, Betty, it's so hard to believe he's guilty," I said. "I mean, why would he do it? Dick's rich as Croesus."

"The rich are greedy by nature. How do you think they got rich?" Betty said.

Betty always talked about "the rich" as if she, herself, weren't one of them. In fact, as one of the top art dealers in the world, Gil Waterman was worth a fortune, even more than many of his clients. Betty was kind of like a Communist married to the Tsar.

The Watermans both said that Trish was particularly upset because Dick's lead counsel, Sy Cronenfeld, had barred her from attending the trial. According to Gil, Cronenfeld had tactfully explained to the Bromires that although Trish was a lovely and generous person, he couldn't be sure how some of the people on the jury, especially the older women, might view Trish, a striking blonde, half Dick's age, wearing knockout clothes and jewels. Cronenfeld didn't want to take the chance.

Betty's take on it was slightly more direct. "Listen, Sy Cronenfeld knows damn well that the sight of Trish and Dick making goo-goo eyes at each other across a crowded courtroom is just too Damon Runyon—even for New York."

A short time later, dinner was announced. Two mirthless butlers stood at either side of the entrance to the dining room, holding identical leather placards to help us locate our seats. The white walls of the large dining room featured two enormous and perfectly hideous abstract paintings by a young contemporary artist. The rectangular, white lacquer dining table was extended to its full length, easily accommodating the thirty guests—fourteen on either side, and one at each end. A single-file column of tall, oddly shaped black vases, each topped with a tight bunch of white chrysanthemums, ran the length of the table. Dozens of black votive candles provided a sort of witches' sabbath light. The whole setting was macabre. As I sat down and unfolded my black linen napkin trimmed with black lace, I reflected on how misfortune can often seriously impair taste.

I was seated between Larry and Roland Myers, a Washington insider and the senior partner of one of the city's most distinguished law firms. Rolly, a handsome African-American in his sixties, was deeply involved in politics, and was referred to as "the Éminence Noire."

When Dick Bromire made his entrance, a marked hush

swept the crowd. Dick was a tall, portly man, who, despite his bulk, had always struck me as oddly graceful in his movements. Tonight, however, his steps were halting and his eyes were glassy. He looked as if he'd either been crying or smoking a banned substance. Taking his place at the head of the table, he nodded to various people with a forlorn smile on his face. Despite the brave front, Dick was obviously in both physical and emotional pain.

I was dying to dish with Larry, but since Roland Myers was my dinner partner, etiquette dictated that I talk to him first. And besides, talking to him was always fun. Rolly was an interesting man with far-reaching connections in the highest precincts of power. When people got into trouble, it was Rolly they sought out for advice. He told me that he'd put Dick in touch with a "jail facilitator," explaining that this was a person who helped "people like Dick" get into one of the better jails. He said he'd done this just as a "superprecaution" in case the worst happened and Dick was convicted.

"It's a relatively new area of specialization," Rolly went on to say with a straight face, "but a fast-growing one now that so many CEOs and people with wealth and influence are facing prison time. Let's be honest here, Jo, if a guy like Dick Bromire winds up in the wrong jail, all the money in the world won't protect him."

The rack of lamb entrée came and the table turned. Despite the plight of our friend Dick, all Larry and I were interested in talking about was the Cole case. I plunged right in: "Okay, Larry, so do we think Russell's dead or not?"

"Hard to tell," Larry said with a sigh. "The guy in Castries wasn't him, obviously, although there was a resemblance. I don't know, Jo, people usually don't just disappear off the face of the earth. But he has. When I was down in Barbados, I saw everyone, from the governor general to the head of the Coast Guard to the guy who filled the yacht with fuel to the men who picked up their garbage. Everyone's mystified. Carla's backed out of all our interviews, as you know. She keeps promising to see me, though. I ain't gonna hold my breath. *But . . .*" he leaned in and whispered to me, "guess who *is* cooperating and talking her head off?"

"Who?"

"Lulu."

"I'll bet."

"And has she given me an earful! Believe me, if *half* of what she says is true . . ."

"But can you trust what Lulu says? Isn't she a little biased?" Despite her apology to me at the opera, I still wasn't overly fond of Lulu Cole.

Larry leaned in farther. "Jo, you can't breathe a word of this. Promise?"

"I'm the grave, Larry, you know me."

He whispered, "Lulu had a *spy* on board that boat."

He registered satisfaction when he saw the stunned look on my face. Suddenly the light dawned.

"So *that's* how she knew he was missing!" I said.

"*Shhh,*" Larry said, motioning me to keep my voice down.

"I always wondered how she found out."

"Well, now you know. He's an Australian named Jeff Martin. He was the sous-chef. He called Lulu the morning Russell disappeared. But he'd been reporting back to her for months. According to Lulu, that boat was a floating nightmare . . ." Larry peered over the top of his glasses and rolled his eyes at me. "Anyway, I'm going back down to Florida tomorrow to interview him. I have to check out Lulu's story because, as you wisely point out, she's not exactly an impartial source . . . I'll see Miguel Hernandez again when I'm down there."

"Yes, now how did *that* go?" I asked him.

"Well, that's a whole other fascinating story. Miguel Hernandez is a very attractive guy who lives in regal splendor in Palm Beach. He's rather shy, but if I said there was no love lost between him and his former stepmother, that would be putting it mildly. I think the only reason he agreed to see me is because he hates Carla so much. He's none too fond of the press, either. It took him a while to loosen up, but when he started talking . . . boy oh boy . . . !"

"Oh, *tell* me, Larry."

"Well, apparently, Antonio didn't leave his grieving widow anywhere near as much money as she thought she was going to get."

"Like how much is not much?"

"Miguel says she only got two million dollars—which, as you know, in that rarified little world isn't even pocket change."

"Jesus, she must have been furious."

"Get this," Larry said with a malicious twinkle in his eye. "A few months before he died, Hernandez showed her a *fake* will."

My mouth dropped. "You're kidding!"

"I kid you not. Miguel told me that his 'wicked stepmother,' as he refers to her, was positive she was getting at least half a billion dollars from his father's estate. And when she found out he'd tricked her, she went absolutely *bananas*."

"God, Larry! That's hilarious!" I thought for a second.

"But then, how come everyone thought she was so rich when she married Russell?"

"She acted rich. She spent her wad on the façade, as they say. Miguel loathes her. Thinks she's capable of anything."

"Murder?" I ventured.

Larry shrugged. "I don't think he'd put it past her."

"Would you?"

He considered a moment. "Not sure. Doubt it, though."

"So what else did he say?"

"He's a very cautious man. I think he trusts me now, and I have a feeling there's more he can tell me. Anyway, I'm going to hop over and see him again when I interview Lulu's spy. They're not far from each other."

"Don't you find all this absolutely fascinating?"

Larry nodded and took a bite of food. "And there's a lot more to learn. . . . But enough about the Coles. I want to hear about *you*, Jo."

"What about me?"

"Oh, a little bird tells me that you have acquired an insect pin!"

Larry was always up on the latest skinny. I laughed, amused at the idea that this nonexistent liaison between me and Lord Vermilion had already reached his ears.

"Max and I are just friends, Larry. We *really* are. No kidding."

"I believe you. He's a rather complicated figure, old Max."

"What makes you say that? Just because he's been married a hundred times?" I said facetiously.

Larry smiled. "I think old Max has a hidden life."

"Don't we all?" I said.

Larry nodded knowingly. "Yes, but Max's is particularly dark, I suspect. You know the English. They always have the grisliest murders and the kinkiest sex scandals."

"So which is Max? Murderer or pervert?" I asked, joking.

Larry chuckled knowingly. "Voyeur, one hears," he said without hesitation.

Just then, Dick Bromire tapped his glass with his knife. I hated to break away from our conversation, but the room fell silent. Trish leaned forward a little with nervous anticipation as her portly husband hauled himself up out of his chair and stood with some effort.

"My dear friends," Dick began in a halting voice. "I can't tell you how much it means to me that each and every one of you has come here to be with me tonight. . . . My dear friend Jo Slater has a motto, which is, 'I may not remember, but I *never* forget.' Jo, if you'll allow me, that's a motto I'm going to adopt for myself from now on." He took a deep breath and continued on in a stronger voice. "I'll never forget those who are here with me tonight . . . and I'll never forget those who are *not*. And to those who are not, I say, '*Good riddance!*' So eat, drink, and be merry, because tomorrow it may be baloney sandwiches for all of us. Ya never know!"

We all laughed politely as Dick sat down, but there was a strange feeling in the air. I remember thinking at that moment, "It's not you are what you eat so much as it's you are who you eat *with*." I coaxed Larry to return to our conversation about Max, and he told me that when he was living in London, Max had the reputation of liking call girls.

" 'Marries high, fucks low' is what they always said about him," Larry said. "A lady I knew told me that among the cognoscenti, there was a joke about Max's 'Taunton Hall Balls'. . . . Apparently, he was into orgies and used to have them regularly at his house."

Clearly Max was a more intriguing figure than I had realized. But I was just as happy we had never gone to bed.

Whispered conversations continued around the table, an indication that the evening was never going to become less lugubrious. Fortunately it ended early, and Larry gave me a lift home, keeping the cab waiting while he escorted me to my door. He made me promise to tell him all about the trial, since he was not going to be able to attend. He pointed his right index finger at me in a very Larry way—that is to say, with an impish gleam in his eye— and said, "I'll call you the nanosecond I get back from Florida."

Seventeen

IN THE THEATER OF SOCIAL LIFE, THE OPENING day of Dick Bromire's trial was the hottest ticket in town. People were dying to see the show. Dick had personally made arrangements for his close friends to have seats in the courtroom, having privately confided to me that the humiliation was so great he couldn't bear for anyone but his oldest and dearest pals to see him under those circumstances. In other words, he wanted to be surrounded by friends who genuinely wished him well, as opposed to people who would dine out on the fact that they had been there.

No such luck.

Despite the freezing cold, Betty and I went to the courthouse together to give Dick moral support. Dick's entrance into the courtroom was dramatic. He looked pained and frightened, like he was walking a gangplank. Several of the people there had been at the party the night before. Betty caught sight of Carla Cole and Marcy Ludinghausen, whom she referred to as "Scylla and Charybdis," sitting together. I wondered aloud what Carla was doing there since she wasn't a great friend of Dick's, to which Betty immediately responded, "Honey, this morning, Forty Centre Street is *the* place to be. Carla's playing the game now. You watch."

During the recess, Carla made a point of coming up to me and Betty and asking how "dear June" was. I found her inquiry not only disingenuous, but slightly sinister. It was beginning to dawn on me that Carla Cole was going to be a fact of social life from now on.

Betty and I went directly from the trial to the hospital to see how June was doing. Charlie was there, as usual, keeping a vigil at her bedside. His thin, lined face looked drawn and tired. We told him all about the Bromires' dinner and the trial, gossiping with him in order to buoy his spirits a little.

"I wish I could be there for Dick, but—" His voice trailed off as his gaze drifted sadly to June. "Oh—they found the car," he said suddenly.

Betty and I perked up.

"Screw the car. Did they get the driver?" Betty asked.

"No. The car was stolen."

"Has there been any change at all?" I asked him, looking at my poor, dear friend who looked uncharacteristically serene in her comatose state.

He shook his head. "I talked to the doctors. They don't think there's brain damage, but they won't know for sure until she, you know . . . comes out of it."

"You should go home and get some rest," I said.

Charlie shook his head. "No rest at home. Carla Cole's started construction."

"Construction? It's only February, for heaven's sakes.

You can only do construction in my building from May to September," I said.

"Same with us. But the board granted her a special dispensation."

"*Why?*" Betty asked.

Charlie bristled. "Hadley Grimes. He's a stickler for building rules except when it doesn't suit him. He wouldn't postpone the meeting for June, but he's letting Carla Cole do major work off season. She's built a special freight elevator to handle all the debris. I get woken up at seven every morning with all the hammering and drilling. I feel like I'm living in the inside of a pinball machine. At least the hospital is peaceful."

As Betty and I left the hospital, Betty said, "Well, I guarantee you one thing: Someone's on the take from Carla, and I bet it's that old Tut-tut Hadley Grimes."

I didn't disagree.

When I got home that evening, there was a message that Max had called. I didn't call him back because it was fairly late in London and I didn't want to disturb him. But he called again at what must have been two o'clock his time. I was just getting ready to have a nice, quiet dinner alone in front of the fire—my favorite kind of evening these days. I was weary of social life, and with June out of commission, a certain spark was gone—exasperating spark though she was.

As always with Max, there was a vaguely seductive tone to his voice. He said he missed New York and he missed me and he was coming back to town in a couple of weeks. He wondered if we could get together for a drink, or dinner, "or a little something more amusing." I intuited that "a little something more amusing" did not mean romance. It meant he was asking would I give him a party. When I suggested it, he jumped at the idea. Max made no secret of the fact that he adored parties—particularly those given in his honor. Betty was the one who said, "Somewhere someone is always giving a party for Max Vermilion."

Max and I made up a guest list. He asked me if I wouldn't mind asking Lulu Cole. I told him I wasn't crazy about the idea, but since she'd been kind enough to invite me to the opera where she and I had declared a truce, I would.

"I'll do it for you, Max," I said. "Just for you."

"Jo, you are a star," he said.

I suggested some friends of my own—several of whom he'd never met. He said he was delighted to meet "new people." I thought of Betty, who was always saying how she couldn't stand new people because, as she put it, "You meet them, you get friendly with them, and then when they get indicted, you have to stick by them. New people today are riskier than unprotected sex."

Fortunately, Max didn't have that view.

"I collect friends the way my ancestors collected bronzes—in great quantity, but with some discrimination," he said.

We completed the list, fixed a date, and I told him I'd get right on it.

"Please wear your little pin," he said flirtatiously.

"Of course—social butterly that I am," I said.

"Dragonfly," he corrected me.

I went to bed fairly early and was awakened out of a fitful sleep by the phone. I picked it up and said a groggy hello. It was Larry calling from Florida. I glanced at the clock—just past eleven.

"Jo, Larry. I'm so sorry to wake you up," he said apologetically. He obviously wanted to talk.

"No, that's okay, honey. What's up? Where are you?"

"Palm Beach."

"How's Lulu's spy?" I asked him, slowly coming to life.

There was a brief silence.

"Dead," Larry said.

That woke me up.

"What?! You're kidding! What happened?"

"The Palm Beach police just paid me a visit at my hotel. I was supposed to meet him for dinner tonight and he didn't show up. I went back to The Breakers and called him several times. There was no answer. They found him and his car in a ditch."

"How come they called you?"

"My name and telephone number and the details of our meeting were in his pocket. He was obviously on his way to see me when he went off the road." He paused for a moment, then said, "It strikes me a little odd."

"What do you mean?"

"Well, Martin was on his way to confirm some unpleasant stories about our friends the Coles, and he dies. Our friend June was about to veto them from getting into her building and she winds up in a coma. Both car accidents. Maybe it's just my old reporter's instincts, but it kinda makes you wonder, doesn't it?"

I sat up in bed. "Oh, Larry, you don't think that Carla—"

"I don't know," he interrupted me, anticipating my thought. "Right now, all I'm willing to say is that it's odd. Jeff Martin was a problem for Carla and so was June. Well, they're not problems anymore."

"She couldn't have done it. She was at the trial today."

"Money may not buy happiness, Jo, but it can buy damn near anything else."

"You're saying she hired someone?"

"I'm not saying anything. I'm just thinking out loud."

"You suspect her, Larry. I know you do."

"Well, I do have a little motto, 'Don't rush past the obvious.' "

Larry told me he was going to stay down in Palm Beach for a couple of days to see if he could find out anything more about Jeff Martin's death and also to see Miguel Hernandez again. We made a dinner date for the Thursday he got back. Needless to say, I didn't rest easily that night. Though I was wary of Carla for my own personal reasons, it was hard to believe she was somehow responsible for June's accident. And yet, as I lay awake in the dark, unable to sleep, I wondered if Larry's instincts might indeed be correct. Was Carla Cole merely a social interloper, or was she a person of considerably more unnerving ambitions?

Eighteen

THE NIGHT LARRY RETURNED FROM PALM Beach, he took me to dinner at Pug's. Larry couldn't go anywhere without being recognized, and as we followed the maître d' through the crowded little restaurant, he was hailed by several friends and fans. We sat across from each other at a secluded table in the back room where we could talk privately. A waiter in a long, white apron took our orders. We quickly got down to business.

Larry had no further information on Jeffrey Martin's death, which the Palm Beach police were now treating as an accident. But he did have some riveting news. He leaned forward, rested his arms on the table, and said, "Jo, I'm taking you into my confidence here. I'm putting all this in my article, but I'd appreciate it if you wouldn't say anything before it comes out, okay? Do I have your word?"

"Of course," I assured him.

He leaned in farther and said in a low, measured voice,

"Courtney Cole has petitioned the court to have her father declared what they call 'presumptively' dead."

I was amazed. I remembered talking to Courtney at the opera that night and thinking how desperately she was clinging to the hope that her father was still alive.

"Why?" I asked, perplexed.

Larry got one of those gleaming expressions on his face that denote gossip of the first order. "Because her stepmother is attempting to plunder her father's fortune."

I cocked my head to one side, uncomprehending. "Carla? How can she do that?"

"Okay, follow me closely here, Jo," he said, using his hands to punctuate his explanation. "Nearly all of Russell Cole's wealth is tied up in a holding company in Tulsa called the RTC Corporation, of which he—Russell Taylor Cole—is the principal stockholder. This company has multiple subsidiaries and vast holdings in real estate and businesses all over the world. Now it turns out that Russell gave Carla both his general power of attorney and his durable power of attorney . . ."

"Why would he do that?" I interrupted.

"It's not uncommon for husbands and wives to give each other their powers of attorney. However, in this case, it could be catastrophic. Apparently, Carla wants to make a gift to herself of the shares Russell owns in the RTC Corporation. If she succeeds, it will mean that with one stroke of the pen, she will become a multibillionaire. Courtney's trying to stop her before she gets control of everything."

I thought back to my conversation with Courtney Cole.

"Larry," I said excitedly, "that night at the opera, Courtney told me that she thought Carla was up to something. This is it! She told me that under the terms of the will, Carla only gets ten million dollars."

"That's right. There's a prenuptial agreement in which Carla waived her rights to Russell's estate. The will leaves everything to Courtney except the ten mil. . . . Remember how she got screwed by Hernandez? Well, she ain't gonna let that happen again. Jo, if this works, it'll be the fanciest finagling I've ever seen in thirty years of covering finaglers."

"But, Larry, how can she sign over his fortune to herself, just like that?"

"She can do anything she wants if she has his powers of attorney. I'm no expert, but I think it's all perfectly legal. Naturally, Courtney's trying to stop it. But, frankly, I don't see how she's going to succeed."

I slumped back on the banquette. "Jesus, Larry. Are you sure this is true?"

"I called Lulu from Florida to tell her about Jeff Martin and she told me. Of course, I had to confirm it with two of my Park Avenue Regulars," Larry said. "And they say it's what's happening."

Whenever Larry didn't want to identify a source by name, he would say the information came from his "Park Avenue Regulars"—a spin on Sherlock Holmes's army of urchin informants known as the "Baker Street Irregulars." Larry's group included spies in high and low places—everyone from court clerks, who called him when there were interesting cases on the docket, to maîtred's at posh restaurants, who called him when celebrities booked reservations, to socialites who called Larry just to gossip. It never ceased to amaze me how Larry seemed to know things that were going on in the city way before anyone else—sometimes even before they happened.

"Is Lulu upset?"

Larry looked at me askance. "*Upset*?! She'll spontaneously combust if she's not careful. This is her absolutely worst nightmare—Carla getting control of her daughter's fortune. She's got a battery of lawyers working on it. She told me she's going to sue the board of directors if they let it happen. Some of them are threatening to resign. But we'll see if they do. Anyway, if Carla gets away with this maneuver, she'll be a multi*billionaire*. No one on the board will want to alienate her then. You know how it works in this town: He or *she* who has the most money wins. Isn't it *fascinating*?"

I loved the way Larry said "fascinating," with a southern drawl and a big, impish grin.

"Oh—and there's another thing," he said just as our food arrived.

"Jesus, *what*?"

"Well, apparently, there's something in the wind about his collection."

"Oh, right. I forgot all about those glorious paintings. My God. They've got to be worth at least a billion."

"More," Larry said, as he cut into one of his miniature sirloin hamburgers.

I thought for a moment as I watched tiny rivulets of steak blood run out over his plate.

"Maybe the court will declare him dead and she'll be stopped in time," I said.

Larry shook his head. "Jo, think about it. It's tough enough to get a normal person declared dead. But any court looking at a man who's been diagnosed with Dissociative Fugue Disorder—a condition where people can disappear for months and sometimes *years* at a time and then show up again . . . well, they're just not going to risk it. If she succeeds, if they ever *do* find poor old Russell, he'll be broke. . . . Six billion dollars . . . Now that's what I call a motive."

I cocked my head to one side. "You know, you kind of have to hand it to her, it's a pretty grand scheme," I said with grudging admiration. "So do you think Russell's dead?"

"I do now," Larry said flatly. "But let me ask you something else, Jo. Don't you find it odd that Carla married two men with well-known, diagnosed psychiatric conditions? Both very vulnerable men. Solitary men. Shy men. One dead. One missing. I find it really . . ." he paused, as if searching for the word. "Coincidental," he said at last.

"Larry, are you saying she *planned* all this?"

"I don't know, Jo. You tell me."

I thought for a moment.

"Well, if the Manolo Blahnik fits. . . ."

Nineteen

M Y PARTY FOR MAX VERMILION PROMISED TO
be a glittering occasion, although not a huge
one because I could only fit forty people into
my dining room comfortably. Max being Lord Vermilion,
the eighth "Oil" Vermilion, as Betty irreverently referred
to him, everyone wanted to be invited. The final list was
a combination of Max's and my friends, a sprinkling of
inevitable *amis mondains*, and a few new and interesting
people I thought it would be fun for Max to meet. Naturally I hired Trebor Bellini to do the flowers, telling him
I wanted to create the atmosphere of a "wild English garden." To which Trebor wisely replied, "No point in com-
peting with Taunton Hall, Jo. What say we stick with a
tame New York apartment?"

The day before the party I was in hostess hell, trying
to pull all the loose ends together, as one does before such
a big event. In the middle of dealing with everything,
Max called and asked me if he could bring along a guest.

"Jo, m'dear, if this is the slightest imposition, you

must tell me," he said in his cheerfully clipped English accent. "We're too good friends now for you not to be completely honest."

His polite request was merely a genteel formality as we both knew I could not refuse him anything.

"It's no imposition at all, Max, dear. Who is it?"

"Carla Cole," he said. I blanched. "Ran into her at a luncheon at Bootsie Baines's today and we had a jolly time together. She spoke so well of you."

I hesitated for a moment in an effort to gather my thoughts.

"Max, Lulu's coming to the party, remember? You specifically asked me to invite her."

"So what?" he said blithely.

"You can't be serious. Lulu loathes and despises Carla."

"Oh, Lulu loathes and despises so many people it's difficult to keep track," Max said, dismissing the idea. "It's just her way, you know. She doesn't really mean it half the time."

"Max, dear, I really think she means it *this* time," I said, trying to remain calm. "May I remind you that Carla is the woman who stole her husband away from her? *And* the woman who Lulu now believes has *killed* him?"

"A bit dramatic, *what*?"

"Sweetie, we're not just talking *amis mondains* here," I said, making a reference to the people in social life one tolerates but doesn't really like. "We're talking arch enemies."

Remembering my promise to Larry, I bit my tongue to keep from telling him that Lulu was currently suing Carla because Carla was looting Russell's fortune.

"All my ex-wives loathe each other, but they behave in

public," Max sniffed. "I have children who don't speak to each other—or to me, for that matter. On their mothers' orders. But we all kiss and act friendly in public. That's life. One's bound to run into someone one loathes here and there. One simply controls oneself, *what*?"

"I think it's a bad idea."

A long silence ensued. "That puts me in rather a bind," Max said at last. "I'm afraid I've already invited her."

"Don't tell me!"

"I was sure you'd be delighted to have her. I know you two are friends. I saw you lunching together at The Forum, remember?"

"Okay. You can bring her under one condition."

"Name it, m'dear."

"You call Lulu and tell her that Carla is coming and you call Carla and tell her that Lulu is coming. That way they can back out if they want to. I'm serious. I'm not going to do it. And I don't want my apartment to become a crime scene."

"Oh, my dear Jo," he said, chuckling, "I *assure* you there won't be a problem."

I hung up with a sinking feeling. I immediately rang Betty and explained the situation.

"So you're depending on *Max* to tell each of them the other is coming?" she said incredulously.

"Well, I'm sure not going to do it, and I think they should both be warned."

"Honey, one thing everybody knows about Max is that he's full of mischief. He loves social scenes the way sports fans love playoffs. I bet he doesn't tell either of them."

"Oh, Betty! What do you *mean*? I can't have them showing up here unprepared. That's like having Churchill and Hitler to the same party—although in this case, it's hard to tell which is which."

" 'Witch' being the operative word," Betty said. "And lest you forget, Max Vermilion is the man who invited *all* of his wives and a few of his current girlfriends to his fifty-fifth birthday party. Gil and I were there. It was like walking into a ring of jeweled pit bulls. The only thing Max likes more than women fighting is women fighting over *him*."

"Do you think I should call them?"

"You could—for all the good it would do."

"I'm sure if Lulu hears Carla's coming she won't come. And vice versa. With any luck, both of them will decline."

"Dream on," Betty said. "Max Vermilion is the biggest social catch around. If you think either of those gals is going to fold in the stretch, think again."

"So you don't think calling them would do any good?"

"Max said he'd handle it, didn't he? So let him," Betty said. "Just hide the good china."

The morning of the party, I sat at the desk in my bedroom with the placement placards spread out in front of me, trying for the hundredth time to seat the damn dinner. I got an inkling of what Metternich must have gone through trying to seat the Congress of Vienna. No matter what I did, someone was bound to be insulted. Rich people are like monarchs, used to absolute rule within their own spheres. Seating a dinner like this one was always bound to give offense to someone. For example, the only way not to offend Lulu was to seat her at Max's table. But Max had called again to ask if Carla could be at his table. Since I couldn't very well seat Carla and Lulu anywhere near each other it meant that if I honored Max's request, Lulu would be offended. And if I put Lulu at Max's table and Carla at another table, Max would be offended. Finally, I split the coveted baby—a.k.a. Max Vermilion—in two. I put Carla on his right and Lulu on his left. That way no one could complain, and they could all kill each other if they felt like it.

That night, I put on a long, white silk dress and pinned Max's diamond dragonfly high up on my shoulder. I didn't look my best because I was a nervous wreck. I went around the apartment lighting all the candles myself to help steady my nerves. Larry was the first guest to arrive. We had a drink and he informed me that the *Wall Street Journal* was doing a big article on Carla Cole and the RTC Corporation.

"The reporter doing the story is a friend of mine," Larry said. "He claims that Carla is inches away from getting control of the whole thing now and there's nothing anyone can do about it."

"Is Lulu still suing?"

"Yes, but she doesn't really have a case. The law is in Carla's favor. Russell set it up that way. Lulu told me she was meeting with the lawyers today."

I looked at my watch with a feeling of panic. "Larry, do you realize that in less than twenty minutes, Carla and Lulu are arriving here for dinner. They're going to kill each other. Jesus, what am I going to do?"

"Check for automatic weapons at the door?" he ventured.

Polite and punctual guest of honor that he was, Max Vermilion arrived on the dot of eight. He looked elegant in an old-style tuxedo that was intended to "last the duration," as he put it. Max didn't approve of men whose clothes were "too new or too fashionable," and his entire wardrobe seemed to consist of many similar bespoke suits made by a Savile Row tailor who had gone out of business at least twenty years ago. He was a marked contrast to those in New York who, unlike Thoreau, are wary of any enterprise which does *not* require new clothes.

Carla arrived shortly after Max. She was dressed in a long, black sheath and had her hair pulled back into a tight chignon. The large diamond-studded choker she was wearing reflected the light and gave her face a glow. She greeted me with the requisite air kisses, one on each cheek, and the smug attitude of an adversary who knows she has won. There was something even more confident about her that night and I suspected it had to do with her impending wealth.

"Jo, darling, thank you so much for including me in on your beautiful party tonight. I hope it is not too much of an imposition."

"Not at all, Carla, dear. I'm delighted you could come," I said, hiding my apprehension under a forced smile. "You know Max Vermilion, of course . . ."

Max bowed slightly, giving her a mock kiss on the hand. "Dear lady, how very nice to see you again." That seemed to be one of Max's stock lines.

"And Larry Locket . . ." I said.

Carla bridled slightly when she saw Larry.

"Ah, Mr. Locket . . ."

"Mrs. Cole," Larry said, shaking her hand with a knowing smile.

"I trust you are not working this evening," Carla said lightly.

"Writers are always working, I'm afraid," Larry said.

Carla made a sad face. "Oh, and I thought we were going to have such a nice conversation together," she said, abruptly turning her back on Larry and talking to Max.

Carla played up to Max with the verve and energy of a skilled coquette. I wondered who this woman really was. Had she, in fact, engineered the disappearance of her husband in order to get her hands on his fortune? Could she possibly have had anything to do with June's accident or the "accidental" death of Lulu's spy? And what, exactly, did she know about me? And how did she know it? No one looking at such a resplendent figure would imagine her capable of murder. But I knew, probably better than anyone in my little set, that murderers come in all forms—even socialites.

The next couple to arrive were the Bromires. Trish, pale as a candle flame, was getting thinner, and Dick, pink as a raspberry soufflé, was getting fatter by the day. Trish became very fluttery around "Lord Max," as she constantly (and erroneously) referred to him. He was, in fact, Lord Vermilion. It was rather touching the way Trish dropped the names of the people she knew in the English nobility, hoping to impress him. This was an old habit of Trish's, something she did with anyone she considered grand. I remember Betty once pointing out to her that it was impossible to impress anyone by telling them you'd just met people they had grown up with. But that didn't seem to deter Trish, who went right on dropping names.

There was a palpable air of doom about poor Dick. The trial was winding down to a grim, some felt inevitable, conclusion, accounts of which we all devoured each morning in the newspapers. Food seemed his only comfort. In short order, Dick washed down several smoked salmon and caviar hors d'oeuvres with successive flutes of champagne. Powerless to curb his compulsive eating, Trish stood by with the air of a beleaguered nanny who has given up on disciplining a willful child.

Ethan Monk drifted in with some friends from the Municipal Museum, Edmond Norbeau, the director, and his wife, Christine, and Justin Howard, the chairman of the board, and his wife, Regina. I watched Carla excuse herself from Max to go talk to Justin Howard, who greeted her warmly, as did his wife. I didn't much like the look of this. The Municipal Museum was my own little bailiwick, and I certainly didn't want Carla butting her nose in there. I immediately scooted over to their group like a polite hostess, and said, "Well, I see you all know each other."

Justin Howard responded by giving Carla a little one-armed hug and saying, "Everyone knows this brave lady."

Carla, Justin, and Edmond excused themselves and retreated to an isolated corner of the room, leaving me and Ethan with the wives. As I talked to Christine Norbeau and Reggie Howard about the current Ingres exhibition at the Muni, I watched Carla, Edmond, and Justin out of the corner of my eye. I knew Edmond well enough to know that he was never that enthralled unless he was deep in conversation about the Muni, his beloved museum. And Justin Howard wasn't about to waste his valuable time at a party like this, which was full of so many potential contributors, unless something big was up. I ran out of things to say about Ingres and dragged Ethan off into a corner.

"What's up with those three?" I asked him.

"Something very exciting, Jo. Carla has agreed to

put up the other half million for the *Judas*! Isn't that wonderful?"

I was horrified, but said nothing.

The Municipal Museum, widely considered one of the most prestigious of all New York institutions, was the social climber's Mount Everest. I dreaded the thought of Carla horning in on my territory.

Nearly all the guests had arrived and I kept glancing at the entrance to the living room, steeled for the arrival of Lulu. It was getting late and I was beginning to wonder if she would show up at all. She still hadn't appeared by the time the last guests, Betty and Gil, arrived.

Gil apologized for being so late.

"It's my fault," he said. "Important gallery opening."

"Dreary cocktail party," Betty whispered in an aside.

Gil took a long look at my glittery array of guests, like a farmer appraising a fine crop ripe for picking.

"Good group," he said. With that, he strode into the crowd, hand out, eyes sharp, bent on doing business.

Betty stayed back with me and surveyed the scene. "Well, I see Dracula," she said, referring to Carla, who was still talking to Justin and Edmond. "But where's Frankenstein?" A reference to Lulu.

"Not here yet. Let's hope she doesn't come."

I saw Max glancing surreptitiously at his watch. He was a great believer in punctuality and it was past the time we should have sat down for dinner. Cyril came in and whispered to me that the chef was getting anxious.

"Tell him we'll sit down in five minutes no matter what," I said.

It wasn't polite to keep my guests waiting because Lulu was so late. I excused myself from Betty and went over to Max, taking him aside.

"Max, dear, what exactly did Lulu say when you told her Carla was coming?"

He looked puzzled. "Was I supposed to tell her Carla was coming?"

"*Max*," I said sternly. "You didn't tell either of them, did you?"

He glanced up at the ceiling as if trying to recall, then back at me. "You know, I honestly forget."

"In other words, *no*."

"Now, Jo, we're all civilized people here, *what*?"

"That remains to be seen," I said, stalking off. I was furious.

I found Betty and told her what Max had *not* done.

"Oh, he really is so impossible," Betty said, shaking her finger at him across the room. "But are we surprised, Jo? This is the man who once switched the place cards at a dinner at Buckingham Palace. It's not exactly a news flash he can't be trusted."

I should have known. One thing was certain, under no circumstances could I now put Carla and Lulu at the same table.

I was just going in to change the place cards when Lulu appeared at the front door. Acting anxious and distraught, she practically threw her chinchilla coat at Cyril. Her brown satin evening suit was oddly off kilter. One shoulder looked lower than the other. Even her black hair, usually so perfectly coiffed, looked unkempt, with stray strings hanging around her face. I noticed she had two diamond bumblebee pins affixed to the lapels of her suit. A Max Vermilion special, no doubt.

"Jo, dear, I'm so, so sorry to be late. *Please* forgive me," she said breathlessly. "I'm beside myself, I really am. I was with the lawyers all afternoon and it just went on and on and on. You simply will not *believe* what's happened! It's an absolute scandal. But I won't bore you with all that now. You must be holding dinner. Where's Max? I must apologize to him."

Before I could stop her, the Chiffon Bulldozer was mowing her way into the living room in search of the guest of honor.

It was one of those social moments that happens so fast that no one thinks anything of it until they realize that in the midst of all the artificial camaraderie, war is about to break out as two arch enemies are brought face-to-face. Lulu paused to look over the crowd before she located Max, who was holding court, standing in the middle of a little knot of admirers—among them, Carla, with her back to the entrance.

Larry and Betty, who were talking privately in a corner, looked out simultaneously and saw exactly what was about to happen. They looked at Lulu, marching toward Max to say hello, then at me, traipsing after her, like a hapless foot soldier following a tank, then back at Lulu, as she reached Max's little group. I veered off and retreated to the corner with them, seeking shelter, dreading the moment when the past and present Mrs. Cole were dragged together by the silken ropes of etiquette.

An ominous hush fell over the room as Lulu, still oblivious to Carla, greeted Max with air kisses and said in a chirpy voice, "Max, darling, *do* forgive me for being so late!" She had suddenly developed a slight English accent.

"Never complain, never explain, Lulu, my dear," Max said. I thought I detected a malicious little twinkle in his eye as he motioned to the rest of the group and said, "I believe you know everyone here."

Lulu said hello to Justin Howard and a couple of others before turning automatically to Carla. When she realized who it was, she gasped. Her jaw dropped and she froze, looking deeply pained, like she'd been punched by an unseen entity. Carla mustered a synthetic smile and graciously extended her hand to Lulu who, still dazed, looked down at it in disgust, as if it were a claw. Looking up again at Carla, Lulu paused for what seemed like an eternity, and then said in a loud, clear voice, *"Thief! Murderer!"*

Gasps swept through the room, followed by an electric silence.

"I love a gal who says what's really on her mind," Betty whispered to me.

In this softly lit setting of antiques and pretty flower arrangements, everyone looked as if they had just witnessed a beheading. All eyes were focused on Carla to see how she would respond.

Carla seemed to be calculating the effects of this encounter. I sensed that she alone among everyone in the room was unmoved by the event. Her cold eyes betrayed her, as if she were merely an interested spectator rather than a main participant. She looked at Lulu with a steely gaze, like a hunter gauging the prey she has cornered, evaluating how best to make the kill. Suddenly, a decision made, her face melted into an expression reflecting a masterly combination of shock, hurt, and disbelief. The face of an actress in a star part, I thought.

Slowly lifting her gaze to Max, who was at a loss, along with everyone else, Carla said, "Max, I think I should go." There was a tearful tremor in her voice.

Max turned to Lulu and said, "Lulu, m'dear, rather bad form, *what*?"

Lulu shot back. "Don't talk to me about bad form, you horny, old hypocrite!"

"Excuse me," Carla whispered, edging past Lulu.

"*I will never excuse you!*" Lulu said in a loud voice. "*You stole my daughter's fortune! You killed my husband!*"

"*Ex*-husband," someone whispered loudly.

Carla left the living room, giving me an enigmatic look as she passed. Max followed her out, muttering under his breath in French. He trotted back in and said to me, "Jo, just seeing Carla home. Back in a jiffy."

Lulu waited until Max and Carla had left, then she stalked out of the room. I ran after her.

"Lulu, I am so sorry, believe me. Max promised me he was going to tell you that Carla was coming."

This seemed to infuriate her even more.

"And you *believed* him?" she scoffed at me.

"I should have called you myself."

"Yes, you should have."

"I don't know what to say."

"Jo, you once hated me for entertaining your arch enemy. Well, now we're even. What goes around comes around, as they say. But I'd watch out for Max, if I were you," she said, pointing an accusatory finger at my diamond dragonfly pin. "He's not worth it, *believe* me."

Larry came out into the hall. Lulu looked at him. Tears welled up in her large eyes. She said, "She's done it, Larry! She got control!"

Larry and I looked at each other. The elevator arrived and Larry escorted her downstairs.

I returned to the living room, where the buzz of whispers was deafening. Seeing Gil and Betty, I threw up my hands.

"Well, there goes the party!" I said.

Betty laughed. "Are you kidding? Honey, this party has just been *made*. What a fucking floor show!"

"Dinner is served," Cyril announced with great solemnity.

"But the main dish just left!" Betty cried.

Uncharacteristically true to his word, Max returned to the dinner after escorting Carla home. He joined us midway through the entrée. He sat down, blasé and charming as always, acting as if nothing much had happened. When I brought up the incident and chastised him for not having told Lulu that Carla was coming, he simply said, "Girls will be girls," and dug into the beef Wellington.

Twenty

NEWS OF THE PARTY SPREAD FASTER THAN cellulite. The next morning, I fielded calls from all over the world. Everyone in social life had heard about "the incident." What they were all dying to know, of course, was why Max had sided with Carla over Lulu. Lulu, who many believed to be romantically involved with Max, was a longtime friend, whereas Carla was a relatively new acquaintance. People wondered: Would Carla soon be wearing a diamond insect pin? And, of course, everyone was curious about me and Max. The rumor now was that he'd jilted me in favor of Carla.

In New York, the best part of any evening is often the day after, when it can be dissected from a distance. In light of that, Larry, Betty, Trish, and I all met for lunch at Pug's in order to conduct the autopsy. Before going to the restaurant, Betty and I had made our daily pilgrimage to the hospital to see our beloved and still comatose June. Betty, who always talked to June as if June could hear her, sat by her bedside and gave her a blow-by-blow description of the party. On our way out, Betty said to me, "Now if *that* doesn't bring her out of it, nothing will!"

Pug's was brimming with pals, as usual, among them Max, who was dining with Charlie Kahn at a nearby table. Charlie usually took friends to his club for lunch, but Max hated club food and he loved Pug's haute boarding school cuisine.

As Larry ate his designer meat loaf, Trish and Betty and I leaned in across the table, speaking in hushed tones so Max wouldn't overhear us. We speculated on the nature of Max's relationship with Carla. Trish was energized by this most recent little scandal because it was a chance to get her mind off her husband's trial. Old New York proverb: Fight scandal with scandal.

"I spoke to Lulu this morning. Obviously, she's upset about the whole money situation. But she thinks it's absolutely disgraceful that Max and Carla are having an affair, given the fact that Carla is still a married woman and she's acting so upset about Russell!"

"Lulu can't have it both ways," Betty said irritably, spearing lettuce leaves with her fork.

"What do you mean?" Trish asked.

Betty paused with her fork in midair. "Lulu called Carla a murderer, right?"

"Right," Trish said warily.

"Well, if Russell's dead, then Carla's a *widow!* She's therefore free to fool around with anyone she damn well pleases." Betty stuffed the lettuce leaves into her mouth and resumed harvesting the rest of her salad plate. "I just think we should be clear about these things, that's all. . . . Sure she's pissed about the money. But I think

she's even more pissed that Carla's moving in on Max.
Let's face it, Lulu would love to be Lady Vermilion."

"I thought Lulu was still in love with Russell," I said.

Betty gave me an incredulous look. "*So*? He's out of
her life. She might as well carry her torch around a castle. But my money's on Carla."

"Why?" Trish asked.

"Because, Trish, my darling, you know as well as I do
that powerful men like women who have been involved
with other powerful men. It makes them feel like they
have something special. Let's face it girls, women are
like paintings: the grander the provenance, the more coveted they are."

"And the bigger their bank account," I added.

"What about you, Jo? Aren't you and Max kind of involved?" Trish said.

"I know that's what everyone thinks, but we're really
not."

"That's too bad. I'd divorce Dick for a crack
at Taunton Hall," Trish said, then quickly added, "Just
kidding!"

"No you're not," Betty said.

"Yes I am!"

Larry was listening to our conversation, shaking his
head in amusement. "You ladies. . . !" he said, chuckling.

"*What*?" Betty glared at him.

"I'm here to tell you that the Carla-Max connection
ain't about romance," he said.

"No? So what's it's about, then?" Betty inquired.

Larry put down his fork and lowered his voice. We all
leaned in toward him like flowers bending toward the
sun.

"The reason those two are so chummy at the moment

is because Carla is putting a roof on Taunton Hall," he said with great authority.

We all exchanged bewildered glances.

"Taunton Hall needs a new roof and Carla is paying for it—to the tune of a cool ten million pounds," Larry said.

"Can't Max afford to put a new roof on his own house?" Trish inquired, echoing my own sentiments exactly.

"Of course he can," Larry said. "But why should he when he can get Carla to foot the bill for him?"

"Larry," I began rather sternly, "Max doesn't strike me as the type who either needs or wants to be in anyone's debt, certainly to that extent."

"He doesn't think of it as being in her debt, Jo. I think Max thinks of it as rather an honor he's bestowing on her. Taunton Hall is one of the great houses of England. I'm sure there'll be a plaque somewhere which says the roof was made possible by the generosity of Carla Cole. It's a charitable contribution. I gather he's delighted about it," Larry said.

"Hey, I'd be delighted if someone wanted to put a new roof on our house," Betty said.

"I'd be delighted if someone wanted to *come* to our house," Trish said sadly, reflecting, no doubt, on the number of friends who had recently deserted them.

Max and Charlie finished eating before we did and they both stopped by to say hello. We all exchanged cordial greetings. I practically had to pinch Trish to keep her from standing up in deference to Max. Trish's pulse just naturally quickened around aristocrats and she became particularly fluttery around Lord Vermilion. Betty, on the other hand, was one of the few people I knew who wasn't at all impressed by titles. She didn't care two hoots what Max or anyone else thought of her. She referred to Prince Charles as "Chuck," and the Queen as "Liz." And probably would have done so to their faces.

"Hey, Maxy, honey," she said, "we hear Carla Cole's putting a new roof over your head!"

Max guffawed. "My heavens! That was fast."

"Is it true?" she pressed him.

"In a manner of speaking, yes."

"Isn't that a little tacky-tacky, Maxy–Maxy?" Betty said in her inimitable hand-on-hip way.

Larry, Trish, and I all glanced at each other in amused disbelief. No one dared talked to Lord Vermilion like that—except Betty. Max laughed. If he was offended, he didn't show it. In fact, he seemed to enjoy it. Max was the recipient of so much nauseating flattery that I suspected he rather delighted in being kidded from time to time.

"First of all, it's not only *my* house, Betty, dear. It belongs to the National Trust. And despite the millions of pounds I've spent on it and continue to spend on it every year, it always needs a vast amount of work. We have a ball every year to raise money for it. You were kind enough to come to one, if you remember. Carla tells me it's Russell's favorite house in England. She wants to do it for *him*."

"As what? A memorial?" Betty said.

Max laughed again. "I don't think it's quite that grim, do you? Frankly, I think she's looking for projects to keep herself occupied until he resurfaces."

"'Surfaces' being the operative word," Betty said pointedly.

Enough was enough, however. Max furrowed his wide brow and grew serious. "Mrs. Cole is having a rather difficult time, you know—as anyone in her position would be, of course. She's a very nice, very generous person who means very well, I think. So wouldn't it be lovely if all you people here in New York were kind to her—particularly you, Mr. Locket?"

This zinger out of left field perked Larry right up.

"Me?" Larry said, pointing to himself with some astonishment.

"Yes, you. One hears that you are doing an article and that you are only listening to one side of the story," Max said. "And, as you can see from last night, that side is rather prejudiced, wouldn't you say? Wouldn't it be nice to get another point of view?"

Max may have thought he'd put an end to a conversation with a polite suggestion that had the ring of a royal decree. But Larry, who was no one to trifle with, particularly when it came to his professional integrity, quickly picked up the gauntlet. He straightened himself up in his chair and, pinning Max with a hard gaze, said, "You can tell the present Mrs. Cole for me that I would be delighted to listen to her side of the story if she would be kind enough to tell it to me. I have repeatedly set up interviews which she has repeatedly canceled."

"She doesn't want to talk to the press, Mr. Locket, which I, frankly, find rather refreshing," Max said. "However, she did tell me that if she were to talk to any of them, it would be to you. And I agreed with her. I do so admire your work—from a safe distance."

With that, Max walked off. Charlie shrugged with mortification and followed him out of the restaurant.

"*Brrrr . . .*" Betty shuddered as they left. "Well, those two cold fish certainly deserve each other," she said, referring to Max and Carla.

"Max isn't cold," Larry said. "He's just very English." He reflected for a long moment. "And he does make a good point. After last night, anything that Lulu says about Carla is going to be very suspect. If I quote her too much, it's going to look like I'm biased. Plus I only have her word for some of the things she's told me."

I could see that Larry was troubled.

"Well, you'll have to discover the smoking gun," Betty said, continuing to eat. "And I ain't referring to Max's third leg."

When I got home that afternoon, there were many flowers and presents and messages waiting for me, all of them thank-yous for the party. Max sent a lengthy hand-written letter on his coroneted stationery, along with a beautiful old book of French furniture designs to add to my collection. He didn't allude to the incident, but dwelled endlessly on the dessert I'd served, which looked like slices of watermelon, but was, in fact, watermelon sorbet with chocolate pits set in a real watermelon rind so one could easily mistake it for the fruit itself—until one tasted it. It was one of my famous "trompe l'oeil" desserts, as I called them. Max loved it. He wanted the recipe for his chef.

Carla sent me a large orchid plant in an antique vase. Her note, written on the back of a postcard, read simply,

> Dear Jo,
>   A memorable evening,
> So sorry I couldn't stay.
>   Love,
>   Carla.

What bothered me was that the postcard was a picture of one of the rooms in the Slater Gallery. These cards were only available in the Muni gift shop. Was she sending me a message?

Someone sent me a cactus plant with no note. I called the florist to find out who it was from. The florist replied, "Lulu Cole."

I thought so.

The most disturbing note came from Justin Howard, however. Justin thanked me for the party, adding a P.S., which said, "And you will be delighted to know that your dear friend Carla Cole is giving the rest of the money to buy the de La Tour *Judas*, thus making the two of you co-donors."

I already knew this from Ethan and it delighted me about as much as watching a fungus grow.

Betty called bright and early the next morning and spoke the five most feared words in New York, "Have you seen Page Six?"

"Listen to this," she said, reading from the paper: " 'Socialite Jo Slater's coveted dinner party for the elegant Earl Vermilion turned into a free-for-all when Lulu Cole, once married to missing billionaire Russell Cole, accused her successor, Carla Cole, of being a thief and a murderess in front of the fancy crowd . . .' "

She read on: " 'The posh gathering was stunned by the first Mrs. Cole's slanderous accusations. At one point, she physically menaced Carla Cole. The much younger woman backed off, not wanting to cause her socialite hostess any further embarrassment . . .' " Betty paused for a moment, then said, " 'The *much younger* woman?' Carla definitely called Page Six herself."

"I wish they'd stop referring to me as a socialite. It sounds so damn dumb."

"Jo, better a socialite than a *sociopath*—which is how Lulu sounds."

"Let's hope she doesn't see it."

"The odds of that are slim and none," Betty said.

And indeed, almost immediately after I hung up with Betty, I got a call from Lulu, whose apoplectic rage about the article was directed entirely at me. She hardly drew breath as she ranted at me.

"Jo Slater, you are a *snake*! First you lure me to that party, *then* you feed me to the press! *Page Six*! That was supposed to be a *private* party! And after I apologized to you and let my daughter confide in you . . . I think it's just despicable! I think *you're* despicable! And as far as I'm concerned, you and Carla Cole deserve each other!"

She hung up without even giving me a chance to offer her an explanation—not that I really had one. Aside from the acute embarrassment I felt over the incident and its airing, I was worried that the public perception was that I was Carla's best friend.

Then the mail arrived and with it a calligraphed invitation from the Municipal Museum to attend a gala dinner for the opening of an exhibit simply called "The Old Masters," the show that Ethan Monk had been working on for years. I was thrilled at first, knowing that this exhibition was the culmination of Ethan's professional career, and that it meant so much to him. I was just about to call and congratulate him when another, much smaller, calligraphed card fell out of the large tissue-lined ecru envelope containing the invitation. It read, "This exhibition has been made possible by the generous gift of Mrs. Russell Cole."

Twenty-one

A S IS OFTEN THE CASE IN NEW YORK, ANOTHER scandal got my mind off my own problems. Dick Bromire was found guilty by a jury of his "poorer peers," as Betty Waterman said. Dick's lawyers made a brief statement before the television cameras, saying that they would immediately appeal. I spoke to Trish afterwards. She was keeping up a brave front.

"The dogs are barking, Jo, but the caravan will move on," she said with disconcerting cheer, prompting me to think she had upped her dosage of Prozac.

The verdict hit our little set like a Scud missile. The ever tasteful tabloids featured huge blowups of Dick's beefy face, with the word "guilty" perched atop his head like a crown of thorns. All the speculation now was about how much time he would have to spend in jail and how rich he would be when he got out. Would he still keep his plane and helicopter? was the burning question on everyone's lips. And though the foul odor of his conviction had some hostesses turning up their noses at him, others remained noncommittal or even sympathetic. They were keeping their options open, remembering how generous Dick had been, and also bearing in mind that he might one day again be in a position to provide them with private air transportation.

The hard facts were that Dick faced a minimum jail term of ten months and a maximum of three years. If he was sentenced to over two years, he might have to go to a real prison, as opposed to one of the regimented country clubs white-collar criminals usually found themselves in—the ones the "jail facilitators" favored. Sentencing was in two months, assuming the appeal did not delay it.

"Forget synthetic antidepressants," Betty told Trish. "Jo and I will give you a large dose of that ladies' homeopathic stress remedy called shopping!"

In Trish Bromire's case, shopping meant spending money on variants of clothes and jewels she already owned many times over. Trish adored spending money, but she was so distraught about the verdict that even trying on shoes, clothes, and jewelry couldn't cheer her up. Then Betty suggested we all drop into Gil's gallery where we could get Trish to agonize over some really expensive art, and thus forget her problems, if only for one haggling afternoon.

The Waterman Gallery was an unmarked limestone town house in the East Seventies, right across the street from Gil and Betty's house. It looked just like all the other houses. If you didn't know about it, you would easily walk by its pretty, classical façade, failing to notice that the wrought-iron bars on the windows were sturdier than average, and that there were at least two security cameras—one above the front door and one perched on a second-story ledge. Gil didn't want browsers, he wanted buyers, serious ones: i.e., people who were rich enough not to quibble over millions. Betty referred to some of her husband's best customers as "million wise, billion foolish." The gallery was one of the hidden treasures of New York—accessible only to those who knew about it.

Betty rang the doorbell and we were met by Tory Wells, one of Gil's assistants, a tall, fresh-faced young blonde with a frisky, coltish air about her. Tory was the quintessential all-American girl. Wearing pearls and a sleeveless black dress that showed off her broad shoulders and long, lean legs to advantage, she spoke with the kind of drawl that reflects a privileged East Coast upbringing. She was also, according to Betty, a whiz with a Ph.D. in art history who spoke four languages fluently—including Japanese—and who Gil's male clients adored.

It was Gil's contention that, great art notwithstanding, it was always helpful to have smart, attractive women around to help sell the product. The fact that Betty was never threatened by any of these bright, attractive staffers was a testament either to the strength of her marriage or to her own self-confidence, or both. Ever since my late husband had betrayed me so completely, however, I was more suspicious of men and their secret lives.

"So nice to see you, Mrs. Waterman," Tory Wells said, aiming her charm-braceleted hand at Betty like it was a gun.

"Hello, dear," Betty said curtly. "Where's my husband?"

"He's in the basement with a client," the young woman said. "The Tiepolo."

"The Tiepolo . . . well, well, well," Betty said knowingly. "Let's go see him, shall we?"

The basement was where Gil Waterman kept old stock, as well as paintings that were too big to display in the gallery. The four of us crammed into the small, old-fashioned elevator. On the way down Betty explained that Gil had acquired a massive Tiepolo painting, but that it was so big and so expensive that he had not yet found a buyer.

The brass-gate door of the elevator opened onto a huge, windowless space, aglow with cold, gray fluorescent lighting, lined with vertical wooden racks into which framed paintings of all shapes and sizes had been slotted.

"They're in the viewing area," Tory said, leading the way across the rough cement floor to a gray metal door at the end of the vast room.

Tory opened the door, and believe me when I say that if I'd seen Gil Waterman on the floor screwing one of his assistants, I couldn't have been more stunned by the sight that greeted me. There were Gil, Ethan Monk, and Carla Cole standing in front of an unframed canvas, so enormous that only half of it was visible. The other half was rolled up on the floor.

"Betty, Jo, Trish," Gil said, stepping forward to greet us. "What a nice surprise. This must be old home week."

I hadn't seen Carla since my party. She immediately walked over and gave me an air kiss, moving right along to Betty, then Trish.

"Trish, darling," she said, taking both of Trish's hands in hers, "I was simply devastated to hear about poor Dick.

But darling, you will get through it, I promise you. Look at me."

Ethan sidled over to me. "So what do you think of it?"

"I take it you're referring to the painting," I said sourly.

"Huh? What else?" Ethan said, uncomprehending. There were times when Ethan's choir boy naïveté infuriated me.

We all paused to study the Tiepolo painting: a mythological scene of Poseidon surrounded by nymphs and sea creatures. Gil crossed his arms in front of him and stared at the majestic canvas with the look of a proud father.

"I bought it straight off the wall of a Venetian palazzo. It's unquestionably the finest Tiepolo in private hands, right, Ethan?"

"It's just remarkable," Ethan said.

Carla said, "What do you think, ladies? Do you like it?"

"Don't ask me, I'm prejudiced," Betty said.

Trish, whose ecclectic taste ran more toward modern and contemporary art, said, "I think it's nice. It's big. And there certainly are a lot of fish."

Carla turned to me. "Jo . . . what do you think? You have such impeccable taste."

"I've always trusted Ethan's judgment," I said.

"But would you buy it?" she asked.

Gil shot me an anxious glance. So did Ethan.

"Probably. If I lived in a warehouse. It's enormous."

"Fortunately, I think it will be just perfect for my new apartment . . ." Carla paused to reflect. "I'll take it!" she said decisively.

The tension in the air diffused slightly as both Ethan and Gil let out little sighs of relief.

Betty clapped her hands in mock joy. "Oh, goody, goody, goody. Now I can go shopping too!"

Later on that afternoon, I called Ethan and asked him point-blank how much the painting cost. He knew better than to try and stonewall me.

"Gil was asking twenty-two," he said. "But I think she bargained him down to nineteen."

Nineteen million dollars. Some bargain, I thought.

Twenty-two

THAT NIGHT, LARRY CALLED ME, SOUNDING very excited. He asked if I was free to spend the next day with him and, if so, would I mind driving us somewhere. I said I couldn't think of anything I'd rather do.

"Where are we going, by the way?"

"A place called Golden Crest."

"Which is?"

"A very private hospital for very rich people."

"Russell Cole?" I asked.

"Among others," he said with a little smile.

Golden Crest was a private sanatorium located forty miles east of Poughkeepsie. The entrance to the facility was an unmarked driveway vanishing into a dense forest. We drove down a narrow, winding dirt road, at the end of which was a gate with an electric eye nestled snugly between the trees. Larry pulled up alongside a little black box on a metal rod a few feet in front of the gate and pressed the red button. The gate slowly opened outward and we drove on through. I noticed there was a camera in one of the trees, moving as we moved, tracking us.

After a quarter mile or so, the woods stopped abruptly and we came to a vast clearing dominated in the distance by a huge, old brown shingled house in the Queen Anne revival style of the late-nineteenth century. With its little turrets and fussy white wood trimming, it looked like a gingerbread mansion. A thin stream of water spouted up from a carved stone fountain in the middle of the circular driveway. I pulled up near the big house next to a couple of other cars, which were parked just short of the dried-out winter lawn. Larry and I got out of the car and stretched ourselves. We were both a bit stiff after the two-hour-plus journey. It was much colder there than in the city. Still, the country air smelled wonderfully fresh and clean. As we headed up the front steps of the house to the wide porch studded with fine antique wicker chairs and rockers, a thin, middle-aged woman with cropped, brown hair and a pinched face appeared at the door. She was hugging a green cardigan sweater around her shoulders.

"Come in, come in," she beckoned us. "It's winter out there."

We followed her into the warmth of the old house, whose dark mahogany paneling and period Victorian furniture gave it the look and feel of a quieter century. The woman kept glancing at Larry, acting like a schoolgirl with a crush. It was clear she was dying to say something to him, but couldn't quite bring herself around to it.

"Would you please tell Dr. Auer that Larry Locket is here to see him," Larry said.

This gave her the opening. Awestruck, she looked at him and said, "Oh, Mr. Locket, you don't have to tell me who you are. I've read every single one of your books and articles. And I was wondering if, before you left, you might be kind enough to autograph a book for me. I brought it along because I knew you were coming."

Larry, always gracious, said, "I'd be honored. What is your name?"

"Doris Spillson, but please call me Doris."

We all stood around for an awkward moment while Doris gazed reverentially at Larry. Then, as if suddenly remembering the reason for his visit, she said, "Let me just go tell Dr. Auer you're here, Mr. Locket."

"Larry," he said.

A beatific look came over her face as though the Sun King had just asked her to call him Louis.

"Larry," she repeated.

When she was out of earshot, I said to Larry, "How does it feel to have an adoring fan club?"

"Honey, it feels just *swell*," he said.

A short time later, Dr. Auer came out to greet Larry. From the look on Doris's face, I gathered this was a rare occurrence. Auer was a stilt of a man who had thinning white hair, a short, white beard, and walked with a slightly arthritic stoop. Dressed in a three-piece suit and tie, he looked like a kind of skinny, road-company Freud. There was a rigid, old-world air about him. When Larry introduced us, Auer looked me straight in the eye, and said, "How do you do, Mrs. Slater?" and gave me a too-firm handshake, as if to prove he wasn't frail. That was the extent of his greeting. No small talk at all. He and Larry walked away down the corridor toward his office.

While Larry was meeting with Dr. Auer, I made my-self comfortable in the waiting room, a little Victorian parlor with mahogany tufted furniture and fringed lamp-shades. There were no magazines or newspapers, just books. I was thumbing through a tattered paperback copy of Larry's second novel, entitled *The Heiress Apparent*, with a main character loosely based on the Demont heiress who got away with the murder of her second hus-band, a stable groom. Larry was a good storyteller and I found myself becoming engrossed in the book all over again when Doris came back, rubbing her hands together, flushed with excitement.

"Isn't that a wonderful book?" she said, sort of crouch-ing down and leaning to one side, as if she were trying to see what page I was on.

"Yes. I haven't read it in a long time. I'd forgotten how good it is."

"Are you a good friend of Mr. Locket's?" she whis-pered, her taut face straining with inquisitiveness. She looked like an anxious whippet.

"Yes, I am," I said.

I saw from the light in her eyes that my stock was con-tinuing to rise.

"He's my absolute *favorite* writer," she said. "Would you like to take a tour of the property while he's in with Dr. Auer? There's a warm coat there you can wear."

"Thank you, I'd like that."

Doris Spillson was a gossipy spinster whose personal range of experience seemed limited to mild expectations or great disappointments—I couldn't quite tell which. She talked to me nonstop as we strolled around the grounds. It was a cold day and the place appeared to be completely deserted. The pretty property was dotted with twelve neat, white cottages, with shutters trimmed in dark green, each named after a tree. As we headed toward Maple Cottage, Doris explained that only twelve patients were ever admitted to Golden Crest at one time.

"Why so few?" I asked her.

"Are you kidding? With the level of service we have to give each one of them, that's all we can cope with."

Doris informed me that every patient had his or her own private cottage and staff. Maple Cottage was vacant, so she showed me into the luxurious little house.

"Each cottage is decorated differently," she explained. "A famous New York decorator came up here and did them. . . . The sheets and towels cost thousands," she whispered. "Rich people like good linens. And with what they charge you here, everything has to be the very best, you know?"

"What do they charge?"

"Around fifty thousand dollars a week. It can be more, *depending*," she said, raising her eyebrows.

"Why so much?"

"Oh, you get the royal treatment here, you really do. Facials, massages, herbal therapy, special diet. It's like a spa with doctors . . . and *drugs*," she whispered.

"Drugs? What kinds of drugs?"

She quickly put her hand to her mouth. "I didn't say a word! They're not illegal drugs. They're just, you know . . . legal drugs that make you relax and feel better. So many of our patients are under a lot of stress."

From the way Doris described it, Golden Crest was a far cry from most of the rehab centers I'd ever heard about. Over the years I'd known several friends and acquaintances who'd checked into treatment clinics for various addictions. But they had all been described to me as fairly utilitarian centers with many more than a dozen residents and usually possessed of a communal spirit. By contrast, this place seemed to be a glorified rest home for very rich, neurotic people who were more interested in a deluxe shelter to continue their bad habits rather than in a lasting cure for what ailed them.

"Oh, you would simply not *believe* some of the people who come here," Doris went on. "I'm telling you that if Mr. Locket came and spent a few months here, he'd have enough material for a dozen books. *Two* dozen! No kidding!"

"I suppose I can't ask you who?"

She laughed. "No . . . ! But, trust me, we've had royalty, billionaires, movie stars, rock stars, heads of state. Important people from all over the world. That's why I just *love* Mr. Locket's books because he writes about all the people I see. Shows you what they're really like and how they *got* here," she said with a little laugh.

As Doris and I walked back up to the main house, she asked me what Larry was working on now.

"The Cole case," I said. "Russell Cole? The missing billionaire?"

She nodded excitedly. "Oh, yes! Such a lovely gentleman, Mr. Cole. I remember when—" She stopped herself, putting her hand to her mouth again.

"That's all right. I know he was here."

We walked on. I could see Doris was champing at the bit.

"Well, seeing as how you already know he was here . . ." she began. "I was very fond of Mr. Cole. Such a nice man. Very shy. I didn't care much for his wife, though. Stuck-up type, you know?" She made a face. "Nose in the air. Never said hello or good-bye. Just treated you like furniture. If you ask me, he didn't much care for her, either."

"How long did Mr. Cole stay here?"

"Oh . . . let's see . . ." She thought for a second. "One time he was here for about three months."

"So he's been here more than once?"

"I really shouldn't say . . ." she said, with the air of someone who is dying to tell what she knows. "But, yes. He's been here four times."

"How recently?"

"I'd have to look back at the records."

"Would you mind?"

She gave me a sheepish little smile. "Well . . . anything for a friend of Mr. Locket's."

I was curious to know if Russell Cole had been in the facility since his marriage to Carla.

Back in the main house, Doris sat down at her desk and called up patient records on her computer.

"All the records, going back twenty years, are right here on this computer and a zip drive." She paused, narrowing her bespectacled eyes as she examined the screen. "Okay, see, here we are . . . Russell T. Cole . . . first time admitted, January 1986 . . . then again March of 1991 . . . then again in April of '92. And then in May of '96." She let me see the screen.

"What are 'visiting records'?" I asked, pointing to a small banner in one corner.

"We keep a daily record of all visitors—including deliverymen. Patients are only allowed visitors on Sundays and they all have to sign the visitors' book. All those books have been scanned and they're in here. I'll give you an example . . ." She called up another screen. It was a photocopy of a page from the visitors' book, "This is Sunday, May tenth, as you can see from the heading. And Russell Cole had one visitor . . . Lulu Cole . . . see, there, she signed her name in the book right there . . ." She pointed to Lulu's signature. "And it's in his records. We keep meticulous records."

She was about to switch screens again, when another name on the list caught my eye.

"Wait! That signature . . . ?" I said, pointing to the screen.

She peered closely. "Another visitor. For someone else who was here."

"Carla Hernandez?"

Doris sighed. "Well, I'm not really supposed to say . . . but seeing as you're a friend of Mr. Locket's. . . . Yes, that's Mrs. Hernandez."

"Antonio Hernandez was here at the same time as Russell Cole?"

She raised her hand to her mouth. "You're going to get me into trouble now."

"I won't say a word. Promise."

"Well . . . yes," she said at last.

This was fascinating news.

"Let me ask you something, Doris. Would it have been possible for Mrs. Hernandez to have known Mr. Cole? Or known what he was in here for?"

"I really shouldn't be telling you this . . ." she said, voicing the last alibi of the inveterate gossip.

"Trust me, Doris. I won't say a thing."

Doris got that same eager look on her face that June Kahn got whenever she was about to spew out really confidential information. A little picture of June's perky face flashed through my mind and made me suddenly sad, wondering if she would ever be the same again.

"Well, this is a very small place," Doris said. "Mrs. Cole didn't come to visit very much. Mr. Cole seemed very lonely. And, well, I used to see Mrs. Hernandez and Mr. Cole strolling on the paths together sometimes," she whispered. "I remember it distinctly because it was the only time I ever saw Mr. Cole laugh."

After concluding his appointment with Dr. Auer, Larry autographed a book for the starstruck Ms. Spillson and we left for the city. In the car, I eagerly told him what the receptionist had told me. But the news that Carla had known Russell Cole long before anyone suspected did not come as a great shock to Larry. On the contrary.

"I need to level with you, Jo. Miguel Hernandez believes that Carla targeted his father *because* he was bipolar. He told me she was seeing one of his friends. That's how they met. This man was even richer than his father, but she dropped him for Antonio. Miguel thinks that's because she found out about his father's history of depression. And he's absolutely convinced she had a hand in his death. But he can't prove it. Carla thought she was going to inherit everything when Hernandez died, but he tricked her with the fake will, as I told you. When Miguel mentioned to me that his father had been a patient here, I remembered Lulu telling me that Russell had been a patient here, too. Something in my brain twigged, and I suddenly wondered if their stays had ever overlapped."

"They did. Your friend, Doris, told me she saw Carla and Russell walking together. She said it was the only time she ever saw Russell laugh."

Larry nodded as if things were falling into place in his head.

"You know what I'm beginning to think, Jo?" he said pensively.

"What?"

"I'm beginning to think that Carla may be more of a planner than anyone gives her credit for. She meets Russell up here, realizes he's vulnerable, and files him away for future use, as it were."

"Are you saying that she targeted Russell just like she targeted Hernandez?"

"Could be. Russell Cole was a good insurance policy in case things didn't work out the way she'd planned with Hernandez. And, of course, they didn't. Hernandez was too sneaky for her. When she was cut out of his will, she went after Russell. It wasn't that difficult because she'd already gotten her hooks into him up here."

"Larry, do you really think anyone is *that* calculating?"

Larry stared out the window at the passing scenery. "Oh, yes . . ." he said absently. "Some people are very, very calculating indeed. It's a difficult thing to prove, though."

My mind drifted back to the way I had met my late husband at a restaurant in Oklahoma City when he was still married. After his wife died, he concocted this ruse about my having met him at Tiffany's where I was working as a salesperson, an attempt to keep anyone from suspecting I'd been his mistress for over a year. I remember Lucius telling me to deny I was a salesgirl. "They'll find out you were, think they've discovered the deep dark truth about you, and they won't bother to look any deeper," he said. "Just give the gossips something good to gossip about and you'll put them off the scent." Lucius taught me that "the lie within the lie" always works. I wondered if Carla and Russell had concocted something of the same sort. Carla's old comment to me that we were "sisters under the skin" was taking on greater resonance as I got to know more about her.

"So do you think she killed Hernandez?"

"I have no idea. But Miguel says his father's death was very suspicious."

"So did he shoot himself?"

"That's how it looked."

"Twice?"

"No. That really is a myth. But there *were* questions about it being a suicide at the time. Differing accounts of where the gun was positioned when they found him, time of death, location of the wound. They cleaned up the scene and flew the body out before anyone could do any forensics."

"But Carla was away in Paris, wasn't she?"

Larry looked at me. "She wouldn't be the first person in history to hire a hit man. Miguel told me that one of the guards on the estate left right after the shooting."

"Did they find him?"

"No. He was a new man. He had given them a phony name and false identification."

"Why didn't they prosecute him?"

"First of all, they couldn't find him. Second of all, I have a feeling that Miguel was none too anxious to have his father's affairs looked into too deeply. I suspect that Mexico's 'pharmaceutical king' may have had a *muy grande* drug problem. That revelation wouldn't have been good for business, to say the least. Thirdly, they wanted Carla out of their hair. The family agreed not to pursue the case as a homicide if Carla agreed not to contest the will. According to Miguel, she walked away with no argument—which tells you something right there, doesn't it?"

"So she may have gotten away with the murder, but not with the money."

"Exactly."

"Well, the girl must have something, is all I can say. And I'd sure like to know what it is."

"Carla Cole is a woman who knows instinctively how to manipulate men sexually. And she purposely picks on wounded game," he said.

We drove in silence for a time, both contemplating the possibility that Carla Cole had set up two rich men.

After a time, Larry said, "You know me, Jo. I don't believe there's such a thing as 'normal' when it comes to sex. Love and let love is my motto. But I do think that people with certain—shall we say—*unusual* sexual proclivities are more likely to have other problems. Compulsive sexual behavior seems to lead to other types of compulsive behavior. Or maybe it's vice versa. Maybe compulsive behavior is the cause of sexual obsession. But one thing I do know for sure from years of watching human nature: you can't keep a strong obsession in a watertight compartment. It's bound to leak out. And even if you think you've got it under control in one area, it has a nasty way of spilling out into another. And, let's face it, who better than a courtesan to understand and cater to obsession? That's her stock in trade."

"Well, she's not exactly obsession-free herself," I said. "Social climbing seems to be her obsession of choice."

"Social climbing . . . the ladder with limitless rungs," Larry reflected. "One of the most fruitless and ridiculous obsessions of them all."

"But an obsession nonetheless," I said. "And it certainly traps a lot of extremely intelligent people."

"Yes, it does. I'm always amazed at the strange magnetism of the rich, and what people—even the most brilliant ones—will do to get to a certain party or be part of a certain set. And, of course, as you and I know only too well, what's the one thing you need above all else in New York to get to the top of the heap?"

I glanced knowingly at Larry as I drove. "*Money.*"

He nodded. "Right . . . but in Carla's case, the marrying, the money, the social climbing—they may all be alibis for a deeper need."

"Like what?"

"Like killing," he said matter-of-factly. "Maybe that's what she *really* enjoys. After all, social climbing and murder are both processes of elimination, are they not?"

Twenty-three

BETTY CALLED ME UP THREE DAYS LATER AND said hello in such a tearful, tremulous voice that I was certain she was going to tell me that our dear friend June had died. I, too, burst into tears when she said, "Oh, Jo, she's going to be okay! She's out of the coma and she's going home!"

I was thrilled and relieved. It was the one bright spot of news in an otherwise desultory climate. I literally got down on my knees and thanked God for saving my dear friend's life.

Betty and I raced over to the hospital, where Charlie was busy checking June out. The doctors had told him that she needed plenty of rest and absolutely no excitement, and to that end Charlie was taking her directly out to Southampton to recuperate. We all made a pact not to tell her that Carla Cole had gotten into her building, agreeing that the news might literally kill her.

Betty and I flanked June's wheelchair as a nurse pushed her down the hospital corridor to the elevator. Her legs covered with a blanket, she looked very thin and fragile. Her core of energy was gone. This was a mellow, gentle June, a woman who spoke softly and hardly moved at all, a shadow of her former, twittery self. As Charlie and the nurse helped her into the back of the limousine that Charlie had amazingly sprung for, June paused, looked up at Betty and me, and said, "Will I see you at the party?"

Betty and I both nodded. As they drove away, Betty said, "Well, some things never change."

Three weeks later, Larry Locket escorted me to the opening night of "The Old Masters" show at the Municipal Museum. It was one of those stellar New York occasions where the social and cultural worlds come together in a glittery mix. Gentlemen in tuxedos and ladies wearing couture gowns and "jewels of mass destruction," as Betty called them, prowled the rooms, ogling each other as much if not more than the extraordinary paintings. After the preview, there was a gala dinner in The Great Hall.

It was an extraordinary exhibition, even by Municipal Museum standards. Ethan Monk had spent three years persuading some of the greatest museums in the world to loan the Muni some of their most valuable treasures: Da Vinci's *La Gioconda*, on loan from the Louvre; Botticelli's *Venus and Mars* on loan from the National Gallery in London; Giorgione's *The Judgment of Solomon*, from the Uffizi; Titian's sensual portrait of *Danae*, and Raphael's *The Holy Family*, from the Hermitage; a Velasquez portrait from the Prado; a series of Dürer drawings from Vienna's Kunsthistorisches Museum— to name a few of the most impressive works.

Though far from being the greatest painting there, the Cinderella of the night was unquestionably *Judas and the Thirty Pieces of Silver*. Recently authenticated by the greatest living de La Tour scholar in France, the painting was now definitely attributed to Georges de La Tour. It was Ethan Monk's great find worth many times what the Muni had paid for it. And Ethan was the brilliant, self-effacing, very popular curator who had put the whole show together.

I knew Carla was going to be there because she had underwritten the cost of the entire exhibition. I figured she would be with Max. Their names were now linked in every gossip column and the rumor was that he had jilted me for her. Max called me occasionally, "just to check in," as he put it. But I never saw him. I began to understand that Max collected people the way his ancestor had collected bronzes, just as he said. He strung his ladies together on an invisible necklace that he wore around his ego.

That night, however, Max wasn't there, which surprised me. Carla was standing in the receiving line between Ethan and Edmond Norbeau. She was dressed in a long gown of black satin, wearing a huge emerald cross on her neck. When Larry and I spotted her, he whispered to me excitedly, "My God, Jo, she's wearing it!"

"Wearing what?"

"The famous de Vega cross," he said. "Hernandez's wedding present to her. If you look at it closely, you'll see it's cut from one *single* emerald, the other four corners of which were made into rings by Louis Cartier in the twenties and sold for about a million dollars each. Staggering prices at the time. It's so big and fragile that no insurance company will touch it. It's supposed to have a curse on it."

"The curse is wearing it," I said.

Neither Larry nor I were particularly anxious to greet Carla that night. Larry was still working on his article and our visit to Golden Crest had planted too many suspicions in both our minds. Ethan spotted us, and in one of those Ethanesque bursts of enthusiasm, he waved us over to say hello. He was generally oblivious to social intrigue.

"Might as well get it over with," Larry said, mustering a party smile.

"Yes, in a place where there are no concealed weapons," I said jokingly.

"Carla Cole *is* a concealed weapon," Larry said under his breath.

Ethan Monk's frazzled, professorial air was muted that night by a dapper new tuxedo and stylish, high-tech glasses that made him look less myopic than his old horn-rims. Ethan was an admitted party hound and hosting tonight's event had spun him into a state of turbo excitement. This triumphant show reflected not only his scholarship, but his consummate diplomatic skills, as well. It was no mean feat getting foreign museums to part with their treasures—particularly in today's climate of danger and suspicion. Little beads of perspiration glistened on his forehead as he enthusiastically pumped Larry's hand and hugged me three times. Wild-eyed and slightly crazed, Ethan reminded me a little of Alice's Mad Hatter.

"Oh, Jo, isn't it a marvelous evening! Everyone's here! I can't believe it's finally happened. This is the dream of a lifetime. Thank you so much for all your support!"

Ethan and I chatted for a moment about the de La Tour, and how wonderful it was that Jacques Sebastien, the world's foremost expert on Georges de La Tour, had given it his imprimatur. Sebastien apparently came across an old inventory from a French chateau that backed up Ethan's belief that the painting was indeed by de La Tour père, not fils. Because the painting itself was impressive and because de La Tour was such a great artist, the story of the reattribution had made the front page of the Arts section of the *New York Times* that very day.

"And here is the other lady who made it possible!" he said, indicating Carla.

I felt a knot in my stomach as Carla extended her hand to me.

"Jo, dear, how lovely to see you," she said, giving me two air kisses, one for each cheek.

I was put off by her unctuousness, but tried not to show it. She then turned to Larry and said, "My dear Larry, how are you?"

"Very well, thank you, Carla. Still hoping for that interview," he said with edgy cheer. I was amazed at how good he was at hiding his true feelings.

"Don't tell me you have not finished with your article *yet*? Are you writing a *book* about me?"

"One day, perhaps. I want to be thorough," Larry said. "And unfortunately, your husband is still missing, so there's no great rush, is there?"

"You know, I am not very good at interviews," Carla said, sighing. "But I am inclined to think you are a fair person and I really do not want you to have any sinister misconceptions about me. I would like for us to get to know each other better, Larry. Off the record, as you say. After all, we have been ships that cross in the night for so many years."

"I'd like that, too," he said.

"I am going to give a little party in my new apartment quite soon. It's nearly ready. Will you come?"

"Only if you invite me," Larry said.

"You will have the first invitation, I promise."

"Let me give you my address," Larry said, pulling out a small, white calling card from his pocket.

Carla refused it. "Oh, I know precisely where you live," she said.

I sensed a threat in her tone of voice, and from the look on Larry's face, I knew he sensed it, too. As we moved on down the receiving line, Larry looked at me and I looked at him. We said nothing. We didn't have to.

Later on in the cocktail hour, Larry and I drifted apart as we each said hello to various friends and acquaintances. It was nearly dinnertime and I was talking with Edmond Norbeau, who had dragged me off into a corner to tell me how wonderful Carla Cole was and how she had expressed an interest in being on the board of the museum.

"She's already given us a great deal of money, as you know, Jo. This exhibition tonight, underwritten by her," he said in his soft, smooth voice, which had just a hint of a French accent, "and, of course, the de La Tour. You and she are the godmothers. But as you well know, Jo, it's not merely a question of money. What I would like, as you might imagine, is for the museum to become the beneficiary of the Cole collection one day. It's a superb collection. If she could arrange that, then I think you would agree we must at least entertain the idea of electing her to the board. What do you think, Jo?"

Over my dead body, is what I wanted to say, but I was afraid that might be a little too close to the truth. I absolutely hated the thought of Carla Cole slithering into my world like this. With what I was starting to learn about her, I thought she might be quite dangerous. Bearing in mind Talleyrand's famous rule of life, "Above all, not too much zeal," I forced myself to act nonchalant about the whole thing.

"You know, Edmond, I really think we must wait and see, don't you? After all, Carla might agree to something which—if Russell turns up—he might not agree to. And then we're stuck with her and no collection—not to put too fine a point on it."

"But she is giving us a great deal of money, after all," he said.

"Yes, but if you elect her because of that, it looks like anyone with a billion dollars can just *buy* their way onto the board of the Muni. Not the best image for us, do you think, Edmond?"

Edmond lifted his long-fingered hand and stroked the side of his thin, Gallic face reflectively. "One sees what you're saying, of course."

"Not that we shouldn't elect her *eventually*," I added, wanting to cover my tracks in case Carla somehow got wind of this conversation. "But I doubt Carla herself wants to create the impression that she's using her money like some sort of a tool to jimmy her way into New York, do you?" I said this knowing that was *exactly* what she was trying to do.

"No," Edmond agreed. "But we certainly would like to get that collection if we could. The whole world is after it."

"I understand."

A soft gong sounded. Edmond and I continued to debate the issue as we started strolling toward The Great Hall, where dinner was about to be served. Carla joined us and as the three of us walked to the glowing dining area, she said, "So, Jo, darling, have you spoken to Max lately?"

"No."

"He is in London. He was simply devastated he could not be here tonight, and he told me to be sure to give you his love."

"Did he?"

"This is Max's favorite museum, you know."

"No, I didn't know," I said.

"Yes, he admires it so much. Actually, Edmond, Max is the one who told me I should be on the board."

I glanced up at Edmond, who was nodding with approval. And why not? Lord Vermilion was a very powerful ally.

Dinner in The Great Hall that night was smallish by Muni standards, in keeping with the exclusivity of the occasion. As opposed to the usual forty or so tables, only twenty round, candlelit tables of twelve floated like little sparkling islands on the dark stone floor. Each table was named for an artist in the exhibition. Larry and I were at the Botticelli table. Trebor Bellini, who usually did all the museum's party decorations, was away in Europe doing a major party for a minor royal. He'd left a new assistant in charge and, unfortunately, the results were less than stellar. The centerpiece of our table, for example, was a naked doll with long blonde hair cascading down her body, standing on an enormous scallop shell—a questionable homage to Botticelli's most famous work, *The Birth of Venus*. As Betty passed by and took a gander at the kitschy display, she remarked, "Well, well, well, if it isn't *The Birth of Barbie*."

Dinner was pleasant enough, as always, Muni dinners

being renowned for good food and good service. There were toasts in which I was mentioned along with Carla Cole. Our names being linked together didn't thrill me, to say the least. Ethan thanked us both for our "supreme generosity." Edmond Norbeau called us both "great Patronesses of the arts." It was all very decorous—except for the spectre of Russell Cole, hanging over The Great Hall along with the medieval banners.

Twenty-four

THE NEXT AFTERNOON, I WENT TO THE Municipal Museum for an executive committee meeting of the board. Unfortunately, the meeting turned out to be one of the most disturbing experiences of my life—and, believe me, if you know my life, that's really saying something.

Everything started off extremely well. About fifteen of us—the chairmen of the standing committees, such as myself, plus key staff members, plus the chairman of the board himself and Edmond Norbeau, the director— all gathered in the main boardroom. Everyone was in an upbeat mood because the previous night's dinner had been such a great success. The *New York Times* and the *Washington Post* had both called the exhibition "spectacular." People were lined up around the block to see it. We all chatted amongst ourselves before taking our seats around the long, mahogany conference table. I had a particularly nice conversation with Justin Howard, the new chairman of the board. My old friend, Roger

Lowry, had retired and Howard was now head of the museum.

The scion of an old and prominent New York family, Howard had first distinguished himself as the president of his family's publishing empire and then gone on to dedicate himself to philanthropy and other eleemosynary activities. In his early sixties, his puggish face bustled with energy and purpose. He was a real charmer, as well as being an astute businessman and a man of culture. In the relatively short period of his leadership, the museum had prospered. Justin and I were not great friends, but I respected him and I believe he respected me. When his appointment was announced, I had given him one of my small dinners. He and his wife, Regina, said it was one of the most elegant evenings they'd ever been to, which pleased me to no end. And they had both been extremely supportive after my now infamous dinner for Max, at which they had both been present.

Just before we sat down, Justin said to me, "I have some very exciting news, Jo. I hope you'll be pleased."

"How wonderful. Can't wait," I said in a polite, chipper voice. Taking a seat beside Ethan Monk, I whispered to him, "What's going on?"

Ethan shrugged. "Don't ask me." He seemed as perplexed as I was.

As chairman of the acquisitions committee, I knew it had to be something very big indeed mainly because I was not privy to it. I was usually privy to all museum business, as was Ethan. And even if Ethan wasn't informed outright, or consulted, as I generally was, he always heard the scuttlebutt through the gilded grapevine. I simply couldn't imagine what was up.

The meeting was called to order and we whipped

through routine business a bit faster than usual, I thought. Justin seemed eager to get to his "news." Finally he rose to his feet—a rare occurrence at one of these events, signaling a matter of great weight was at hand. He cleared his throat, adjusted his stance, and before he began, glanced conspiratorially at Edmond. The atmosphere crackled with expectation.

"Ladies and gentlemen, I have a very important and exciting announcement to make. It is my great honor, privilege, and pleasure to inform you that Mrs. Russell Cole has graciously donated the Cole collection to our museum."

Little gasps of astonishment rippled through the boardroom, followed by nods and murmurs of approval, then a round of solid applause. Justin and Edmond looked at each other and preened. For years, every museum of note in the country had courted the Cole collection. This was a major coup for the Muni, and a major blow for me—mainly because I sensed all too well what was coming next.

Justin continued: "As all of you here know, the Cole collection is perhaps the finest of its kind in private hands. Over the years, many museums have coveted it, and it gives me great pleasure to be able to tell you that our beloved Municipal Museum will be the beneficiary."

There were more mutterings of approval. Amid the palpable excitement, I tentatively raised my hand.

"Yes, Jo," Justin said, beaming down at me.

"This may be a rather stupid question," I began. "But as I understand it, Russell Cole is still presumed to be missing, not dead. Is it conceivable, Justin, that if he were to turn up one day, he might possibly contest this gift?"

"That's certainly not a stupid question, Jo. Edmond

and I had exactly the same concern," Justin gallantly replied in his patrician voice. "The fact is that Mrs. Cole has told me that Russell had already made up his mind to give us the collection shortly before his tragic disappearance. Still, we're very cautious, as you know, and we've gone over this thing thoroughly with Bart Jehovie. Bart, here, has assured us we're covered on all fronts, no matter what happens, haven't you, Bart?"

Bart Jehovie, the dark-haired, long-faced, brilliant lead counsel for the museum, who Ethan said looked like an El Greco, was seated on Justin's left. He looked up and gave his chairman a solemn nod. Everything the Municipal Museum did or ever got involved in was always vetted by Bart Jehovie and his able team of lawyers. Normally, at this point in the meeting, Bart would have been asked to get up and explain the particulars of such a bequest. However, it was clear that Justin was so excited by this triumph, he wanted to keep the floor all to himself for the time being.

Justin went on, "Mrs. Cole will finance the new wing that will house the collection." Again, he paused for effect. "She is donating one hundred million dollars to the museum for that purpose."

One hundred million dollars.

More gasps as that figure hung in the air like a blazing chandelier for all to admire.

I felt sick.

Suddenly, Seymour Heffernan, the slick billionaire businessman who was chairman of the finance committee, piped up. I had never much cared for Seymour or for his pushy, third trophy wife, Tiffany. I suspected they had no real interest in the Muni except as a social catapult. His too-polished hair, fingernails, shoes, and manners only heightened by contrast a kind of innate crudeness. Heffernan measured everything by money—arguably a valuable trait for a finance committee chairman, but one that didn't particularly appeal to me. He claimed to be knowledgeable about "paintings and art," as he always said, but Ethan took him to lunch once and told me that Heffernan could stuff what he knew about art through the boutonniere of one of his too-loud English suits. Betty, who knew him as an erstwhile client of Gil's, told me, "Gil simply refuses to deal with him anymore mainly because he loathes his taste in art. Victorian paintings of horny cardinals are not exactly Gil's thing. You should see their apartment. It looks like a bordello."

Today, however, good old Seymour Heffernan asked the billion-dollar question.

"Justin, if I may be so bold," he began in that fake, solicitous, diamond-in-the-rough voice of his. "We only have her word for it, right? What happens if the guy turns up one day and says he never said anything like that?"

I could have kissed him, his spoiled wife, *and* his horny cardinal paintings.

Justin was cool under fire.

"I'll let Bart elaborate on all this a little later on. But let me just give you the headline, Seymour. The one hundred million dollars that Mrs. Cole is giving us for the wing comes directly from her own private funds. The Cole collection, some of which they acquired together, is in a separate trust, over which Mrs. Cole has discretion. Bart, that's about right, isn't it?"

Justin glanced at Bart Jehovie, who was shaking his head in mild amusement. "It's slightly more complicated than that, Justin. But you're doing fine. Go on."

Murmurs of approval.

"Thanks, Bart," Justin said with a smile. "To make a long story short then, if Russell Cole does indeed come back home safely—and God knows we all hope and pray that he will—and for some reason, he doesn't agree with his wife's decision and he wants his collection returned, we will return it."

Murmurs of disapproval.

Justin held up his hand. "No, no, hear me out, please! In the hundred and forty-seven years of its existence, the Municipal Museum has never had a scandal. And we're not going to have one under my watch. It's my understanding that if such an unfortunate event were to occur—and I don't mean Russell's return, of course! That would be wonderful—I mean if he wants his collection back," he quickly added, "then we would simply give it back to him. Particularly because all of this has cost us absolutely no money. The worst that could happen? We have a beautiful new *empty* wing, which we can easily fill with treasures from our storerooms or with another collection, for that matter."

Murmurs of approval.

Justin went on: "Mrs. Cole has made only one stipulation and one request . . ."

I braced myself.

"The stipulation is that she be involved in choosing the architect who will design the wing and in the final design of the wing itself. She's not insisting on final approval, but she does want to be involved . . ."

Murmurs of approval.

Then came the bombshell.

"The request is that she very much wants to join the board of the museum."

Murmurs of disapproval.

Justin put his hand up to quell the apparent discontent. Each and every person there at least imagined they had paid their dues to the museum and no one likes an upstart, no matter how much money she is prepared to give.

The group was like some sort of Miss Manners mob— politely swaying this way and that with each new snippet of information. They were against Justin now, but at least he had their attention. Justin swept his hand through his salt-and-pepper hair and threw his head back, preparing to use his eloquence to convert everyone to his point of view. I knew he couldn't risk losing such a coveted collection.

"Granted, this request is a little unorthodox. But ladies and gentlemen, the gift is magnificent! The generosity is *unparalleled*—particularly in this day and age when, as all of you here know only too well, both private and corporate giving to institutions—even great ones like ours—is at an all-time low."

There was a lull signaling that the sympathies of the mob could go either way.

"The Cole collection is a chance for us to enrich this great museum even more in an area where we could, quite frankly, use some improvement," Justin went on. "And I think Mrs. Cole's request to join our board is certainly not unreasonable under the circumstances—to say the least. But, as we all know, under our own peculiar rules of governance here at the Muni, we need unanimous approval. One no vote and . . ." He raised his eyebrows and gave a little shrug. He didn't have to finish the sentence.

By charter, the Municipal Museum operated under an antiquated election process, much like the old clubs in New York and London, where the term "blackball" originated. One no vote and the candidate was vetoed. It was generally accepted, however, that if someone was good enough to be proposed—particularly by the chairman or the director—he or she would automatically be elected. In fact, in the twenty-odd years I'd served on the board of the Muni, only one proposed candidate ever failed to be elected, and that was because on the eve of the vote he was indicted for fraud.

Justin went on, "I've taken the liberty of telling Mrs. Cole that she will be proposed as a board member at our next meeting—in a month's time. That will give you all ample opportunity to think about this. It's an important decision, so I know you'll think seriously. Also, please bear in mind that if we don't approve her, we will possibly— probably—lose the collection."

"She's a shoo-in," Ethan whispered to me.

Bang!

The shot through my heart.

Carla Cole was going to sit on the board of my beloved Municipal Museum.

Next thing I knew she would probably want to be on the acquisitions committee. And then chairman of the acquisitions committee—my job. And then, knowing her, chairman of the museum. The top was not high enough for this gal's ambition. She was climbing that "ladder with limitless rungs," as Larry called it, with a vengeance.

I couldn't protest, even though I was dying to. There were too many big mouths in that room and I knew that if word ever got out that I'd said anything against her, it might be quite unpleasant for me. I just gritted my teeth and smiled politely, hoping someone else would point out what a controversial and divisive figure she was—definitely not the sort of person the Municipal Museum wanted on its board. I decided to bide my time. I had a month to lobby against her behind the scenes.

The meeting concluded and we all got up. Ethan and I walked out of the boardroom together. He knew me well enough to know that I was upset.

"What's wrong, Jo?" he asked.

"Well, quite frankly, I'd always thought of the Muni as one of the last places you couldn't buy your way into."

"Oh, come on, Jo. You know that's not true. Money's the only thing that really talks in this town."

"I understand. And I wish it would shut up for once."

That evening, I came home to find a calligraphed invitation with a blue velvet ribbon threaded through the top. It looked like a royal proclamation. It read,

Carla Cole

requests the pleasure of the company of

Mrs. Jo Slater

at a small dinner dance

on Saturday, May the twelfth

at eight-thirty p.m. o'clock

831 Fifth Avenue

I saw this as the beginning of a long reign of a rival queen in whose court I might very well become a prisoner. A little handwritten note at the bottom of my invitation read, "I know you will be with me on this glorious night, dear Jo." I took it not as an invitation, but as a command.

For the next couple of weeks, I did some not-so-subtle lobbying of my own. I took every single Muni board member out to lunch at Le Poisson, or the Fish Tank, as it was affectionately called by regulars, the last of the truly luxurious French restaurants in New York. The old-world atmosphere of the place, with its soft, flattering lighting, towering flower arrangements, delicious food, discreet service, and shiny, well-heeled patrons, offered a convivially formal setting for those who like that sort of thing and who can afford it. I felt it was the perfect venue to bring up the subject of Carla Cole.

Though I never came right out and said I was against her being on the board, anyone reading between the glasses of fine white wine knew that I was not exactly in her corner. My position was not so much against her, but more of a "let's wait and see" attitude. I knew, of course, that once a person has been blackballed from the board, that's it. No second chances. Conversely, once someone was elected to the board, it was difficult to get them off until their term expired. And even then, it was tricky, particularly if the person in question had great financial means.

Even though all Municipal Museum business was highly confidential and board members took that very seriously, this was, after all, New York. I was a little worried Carla might get wind of my subtle sabotage, so I was always careful to preface all my conversations with the assurance that she was a friend of mine and that I was thinking more in terms of the reputation of the Muni.

"No one—especially Carla—would want to give the impression that a seat on our board can be sold to the highest bidder," I said, knowing full well that was how more than one of my luncheon companions had secured their positions, though they would never admit it. I appealed to their snobbery, however, by making a seat on the board of the Muni seem like one of the grandest status symbols that there was in New York, an honor conferred only after years of service and scrutiny. When anyone brought up the subject of the Cole collection and Carla's proposed grant, I merely suggested that it would behoove us to hold off and wait and see if Russell returned.

Twenty-Five

CARLA'S PARTY WAS THE VERY NIGHT BEFORE
the Muni board meeting. Long after the fact, I
realized to my chagrin that this was not luck,
fate, or a coincidence. It was well planned.

Our little set was all atwitter with excitement. Word
had drifted down from various sources that Carla's apartment was the single most spectacular abode in New York,
if not the western hemisphere—a not-to-be-missed,
once-in-a-lifetime, must-see extravaganza. No one I
knew had actually seen it, except Dieter Lucino, the decorator, of course, and his army of assistants who, like
members of Marco Polo's caravan, brought back tales of
its wealth and luxury beyond measure.

"I can't wait to see this fucking apartment," Betty said
to me on the phone that morning when we were confer-
ring on what to wear. "I hear it makes Versailles look like
a Holiday Inn."

I, of course, was dreading the whole event. I hated
going to a party whose hostess I didn't much like or trust.

Like Larry, I had the nagging suspicion that Carla was far, far more calculating than anyone could imagine. But I couldn't prove it. Carla Cole was a fact of social life now. I knew I'd have to deal with her unless I stopped going out or else moved away from New York altogether—neither of which I intended to do.

That afternoon I went to the hairdresser, a wonderfully old-fashioned salon called Mr. K's, located in the Waldorf-Astoria. Mr. K himself was a grand old gentleman who had been in business since the days when hats, neat hair, and good manners were the rule and not the exception they are now. In his heyday, he had famously styled the coiffures of queens, socialites, and first ladies. Now, at the age of eighty-one, he still went to work every day to cater to his loyal clientele. I'd been going to him steadily for years, except for that unfortunate interlude of five years when I could barely afford a cut-rate barbershop, let alone an elegant beauty salon. I always ran into at least one or two people I knew at Mr. K's. Like Pug's, it had a precious atmosphere of comfort and security, and a certain antiquated style.

I was just about to sit down and begin my color treatment when I heard a voice at the far end of the room cry out, "Jo!"

I looked around and spotted a woman seated in the corner waving at me. It took me a few seconds to recognize Ellen Grimes, Hadley Grimes's wife. Her hair, standing on end, wrapped in gridlike rows of neatly folded tinfoil, made her look like a hi-tech bride of Frankenstein. I walked over to chat with her for a moment. Ellen Grimes was a chunky, square-jawed woman whose leathery, lightly tanned skin—the product of outdoor sports and sunshine—would have made a rather at-

tractive Birkin bag. She spoke in a kind of boarding
school lockjaw, called her mother "Mummy," her father
"Dads," her husband "Grimesy," and her children "the
brood." We hadn't seen each other in ages—with good
reason.

"I've decided to go platinum blonde," she announced
to me. "Grimesy won't approve, I'm sure, but I need a
change. It was either that or another face-lift. I take it
you're going to Carla Cole's tonight, aren't you? Of
course you are. The whole building is in an absolute uproar with all the catering trucks parked outside and the
people coming and going. It's going to be amazing. Isn't
it something about Russell Cole? Is there any more news?
Hadley just adores Carla. Don't you? And how's poor
June? Thank God she's in Southampton! Think if she
were here and not invited! Is she okay, by the way? I
mean surviving? What are you wearing? Something long,
right? I had to go get Mummy's jewels out of the safe de-
posit box this morning. Vault occasion. Jewelry's so
ridiculously expensive to insure these days, isn't it? I
wouldn't *dream* of keeping it in the house, would you?"

Ellen hadn't changed. She cruised along at her own al-
titude, her speech a flowing stream of consciousness, asking questions she either provided the answers for herself
or never expected to have answered. But Ellen was a gossip and, as my mother used to say, "Even a blind chicken
sometimes finds a kernel of corn." When asked the right
questions, Ellen could spew out interesting information
faster than Old Faithful.

That afternoon I learned from Ellen that Carla Cole
had spent over a hundred million dollars decorating her
apartment, that she maintained an army of servants who
lived in the bowels of the building, that she was an ex-

tremely stingy tipper, which is why all the doormen and elevator men and building staff loathed her, and that her limousine blocked the entrance of the building so often that the other tenants had lodged a complaint with the board.

"It's amazing how she's gotten the apartment ready so quickly," I said, just to make conversation.

As is often the case in life, this offhand remark elicited a riveting response.

"Well, she did order everything last year, so it was all set to go," Ellen said.

Pause.

I looked at Ellen who caught my eye and quickly looked away as if she'd said something she shouldn't have.

"Wait a minute," I said. "*Last year?* She only bought that apartment five months ago."

Ellen clapped her hand to her mouth. "Me and my big mouth."

"*Ellen?* What's going on?"

"Nothing. I got confused."

"No, you didn't. What do you mean, she ordered everything *last year*?"

Ellen stared at me with scolded puppy eyes. "Oh, Jo, Grimesy will murder—*meurdah*—me if I spill the beans!" She pronounced "murder" the way her husband did in haute mid-Atlantic.

"The beans are spilled, Ellen. Let's get cooking." Behind her contrite façade, I knew she was dying to tell me.

"Well," she said at last, breathing a deep sigh and lowering her voice to a confidential tone, "Marcy agreed to sell Carla that apartment almost a year ago. Last spring, in fact. According to Marcy, Carla went over there for tea and absolutely fell head over heels in love with it. And why not? I mean, it *is* the grandest apartment in New York, after all, run-down as it was. So anyway, Carla said to Marcy she absolutely *had* to have it. Marcy said she was ready to plunk down the money right then and there, but that there was a slight problem."

"What?"

Ellen paused. "Russell."

"What do you mean?"

"Jo—if you breathe a *word* of this—"

"I *won't*. Go *on*." I was on tenterhooks.

"Well, apparently, Russell wasn't keen on moving to New York. . . . No, let me put it another way. Russell was *dead set* against moving here. Carla told Marcy she was sure he'd change his mind if he saw the apartment. So they both came and had tea with Marcy. Marcy said that Russell was too polite to say anything, but that she could tell he absolutely *loathed* the place! He kept saying, 'Isn't it a little big?' as they walked through all the rooms. You know Russell. He's so low key—even that boat isn't as big as it could have been with all his moolah. Well, anyway, Marcy was upset he didn't like it because, of course, at that point she was *dying* to unload the thing and how many buyers are there at that price? Let's be honest. She thought it was over when they left. But then she got a call from Carla."

"When?"

"Oh, right after they went to look at it. Carla called her the next day and said that she was going to go ahead and buy the apartment and have it all done up the way she knew Russell would like it. She told Marcy that if Russell could just walk in and 'put his toothbrush in the cup'— that was her expression, don'tchya love it?—he would adore it. Marcy was a little stunned because she was sure Russell had really hated it. Anyway, it didn't seem to matter because Carla went in there a week later and took measurements and had her architect order doors and windows and cabinets and furniture and everything."

"*Before* she bought it?"

"Oh, yeah, *way* before. Well, anyway, later Russell disappeared and Carla went ahead and bought the apartment. But then she ran into this snag with poor June and almost didn't get into the building. . . . Jo," Ellen said, leaning in confidentially. "Can you imagine if Carla *hadn't* gotten in? After ordering—well—*millions* of dollars' worth of stuff made specially for that particular apartment? The mind boggles!"

I couldn't quite believe what I was hearing. I needed to make absolutely sure of what Ellen was telling me.

"Okay, let me get this straight. Carla had a deal with Marcy Ludinghausen to buy that apartment months ago? *Before* Russell disappeared?"

Ellen nodded. "Yup. So Marcy says."

"And she ordered furniture and everything?"

"Curtains, furniture, fittings, carpets, this incredible floor . . . but you *can't* say anything, Jo! *Promise?*"

"Why can't I?"

"Because Marcy told me in *strictest* confidence . . . although I suppose it really doesn't matter now that Carla's got the apartment," she said with a shrug. "But I mean, who could afford to pay that ridiculous asking price except the Coles? Oh, maybe some drug dealer or a rock star or someone like that. But no one who could actually get *into* the building. So Marcy held out and refused to lower her price—even though all the real estate agents told her to. She knew Carla would come through in the end. I mean, she kind of had to. She'd already spent millions. But I guess when you're that rich you can afford to order things for places you don't own yet."

"Ellen, let me ask you something. What if June *had* blackballed her?"

Ellen thought for a moment. "Well, that would have been *awful*. She would have had to scrap everything or else buy some other place and have everything refitted. Actually, it would have been a complete *disaster*. Hey, wouldn't it be marvelous to have that kind of money— where you could just throw away millions of dollars without thinking twice? Of course, it's terribly sinful and such a waste," she added piously. "But still, it would be nice. Anyway," Ellen went on in a chipper voice, "it all worked out in the end."

Yes, I thought to myself, in the end of Russell Cole.

Twenty-six

THAT EVENING, LARRY LOCKET ARRIVED AT
my apartment, looking spiffy in his tuxedo. It
was a balmy May night and we decided to
walk the few blocks to Carla's apartment building.

"Let's get as much air as we can before we're stifled
by wealth," Larry said as we strolled arm in arm down
Fifth Avenue.

"Larry, dear, I found out something very interesting at
the hairdresser's today," I said as we walked.

"I'm listening."

"Did you know that Carla had a deal with Marcy Ludinghausen to buy her apartment almost a *year* ago?"

Larry stopped dead, turned to me, and raised his eyebrows. "No. What do you mean?"

"According to my source, Carla took Russell to see
the apartment a year ago and he hated it. Carla thought
that if she went ahead and bought it anyway and fixed it
up the way he liked, she could get him to change his
mind. So she ordered millions of dollars' worth of fix-

tures and fittings and furniture for the place long *before* it was hers."

Larry narrowed his eyes. "She ordered things for an apartment she didn't own yet?"

"Exactly. Millions of dollars' worth of things. Apparently, Russell didn't want to move to New York. But then he disappeared, so she went ahead and bought the apartment without him. Of course, June was going to prevent her from getting into the building. But then June had an accident."

Larry was fascinated. We continued walking. "Who told you this?"

"I swore, Larry—"

"Jo, please. The source here is important. I promise I won't betray you."

"Okay," I said reluctantly. I trusted Larry. "It was Ellen Grimes, who's married to Hadley Grimes, the head of the board."

"And how does Ellen know this?"

"She got it from the horse's mouth. She's Marcy Ludinghausen's best friend."

"That's a primo source," Larry nodded. "You think she'd talk to me for my article?"

"Oh, no, Larry, *please!* Ellen *swore* me to secrecy."

"Don't worry. But there must be another way to verify this information. I mean, Jo, this is another one of those what I call 'rich people motives.' She wants a big apartment. He doesn't. So she kills him, gets a hold of all his money, and buys it herself."

We both laughed grimly.

Our decision not to take the car was a prescient one. The dozens of shiny, black limousines encroaching upon the entrance of 831 Fifth Avenue resembled an infestation of beetles. Each car inched slowly up to the scrolly, wrought-iron doors of the building, egested its human cargo, then crawled off into the twilight. The entrance hall of 831 was a fairly unprepossessing space, given the fact that above its checkered marble floor were grand apartments as big as houses, many of them filled with museum-quality treasures. I noticed three men in dark suits lurking in a corner, eyeing the guests as they entered.

"Security," Larry whispered.

"Whose?"

"Probably some dignitary or muckety-muck."

A wave of nostagia hit me as I entered the lobby. How many times had I been in that building to visit my late friend Clara Wilman and my dear June? I wondered if I could bring myself to shake hands with Carla Cole tonight, harboring this awful feeling that she'd had a hand in June's accident and so much more treachery. But being charming—even to people you suspected of terrible misdeeds—was all just "social life," as June herself always said.

Larry and I stepped into the elevator with a crowd of *amis mondains* whom we both knew. At first everyone greeted everyone in a fluttery, repetitive way—what Betty called the "Hello Darling Syndrome"—triggered when people are trying to suppress a palpable air of excitement before a big event. The journey to the penthouse, however, was made in relative silence. No one uttered a word as the wood-paneled car whooshed upward. A couple of the men cleared their throats and the women surreptitiously appraised one another's gowns, jewels, hair, and makeup. Someone was wearing too much perfume.

As we approached the top floor, we heard the strains of a string quartet playing classical music. Finally the elevator stopped. Its mahogany door slid open, and one by one we all stepped out of the boxy car into another century. Two footmen in blue velvet livery stood at attention on either side of an arched entranceway leading into a vast reception hall, the floor of which was real lapis lazuli. The deep blue stone was like a little sea, glittering with golden grains of pyrite. There were no electric lights. Dozens of candles burned brightly in the huge, silver Regency chandelier and in antique silver wall sconces sculpted in the shape of shells. The veneer of brilliance created by the candlelight was unlike anything achieved by electricity.

At the far end of the hall, spread across the wall like a mural commissioned just for that space, was the enormous Tiepolo painting Carla had bought from Gil Waterman. In this setting, the mythical ocean scene depicting a golden-bearded Poseidon, holding a golden trident, leering at a bevy of nymphs frolicking away in the foam-tipped waves, seemed even more magnificent. A few sea monsters slithered through its painterly water. They reminded me of a couple of the guests. The blue of the ocean deepened gradually toward the bottom so that the lapis lazuli floor appeared to be a continuation of the painting.

In front of this spectacular backdrop stood Carla Cole, in a draped, white crepe gown with a diamond moon crescent perched atop her sleek chignon coiffure. She looked like a sea goddess arising from the crest of a wave. Her diamond earrings, practically the size of sand dollars, were like two spotlights on either side of her face. I watched her as she shook the hand of each guest, inclining her head slightly, affecting a regal air of noblesse oblige. Sometimes when she extended her hand to greet a guest, the line of sight that encompassed both her and the painting made it appear as though it were she, not Poseidon, who held the trident. Beside her stood Max Vermilion, looking very fit and elegant in one of his vintage tuxedos. A grieving spouse she definitely was not.

I got a little frisson when I saw Max. Even though he and I were definitely not meant for each other, I didn't particularly like it that he was squiring Carla around. Max was a powerful friend and the two of them made a formidable couple. That didn't bode well for keeping her off the board of the Muni, and the board meeting the next day was very much on my mind that night.

I whispered to Larry, "Just asking . . . do we think having Max here as the queen's consort is in the best of taste, given the fact that her husband is still missing?"

"Well, she's either positive he's coming back, or positive he isn't," Larry said. "My money's on the latter."

Betty, who looked like a big carrot in an orange silk gown with green ruffles around the neck, stopped by on her way to the powder room and whispered, "Hey, Jo, you think Russell's buried under this lapis lazuli ocean?" She laughed. "And check out Carla's waist carefully when you shake hands." She raised her eyebrows knowingly and moved on.

As Larry and I were waiting in the reception line, I felt a tap on my shoulder. I turned around and saw Trish Bromire, who had apparently decided to tone down her look since Dick's conviction. Eschewing her usual loud colors and garish jewels, she looked the best I'd ever seen her, wearing a severe gray velvet dress and a striking antique garnet necklace and matching earrings. Garnets, not rubies. She kissed Larry hello, then kissed me and whispered, "Jo, you don't think Carla invited us here just to snub us in public, do you?"

"No, sweetie. Everyone understands these things happen."

"You mean people getting convicted of federal crimes?" Trish said ingenuously.

I decided not to elaborate on my remark. "Where is Dick? I want to give him a hug."

"Oh, he'll be here. He's with the lawyers. They're deciding whether or not to appeal. I came on ahead. I didn't think it was proper to be late, particularly under the circumstances. We have to be so careful now. Of course, if I'd known it was going to be such a zoo, I'd have waited for him," Trish said, waving to three different people as she spoke. "Most people have said hello to me. Isn't that nice? I guess it means they still like us."

"We love you, sweetie," I said, giving her a hug.

"Of course we do," Larry concurred.

Dick arrived shortly thereafter and joined Trish behind us in the receiving line. Larry shook his hand ostentatiously and I gave him a big kiss. But he seemed wary—even of me. In my view, it was very clever of Carla to have invited the Bromires because, despite Dick's recent travails, they still had a lot of friends in New York.

When Larry and I reached Carla, she seemed particularly happy to see us both. Her face brightened noticeably as she greeted the two of us.

"Ah, my dear Jo, and the brilliant Mr. Locket, how divine of you both to come! I hope you will enjoy all the surprises I have in store for you tonight."

Why was it that everything Carla said sounded like a threat to me?

I checked out Carla's waist, as Betty had told me to. There, partially hidden underneath the Grecian folds of the dress, were not one, not two, but *five* diamond insect pins on a white satin belt.

Max!

I got one insect pin merely for being his friend. But *five* definitely indicated a deeper relationship.

Larry and I smiled politely and quickly moved on to Max, who also gave us both a warm welcome. Just then Betty waltzed up to us, pointed at the great ocean painting, and said, "Do we think that choice of artwork is, shall we say, *appropriate*, when half the world thinks your husband is fish food?"

Gil, who was just behind her, disparaged her comment. "Betty, that is a *great* painting and you, my good wife, are enjoying the proceeds of its sale."

"I don't care. The theme is macabre," she said imperiously. "Couldn't she have picked a forest instead of an ocean? C'mon, kids, let's go snoop around the rest of the palace." She waved us all to follow.

Trish, Dick, Betty, Gil, Larry, and I all trooped through the apartment, which I had seen in two previous incarnations. When Clara had it, it was an ode to understated elegance. Clara Wilman believed that a kind of grand coziness was the ultimate luxury. She had decorated the apartment as if it were a great English country house, filling it with carved William Kent furniture, large, comfortable couches, and beautiful paintings of landscapes, horses, and dogs. Wandering around the apartment, one's eye was constantly amused by oases of beauty: the hand-painted trompe l'oeil scenes in the smaller sitting rooms, and precious collections like the tiny, jeweled flowers in real jade or crystal flowerpots or the menagerie of silver animals made by Fabergé for the Grand Duchess Tatiana.

Marcy Ludinghausen's taste ran screaming in the opposite direction. Marcy, once married to an avant-garde artist, was still in her downtown period when she bought the apartment. She and Baron Ludinghausen, an ersatz art dealer among other things, both favored Andy Warhol paintings, neon sculptures, and beanbag chairs. The place looked like a sixties Soho art gallery and was just about as comfortable, as I remember from the one time I went there.

And now it was a whole other incarnation, one that Betty described as "Late Catherine the Great." The furniture was all ormolu'd and gilded within an inch of its life. Each room had a plethora of magnificent pieces. Huge tassels dangled from sofa arms, chair seats, and cabinet keys. The silk-brocaded walls were crammed with paintings in ornately carved gilt frames. I recognized some pictures from the Cole collection, but not many, and the ones that were there seemed oddly compromised by the magnificent seventeenth and eighteenth-century furniture surrounding them. The apartment was a very grand, very expensive mishmash of styles. It lacked what Clara Wilman had called "a presiding eye." It was just rich-rich-rich.

Fingering a giant tassel, Betty wondered aloud, "Is there a period called rococo-a-gogogo?"

"There is now," Larry said.

Dinner was served in a miniature re-creation of the Hall of Mirrors. Carla had transformed her dining room into that legendary space in the palace of Versailles, complete with towering torchieres, smoky mirrors, and footmen in livery. The pampered people in our little set are very competitive, and that night Carla Cole raised the bar a good ten notches. For those who prided themselves in large measure on their dwellings, their possessions, and their party-giving, the entire evening was a form of exquisite torture. It was as if at every step of the way, Carla was saying, "Top that!"

Betty walked into the dining room and said, "Mirror, mirror, on the wall, who's the richest of them all?"

Larry, who was seated next to me, and who noticed the footmen eyeing one another across the table, said, "What do you bet they're all out-of-work actors? And what must they be thinking?"

"What must *any* of us be thinking?" I said as a bowing waiter presented me with a silver bowl in which a huge tin of fresh Beluga was encased in shaved ice. He handed me a large gold spoon. I dug in.

During the appetizer, the conversation was muted by awe—an unusual occurrence in a group where profligate spending is not exactly unknown. Gradually, however, the great wines and the delicious food loosened everybody up so that by the time the waiters in white gloves had served the main course, we were all chattering away like yardbirds—beginning to focus on the cracks in the façade. The bitchy comments started. No matter how perfect things are, it is the special talent of New Yorkers to be able to find fault with them. A "perfect" evening to us is an evening we can criticize.

At several points during the meal, I found myself looking down the table, thinking that if Carla were trying to buy her way into New York society, she had certainly succeeded that night.

Justin Howard was seated on my left. We briefly discussed the Muni board meeting the next day.

"Jo, a little bird tells me you've been lobbying against Carla going on the board. Is that true?"

"I don't think she deserves a place on the board just yet. In time, though."

"This is a woman who doesn't like to wait, Jo."

"So I see," I said, glancing around. "But who's she going to give that collection to, Justin? Los Angeles? Washington? Boston? Look for yourself. She obviously wants it in New York."

Over the years, I had learned a lot about the pathology of privilege, having been both its beneficiary and its victim at different times in my life. Extravagance on a nuclear level—as this was—always represented something else. What we were watching was usually not what was really going on, but rather an elaborate smoke screen to cover up some deep deception. Just what that deception could be was unclear to me now, but I had no doubt it would come to light eventually. Then Justin would thank me for my caution.

After dinner, coffee was served in the enormous living room. Holding a delicate red-and-gold demitasse in hand, Carla approached me and artfully steered me off to one side of the room, away from the crowd.

"Jo, I understand the Municipal Museum board meeting is tomorrow," Carla said. She looked at me soulfully. "*Are* you going to support me, *cara*? I have heard rumors that you are a bit—how shall I say it?—hesitant."

I've never been one to beat around the bush. I consider myself a pretty straight shooter. There was no point in lying to her, particularly as she would find out the truth soon enough.

"Carla, I'm not against you coming on the board. I just

think it looks better for the museum, and for you, quite frankly, if we wait a bit, that's all."

"But why, Jo? Why should I wait? I am giving one of the great collections in the world to the museum and building a wing to house it. I think I deserve a place on the board, don't you?"

"There are people on the board who have donated a lot of money and great collections to the museum who didn't get on the board right away, Carla. In fact, the Muni prides itself on being an institution where you have to pay your dues. You can't just buy your way in. I didn't get on the board until two years after Lucius and I donated the Slater Gallery."

She looked at me with glittering eyes and said sweetly, "You are not jealous of me, are you, Jo?"

It was a fair question, deserving of a thoughtful answer.

"Oh, perhaps people will think that," I said. "But the simple truth is, I just don't trust you, Carla. I don't trust you as far as I can throw you."

She put her hand to her chest and stepped back, feigning hurt. "Jo! I am wounded!

"I'm sorry. It's the truth."

She was silent for a long moment. "Jo, dear, is there *nothing* I can do to make you change your mind?"

"Well, as a matter of fact, there is something, yes."

"Please, *tell* me what it is! I will do anything!"

"Bide your time a bit. Don't be so anxious. I'm not saying you shouldn't get on the board one day, Carla. You should. But wait a while. Learn about the museum. Understand what it is you hope to accomplish there. Make it about the institution itself, not about the social advantages it affords you."

She looked at me quizzically. "But what makes you think I am not interested in the museum?"

"Do you know much about the Muni?"

"I know it is one of the greatest museums in the world. Isn't that all I have to know?"

"No. You have to know what makes it great. And it's not just the art. The Muni is a living, breathing institution. It has pioneer conservation programs, community outreach programs, international exchange programs, teaching facilities. We're like a great university. People come from all over the world to study with us and contribute to our community."

"Yes, I know all that is marvelous," she said impatiently. "But most people come to see the paintings, no? And the Cole collection will be a great attraction."

"Indeed it will."

"I do not believe in waiting," she said. "I can do a lot of good for the Muni right now. I have the money to do all sorts of wonderful things for it. And I think I should be given the chance."

There was no use arguing with her.

"Carla, if you must know the truth, I'm going to abstain in tomorrow's vote. I won't be the one to veto you."

She stared at me for a long moment.

"How lovely you look tonight," she said, pointing to my sapphire earrings. "I find sapphires a rather cold stone. But they suit you very well, Jo. They are good for your coloring. I prefer diamonds."

"So I see," I said, noting her enormous diamond earrings.

"I know of some wonderful diamond dealers," she went on. "It is such a funny world—the world of diamond dealers. Very small. Like your little world here in

New York. Everyone knows each other. . . . They say that diamonds are the best investment. Have you ever bought diamonds for investment purposes, Jo?"

"Yes, as a matter of fact, I have. I do. I have quite a good dealer myself."

"Really? I would love to meet him."

"I'm sure that can be arranged," I said, holding her gaze without flinching.

I refused to be intimidated by this woman, even though she was making it quite clear that she knew about Oliva and the blackmail payments I sent her.

"Well, I must attend to my guests," she said. "Please think about what we have discussed."

"I've thought about it, Carla, believe me."

"Have you? Have you *really*?" she said, glaring at me with a disconcerting smile on her face. There was a hint of true madness in her expression.

Then she walked away.

This was as clear a threat as I'd ever had in my life. I was unnerved. I paused to think for a moment and calm down. It was obvious that Carla either knew or knew *about* Oliva and the fact that she was blackmailing me. But how? From where? The real question was: What exactly did Carla know about the crime itself? Somehow I doubted she knew the details. From the little I knew of my blackmailer, I couldn't believe she'd be dumb enough to tell anyone what she had on me. Why would this canny, sexy sociopath give away the nature of the valuable information she possessed? It simply wasn't in her interest to dilute such a lucrative secret by revealing it to anyone else. So while I could picture Oliva telling someone she had a strong hold over me, I just couldn't picture her telling anyone exactly what that hold was. And besides, I figured that if Carla really knew what I'd done, now would have been the time to use that information. It would have been great leverage against me in getting what she wanted. And she desperately wanted to go on the board of the Muni.

But, again, all this was speculation on my part. I couldn't know anything for sure. It was this uncanny ability of Carla's to keep me off balance that I hated most. I couldn't get a handle on what she was up to. By hinting at things rather than declaring them outright, she created a climate of fear and ambiguity. She seemed to understand innately that the big, black spider of uncertainty was the one thing in the world I couldn't bear.

Larry and I and the Watermans joined the procession of guests slowly making their way downstairs. Carla had demolished a rabbit warren of maids' rooms to create one huge ballroom, complete with an orchestra platform and marble columns, and elevated tiers set with small, round tables and shaded candlelights, just like an old-fashioned nightclub.

"How she got all this done in four months is beyond me," Betty said. "It takes me four months to get a sink fixed in this town."

"I bet the floor opens up to be a swimming pool," Larry said.

A band was playing a smooth medley of Cole Porter tunes. Some guests immediately glided out onto the highly polished marble dance floor and started fox-trotting. Others sat down at the tables and ordered champagne cocktails from waiters dressed in white pants and blue jackets with gold buttons and braid.

"Welcome to hookerina heaven!" Betty cried. "If Russell *is* alive and he comes back and sees this, he's going to *die!* Death by vulgarity! A new weapon."

"Not that new," Larry said dryly.

Betty turned to me. "You're very quiet, Jo. What do you think?"

"You know, Betts, I prefer not to think tonight. It's not the setting for it."

I noticed Carla hurrying toward the bandleader. Still conducting, he leaned down and she whispered something in his ear. He immediately stopped the music. People quit dancing and the room fell silent.

"Ladies and gentlemen, may I have your attention, please?" the bandleader said, speaking into the microphone. "Mrs. Cole wants me to announce that she's lost an earring."

There were murmurs throughout the room. No one had failed to notice those klieg light diamonds.

"If everyone would please take a moment to look around," the bandleader went on, "Mrs. Cole would be very grateful!"

"I wonder how it feels to have four million dollars drop off your ear," Betty whispered.

Everyone took a cursory look around the floor. Then the music struck up again and people gradually resumed dancing. Carla strolled back our way. She seemed cool enough.

"God, Carla, you must be frantic," Betty said. "I hope you're insured."

"No, no, darling. I do not insure my jewelry. Why bother? You can't ever replace it exactly. And it's just a material thing, after all. I do not get upset over material possessions . . . not since Russell," she said with a meaningful expression.

"This is why I have pierced ears," Betty said.

"I am certain it will turn up. And if not . . . ?" Carla said, dismissively waving her diamond-braceleted hand, "*C'est la vie, n'est-ce pas?*"

I was surprised when Max walked over to the table and asked me to dance. Betty winked at me as Max took my hand and led me out onto the dance floor. He held me rigidly in his arms and we began a bouncy fox-trot around the room. Max was a good dancer, if a tad too energetic for my taste. He was what Betty called a "pumper"—that is, a man who pumps your arm as he dances with you like it was the spigot of a well from which he is trying to extract the last drop of water.

"So m'dear, how are you?" he asked. *Pump, pump, pump.*

"Fine, Max. And yourself?"

"Oh, limping along, you know. . . . Sunset years, a bore, *what?*" With that, he did a particularly energetic twirl.

"Feels like you're still at high noon," I said, struggling to maintain my balance.

Max laughed and we slowed down a bit. "Jo, may I speak frankly to you?"

"Since when have you not?"

"Point taken. I believe you're aware that our hostess has her heart set on going on the board of the Municipal Museum. A little bird tells me you don't want her on."

"Just one little bird? I'd have thought the whole flock would have chirped in your ear by now."

"Why don't you want her on that board, m'dear?"

"As I just explained to Carla, I think the board should wait a bit before electing her, that's all."

"Why should you wait? She's giving you a brilliant collection, plus the money for the wing. Can't do better than that. I think you should all be *grateful*. I mean, what sort of people do you want on that board anyway? Seems to me Carla's absolutely the perfect addition."

As Max got more blustery, he pumped harder. My arm hurt. I finally just stopped dead.

"Did she put you up to this?" I asked him.

He looked away evasively. "Well, of course, she knows we're friends. She did ask me if I'd put in a good word. You New York ladies are rather a tough crowd, *what*?"

"We're like anywhere else. You have to prove yourself first, Max. I don't see people walking into London society with the greatest of ease, either."

"Oh, London's very different, m'dear," he said, resuming our dance. "We all grew up together. Known each other for years and years. Whereas practically everyone I meet in New York is from somewhere else. Know someone for a month in New York and you consider them lifelong friends, whereas in London three years is barely enough time for a nodding acquaintance. The so-called establishment here invented themselves. They weren't born to it."

I marveled at Max's cool snobbery.

"Yes, well, some inventions take longer to get patents than others," I said, referring to Carla.

We danced for a few more moments, then we both called it a night. As Max escorted me back to the table, he said, "You know, I'm rather surprised at you, Jo."

"Why?"

"Oh, I thought that you, above all people, wouldn't allow any kind of pettiness to get in the way of your good judgment. I somehow imagined you'd see through to a person's core, *what*?"

"Well, perhaps I do, Max. Perhaps I do . . ."

He gave me a little smirk, deposited me with Larry and the group, and left.

When I told Larry what had transpired on the dance floor, Larry said without hesitation, "Oh, they're definitely having an affair."

Toward the end of the evening, just as Larry and I were leaving, one of the footmen took me aside and asked if he could look inside my purse.

In the haze of after-dinner drinks and champagne, the missing earring had faded from most people's minds. Still, I figured the reason he was asking to search my bag was because he thought I'd taken it. I was outraged.

"You must be kidding! You certainly don't think *I* stole Mrs. Cole's earring, do you?"

Larry came to my defense. "Young man, you've got some nerve."

At that point, another footman stepped forward and said, "I'm sorry, ma'am, but I saw you pick it up off the dining room floor and put it in your bag." He pointed to the blue satin evening purse that matched my dress. I remember I had a fleeting thought that there was something oddly familiar about this footman, but I was so angry I couldn't focus on that for long—only on the fact that I was being accused of this horrible deed. I tried to maintain my composure. People were beginning to look at me and ask what was going on.

"You're mistaken," I said calmly. "You must have me confused with someone else."

The crowd was clearly with me. But the footman was

still demanding to see the contents of my purse. Suddenly, the crowd parted and Carla came rushing through, very anxious.

"What is going on here?" she demanded.

The footman explained that he saw me pick up her earring and put it in my bag. Carla listened with a stoney expression, then said to him, "That is utterly ridiculous!" She turned to me. "I am so sorry, Jo."

It was at that point that Max Vermilion piped up with a democratic suggestion. "I say, why not search *all* the ladies' purses and turn out the men's pockets, too? Maybe somebody did pick it up and just forgot. It's a damn valuable object, *what?* Might as well give offense to everyone while we're at it."

Everyone thought he was joking, but I knew he was dead serious. The social consequences of searching all our purses would be as lethal as the time a grande dame in Paris lost a diamond bracelet at one of her parties. She wrote form letters to nearly all her guests, asking whoever took the bracelet to send it back anonymously, no questions asked. The scandal that letter caused was compounded by the fact that some guests at the party didn't receive it. Three royals and two billionaires who'd been in attendance were deemed far too grand to have pocketed such a trinket, so the hostess didn't write to them. Her reputation was never recovered, unlike the bracelet, which was found months later by a zealous maid cleaning deep in the folds of an upholstered couch. But that's another story.

Right now, the guests were silent, standing firmly behind me. Everyone thought it was an outrage to be physically searched. In order to curry favor with Max, however, Bootsie Baines broke ranks.

"Well, anyone is welcome to search *my* purse, if they want to—provided they don't mind a soiled hankie," she said.

With that, Bootsie walked over to the hall table, opened her purse, and dumped out its contents. Her long-suffering husband followed suit by turning out his pockets.

"I think if you have nothing to hide . . ." she said sanctimoniously, looking directly at me.

Max kissed her good night and muttered "good show" under his breath.

At that point, several other ladies volunteered to have their purses seached, as well. But the crowd was still divided and outrage swelled. Discontented murmurs escalated to very vocal indignation. I thought it ironic that this ersatz Versailles was about to see another mob scene.

Finally Carla raised her hand and cried out, *"Basta!* Everybody *stop!"*

The crowd hushed up as she turned to the footman and pointed an accusatory finger at him.

"Young man," she said in a loud voice so that everyone could hear. "You have caused a great deal of embarrassment to me and to my guests. You are obviously a liar. Please leave my house immediately."

The footman, protested. "But, ma'am, I *saw*—"

"Immediately!" Carla cried, cutting him off.

As the footman turned and made his way through the crowd, his angelic face was clearly on the verge of tears. He still seemed vaguely familiar to me, but I just couldn't place him.

Carla turned back to me and said, with a very contrite expression, "Jo, dear, I am deeply sorry for all of this trouble. Obviously that silly young man was mistaken. Please accept my profound apologies."

"It's all right, Carla. It's not your fault."

Larry took my arm and we started for the door. I just wanted to get the hell out of there. However, before getting into the elevator, a few other women were allowing their bags to be searched and some of the men were turning their pockets inside out. I watched a procession of women, including Trish Bromire, Marcy Ludinghausen, Ellen Grimes, Christine Norbeau, and Regina Howard all turn their bags upside down and dump the contents out. Trish and Dick, eager to be cleared, allowed themselves to be searched twice. Only curmudgeonly Betty refused.

"They wanna seach me? Let 'em go ahead and *strip*-search me in front of everyone. That'll be a pretty sight!" Betty whispered to me.

I still felt awkward. Since I was the one who had initially been accused and my indignant reaction had basically started the whole thing, I thought I should at least volunteer to have my bag searched.

Betty was outraged when I told her. "Don't you dare, Jo! Don't you see how fucking *nuts* this is?! Rich people are really insane!"

But Larry looked at me and shrugged, as if to say, "What the hell." He turned out his pockets like the other men were doing. Betty stalked off. But I was too chicken. With grand distaste, I handed my bag to the footman near the door, who opened it and rummaged through the contents. He got a quizzical look on his face, went over to a nearby table, and turned my purse upside down, dumping its contents out on the top. A little crowd, including Carla, Larry, Betty, Gil, Justin Howard, Max, and Ethan Monk, was casually watching this now-routine procedure.

No one's gasp was louder than mine when sparkling amid the grouping of my gold compact, a lipstick, small comb, house key, and tissues was Carla's huge diamond earring. A bloody knife couldn't have shocked me more.

"Oh, shit," Betty said softly. "Talk about a smoking diamond."

I didn't know what to say. I looked around for allies, but people were sort of frozen, too shocked to react. I do recall the incredulous look in Justin Howard's eyes, as if he suddenly saw me in a brand-new light.

Finally, I said, "I have absolutely no idea how that got there."

"Well, I do!" Betty piped up. "Someone obviously *planted* it!"

There were murmurs all around. Justin Howard shook his head in dismay and walked off with his wife. Others followed him. I could see that no one except my closest friends believed me. Finally, Larry plucked the earring off the table with two fingers. He held it up with obvious disgust, as if it were a used tissue. He walked over and handed it to Carla.

"Here is your earring, Mrs. Cole," he said. "I happen to believe Mrs. Slater."

I hurriedly stuffed the contents back into my bag. Larry walked me to the elevator. It was so quiet, you could have heard a name drop. Just as the elevator arrived and we were getting in, I heard Carla say in a loud voice, "I am certain she took it just as a joke. After all, what can one do with *one* earring?" There was laughter all around. At my expense.

I was shaking by the time Larry and I got home. We sat in my library and I had a stiff drink. "Just think if I hadn't let them search my bag," I said. "I would have come home and found the damn thing. And then what would I have done?"

"Mailed it back anonymously," Larry said. "You didn't take it, after all. Someone planted it."

"Oh, I know . . . Still, it was a win-win situation for her, no matter what I did. She set me up, Larry. The Muni board meeting's tomorrow and she set me up. You should have seen the look on Justin Howard's face. She's going to get on that board now, you watch."

"Jo, anyone who knows you—"

"No, Larry . . ." I interrupted him. "Think of my past. I was once suspected of murder. Theft is mild by comparison."

Even Larry, wordsmith that he was, had no comeback for that.

Twenty-seven

A MARKED CHILL GREETED ME AT THE MUNI board meeting the next afternoon. Nearly everyone there had been at Carla's party, and those who hadn't been wanted to be invited to the next one. There or not, by now they'd all heard about the earring debacle. People lowered their voices as soon as I walked into the room—a sure sign I was the main topic of discussion. Justin Howard was talking to Edmond Norbeau in a far corner, near one of the windows overlooking Central Park and the Tiffany Wing of the museum. I distinctly saw him glance at me as I entered, but he didn't immediately rush over and say hello as he normally would have. Instead, he lowered his eyes and quickly turned his back, continuing to talk to Edmond, pretending he hadn't seen me. I figured this was a harbinger of things to come.

Ethan Monk, always loyal, immediately rushed over and gave me a warm greeting.

"Well, that was quite some party last night, wasn't it?" he said, attempting to diffuse the awkward situation.

"Forget it, Ethan," I whispered. "They're going to hang me out to dry. You watch."

"I won't let them, Jo," he said, patting my arm in sympathy.

People milled around, speaking in hushed tones. Several glanced my way, and if they caught my eye, they gave me embarrassed smiles. I just nodded with a fixed grin on my face as if to say, "I know you're talking about me and I don't care." But I did care.

The meeting was finally called to order. I sat next to Justin, who gave me a polite if tepid hello. Clara Wilman, my mentor, had always taught me to hold my head up high no matter what. I had nothing to be ashamed of. I'd been framed. And although no one believed that at the moment, I knew it was the truth. So when Justin said a perfunctory, "Hello, Jo, how are you?" I responded in a very cheerful, positive way, "I'm very well, thank you, Justin. And you?"

Justin looked at me incredulously and kind of rolled his eyes without really meaning to.

"Fine, thank you," he said and turned away.

The meeting soon got under way. A summary of the minutes from the last meeting were read and some museum business was gotten out of the way. I noticed that people were taking potshot glances at me throughout the session. If I happened to catch an eye, that eye quickly darted away. When it came time to vote on Carla Cole's election to the board, Justin Howard cleared his throat and said, "And now, ladies and gentlemen, the time has come to vote."

I was well aware of the surreptitious looks in my direction. Justin continued, "I move the nomination of Carla Cole to the board of the Municipal Museum. Will anyone second the motion?"

Edmond Norbeau raised his hand and said a somber, "Second."

"Thank you, Edmond," Justin said. "Well, now, I think we've all had ample time to reflect on this nomination. Does anyone feel the need for a discussion at this point?"

I raised my hand. Justin raised his eyebrows.

"Yes, Jo?" he said, somewhat testily.

I had prepared a little speech in my mind. However, facing that roomful of hostile faces, I hesitated.

"Jo? You wanted to say something?" Howard said.

I took a deep breath and geared myself up. I had to defend myself and the museum I loved.

"I'm not going to beat around the bush," I began in a somewhat tremulous voice. "You all know what happened last night. But I swear to you that I did *not* take that earring, which means that someone planted it. If you believe me, then I think you will also agree with me that now, more than ever, it is imperative that we wait before electing Mrs. Cole to this board. If she, indeed, used that incident to manipulate your votes, I don't think she's a worthy candidate. That's all I have to say."

Ethan gave me a sympathetic nod. Justin Howard paused to clear his throat, then said, "We all know how you feel, Jo. But I believe that waiting would be counterproductive. I doubt it escapes anyone here that the director of the Metropolitan Museum and president of the Museum of Modern Art were both at Mrs. Cole's party last evening. The incident in question notwithstanding, let me put this as strongly as possible, We do *not* want to lose the Cole collection if we can possibly help it. . . . Now, shall we vote?"

He paused and looked around the room, focusing for a moment on everyone, except me. "All in favor of Carla Cole, please raise your hands and say aye."

Hands shot up all around the table, along with a droning chorus of ayes. It included everyone I had taken to lunch who had promised not to vote for her.

Everyone except Ethan.

"All opposed, please raise your hand and say nay." Justin looked directly at Ethan.

Justin didn't seem worried about me because I had previously told him that I was going to abstain. However, that was before the incident last night. Knowing what she had done to me and suspecting what she'd done to Russell, June, and Lulu's spy, I certainly didn't want Carla Cole's nefarious presence polluting the board of my beloved museum. As I had not actually given Justin my word, but merely mentioned I would abstain, I decided that now was the time to take a stand.

"All opposed?" Justin said again.

I raised my hand and said, "Nay."

Discontented murmurs rippled through the room. People glared at me in contempt. I ignored them.

Justin shook his head. "Abstain?"

Ethan raised his hand. "Abstain," he said.

Ever the diplomat, Ethan.

It was at that point that I noticed the rather gleeful look that passed between Edmond and Justin. Justin rose to his feet.

"Ladies and gentlemen, as you all know, under the by-laws of the corporation, one nay vote or 'blackball,' as it is called, can prevent the election of a person to this Board. However, Edmond and I strongly believe that Carla Cole would also be a tremendous asset to the Museum. And perhaps more importantly, we are convinced that we will lose the Cole Collection if she is not elected. It is, therefore, with great reluctance and sadness, that I

am going to invoke what is known in the bylaws as The
Marchant Exception."

I was so flabbergasted at the insulting implications of
this that I could hardly believe my ears. And indeed, there
were gasps all around the table because everyone immediately understood what a slap in the face this was to me.

The Marchant Exception stated that if there is only
one vote against the election of a candidate, the chairman has the power to override that single vote and elect
the candidate—provided, of course, that he has a two-
thirds majority consent of the board. It was created in
1929 when Hiram Marchant was blackballed from
going on the board of the Muni by his brother-in-law,
Frank Lanier. Marchant, a popular and powerful figure
in the community, had just donated a hundred thousand
dollars to the Museum despite the Crash. By contrast,
Lanier was a rotter who had swindled Marchant out of a
large sum of money. Sympathies were certainly with
Marchant, who had refrained from pressing charges
against his brother-in-law in order to avoid a scandal
and protect his wife, who was Lanier's sister. Everyone
on the board knew that Lanier had blackballed
Marchant out of pure jealousy and spite. In an
unprecedented move, Lanier's blackball was overridden
and Marchant was elected to the board. Lanier was
asked to resign. This occurrence was written into the
bylaws and known as "The Marchant Exception."

"Of course," Justin went on, "we don't have a truly
comparable situation here. Jo Slater, I needn't tell any of
you, is a most valued and revered member of this board.
But"—a New York but—"I do believe that Carla Cole
would be such a valuable board member that I must override the blackball."

Justin paused for a moment. I could see this was not easy for him. Little beads of sweat popped out on his wide forehead.

"So, that being the case," he went on, "all those in favor of invoking the Marchant Exception which gives me the power to override the veto, please raise your hands and say, 'Aye.' "

The response was slightly slower this time as people considered the magnitude of their decision. Invoking this exception was a huge matter, not to be taken lightly. It was lost on no one that a vote for this measure was a vote against me. I watched as each of the members looked around to see what their cohorts were doing. Seymour Heffernan, the Chairman of the Finance Committee, who I didn't particularly like and who obviously didn't like me, was the first to raise his hand and say a sharp, "Aye." Then, like dominoes falling, everyone around the table followed his lead. People purposely avoided my eyes. Edmond Norbeau, with whom I had worked side by side over the years, said the softest, "Aye," of all. He looked truly pained, despite the fact that he and Justin had obviously discussed this way in advance. With the count in, my posture stiffened and I stared straight ahead, feeling utterly humiliated.

"All opposed?" Justin said.

I knew it would have been most undignified and unseemly for me to oppose a measure which was so clearly designed to embarrass me. I thought it wiser to hold my head high and say nothing than to voice some petty, self-serving protest which wouldn't have done any good anyway. But dear Ethan came to my rescue. This time he didn't abstain. He raised his hand and said in a loud voice, "*Opposed! Vigorously opposed!*"

His gallantry brought tears to my eyes. I could have kissed him.

"The ayes have it," Justin said. "As Chairman, I therefore invoke the Marchant Exception. I override the single veto of Carla Cole and declare her elected to this board."

"And I resign," I said, getting up and leaving the room.

That evening, ever loyal Ethan sent me a big bouquet of white roses and a note which read,

> *I am sick at heart.*
> *Please reconsider.*
> *Love,*
> *Ethan*

It was a sweet gesture and I called to thank him.

"Oh, Jo," he said immediately, "I'm so happy you called. Listen, you've just got to reconsider your decision. I can't stand it that you're not on the board now. Please, talk to Justin, will you? I'm sure he'll understand."

"I'm certainly not going to call Justin. In my view, he owes me an apology. If he wants to talk to me, he knows where to find me," I said.

I still had my pride.

"But, Jo, she'll take over the museum. You know she will."

"They asked for it. If you invite a shark in to swim, you can't complain if it attacks you."

"Then think of *me*," Ethan said plaintively. "It won't be any fun there without you."

"Sweetie, I'm sorry. But what's done is done."

I hung up with the gnawing feeling that I'd played

right into Carla's hands. I was mulling on this thought when Cyril came into the library carrying a silver tray with a single letter on it.

"Hand delivered just now, madam," he said, offering it to me.

It was from Carla and it read,

> *Dearest Jo,*
>
> *I was so sorry to hear of your resignation from the board of the Muni. I was so looking forward to working with you. I feel we could have done great things together. Still, I wish you the best of luck and I sincerely hope that I was not a factor in your decision. I am looking forward to seeing you again very soon.*
>
> *Love,*
> *Carla*

It did not escape me that it was written on Municipal Museum stationery.

Twenty-eight

THE NEWS THAT I HAD RESIGNED FROM THE board of the Muni ripped through New York faster than a stocking run. Charlie Kahn called to offer his condolences to me. He also had an ulterior motive. He wanted me and Betty to break the news to June that Carla had moved into their building. Having been forbidden a telephone or stimuli of any sort, including *Nous* magazine, June was reduced to listening to classic books on tape, blissfully unaware of this horrible development.

"I haven't dared tell her yet, Jo," Charlie confided. "I don't want to upset her progress. She's doing so well— recovering by leaps and bounds."

When Betty heard this, she said, "Yeah, she's leaping to conclusions which are bound to be wrong!"

Betty and I knew the real reason Charlie didn't want to take on the task of telling June the bad news.

"Let's face it, he's scared stiff of her," Betty said.

I knew also that he hated scenes of any kind. Charlie

Kahn was the last of a dying breed: a native New Yorker who was "to the manner born," a gentleman and a truly courtly being who loathed publicity and disruption of any kind. He also had a streak of mischief in him—but that's another story. I knew him to be both utterly devoted to and terrified of his flighty wife.

Betty agreed to go with me to see June. The two of us drove out to Southampton just for the day, charged with informing our volatile friend that Carla Cole had successfully moved into her territory and was now a firm fact of all our lives. Quite frankly, I was thrilled to be getting out of the city. The whole Muni "excommunication," as Betty called it, had left me feeling very low indeed. It was just one more example of how absolute money corrupts absolutely—not just the person who has it, but the people around it. The fact that my beloved museum, for which I had worked for nearly twenty years, had succumbed to the wiles of this financial Circe was devastating. I relished the idea of going out to the country and seeing some green that didn't have to do with money, for a change.

Betty and I felt like two envoys on a "delicate diplomatic mission," as I called it. As I fought the endless traffic on the Long Island Expressway, we debated the best way to tell June about her new neighbor. We tried out all kinds of subtle approaches, everything from sneaking it into the conversation as an aside, to throwing it away as a parting shot. Quickly wearying of the tactful approach, however, Betty finally said, "Hell, Jo, why don't we just come right out and say it: 'Junie, there's a new queen in town and she's in your palace in a much grander apartment!' "

Somehow, I thought not.

Halfway there, we grew tired of talking about June. Betty segued onto me. We went over the earring debacle ad nauseum, then Betty chastised me for quitting the board of the Muni.

"What in hell were you thinking, Jo? Are you nuts letting them force you out like that? Carla obviously set you up. How could you have let her get the better of you?" Betty asked incredulously.

"First of all, they didn't force me out, Betts. I resigned. Maybe I was hasty, but invoking the Marchant Exception—?"

"What the fuck's that?"

I explained to Betty exactly what had happened. Naturally, that was not what she had heard. She'd heard that Justin Howard had gotten up and banged his fist on the table, demanding my resignation, and that all the other board members had hounded me out of the room with catcalls. Typical New York: Things aren't bad enough that people can't wait to make them sound much worse.

"Listen, Betts, let's get one thing straight here, okay? Justin did not *demand* my resignation. I resigned on my own. But I have to admit, it was bad. My God, he compared me to that swindler brother-in-law of Marchant's by using an obscure rule that hasn't been invoked in eighty years. I couldn't just sit there and take that, could I? Anyway, I don't want to be on the same board as that woman. Let them all stew in their own juices, as far as I'm concerned."

"But Jo, the Muni! The Slater Gallery . . . that's your baby. Are you gonna abandon your baby?"

"I've dropped off that board before, Betts, as you well know." I was referring to the unfortunate time I'd been subtly asked to resign by the former president, Roger

Lowry, because my fortunes had dipped so low. "I'll be on it again one day, once this interloper derails."

"Don't bet on that train wreck anytime soon," Betty said. "I can't tell you the number of people who've called asking me how they can get in touch with her so they can invite her to things just so she'll return the favor. Everyone is *dying* to see that ghastly apartment of hers. New York is so shameless. Of course, when anybody asks me if I've got her number, all I say is, 'And *how*.'"

Betty was nothing if not loyal.

We arrived at the Kahns' house at around one. They had a large, gray-shingled "cottage," as they're called, just down the road from the beach near the Southampton Beach Club. Though the grounds were beautiful, with a great view of the ocean, inside the house was inappropriately decorated with overgilded furniture, overstuffed couches, and an endless array of knickknacks. Every available surface was covered with carved ivory elephants and pink quartz pigs and other similar dust magnets. I remembered Lucius's description of the Kahns' house as "the Ile St. Louis on Mott Street."

"It's the only house you go to where you have to put your drink down on your lap," Betty said, referring to the lack of space on any table.

But it was June's penchant for nineteenth-century china figurines of monkeys dressed as clowns and jesters that had always been a mystery to me. Her vast collection of costumed simians looked particularly out of place, not to say ridiculous, on the living room mantel of a summer house. But that was our June.

I remember dear Clara Wilman once told me that the essence of great taste was "the appropriate made supremely comfortable." By that she meant you didn't decorate, say, a beach house with marble and gobs of gilt. June rode roughshod over this dictum, for in each of her abodes the inappropriate was made supremely uncomfortable.

Betty and I knew the house well and when Charlie opened the door for us, we barged right in, said fond hellos, then immediately headed upstairs to June's bedroom, where Charlie told us she'd been confined on doctor's orders. We were a bit cautious about entering the room, fearing we would disturb the patient. Betty knocked gently on the door a couple of times and got no answer.

"Maybe she's asleep," I said.

Betty turned the doorknob slowly and cracked the door so we could peer in. If we had walked into that frilly pink-and-white bedroom expecting to see a woman subdued by her near brush with death, we were sorely mistaken. Far from resting, June was propped up on a hospital bed, barking into the phone, taking notes on the yellow legal pad resting against her knees. Though still pale and thin from her ordeal, she nonetheless seemed quite feisty.

"Well, that's just not acceptable!" she was saying as she scribbled furious circles over the notes she'd been taking. "And if you can't help me, I'll find someone who can. . . . No, no, no, I *will* listen to reason. I just won't listen to *you*! . . . Because you're not being reasonable, that's why! . . . Yes, yes, I understand . . . but you're a lawyer, for heavens's sakes! You're *supposed* to be amoral! . . . Yes, and the same to you, too! Thank you! Good-bye . . . and good riddance!"

She hung up the phone and turned to us as if she'd just seen us an hour ago.

"Well, that was my lawyer," she announced, still flushed with rage. "Or my *ex*-lawyer, I should say. Do

you know that Carla Cole got into my building! The
board voted her in when I was on my deathbed. My
deathbed! How dare they?! I intend to sue. And you know
what he just had the nerve to tell me? If I sue the board,
I'll be suing myself because I'm the president of the
board! He says he can't handle the case in good conscience. *In good conscience*! Can you *imagine*? A lawyer
with a conscience?! So I said, 'Then handle it in *bad* conscience! Just help me!' He won't . . . he refuses . . . silly
little man!"

"So much for our delicate mission," Betty said in an
aside to me.

"What mission?" June said, overhearing.

Betty and I gathered around her bed and we both
kissed her hello.

"Junie, it's so wonderful to see you," I said.

"You, too, sweetie. Hi, Betty, dear . . . what mission
are you talking about?"

Betty glanced at me, then said, "Charlie asked us to
break the news to you that Carla got into your building."

June threw up her hands. "Don't tell *me*! I know *all*
about it! In fact, I may call Carla and ask her where I can
find a hit man to rub out that rotten old Tut-tut Hadley
Grimes! A hit man is just the sort of person *she'd* know,
don't you think? She'll probably have hit man parties
once she gets started," June said, only half joking. June
thought for a moment, then heaved a great sigh. "Oh,
well, I suppose I have to be realistic . . ."

"It would be a nice change," Betty muttered under her
breath.

"I heard that, Betty Waterman!" June snapped. "We're
just going to have to start looking for a new apartment. I
will *not* share my lobby with that murderess."

When June had first hurled that accusation at Carla, I'd been skeptical. Now I was inclined to agree with her assessment of her new neighbor.

Colleen brought us up a tray of sandwiches and coffee for lunch. The three of us sat in the bedroom, gossiping. Betty and I filled June in on all that had happened since she had been "out of commission," as she now liked to put it. She sat there seething as we gave her the blow by blow about Carla's grand apartment, the famous party, the egregious earring incident, Carla donating the Cole Collection to the Muni, and my resigning from the board. Fresh and juicy as the sliced white champagne peaches that Colleen brought us for dessert, the conglomeration of bad news seemed to completely restore June to both the pitch and color of her old self.

"This woman must be exposed!" she cried.

Betty and I wholeheartedly agreed. I told her that Larry Locket was on the case and that was some comfort to both of them.

"Well, if anyone can get to the bottom of this rotten barrel, it's Larry," Betty said.

I also confessed to them that I was a little afraid of Carla, and I asked June what, exactly, she remembered about being hit by that car.

"That's the awful thing," she said. "I don't remember anything about it. The last thing I remember is running off that stage when I saw Carla coming up to accept her prize. Charlie tells me they found the car and it was stolen. So I guess we'll never know who did it."

"Maybe not . . . but I have my suspicions," I said.

"You think Carla. . . ?" June said.

"I just find it interesting how she manages to dispose of people who get in her way, that's all."

An hour later, Charlie Kahn said good-bye to us at the door and thanked us profusely for our visit. On the way back to the city, I said to Betty, "Well, it's good to see Junie getting back to her old self, isn't it?"

To which Betty replied, paraphrasing Shakespeare, "'Age cannot wither, nor comas stale her infinite anxiety.'"

Twenty-nine

THE TRAVAILS OF THE RICH BEING FAR MORE fun to contemplate than the real threats of life, the scandal involving Carla and myself became a subject of great speculation, at least in New York. Just how Carla Cole's four-million-dollar D-flawless diamond earring came to be in my evening bag, whether I'd really taken it or whether it had been planted, Carla's unorthodox election to the Muni board, and my own abrupt resignation, were ongoing subjects of conversation at the various breakfasts, lunches, and dinners around town. Items about Carla Cole's party were featured in every gossip column in town, using the egregious earring incident as a peg.

"Grande Dame Dethroned" was the way Page Six headlined their article:

Jo Slater, New York's reigning queen, is having some trouble hanging onto her tiara these days. At what insiders are calling the "coming out" party of

Carla Cole, the wife of still-missing billionaire Rus-
sell Cole, Mrs. Slater was caught trying to pocket
one of Mrs. Cole's pricey diamond earrings. The next
day, Mrs. Slater tried to block Mrs. Cole's election to
the ultraprestigious board of the Municipal Museum,
claiming she'd been framed. In a major upset, how-
ever, Mrs. Cole was elected to the board and Justin
Howard, the chairman of the museum, repeatedly de-
manded Mrs. Slater's resignation. Mrs. Slater re-
fused at first, but then, after a fractious and tense
hour, she reluctantly agreed to resign from the board
to the relief of all concerned . . .

When I read this wholly fictitious account of what had
happened, my only thought was that accurate reporting,
like old-world craftsmanship, was definitely a thing of
the past.

Nous magazine, being a monthly, carried the story
sometime later. This was the account of Carla's party that
everyone had been waiting for. To her credit, Miranda
Somers was the only one of all her colleagues who failed
to mention the earring debacle when describing that infamous evening. Her "Daisy" column concentrated instead
on the sumptuousness of the apartment and the guest list.
She described everything in detail—from the footmen to
the décor to the food, and, of course, what everybody was
wearing. She wrote about Carla Cole's "stunning diamond earrings, the size of plover's eggs," mentioning in
passing that one had been "accidentally misplaced" during the night, but was later "mercifully recovered in front
of the glittering crowd, which glided like gods and god-
desses atop the breathtaking lapis lazuli floor, whose
golden flecks are sprinkled like fairy dust over a deep

blue sea." Okay, Miranda. I was so grateful she didn't mention my humiliation and resignation from the Muni board that I forgave her the hyperbole.

Betty called me to laud Miranda's restrained coverage. "Writing about Carla's party without mentioning the earring thing is like writing about my daughter's wedding without mentioning the rain. Miranda's such a good egg," Betty said. "If only people like her could write the news. Life would be so sunny and we'd never be troubled by terrorism, plagues, and poverty. Just bad outfits—which is terrorism of a sort, come to think of it."

That being the case, I thought, Betty was the Osama bin Laden of fashion.

Shortly thereafter, Carla Cole flew off to London in her private plane to attend the Taunton Hall Ball, an annual spring event where rich Americans paid dearly to hobnob with English royals and continental aristocrats. By invitation only, the cheapest ticket was five thousand dollars, which only got you to the ball itself, not to the coveted dinner beforehand. Dinner tickets were ten thousand dollars apiece and rumor had it that Carla bought four tables—in Russell's name—which came to a little less than half a million dollars. The proceeds from the ball went to the Taunton Hall Trust, of which Max Vermilion was the chairman. The purpose of the trust had always been the upkeep of the grand house itself. In recent years, however, in the wake of terrorism, war, famine, disaster, and waning revenues, the trustees started providing scholarships for art and music students, in an attempt to show they were as interested in human beings as they were in gardens, grounds, and furniture.

Betty, Gil, and Ethan all traipsed off to Los Angeles

for the opening of a new museum. They invited me to go along with them up to the Auberge du Soleil, a splendid inn in the Napa Valley, where the three of them always stayed for a couple of weeks in the spring, but I begged off. Betty called me from the inn to tell me that she had just spoken to Trish Bromire, who told her Dick was not going to appeal.

"Hi-ho, hi-ho, it's off to jail he goes," she sang in her inimitable Betty way.

I was stunned. "You're kidding!"

"Nope. Trish told me that Dick did a lot of soul-searching in Southampton." She paused to reflect. "*Soul Searching in Southampton* by Dick Bromire. Think that would sell? Just kidding . . . anyway, he's decided that he wants to get the whole thing over with as soon as possible. His lawyers apparently told him not to waste his money on an appeal. Rather a novel concept for the legal profession—don't you think?"

"I know, but why not appeal? What's he got to lose?"

"They convinced him that in their opinion there were no grounds for reversible error."

"Whatever that means."

"It means he's guilty," Betty said tersely.

"Oh."

"Plus the fact, he's watched all these other CEOs stay out on appeal, just marking time until they finally have to go to the slammer. Let's face it, Jo, is there anything more depressing than trying to make dinner conversation with a man who has a jail term hanging over his head?"

"You have a point."

"It won't be that long a stretch. A few months max. Trish told me she's going to get an apartment near the jail, wherever it is, and visit him every day. The only thing she's worried about is that he might die or get raped. But I don't think they'll send him to that kind of prison, do you?"

"Let's hope the jail facilitator does his job. How the mighty have fallen, eh, Betts?"

"Look on the bright side. The fallen are still mighty if they have a lot of money."

I hung up thinking what a perfect needlepoint pillow that would make for Dick Bromire.

Trish called me herself to tell me the news. She said that she and Dick were staying in Southampton to savor Dick's last few weeks of freedom.

"Dick's fate is in the hands of a higher power," Trish said.

"Right. The judge."

"No," she said sanctimoniously, "the Judge of judges."

Oh, dear. I dreaded to think of Trish Bromire being born again.

Thirty

IT WAS BLACKMAIL PAYMENT TIME AGAIN. I
traipsed down to David Millstein's office and
picked up my diamonds to send them on, as
usual, to that PO box in Las Vegas. This time I debated
whether or not to put a note inside the envelope, asking
Oliva if she indeed knew Carla Cole, since Carla was always hinting to me they were acquainted and that Oliva
had told her about her dealings with me. From the little I
knew of my blackmailer, I figured this was a woman who
operated on the fringes of both society and the law. If
Carla did know her, I thought it might be useful to know
exactly *how* they had become acquainted. Perhaps such
knowledge would reveal something unsavory about
Carla's past, something I could use to turn the tables
against her for a change. I wrote the note, but at the last
minute decided not to send it, mainly because I didn't
want Oliva getting in touch with me for any reason. It
was just too risky. I sent the diamonds alone, in an unmarked envelope as usual.

As I walked up Fifth Avenue, I reflected that I'd acted a bit precipitously by resigning from the Muni board. However, the humiliation of the moment had simply been too much for me to bear. I knew that I'd been cleverly framed by Carla, although I doubted that even she could have predicted such a satisfactory outcome in her favor. Once again, I found myself marginalized in the world over which I had once reigned. The dazzle of Carla's wealth combined with the newness of her presence blinded people to her true nature. My only recourse now was to discredit and expose her for the scheming predator I believed her to be. For that, I turned to my great ally in this cause, Larry Locket.

With all my dearest friends out of town, I grew even closer to Larry during this period. Bonded by a common fascination with the Cole case and with Carla herself, we talked on the phone every day and saw each other at least three times a week, either for lunch or dinner. Larry sometimes read me parts of the article he was working on. It was a fascinating, meticulously researched description of the whole drama. But even though Larry and I had our suspicions that Carla had orchestrated Russell's disappearance, as well as other "accidents," so far there was no hard evidence against her. It was all innuendo, like the lady herself.

Larry was particularly interested in Carla's relationship with Max Vermilion.

"What I can't figure out is this: is she using Max, or is Max using her?" he said to me on the phone.

"Maybe both," I replied. "She wants social acceptance. He wants money for his house. It's a marriage made in commerce."

"Maybe. But Max is a canny old bird, you know. He

loves being fawned over, but he likes them to have a little class, don't you kid yourself. And there are plenty of rich women for him to choose from."

"There's rich and then there's rich-rich. Not many have six billion dollars at their disposal."

"True . . ." Larry said thoughtfully. "She's over in London now at Max's ball, you know. Have you ever been, Jo?"

"No. Have you?"

"Once. I went because I wanted to see Taunton Hall. It's not a bad evening of its type, mainly because the setting is so spectacular. But balls for furniture aren't my thing. Once was enough."

"Max seems very fond of Carla, I must say."

"Yes, but you know as well as I do that you can never tell what people are really up to when you only see them socially. Everyone's friendly at a party."

"Except Carla Cole's parties," I added grimly, thinking of my horrible experience with the earring.

"Well, that wasn't a party. That was a declaration of war. The lioness's den," he said with a strange little laugh.

I got the feeling that Larry was frightened of Carla, although he never came right out and said so. I was a little frightened of her, too.

And then came the rat incident.

Larry returned home from a dinner party late one night and found a cardboard box on his doorstep. Inside the box was a dead rat lying on top of a newspaper clipping. The clipping just happened to be from a recent Page Six, in which the staple We Hear section had a squib about Larry,

We hear . . . that Larry Locket is sharpening his mighty pen to write the tale of missing billionaire Russell Cole for Vanitas *magazine, and that he won't stop until he gets to the bottom of the intriguing story, which may prove to be as deep as the Caribbean Sea . . .*

Larry called me up that night, apologizing for the lateness of the hour. He told me what had just happened and tried to laugh it off.

"Who do you think put it there?" I asked him.

"Oh, Carla, definitely . . . I mean, not she herself. I'm sure she had someone plant it. But it's a warning from her."

I offered to come over at once, but he said that wasn't necessary.

"I'm used to intimidation, Jo," he said. "It's part of the territory. I found it rather amusing, that's all."

His manner was light and offhand, but I could tell he was shaken, which wasn't like Larry.

"That's not the real reason I'm calling, though. Can you come over for breakfast in the morning, Jo? I have something I'd like to show you."

Breakfasts weren't exactly my thing, but I was concerned about him, so the next morning I got up early and went over to see him.

Larry Locket lived in a secluded, little-known spot in the city located just off Lexington Avenue in the upper Sixties, called the Association. Nestled in the shadow of an old church, it was a quaint cluster of turn-of-the-century houses surrounding a communal square. Like so many of the most interesting places in New York, the little enclave was hidden from public view.

Having no open access, it had remained over the years a place of great serenity and refuge, a throwback to another era when neighbors all knew each other by name and greeted one another with friendly nods as they took their daily constitutionals.

Larry had once explained to me that houses in the Association were hard to come by. They were put on the market infrequently, and when one did come up for sale, a tacit agreement between all the homeowners dictated it must first be offered privately to residents of the garden, who would quietly put the word out to family and friends. Only when those possibilities were exhausted was the precious commodity given over to a single real estate agent—one handpicked by the president of the Association. It was important to everyone that new homeowners blend into the carefully cultivated atmosphere of cooperation and trust. For as long as anyone could remember, there had never been a robbery or any violent crime within the Association. Such was the unblemished record of safety that some people occasionally forgot to lock their doors.

It was a balmy spring morning as I walked through the garden dotted with stately old shade trees and bordered with neat, well-tended flower beds. Larry's brick Victorian-style house was located halfway around the south side of the square. I had been there countless times. I rang the bell repeatedly before Larry answered. He finally appeared at the door in slippers, wearing a bathrobe over a pair of pajamas. There were dark circles under his eyes.

"Oh, Larry, I woke you up . . . I'm so sorry!" I said.

"I wish. I haven't slept a wink," he confessed, letting me in. "Come in, come in. I apologize for not being dressed yet."

He seemed grateful I was there and offered to make me some breakfast. I just wanted some strong coffee. He fixed us a little tray of coffee and biscuits and led me upstairs to the second floor, where his office took up nearly the entire space.

Every time I walked up those steep, highly polished wooden steps, I nearly slipped.

"Your stairs are lethal," I said. "You ought to get a runner."

"You always say that," he said with a smile. "And I always say I will . . . one of these days."

Larry had combined three rooms to make his office. The large space, decorated in beiges and browns, lined with custom-made bookcases and antique wooden file cabinets with brass handles, was where he really lived. His black computer sat catty-corner to the large English partners desk. The sweetish aroma of old pipe tobacco smoke permeated the atmosphere. The sole photograph, nestled into the bookcase nearest his desk, was a small, fading color candid shot of a pretty, dark-haired young woman sunning herself on a rock in a mountain landscape, all smiles and health. It was a picture of Larry's dead wife, taken shortly before she was murdered twenty-some years ago.

"Sorry about the mess," he said as we walked around a little obstacle course of newspapers and books, which were stacked in neat piles on the floor. "When I'm working, it's hopeless in here."

He set the tray directly on top of a bunch of magazines on the glass coffee table in the sitting area. He motioned me to sit down on the comfortably worn, old leather couch. He sat on one of two chairs flanking the low table. He poured me a cup of hot espresso. The strong coffee gave me a welcomed jolt.

"First of all, the rat . . ." he began. "I mean, it's not exactly like finding a horse's head in my bed, Jo, but it's a little disconcerting, I have to confess. It's usually so safe around here, I'm always forgetting to lock my door."

"So you think it's a message from Doña Carleone," I said facetiously.

Larry chuckled. "Well, it's a little coincidental the beastie would be wrapped in that particular article saying I was writing about her, don'tchya think? But who knows? Let's face it, Jo, Carla Cole's not my sole enemy in life."

That was an understatement. Larry was known for taking on the rich and powerful, many of whom had publically vowed to get even with him one day. In the course of Larry's career, he'd had many threats against his life, but he never backed away from a confrontation where justice was at stake. I thought of Larry Locket as a modern-day David going up against a slew of rich Goliaths. Not many people had stood their ground as often or as successfully as Larry against such a varied array of formidable foes.

Larry rose from his chair and went over to the antique wooden file cabinet set into the far wall behind his computer. He stooped down, pulled out the bottom drawer, and pointed to a deep pile of mail strewn inside.

"Hate letters, crazy letters, macabre artwork. Hardly a day goes by when I don't get something from one nut or another. They write to the magazine and the magazine forwards them to me. The number of letters I got on Carney alone would've filled three of these drawers. I put them all in a box in storage."

He was referring, of course, to Jackson Carney, the scandal-drenched circuit court judge who had vigorously denied any romantic involvement with one of his young law clerks after she was found drowned in the East River. Larry uncovered evidence that Carney, a self-proclaimed devoted family man with a wife and four children, was indeed having an affair with the young woman. He wrote a blistering article about the case, revealing Judge Carney to be not only a chronic womanizer, but a pathological liar to boot. The article helped wreck Carney's career. He was not re-elected to the bench.

In fact, there were many instances when Larry had used his great instincts and investigative powers to either rake up cold cases or pursue current ones that looked as if they had derailed. Like an infamous "Daddy Deer" trial in Seattle, in which Michael Posner, the twenty-four-year-old heir to a timber fortune, was accused of murdering his wealthy father on a hunting trip. Young Michael maintained he mistook his father for a deer. He also claimed his father had abused him for most of his adult life. Consequently, it was dubbed the "Daddy Deer" case by the tabloid press. The trial ended in a hung jury, so the judge declared a mistrial. Larry strongly believed that Posner was lying about the abuse and that he had shot his father on purpose in order to get his hands on the family fortune. Working with the local authorities, Larry discovered a disgruntled ex-girlfriend of Posner's who showed him letters the young man had written to her, boasting of how he was going to shoot his father one day and make it look like an accident. Posner was convicted in a second trial. He had vowed to get even with Larry from prison.

Or the infamous Deke Wilson trial in Los Angeles, which had people glued to their TV sets for months. Wilson was the rap star accused of hacking up his girlfriend and stuffing her body parts into a Styrofoam cooler, which he allegedly threw off his yacht into the Pacific Ocean. The cooler was found, along with DNA evidence connecting Wilson to the case. The trial exposed the hedonistic and violent lifestyle of a megastar in the music business, and shone a spotlight on all the toadies who catered to him, giving him drugs, women, money, whatever he wanted. The prosecutor, who seemed more interested in his television persona than he was in a conviction, stretched the case out for months with boring expert testimony, endless sidebars, and long-winded rulings. The jury acquitted the charismatic performer in less than an hour. Wilson then found God. Larry wrote a blistering denunciation of the way the trial had been conducted and ridiculed Wilson's conversion. Wilson told a tabloid that Larry Locket was the devil and some God-fearing Christian should kill him.

Larry's life was nothing if not confrontational. He shut the drawer, walked back to his chair, and sat down again, crossing his legs. Larry looked dapper even dressed in his bathrobe and pajamas, which were from Turnbull & Asser. He was wearing velvet monogrammed slippers.

"So how far along are you on your article?" I asked him. "Are you almost finished?"

"No, no. Lots more work to be done," he said, motioning to the piles of notes, clippings, and photographs strewn across his desk. "What do you think of this for a title: 'Cole Storage, the Tale of a Missing Billionaire.' "

"Great," I said.

"And what are these?" I said, picking up some photographs on the coffee table.

"Courtney gave those to me. They're some pictures she took on board *The Lady C* a couple of years ago. Apparently, Carla doesn't like to have her picture taken. And she didn't let Courtney take too many pictures of the boat, either."

"Now that you mention it, there were no photographers at her party for Missy Waterman. I thought that was a little strange, given that it was a bridal dinner."

I started thumbing through the pictures. They were views mostly, but there was one group shot of the crew.

"He looks very familiar," I said, pointing to a fair-haired young man standing in the back row.

"You met him. That's Jasper Jenks. He was the captain of the yacht when Russell disappeared. But he was only the bosun when that was taken."

I looked harder at the photo. "My God, Larry . . . I think . . . wait . . . you know, that could be the *footman*!"

He squinted. "What footman?"

"Remember the footman who accused me of taking Carla's damn earring that night? I think that's him. I *knew* he looked familiar at the time. Don't you remember the footman who said he saw me put the earring in my bag? The one she very grandly told to leave? I think that's him."

"Jo, are you sure?"

"Not sure, but I think so. I mean, someone planted that earring and framed me. I bet it was him."

Larry looked at the picture thoughtfully. "That's very interesting indeed," he said.

"You think I'm right? Could it have been him?"

"Well, here's the deal with Jenks. They fired their regular captain right before the trip when Russell disappeared, and promoted Jenks from bosun to captain. In order to do that, they had to re-register the boat in the Cayman Islands, because this fellow is from Australia and an American-registered vessel can only be com-

manded by an American captain. And that's one of the
big things that's been gnawing at me: Why did Russell
Cole replace his old captain right before that trip? Jenks
had no command experience, so why would Russell have
entrusted his precious yacht to him?"

"That's exactly what Gil Waterman said the day he
disappeared. I thought maybe Carla had a crush on him or
something. What do you think, Larry?"

"Well, there are a few possibilities, but one is that
Jenks may have been in on the plot—if there was a plot."

"And you think there was?"

"I do. If Russell was killed on board the boat—and I
suspect he was—Carla would definitely have needed
help, both with the murder itself and disposing of the
body. Given my theory that rich people like to hire others
to do their crimes, maybe Jenks is our killer." Larry's
eyes glittered with intensity.

"But you can't prove it."

"No . . . but now that I suspect it, I know what to look
for." He shook his head. "I wish to hell I'd been able to
talk to Lulu's spy."

"Carla's very clever at covering her tracks, isn't she?"
I said.

"Well, maybe not as clever as she thinks," Larry said.
"Have a look through the rest of the pictures, Jo. I'll just
go change."

He put down his coffee cup and left the room. I
thought I detected something odd in his manner. I continued thumbing through the photos, and then I came to one
that arrested my attention. It was a shot of some big costume party taken aboard *The Lady C*. Off to one side were
two women in similar halter dresses, wearing matching
blonde wigs. They were holding drinks with little paper

umbrellas in them, mugging for the camera. One of the women was Carla. Despite her animated expression, her eyes were, as usual, as lifeless as two stones. However, it was the woman beside her who really caught my attention. It was Oliva, my blackmailer. I recognized her, despite the blonde wig.

I sat for a few moments just staring at that picture, wondering if Larry had made the connection and if that were the real reason he'd wanted me to look at the photographs. He finally came back into the room, dressed in beige trousers, a blue blazer, and the colorful shirt and tie that were his trademarks. He stood at the door and lit his pipe, eyeing me through the smoke.

"So what'd you think of the pictures, Jo?"

I was flustered. "Well, they're interesting. Courtney took them, did she?"

"Yes. A couple of years ago on her last visit to the yacht." He walked behind me and looked over my shoulder. "That's an interesting one there, isn't it? I was struck when I saw it. Isn't she the spitting image of Countess de Passy?" He pointed at Oliva with the stem of his pipe. "Of course, it can't be the countess because she was dead by the time that picture was taken."

I pretended to examine the photograph more closely. "Um, now that you mention it, there *is* some resemblance. I wouldn't say she's the *spitting* image, though."

"That's just because she's wearing a blonde wig. But with dark hair. . . ? She'd be a dead ringer for your old nemesis."

I glanced up at Larry, who was staring down at me with an enigmatic smile. "So, um, do we know who she is, anything about her?" I asked him, terrified his answer would be yes.

"No. She was just a guest on board the boat that night."

I put the pictures back into the envelope and handed it to Larry. He walked over to his desk and sat down, laying the envelope aside. I remained silent. Facing his computer, Larry stared at the document on the screen.

"Is that your article?" I asked him.

"Just notes. . . ." He sighed. "I don't know, Jo . . . for the first time in my career, I feel I'm at a loss."

"How do you mean?"

"Well, contrary to every other assignment I've had, it seems that the deeper I get into this particular story, the more I *don't* want to know."

He turned and looked at me pointedly. I knew what he was thinking. We both knew what was being left unsaid. I felt sure that by showing me those pictures, Larry was hoping I would confide in him. And I knew that if I ever told another living soul the truth about my life, it would be Larry Locket. But I just couldn't bring myself to do it. Not that day, anyway.

"Writing is such an odd process," he went on. "No matter what the subject, the writer is always, in some sense, writing about himself or discovering something about himself. Writing is like friendship in a way— always bigger than the sum of its parts. I want you to know, Jo, that I consider you a dear friend."

"And I you, Larry."

Larry went on, "I also want you to know that if, in the course of my investigation, I uncover something that will be detrimental to our friendship, I will not write this article."

This was an amazing moment. "Larry . . . I can't ask you to do that."

"I know. You didn't ask me. I'm just telling you. I've

been in this business a very long time, Jo. I know people who would chop up their mothers to get a good story. But to me, no story is worth a good friendship. I guess I've just been around too long. I know that stories are a dime a dozen, but real friends are very rare."

"Thank you, Larry."

He exhaled fiercely. "That having been said, however, there's something about Carla Cole that is so deeply disturbing to me that I really feel she needs to be exposed. I've never run across anyone like her before. Oh, she's shiny, polished, and polite, all right. And when you look at her, it's impossible to believe she's done what I suspect she's done. . . . This may sound odd, Jo, but she kind of reminds me of the time I visited the Hatterson house."

One of Larry's most famous cases involved a twenty-year-old unsolved murder that had taken place on Long Island. Mary-Ann Keating, the beautiful, seventeen-year-old daughter of John Keating, who was then president of the elite Millstone Club, was found raped and bludgeoned to death on the beach near her parents' house in East Hampton. The young woman's murder was never solved, although police at the time strongly suspected the involvement of Gregg Hatterson, the nineteen-year-old son of Julian Hatterson, a billionaire from New Jersey, whose house was two doors down from the Keatings.

Over the years, the case went cold. It caught Larry's interest when he befriended John Keating at a meeting of a victims' rights group in New York. Keating told him he had always suspected "the young Hatterson boy" of killing his daughter because she had rejected him. The disconsolate father kept tabs on young Hatterson and told Larry he had been in and out of trouble with the law for most of his adult life. Larry tracked Gregg Hatterson down. He was an alcoholic, living on the remnants of a trust fund. Larry learned that over the years Hatterson had boasted to several of his friends that he had "gotten away with murder." Working with a retired private detective, Larry gathered enough circumstantial evidence to get the case reopened. New DNA technology proved that Gregg Hatterson and Mary-Ann Keating had been together that night. His semen was on her clothes. Eventually indicted and convicted of manslaughter, Gregg Hatterson was sent to prison for his old crime. Meanwhile, Julian Hatterson had vowed revenge on the man who put his son away. That man was Larry.

I asked Larry what he meant when he said Carla reminded him of going to the Hattersons.

"Let me see if I can explain it. I remember going out to East Hampton on this beautiful May day and walking all around the Hatterson property, looking at the trees and the greenery, smelling the sweetness of spring, feeling the warmth of the sunshine on my skin. The house is one of those huge, old, grey-shingled cottages. Very well tended. Very proper. All the hedges neatly trimmed, the grass freshly mowed. I went inside. It was filled with pricey early American furniture. Everything was so perfect it was hard to believe that something so horrendous had once happened there. And yet, after a while, I got this eerie, cold feeling. I could feel the crime all around me, like the vibration of it was still in the air, a secret that the place kept for years and years . . ." He paused, lost in thought for a moment. "Anyway," he shrugged, "being with Carla Cole kind of reminds me of that day."

"You make her sound supernatural."

He smiled. "No, Jo, that's the writer's imagination— the instinct, the alchemy we rely on to tell us what's true

and what's not. With Carla, I sense this terrible chill behind her beautiful façade, just like in that house. You can
just feel it, you know, this evil vibration."

He had Carla's number, all right.

We talked a little more about the article. It was all I
could do not to confess everything to him that morning.
But something stopped me. I couldn't bring myself to
take the chance, nor to burden him with that terrible
knowledge. We finished our coffee and I got up to leave.
Larry walked me downstairs to the front door.

"Thanks for coming over, Jo. You're a good friend."

Just as I was leaving, I turned and said, "Larry, tell me
something. Why do you keep all that hate mail? Why
don't you just get rid of it?"

"Partly for insurance. I keep the particularly bizarre
and vicious ones in case I get bumped off one day. It'll
give the police some leads," he said with a grim chuckle.

"Nothing's going to happen to you," I said, kissing
him on the cheek.

"Dead rats notwithstanding?" he said with a wink.
"But I also keep them for another reason."

"What's that?"

"If ever I get too complacent, I'll just reach down into
that drawer and pull out one of those letters to remind
myself that there are real crazies in this world. And real
evil."

I walked home from Larry's house, deep in contem-
plation. I suspected that he was beginning to put the
pieces of the puzzle together, and that it was only a matter of time before he figured out the truth about my involvement in Monique's death. Once he figured that out,
the only question would be: Could he unmask Carla and

protect me at the same time? If not, would he abandon what was arguably the biggest story of his career? Knowing Larry, I felt he would, in order to protect me.

But who was Carla Cole? And what did she really want? Was there a purpose to her mayhem? Or was she like some sort of serial killer socialite, doing away with people just for the thrill of it? Some people think that great wealth puts them above the law and entitles them to do whatever they want to whomever they please. Had great wealth corrupted Carla? Or was her corruption always there, looking for a venue?

I was also beginning to wonder if it was pure coincidence that the Coles had come to Barbados for the wedding. True, Russell was Missy's godfather, but according to Betty, he had never taken the slightest interest in her before. Was it possible all this had been a setup and I had been the dupe? The facts spoke for themselves; Carla was on the board of the Muni and I was off.

It seemed to me that what Carla wanted was to conquer that mirage commonly referred to as New York society. She was certainly not the first, nor would she be the last, to want to reign over the Big Golden Apple, to hold sway over its great institutions, have access to the most private precincts of privilege, give the parties everyone wanted to go to, and most importantly, to exile those whom she did not like to the B-list and make their frivolity in wanting to be included seem even more inconsequential than her own desire to exclude them. Social life in New York was more competitive than the Olympics.

I've always thought of social life as an obsession, rather like murder, in that its importance lies solely in the mind of the perpetrator. Carla's mind was an intricate maze. Getting to its center was a dangerous puzzle. The Minotaur was always lurking.

It even frightened me to criticize her because it put me in mind of my late friend Clara Wilman's famous dictum, Tell me what you criticize and I'll tell you who you are.

Sisters under the skin . . .

Thirty-one

FOR THE MOMENT, HOWEVER, I TRIED TO PUT
Carla and Oliva out of my mind. Without the
Municipal Museum, I no longer had a focus
for all my energy. I had to find a new way to contribute
to the community. This is not as easy as it sounds, particularly when you've dedicated your whole life to one institution. I realized more and more how the Muni had
been another home for me—a home from which I was
now exiled.

I was sitting in my library one evening, looking over
the financial reports of several, smaller institutions,
weighing the possibility of my involvement with them,
when the phone rang. I picked it up and immediately recognized the throaty voice at the other end of the line.

"Hello, Jo. It is Carla. How are you?"

"Fine, no thanks to you. What do you want?" I said
curtly.

"Jo, dear, I would love you to come and have tea with
me tomorrow, if you are free."

"Why? So you can accuse me of stealing something else?"

"Oh, Jo, what a ghastly misunderstanding that all was. You know, the more I think about it, the more I realize that someone must have put that stupid earring in your bag as a joke. And the footman thought that it was you. We older ladies all dressed up must look alike to these young men, no?"

I didn't want to tip her off to the fact that I suspected Captain Jenks was the footman who had accused me.

"Carla, I can't imagine we have anything to say to each other at this point."

"But I would like to talk to you about something."

"What?"

"It is not something I can discuss with you over the telephone. It is a matter of some delicacy. Please, Jo. Do me this favor."

I casually wondered what Churchill would have done if Hitler had invited him to tea. I hesitated, then agreed to go mainly out of sheer curiosity.

"All right, I'll come. I'd like an official taster there, please."

She didn't get the joke.

"I am certainly not going to poison you, Jo! You will be quite safe, I promise," she said seriously. "Shall we say four o'clock, *cara* Jo. I am looking forward to it."

I wasn't.

Just like its occupant, Carla's grand apartment looked coarser in the daylight when sharp edges are more apparent. Far from Miranda Somers's description of a deep blue sea covered with fairy dust, the famous lapis lazuli floor looked like nothing more than what it was: a giant expanse of cold, blue stone, flecked with pyrite. All the gilt and grandeur was oppressive, like the clutter of an antiques shop. Mercifully, there were no footmen in livery around to greet me. In fact, Carla met me at the door herself, all smiles and charm, acting as if we were the greatest of friends.

"You know, Jo," she said airily as she led me through to the living room, "I do so wish you had not resigned from the museum. You and I could have had such fun together planning the Cole wing."

She motioned me to sit down on the brown silk moiré couch in front of a red coromandel screen. She sat cattycorner on an Empire chair with two gilded eagle's heads at the end of each armrest. A butler came in carrying the tea service on a large silver tray. He laid the tray down gingerly on the crackled laquer coffee table in front of us.

"Will you have some tea, Jo? Or would you prefer something more substantial?"

Figuring I was going to need alcoholic assistance to get me through this, I said I wouldn't mind a glass of wine if it were being offered.

"Would you like a glass of champagne? I will join you."

"Champagne's fine, thanks."

Carla didn't have to say anything to the butler. He gave her a little bow and left the room.

"So . . ." she began, "do you think your friend Clara Wilman would approve of what I have done to her old apartment?"

I looked at her squarely. "Carla, I ask you again. What do you want?"

"There is no need to be so tense, Jo. We are going to have a lovely chat. Can you not just relax?"

"No."

The butler returned with a bottle of Cristal champagne in a silver ice bucket and two champagne flutes. He poured us each a glass. Carla raised her glass to me for a toast.

"To friendship," she said.

I didn't respond. I just drank down the delicate flute in one gulp. The butler poured me another, then Carla rudely motioned him to leave the room.

"Well, let me tell you all about London," Carla said, daintily picking a cigarette out of a gold box on the coffee table. "I went to Max's ball and it was absolutely divine. Max sends his love to you, of course. He was so sad you were not there. People came from all over Europe so it was rather a chic crowd for England. Englishwomen have no idea how to dress, most of them. They have got bad clothes and great jewels. You see some of those old dowagers wearing the most extraordinary diamond parures. Inherited, of course. But Max appreciates stylish women. He really does. He has a wonderful eye, Max . . ."

I listened to her go on about Max and his eye, wondering where this was all heading.

". . . And, of course, Jo, he is extremely fond of you."

"Well, I can't think why, because we don't know each other very well," I said, thinking how it was Max who had started the searching of the evening bags at the party, which led to my embarrassment. I didn't trust old Max any more than I did Carla at this point.

"Your opinion means so much to him. He respects your taste and your integrity . . ." She put down her champagne glass and finally lit the cigarette she'd been holding. She exhaled a fine plume of smoke. She stared down and thought for a moment, obviously troubled by something.

"Opinions of others matter a great deal to Max," she said at last.

"Really? It's always been my impression Max didn't give a damn what anyone thought."

"That is only what he pretends. It is all part of that British affectation. He cares, believe me. He cares a great deal what others think. Especially—how shall I put it? He cares what other people think in regard to himself."

"I'm not following you."

"Max likes his surroundings to be elegant. He does not want to be associated with tawdriness of any sort."

"That makes two of us. But you can't always get what you want," I said, pointedly looking at her.

If Carla got my little barb, she ignored it.

"What I mean is, Jo," she went on, "Max would not like to be connected with anyone or anything which had a dubious reputation."

I began to see where she was headed, but I didn't say a word. I just waited and let her go on.

"You know, Jo, I did not grow up poor. I grew up worse than poor. . . . I grew up on the fringes of wealth, so that from a very young age I understood its real power. But on the other hand, I also understood very well what it was like not to have it."

"And just where *did* you grow up, Carla?" I was interested.

"That is not important," she said irritably, waving her hand in the air as if she were brushing aside a fly. "What is important is that I grew up understanding that money can buy quite a lot, but *wealth* can buy *anything*." She smiled. She looked like a cat when she smiled. "I always wanted to be not rich, Jo, but *wealthy*. So wealthy that I could command my own life with a great degree of certainty. It was my dream ever since I was a little girl and had to watch the humiliation that comes from being no one and nobody in this world. Wealth makes you invulnerable to everything—except illness, of course. But even then, you can get the best doctors with a lot of money." She paused to take a little puff of her cigarette. ". . . And I am happy to say that I achieved my dream. You are looking at a woman who can buy anything, Jo— *anything* she wants. That is rare for a woman, no?"

"I'm thrilled for you, Carla. But you can't buy me, if that's what you have in mind."

She leaned forward and said solicitously, "But I do not have to *buy* you, Jo. You are my *friend*."

In her mouth, the word "friend" gave me a chill.

She went on, "Now, people will tell you that if they were rich, they would want all sorts of material things. Houses, planes, jewels, furs, what have you . . . But I will tell you what rich people really want more than anything."

"I'm all ears," I said.

"Privacy," she said simply. "We want complete and total privacy. That is what we really crave, is it not? You yourself are rich, Jo. You know that I am speaking the truth."

"I'll take your word for it."

"And anything that infringes upon our privacy— whether it is something as mundane as the noise from a neighbor or a photographer snapping our photo at an inopportune moment—is troublesome and irritating."

"Okay . . ." I began to see where she was headed.

She took a drag of her cigarette and readjusted herself

in her chair, crossing her shapely legs. She sighed hard. "Max and I had a long talk about this in London. You know, I am becoming quite fond of Max and he of me, I think. He has been so kind to me since Russell disappeared."

I could just see those sugar plum visions of herself as Lady Vermilion dancing in her calculating little head.

"And just how is the search for your missing husband progressing?" I interjected in a purposely mean-spirited way.

She ignored my insinuating tone of voice. "Sadly, there is no more news. There has not even been a dubious sighting in weeks and I am beginning to fear the worst. But I will never give up hope! He has disappeared before and he has returned before. And he will return again, I know it! I *feel* it!" she announced rather melodramatically.

I shifted in my seat, wondering how she managed to keep a straight face.

"Anyway," she went on, "as I was saying, Max loathes publicity. Oh, he likes to have his picture taken at grand events, who does not? It's rather amusing to see oneself in the pages of a magazine. But he really does not relish any sort of intrusion into his private affairs. And so I think it is rather difficult for him to be associated with me at this point, given the interest of the media in Russell's disappearance."

"That's too bad. But what can I do about it?"

"Jo, it is all dying down now—this awful publicity. Thank God! I would hate for it to suddenly flare up again. So would Max."

"*And*—?" I said impatiently.

"And, well, what concerns me now is that I feel that my privacy is about to be invaded."

"I'd say it's been pretty invaded already, wouldn't you?"

"Yes, but not quite in this way."

"What way are you talking about?"

She sat up a little straighter in her chair. "Your friend Mr. Locket is writing an article about me."

"Not just about you. About the whole case."

"Yes, but I know that he has some rather mistaken notions about me. Lulu is cooperating with him and she must have told him terrible things about me."

Now I definitely got where she was headed.

"Why don't you give him an interview, then, if you're so worried?" I asked.

She shook her head. "Max thinks that would be a great mistake. He says it is always an error when people try to tell their side of the story. Silence leaves so much more to the imagination."

"Well, old Max has got a point there, Carla. But, on the other hand, if you leave too much to people's imagination, they may not like you. They may, in fact, suspect you of evil deeds. So if you don't talk to Larry, you take your chances, don't you?"

"Any article about me would naturally include Max. We have been seeing a great deal of each other. Max is very concerned what Mr. Locket might say about him."

"What can he say? That Max has been married a lot? That he has a dark side?"

Suddenly stoney-faced, Carla leaned forward and pinned me with a dead-eye gaze.

"Tell Mr. Locket that it would be very unwise of him to publish his article."

I was dumbfounded.

"Is that a threat?"

Her hand shot up in protest. "Not at all! A strong request."

"Like that dead rat you put on his doorstep?"

She feigned innocence.

"What are you talking about?"

I shook my head in vague amusement. "You don't know Larry very well if you think he's easily intimidated. But if you don't want him to publish that article, why don't you call him up and tell him yourself. Why tell me?"

"Because I feel it would have so much more weight coming from you, Jo."

"Why is that?"

"Because you know him. And you know me . . . and you know the friend that you and I have in common," she said in a sly voice.

"What friend is that?" I said, understanding full well who she meant.

"You know . . . our friend from Las Vegas?"

I took a deep breath, gearing myself up. "Okay, Carla, since we're being very frank here . . . I saw the picture of you and Oliva on your boat."

She lurched back and furrowed her brow. "Oliva? Who is Oliva?"

"Our mutual friend from Las Vegas."

"I do not know anyone by that name."

"I suspect she goes by a variety of names. And although I think you know that I pay *support* to her," I said, carefully choosing a word other than blackmail, "I doubt you know the reason why."

Carla cocked her head to one side. "No? How can you be so sure?"

"Because you definitely would have used it against me by now."

Carla feigned hurt. "You do not think well of me, do you, Jo?"

I couldn't help laughing. "Carla, we are so far beyond whether or not I think well of you. . . . I suspect our mutual friend told you some things about me, told you she had some hold over me. But I seriously doubt she was dumb enough to tell you what that hold is because that would take away her power. And she's a smart cookie."

Carla gave me a crooked little smile. I knew I was right.

I went on: "However, the very fact that you know this woman tells me a lot about *you*, Carla, dear. She's not the most savory character in the world, as you know. And I'm sure that many people would be very interested to know exactly where you two met and how you came to be friends. I think Max would be particularly interested in that information."

Carla leaned over and stubbed out her cigarette in the pretty, flower-pattern Sevres porcelain dish on the coffee table. She then stood up abruptly. I stood up, too. We were just about the same height and our eyes locked.

"Jo, my darling, do you not know me by now?" she said with icy sweetness. "Do you imagine that I will let you or Larry Locket or our mutual friend in Las Vegas stand in my way? As you have seen, it is much better to be my friend than my enemy. I can do so much for you as a friend . . . And so much *to* you as an enemy. Why take the chance? It's just one silly little article, Jo. Larry will find another subject for his great talent—one who is far more worthy than myself. Please tell him to leave me and my darling husband alone. We would be most grateful . . . and so will he, I promise."

* * *

I called Larry the minute I got home and started to tell him about my meeting with Carla. Sounding rushed, he cut me off.

"Jo, listen, I'm really sorry, but I can't talk to you now. I'm catching a plane for Florida and I'm late."

"Why are you going back to Florida?"

"It's a long story. I'm seeing someone there," he said.

"Larry, Carla means business. She really doesn't want you to publish this article."

"Well, that's too damn bad."

"I know. I told her, fat chance."

"Besides, I may have found the smoking gun," he said.

"What do you mean?"

"Look, I'll call you when I get back, okay? I'll have much more news then."

"Larry . . . please be careful."

"Oh, don't worry," he said. "I've been threatened by the best of them. And I'm still here."

He hung up.

For the next few days, I thought a lot about my meeting with Carla. True, she had me a little worried. However, it pleased me to think that I had her a little worried, as well. Carla was obviously very concerned about her reputation and particularly about what Max Vermilion thought of her. Once again, I toyed seriously with the idea of getting in touch with Oliva to find out exactly how she and Carla knew each other. But each time I sat down to compose the note I would send to her, I came to my senses when I thought it through.

If Larry had noticed the striking resemblance between Oliva and the late Countess de Passy, then others would surely notice it, too. While it wouldn't mean much to most people except as something of passing interest, it would mean a great deal to one person, if he ever saw her, that dogged and doglike Detective Shreve. I still feared Shreve for he'd figured out exactly what I'd done, and told me so at the time. But he also admitted he couldn't prove it. However, I knew that if he ever laid eyes on Oliva and then discovered she and I had known each other around the time of the countess's death, well . . . that wouldn't be good for me—to say the least. But that's another story.

For the moment, at least, I naïvely imagined myself to have somewhat of the upper hand with Carla. That was shortly to change.

Thirty-two

WHEN I DIDN'T HEAR FROM LARRY FOR A FEW days, I got worried. I left lots of messages on his answering machine and cell phone. He finally called to apologize for his silence and say that he was "doing fine, up to my ears, hot on a great lead." I told him a little more about my conversation with Carla Cole, but he didn't seem too concerned.

"Jo, if I have what I think I have, all I can say is she better run for cover."

He told me he'd be home in a few days with some "fascinating stuff." We set a date for lunch at his house.

The evening before I was to meet Larry, I was sitting in the library, just finishing up some correspondence when Cyril came in.

"This just arrived for you, madam," he said, handing me a manila envelope.

"At this hour?" I said. It was nearly ten o'clock.

I thanked Cyril and told him he could go home. Then I turned my attention to the package. Taped to the outside was a small ecru envelope with my name, Jo Slater, written in a scrawly hand on the back. The initials, EV, were written on the bottom righthand corner. EV stood for *"en ville"*—"in town," which was the European equivalent of "by hand." It was a bit pretentious, given that we were not in Europe, and I suspected that the package was from Carla.

I detached the small, white envelope and opened it. Inside was one of Carla's note cards with her gold initials monogrammed at the top. Now the intertwined letters looked to me like Max's coronet. Written in the same scrawly script was the following message,

> *Cara Jo,*
> *I promised you that one day I would give you a present you would not be able to refuse. Here it is.*
> *Carla*

I stared at the manila envelope for a few seconds, wary of its contents. I felt curiously vulnerable sitting there alone in my library at this hour when it was dark outside and the city was relatively quiet. I got up from my chair, went over to the desk, and removed the carved ebony-handled letter opener from its cradle. Inserting the sharp, shiny blade into the corner seam of the manila envelope, I ripped it open in one stroke. Inside was a two-page clipping from a Las Vegas newspaper dated two days earlier. At the top was the headline, *"Mystery Life, Violent Death,"* and a subheading, which read, *"Woman's Secrets May Stay Hidden."* The article began,

> *The woman known to her neighbors as Ginger Brown remains as much a mystery in death as she*

did in life. Brown was stabbed to death in her apartment, where she lay undiscovered for at least two days. Her body remains in the Las Vegas morgue unclaimed, and officially unidentified. Police described the killing as "particularly gruesome."

Brown's murder has sent the chill of fear through the quiet residential community where she lived. According to an officer at the scene, there was evidence of a struggle, but robbery did not appear to be the motive. The perpetrator has not been apprehended and there are few leads.

Neighbors admit to knowing very little about the woman who lived in apartment 7B. They described her as "very secretive and not very friendly." Police discovered that Brown had several credit cards and other forms of identification in different names among her belongings, and they believe she may have been a bunko artist, although she apparently had no police record. Police also found a C.V. among her possessions, but Ms. Brown wasn't what she claimed to be. On the résumé, Brown claimed to have two language degrees from Ohio State University, but the school has never heard of her. She claimed to have worked as an actress in movies, but the Screen Actors Guild did not list her as a member. She also claimed to have worked as a dealer in one of the major casinos, but no casino in Las Vegas had a record of her and her fingerprints are not on file. . . .

The article went on to say how much of the dead woman's life was simply fabricated or unknown. Her neighbors said she traveled a lot and was away for long periods of time, but never let on where she went. The police found a bank account in which she had over a quarter of a million dollars.

"We'd sure as heck like to know where she got all this money," the detective in charge of the case told reporters, "but her deposits were all made in cash."

I don't know whether it was denseness, fear, or fatigue that made me unable to see why Carla had sent this clipping to me as a "present." It was only when I turned to the second page of the story that all suddenly became clear. There were two pictures: one was of the apartment complex where the dead woman lived and the other, a snapshot of the victim herself, which had apparently been stapled to her phony résumé. The photograph was of a prim woman wearing a corporate smile and pearls. The instant I saw it, I felt a pluck of terror. Ginger Brown was Oliva—my blackmailer.

I was off the hook. Carla had indeed given me the one present I couldn't refuse: a death.

I arrived at Larry's at noon the next day. Mrs. Barnes, his old housekeeper, answered the door in a blue uniform with white collar and cuffs. Like the Association itself, Mrs. Barnes was a throwback to another era. A stout woman with tightly curled white hair, a constant frown, and a determined manner, she spoke with a brogue and bristled with an air of disapproval. She was also somewhat deaf, or at least "deaf when it suits her," as Larry said.

"Hello, Mrs. Barnes," I said as the older woman stepped aside to let me in.

"Mr. Locket's expecting you. He's upstairs." Upstairs

meant the office. "You know the way. I'm just making lunch," she said, retreating to the kitchen.

I walked upstairs to the office, where Larry, pipe in hand, dressed in corduroy pants and a tweed jacket, was standing hunched over his desk. The day was overcast. I glanced out at the garden where the thin vines of a climbing plant looked like a crazy spiderweb outside the multipaned window.

"Hi, there," I said, trying not to show my apprehension.

I had the manila envelope with the newspaper clipping inside tucked into my purse. I was still debating whether or not to tell Larry about it. He was concentrating hard on something on his desk.

"Come take a look at this, Jo," he said without turning around.

I peered over his shoulder. There were two fairly large sheets of paper spread out on his desk, one above the other. They each had fold marks on them. They looked like blueprints.

"What are they?" I asked him.

"Naval architectural plans," he said reflectively.

"Where did you get them?"

"That's why I went to Florida. Jeffrey Martin's sister called me. Have a look at this," he said, handing me a black ring-binder notebook.

I opened the notebook, which was filled with plastic sheets encasing more folded schematics of the boat like the two spread out in front of Larry.

"That notebook contains all the specs of *The Lady C* from Feadship," he said. I knew from my various travels that Feadship was the greatest yacht builder in the world.

"So *The Lady C* was a Feadship. Figures."

"Nothing but the best for the Coles. All Feadship yachts keep a notebook like that on board, filled with the specs of the boat. Feadship headquarters keep a duplicate so the captain can confer with them if there's something the engineer can't fix. That notebook was in Jeff Martin's safety-deposit box in a package addressed to me."

"To *you*?"

"Yup. He obviously intended to give it to me before he died. His sister just got the box open and found it. And she called me immediately."

"Those look identical," I said, examining the two sheets of paper he was studying.

"They do, don't they? Well, they're not. The top one here is from that notebook. This bottom one, though," he said, tapping the paper with the mouthpiece of his unlit pipe, "was in an envelope taped to the inside cover. I've literally spent hours trying to figure out what this one spec was doing in that envelope, particularly when there's this duplicate here from the book . . . And I think I've just discovered the reason. Look here, Jo. . ."

Larry traced an area on the top blueprint with the mouthpiece of his pipe. Then he traced the corresponding area on the bottom blueprint. "These are obviously the same section. But you see how they differ ever so slightly? The bottom one seems to have an extra passage right there," he said, gliding the stem of his pipe back and forth over the spot. "It's very difficult to see at first."

"I see it. There's like a little tiny alcove there."

"Or a hidden room, perhaps?" Larry said, casting a sly glance.

"So what do you make of it?"

Larry straightened up and stretched his arms in the air. He looked exhausted.

"Let's sit down a minute, shall we?"

We sat around the coffee table. Larry took off his glasses and rubbed the bridge of his nose. He lit his pipe and sat back in the chair, puffing on it in spurts as he spoke.

"When I was down in Barbados, I interviewed the captain of the Coast Guard. He told me that he and his officers searched that yacht from top to bottom the minute they got on board. They found nothing, of course. Being my usual suspicious and macabre self, I asked him if there was a way to dispose of a body so close to land. He said the best way would be to hide it, then smuggle it out with the trash. Like all megayachts, *The Lady C* has an enormous amount of storage space. The captain assured me they went through all the garbage and all the storerooms with a fine-tooth comb. They didn't find anything. Obviously. See now, that argues for Carla's case—that Russell is having one of his episodes."

"I know what you're thinking, Larry."

He nodded slightly. "You're thinking the same thing: if Carla had a place to hide the body so that when the Coast Guard searched the ship, they wouldn't find it, then. . ."

"Then she could get away with murder."

"Precisely," Larry said, flicking his eyes onto mine. "All she'd have to do would be to hide the body until they could sail out to sea where she could dump it. It's a brilliant plan. She kills him. Hides him. Dumps him. Then she uses his past history to invent this fiction about how he's suffering from an episode of Dissociative Fugue Disorder, but that he's bound to turn up again. This gives her time to rearrange all the money, knowing damn well, of course, that Russell is never coming back. But she also knows that no one can prove that and that he'll never be found."

"But why go to the trouble of hiding the body? Why not just take the boat out to sea, conk him over the head, and throw him overboard in the first place?"

"Because she's got to be near land for her story to hold up. There's got to be a really plausible explanation for why he's gone. Anyway, it's risky dumping him at sea. The body might be found too quickly for her to get her hands on the money. You can't always depend on the sharks, you know."

"Except in Manhattan, where they never let you down," I said.

Larry chuckled. "Indeed . . . no, Carla and whoever helped her—and she certainly had to have help—they needed a way to dispose of Russell's body so it wouldn't be found and it would look like he'd just gone off on one of his episodes. I think Jeff Martin figured out exactly what she'd done. That's probably why he was killed."

"So his death definitely wasn't an accident."

"Now that I see this? No. I definitely think he was murdered. It's a brilliant plan, Jo. My hat's off to her."

"So let me get this straight: Carla has Russell's powers of attorney, but she knows she needs time to use them."

"Right. She can't afford to have him turn up dead because according to the will, she inherits next to nothing. So she has to convince the world that Russell's just having one of his episodes. And now it doesn't matter if he's dead or alive."

"What do you mean?"

"She's got control of the money," Larry said.

We sat in silence for a time, contemplating this diabolical plan.

"How did Martin get a hold of this other plan?" I asked, after a time.

"I have no idea. Maybe it was on the boat. But it obviously wasn't among the official Feadship specs. . . . The only thing I can think of is that's it's a plan from the interior designer."

"Do we know who the interior designer is?"

"Her name was Melody Hayes."

"*Was*?"

"She's dead."

"Jesus, Larry! Not killed?"

"No, cancer. Six months ago. *The Lady C* was designed by Peter de Hoch, a very famous naval architect. She was his last commission, in fact. He died about four years ago, well into his eighties. Melody Hayes designed the interior for three of his yachts—*The Lady C* being one."

"Well, that's just great. So we can't talk to either of the designers, right?"

"Right. It's amazing, isn't it? In my view, you can chalk all this up to one of three things: a coincidence, a curse, or Carla. Take your pick," he said.

I rolled my eyes. "I think they're all the same, at this point."

"Yes, but we do have this blueprint," Larry said. Folding it up, he inserted it into his breast pocket. "And I'm not letting it out of my sight," he said, tapping his chest twice. "Come on. Let's go have a bite to eat, Jo. I'm starving."

Thirty-three

LARRY LED THE WAY DOWNSTAIRS TO THE DINing room, where Mrs. Barnes had set up a buffet lunch for us on the sideboard. I helped myself to some of the cold cuts and salad, but I had no appetite. We sat down catty-corner to each other at the ancient, wooden refectory table that Larry had salvaged from an abandoned monastery in Umbria.

Unfurling a large, linen napkin and placing it fastidiously on his lap, Larry dug into his food with gusto.

"Here's the thing, Jo. I'm beginning to see that that yacht has a personality, too—one that is just as circuitous and complicated as that of its former owners. Of course, I have no idea if we could ever actually *prove* anything, but given this set of conflicting plans, I'd certainly like to get a firsthand look at that boat."

I was distracted, I could hardly concentrate on what he was saying.

He looked up at me with one of his leprechaun smiles. "We could, you know."

"How?"

"Carla sold it to a dot-commer from Virginia who charters it out. I have the name of the charter company he uses. The only thing we need is money. It costs a hundred and fifty thousand dollars a week, not counting fuel, food, and tips, and it's available in one month's time. . . . I also found out that the Coles' old captain is in charge of the yacht again. Mike Rankin, he's called. It'll be very interesting to talk to him about his successor. Putting Jasper Jenks in charge was like asking a buggy driver to ride a racehorse. And the thing is, the Coles always did extensive background checks on their staff. They were very careful about who they hired and they always hired the best people. Given their resources, they could have had their pick of great captains. So why did they hire this inexperienced young man . . . ? Unless Carla was counting on a level of incompetency . . . or an accomplice." Larry raised his eyebrows and looked at me. "What's wrong, Jo? You're not eating."

I paused. "Larry . . . do you really have to write this article?"

He guffawed, holding his knife and fork in the air mid-bite. "What do you *mean*?!"

"I mean, do you really have to write this article?" I said more slowly. "Is it something that you absolutely have to do?"

He furrowed his brow. "Well, I won't go to jail if I don't. But the thought just doesn't occur to me. I've been working on it for months. This is an absolutely fascinating case, I mean, with this new evidence . . ." His voice trailed off.

"But what if . . . what if I asked you not to?"

He put his knife and fork on the plate and propped his

elbows up on the table, folding his hands. He stared at me very hard. "Well, I'd certainly want to know why."

I didn't answer him for a few seconds while I collected my thoughts.

"You once told me that if I asked you not to write it, you wouldn't."

"That's not precisely what I said. What I said was that if in the course of my travels, I uncovered something that would be detrimental to our friendship, I wouldn't write the article."

"I know. You said that good stories were a dime a dozen, but real friends were rare. So I'm asking you, as a real friend, not to write it."

Larry lowered his eyes and thought for moment. Then he looked back up at me. "I can't do that now, Jo. I'm too far into it. And I haven't discovered anything that could possibly hurt you. Whereas I really do think that Carla is a menace. And she must be stopped."

I swallowed hard.

"Larry, you don't understand how dangerous she really is."

"Oh, but I do. I'm just beginning to get the full picture."

I shook my head. "No, you aren't. You just have no idea. . . . Please, I beg of you, don't pursue this."

He reached across the table and took my hand with a look of great concern on his face. "Something's happened, Jo. What is it? Tell me."

I stared at his hand for a long time. This was the moment of truth. If ever I were going to confess to another living soul about the sordid secret of my past, it was now.

Larry looked at me quizzically. "What's the matter, Jo? Please tell me."

"Larry," I began softly, "how long have we been friends?"

"Several lifetimes," he said without hesitation.

I swallowed hard. "What if I were to tell you something that would be difficult for you to know . . . ?"

"Go on."

I took a deep breath, resolved now to confide in him. "Something that no one else in the world knows . . . ? Something that if it ever got out, I'd be chopped foie gras . . . ." I said with a weak smile.

"If you mean, will I keep my mouth shut? I think you know the answer to that. As far as my friends are concerned, I'm a tomb."

"But the burden of *knowing*, Larry. The burden of *knowing* . . ."

"I know a lot of things, honey. Believe me. Things I'll take with me to my grave. But you mustn't tell me anything you'll regret my knowing. Our friendship is too important to me for that."

I burst out laughing.

"What's so funny?" he said, obviously disconcerted.

"The dreaded Countess de Passy said almost those exact same words to me once. We were walking on the beach in Southampton and I was about to tell her the real story of how Lucius and I met—something I'd never told another living soul up until that point. I think the real reason I wound up telling her was because she said that she didn't want to know anything that would damage our friendship in any way. I believed her. Of course, what I didn't know at the time was that she knew the whole story already because my son-of-a-bitch husband had told her all about it. And then, of course, she betrayed me."

"Well, I always think that time is the real measure of a friendship and you've known me long enough and well enough to know that I won't do that, Jo. I'm very fond of you, as you well know. I could never break any confidence of yours."

"Not even if it would mean getting one of the biggest stories of your career?"

Larry laughed. "My career's had enough big stories. No story is worth sacrificing our friendship, Jo."

With that, he got up and closed the door so Mrs. Barnes wouldn't overhear us. He sat down again and leveled me with one of his intense gazes.

"Before you say anything, though, let me ask you something. Would this thing you are about to tell me have anything to do with the countess and her will and the way she died?"

No fool, Larry.

"It might."

"I'm sure you're aware then of the rumor that was going around at the time."

I raised my eyebrows. "Which one?"

"That you pushed her off that balcony when you found out she'd left you back the fortune she stole from you. It was just a rumor, mind you."

"Did you believe it?" I asked him.

The air was electric with tension. Larry, who hadn't taken his eyes off me, was silent for a long moment. Finally he said, "I believed that the Jo Slater I knew then would not have surrendered to her apparent fate without a damn good fight."

After a long silence I said, "But did you believe me capable of premeditated murder?"

"You mean hands-on premeditated murder? Murder

that you commit yourself, not that you hire someone to commit for you?"

"Yes," I said. "Hands-on premeditated murder. . . . Larry, may we speak hypothetically?"

"Isn't that what we've been doing?" he said with a wink in his voice.

"Of course." I smiled. "Hypothetically, it was a little more complicated than that."

"What do you mean?"

"Hypothetically, I didn't find out that the countess had left everything to me in her will. Monique de Passy was not a generous soul. . . . When my husband died and left her everything that should have been mine after twenty years of marriage, I felt desolate and betrayed. But I tried to get on with my life, Larry. I really did. Monique thwarted me every step of the way. To make a long story short, I became obsessed with getting even with her. Then one day I walked into a bar and saw a woman who I could have sworn was the countess. She was her twin. And it was then that I got the idea of how to get my revenge. Monique de Passy didn't write that will. *I* did. I wrote a phony will for the countess in which she left everything to me—the whole fortune that should have been mine in the first place. Then I hired this dead ringer I'd seen in the bar to impersonate her, go to a reputable lawyer's office, and get that forged will signed."

Larry cocked his head to one side, looking puzzled. "But the signature," he said immediately. "They can always detect a forgery."

"Well, it just so happens that in New York State, if a person is incapacitated because of a physical injury, they can direct a lawyer to sign their will for them in the presence of witnesses. I told Monique's double to go in there with an injured hand and say that she couldn't sign the will herself. One of the lawyers signed it for her so the signature could never be questioned. Of course, in order for a will to be meaningful, the testator eventually has to die."

Larry's face contorted into an odd cross between admiration and incredulity. He continued to stare at me as the realization of what necessarily had to follow this deception deepened and settled in his mind.

"And she did die," he said. "As I recall, she committed suicide by jumping off her balcony. It was in the papers. I believe you were the last person to see her alive."

"That's right."

There was a long silence while Larry just looked at me.

"*Did* you push her, Jo?" Larry said at last.

I hung my head. "It all happened so fast."

"What exactly did happen?"

"You remember my beautiful Marie Antoinette necklace?"

"Of course. Your trademark."

"Yes, well, I had to sell it to her because I needed the money. But I just couldn't bear for her to have it. I picked it up and threw it over the balcony. She lunged for it and she fell. I didn't push her. I swear. It was her own greed that propelled her over the side. But I confess I was happy to see her fall."

I don't think Larry quite believed my account of the events. He had the vaguely horrified yet captivated gaze of someone whose path has just been crossed by a lustrous insect.

"Do you think I'm evil?" I said at last.

"Evil? No. Certainly not," he said firmly. "Evil, like

genius, is a much overused word, a word that must be reserved for the very, very few. If you say Mozart was a genius, for example, you can't really say too many others are. And if you say that Hitler was evil, that, too, raises the bar. . . . The man who murdered my wife—now *there* was an evil person. He killed purely for his own pleasure and for no other reason. He thoroughly enjoyed inflicting excruciating pain on her and watching her die inch by inch over the course of days." As he spoke, a little film of perspiration sprouted on his brow. "If I ever told you what he did to her and the length of time he took to do it, you'd understand what evil really is."

I reached out my hand to him. "Larry, I'm so sorry . . ."

"No, no . . . I'm sorry," he said, wiping his moist eyes with his napkin. "I don't know why, but it's still so fresh and painful."

I said nothing, waiting for him to recover. Finally, he cleared his throat and said, "Anyway, I reserve the evil category for those who relish and revel in the suffering of others. That's not you, Jo."

"Maybe not. But you could say that Carla Cole and I aren't really all that different. I mean, if she has, in fact, killed Russell for the money, how is that different from me? She even said that to me—that we were 'sisters under the skin.' That really upset me."

Larry leaned forward, focusing in on me again. "But *did* you want her dead just for the money, Jo?"

"*No!*" I slammed my hand on the table. "Monique took so much more from me than money! My God, Larry, she took my husband, my identity, my *life*. She effectively *murdered* me, only I was still alive and around to watch her *become* me. This was identity theft on a grand scale. I tried to let it go, but I couldn't. She became an obsession. I just couldn't stand by and let her *be me*. It was as simple as that. I had to get rid of her. I *had* to. It seemed so . . . so, I don't know, so . . . *necessary* at the time."

"And now? Does it still seem so necessary?" Larry asked.

Another silence engulfed us as I let the anxiety of talking about Monique drain out of me.

"Well, it's done," I said at last. "Here, look at this." I pulled the newspaper clipping out of my purse and handed it to him.

He gripped his tortoiseshell glasses and read the story carefully. He raised his eyebrows the minute he saw her picture.

"This is the woman with Carla on the boat," he said, looking at me.

"She's the woman I hired to impersonate the countess and sign the fake will. She was blackmailing me and Carla knew it." I paused to take a sip of water. My throat was dry. "Carla told me that one day she'd give me a present I couldn't refuse. Well, this is it. She had that woman killed."

"What? Just as a favor to you? Are you kidding?"

"No, no. Listen to me. Last week, Carla called me up and invited me for tea."

"And you *went*? After what she did to you?" he interjected.

"I was curious."

"You should have been a reporter, Jo," he said with a wry smile.

"Anyway, Carla told me she was worried about your article. She asked me to ask you if you'd quit writing it."

"*Really*? That's fascinating. She must know I'm getting close to something."

"Maybe, but she claims the reason is that she doesn't want her privacy invaded. She's also worried about what Max Vermilion is going to think of her when it comes out. Naturally, I told her I couldn't help her, that there was no way I was going to persuade you not to write it. Then she threatened me again, insinuating she knew I was being blackmailed. But this time I called her bluff. I told her that I doubted she knew the *reason* I was being blackmailed or she certainly would have used it by now. And then I turned the tables on her."

"How?"

"Well, I said my blackmailer was a pretty unsavory character and maybe Max would be interested in how *she* happened to know such a creature. I think that worried her a bit. Anyway, I naïvely imagined that I'd gotten the upper hand for a change. Then that clipping arrived."

"When?"

"Last night. I couldn't believe it when I saw it. But, Larry, she didn't get rid of that woman for me or even for herself—although I bet they had *some* relationship! She got rid of her to show me what she's capable of. She'll have you killed, too, Larry. She really will. She won't let you publish that article. I know that you're pretty fearless, but I don't want to lose you, if you don't mind. So will you *please* reconsider, Larry? *Please*? For me?"

He shook his head and was silent for a long time. Finally he spoke: "Jo, you realize that now, more than ever, I can't back off."

"But you see what she's capable of!" I said, exasperated.

"That's exactly why I have to get to the bottom of

this—precisely because she is capable of such horror. I have to expose her if I can. This is what I *do*, Jo. This is my life. After Helena died, I thought of becoming a monk. I also thought of killing myself. But as you can see, I chose the more infernal path, writing. I made a silent promise to Helena that I wasn't going to let someone get away with murder just because they have a lot of money. And I'm not going to break that promise, not now . . . I intend to rent that boat even if I have to go into hock to do it. I'm going to find that hidden room and see what's in it. Carla knows I'm onto something and I want to find out what that something is."

I admired his courage.

"Okay," I said after thinking it over. "If I can't dissuade you, then I guess I'll just have to help you. I have money. You arrange the trip and I'll pay for it."

Larry called the charter company and booked *The Lady C* for a two-week cruise in July, only three weeks away. Though summer isn't exactly the peak season for the Caribbean, Larry felt it was important to go back as soon as possible to exactly the same spot where Russell Cole had disappeared. He told me he spoke to Captain Rankin and arranged for the yacht to meet us in Bridgetown in Barbados. I set about preparing for the trip.

Carla phoned me two days later.

"Did you get my little present, Jo, darling? Isn't it nice that there is no need for you to buy any more diamonds, except for those you want to wear? Are you not happy about that? And I want you to know that there is no need for you to write me a thank-you note."

That low, purry voice of hers gave me the creeps. I had no idea how to respond.

"What do you want, Carla?"

"I understand that dear Larry is back from Florida, and I was wondering if you had a chance to speak with him about the article. And if so, what did he say?"

I didn't like it one bit that she knew where Larry had been. She was obviously having him followed. I wondered how much more she knew. Did she know about the specs, or about my having rented *The Lady C?*

"Call him yourself, Carla," I said and hung up.

I immediately phoned Larry.

"She knows you went to Florida," I told him.

He didn't seem too concerned. "Oh, I'm sure she's having me tailed. So what? I've been tailed before."

"But what if she knows about the blueprints? She'll try to get them, won't she?"

"They're well hidden. Anyway, they don't prove anything."

"What if she finds out we rented the boat?"

"Jo, I told you. This just comes with the territory. I'm pretty sure that Carla's swept her path clean. In thinking about it, I doubt she would have left any incriminating evidence on that boat. But you never know. And I just have a hunch about that room. Anyway, I want to see it. I've spoken to Captain Rankin at length. I told you, he was the Coles' old captain—the one they fired to hire Jenks."

"Larry, is there a chance that Russell's still alive? I mean, I know she's evil and she had that woman killed, but do you think Russell really *could* be having one of his episodes, and she just took advantage of that?"

"It's possible, I suppose. But then you have to wonder why she's going to such great lengths to shut me up."

"Have you written a lot more of your article?"

"A good chunk, yes. I haven't shown anything to my editor yet. I've shown more to you. I just have a hunch about that boat. Anyway, don't worry so much. We'll have fun, Jo. I like this Rankin fella. I trust him. I really do. I think he's—" He stopped, midsentence. "Wait a sec, there's my other line."

Larry put me on hold and came back seconds later. "Speak of the devil . . ." he said.

"Carla?" I asked incredulously.

"You got it. Call you back."

I waited nervously by the phone. Five minutes later, Larry called me back.

"Jo?" he said, sounding shaken.

"What the hell did she want . . . ?" He didn't say anything. "Larry, what's wrong?"

I heard him take a deep breath to collect himself. "She told me I should stop trying to avenge my wife's death by attacking innocent people."

"She's so full of shit." I was angry.

"She also said, 'Remember how Helena died.' She said her name, Jo. She must have researched the case."

Although I didn't know the particulars of his wife's death, I understood from Larry and others it had been a particularly gruesome murder.

"*Oh my God* . . . Larry, will you please, *please* be careful?"

"Don't worry, I will. But I wanted to tell you this before we were so rudely interrupted. I think Rankin's on our side. He's discreet, but I believe he shares my concerns about Our Miss Carla." He paused for a moment, then said, "Jo, I don't say this lightly. She is one dangerous lady."

Over the next few days, Larry and I spoke on the phone several times, finalizing the details of our trip. Larry never alluded to the dark secret I had confided in him, but I knew he had to have thought about it. How could he not? I thought about it all the time.

Thirty-four

ON JUNE 19TH, AT A LITTLE BEFORE FIVE o'clock in the morning, my phone rang, waking me out of a deep sleep. It was Betty calling from California. Her voice was somber and urgent.

"Jo, I'm so sorry to wake you up, but we just got back from a party and turned on the TV." She paused. "Have you heard about Larry Locket?"

"No, what?" I was still drowsy.

"Oh God, Jo . . . he's dead."

I shot up from the pillows. "*What?!*" Panic surged through me. "*Oh my God!*"

"Turn on your television. It's on CNN right now."

I fumbled for the remote on the night table and flicked on the set. The TV screen bloomed in the dark room. My hands were shaking so hard I could hardly find the station. Finally, I tuned in to CNN, where a sunny blonde morning anchor was standing in front of Larry's house in The Association, talking into a mike. There were policemen, firemen, and paramedics milling around in back of her. Dark smoke billowed from the house. I forgot that Betty was on the phone as I listened to a recap of the crime.

". . . And if you're just joining us, some very sad news today. Lawrence Locket, the world-famous crime writer, himself became a victim in the early hours of this morning in his own home . . . I'm here in front of Locket's townhouse in The Association, one of the most secluded and safe areas of New York City. After talking to neighbors, police are speculating that sometime during the night, Mr. Locket returned home and surprised a robber who had broken into his house. The robbery turned violent and Mr. Locket was apparently bludgeoned to death . . ."

A picture of Larry flashed on the screen.

". . . The robber then set fire to the house and fled. This very exclusive community in which Lawrence Locket lived has never experienced a violent crime in its hundred-and-forty-year history. Now its most famous resident is dead and police say they have no leads—although they concede that because of the nature of his work, Mr. Locket had a lot of enemies. Whether this was planned or just a haphazard break-in that ended in violence and arson is yet to be determined. For now, though, Lawrence Locket, the man who was always digging up crimes in unexpected places, has himself been murdered in a most unlikely place—his own backyard. Again, Lawrence Locket, dead at the age of sixty-seven, the victim of an apparent robbery arson gone bad. . . . This is Dawn Dressler, CNN. . . ."

They switched over to the main morning anchor, who said there would be "more on the amazing life of Lawrence Locket later on in the show . . ."

I turned off the TV and picked up the telephone. "Betty? Are you still there?" I said weakly.

"I'm here, Jo . . . poor Larry. It's just *unbelievable*. You must be in shock . . . Jo? You okay?"

"Let me call you back."

I felt faint. I hung up and headed toward the bathroom. I felt like I was walking through cobwebs. I turned on the bathroom light and caught sight of myself in the mirror. A haggard face, drained of all color, stared back at me.

My dear friend was dead.

Murdered.

And I knew who did it. I knew, too, that no one would ever believe me. Not in six billion years.

I splashed cold water on my face and neck. A fearful sadness overwhelmed me. I felt an immense emptiness. I burst into tears.

For the rest of the day I sat glued to the television set for any new scraps of information. I watched the biography of Larry Locket's life, which played over and over again on all the stations. I knew most of it already. Larry was born in a suburb of Atlanta. His parents owned a mom-and-pop insurance company and in subsequent interviews, Larry said it was the insurance business that gave him his "first taste of human larceny," and sparked his interest in crime reporting. He graduated from a local college and the Columbia School of Journalism and then went to work as a cub reporter, covering the courts for the *New York Times*. In New York he met and married his only wife, Helena Gervasi, a paralegal at one of New York's top law firms. The black-and-white photograph of young Larry and Helena at their wedding was poignant, particularly if you knew what happened to Helena a scant three years after it was taken.

Helena disappeared one afternoon. Ten days later, a partially burned and decomposed body was found by a hiker on a muddy trail in the Pine Barrens in south central New Jersey. Seasoned officers at the scene called it "one of the most sadistic murders" any of them had ever witnessed. The body was soon identified as that of Helena Gervasi Locket. After ten months of dogged detective work, her alleged killer was identified. A circumstantial case was brought against Grant Mortenson, a rich client of the law firm for which Helena Locket had worked. Mortenson was an attractive, clean-cut, thirty-seven-year-old man who had apparently developed an obsessive crush on Helena Locket and stalked her for a number of months. There was innovative tire-tread analysis that linked his Jeep to tire marks at the scene.

However, at his trial, a high-priced legal team made it appear as though their relationship had been consensual. Mortenson took the stand in his own defense. He told the jury how much he had cared for Helena and how she had cared for him. He said she was even thinking of getting a divorce and that her death had "shattered" him. His lawyers produced the foremost expert in tire-tread marks to debunk the prosecution's contention that Mortenson's Jeep had been at the scene of the crime.

Mortenson's legal team successfully smeared Helena Locket's name and refuted key evidence. And because Mortenson himself was rich and good-looking, and because the presiding judge in the case seemed more interested in impressing the media than in the trial itself, Mortenson was, incredibly, acquitted. Several of the jurors interviewed after the verdict said Mortenson had made a "credible" witness, and that given the circumstances and testimony of the defense's experts, there were grounds for "reasonable doubt."

Helena's death and her killer's acquittal was the turning point of Larry's life. Although Larry had alluded to it many times during the course of our friendship, I never fully understood just how gruesome or heartbreaking it had been. Larry had told me he'd thought about hiring someone to kill Mortenson, and now I understood why. The biography aired an old interview he gave right after the trial where he had predicted that Mortenson's pathology was so deep and furious that he would surely kill again. A scant ten months later, Larry's grim prediction came true. Mortenson killed another woman, and this time there was hard evidence linking him to the crime. The disturbing thing about this murder was that it gave a further glimpse into the horrors and the suffering that Helena Locket must have endured. Larry attended his trial and wrote about it for *Vanitas* magazine. Mortenson was convicted and he received a life sentence without the possibility of parole.

The biography then went on to show the highlights of Larry's amazing career. There was footage of him at other high-profile trials he covered and on the sets of the movies that were based on his best-selling books. He had been a great advocate for victims' rights and they showed a poignant interview with him where he said in his laid-back southern drawl, "It's an obscenity when people get away with murder just because they have money. Justice may be blind, but she's not deaf and dumb. The law must not be for sale."

The final frames of the biography concentrated on a studio portrait of Larry, which had been used on the back cover of his latest book. There he was, frozen in time, dapperly dressed, glasses perched on the tip of his nose, pipe in hand, looking as leprechaunish as ever. His own voice, taken from a radio interview nine months earlier, was broadcast over the image: "Look, quite frankly, there are some blows in life from which you don't recover. You just have to learn to live with them and, hopefully, turn your own sorrow into something positive. I hope I've helped a few people along the way."

As his name and the dates of his life appeared in black script under the photograph, I sat there sobbing.

For the next few days, the media was saturated with stories about Larry Locket's brutal murder and his extraordinary life. The police continued to report that there were no leads. As Larry had no living relatives, Betty and I took it upon ourselves to organize a memorial service for him. The morning of the service, I opened up the *New York Times* and read the following headline on the bottom of the front page: "*Cole Collection Donated to the Municipal Museum.*"

The article began:

> *Justin Howard, chairman of the Municipal Museum, announced today that Carla Cole, the wife of missing billionaire Russell Cole, has donated the couple's famous collection of Impressionist and Post Impressionist paintings to the museum, along with a landmark pledge of one hundred million dollars, which will be used to build a wing to house the art. The collection, along with the grant to build the wing, is estimated to be worth well over one billion*

*dollars and therefore constitutes the largest single
donation in the history of the Municipal Museum,
and indeed the largest ever given to any museum in
this country.*

*Edmond Norbeau, director of the Municipal Mu-
seum, said of the gift, "We are profoundly grateful
to Mrs. Cole for her breathtaking generosity. The
Cole collection and its special wing will be a stunning jewel in the Municipal Museum's crown."*

The story went on to say how Carla Cole was becoming
"a new force to reckon with, both socially and economi-
cally." It referred to her as a "philanthropic juggernaut"
and a "financial wheeler-dealer," heralding the increasing
numbers of women who are important benefactors in this
country. Tagged onto the very end of the article was the
information that Courtney Cole was petitioning the court
to have her father declared legally dead and that she was
suing her stepmother for "fiduciary malfeasance."

Betty called me to discuss the article, and, as usual, cut
right to the chase: "Courtney Cole can petition and sue all
she wants," Betty said, "but there's no body. So for all we
know, Russell Cole could be painting nudes in Tahiti."

I detected a note of sympathy in Betty's voice.

"Don't tell me you're on *Carla's* side now?" I said,
horrified.

"Christ, don't say *that!* It's just that Russell's had
such a goofy history. I mean who the hell knows? All I
can tell you for sure is that the woman is buying so
much art from Gil, it's ridiculous. She's going into contemporary art and you know what that means . . . A fortune! Did you know that she hates the Impressionists?
She couldn't stand Russell's taste in art. She either

wants Old Masters or contemporary. That's what Gil tells me. Isn't that amazing . . . ? By the way, what are you wearing to Larry's memorial?"

"A shroud. To match my mood."

I couldn't even tell Betty my suspicions about Carla's involvement in Larry's death. She would have thought I was crazy. Given Carla's new role in the city's fortunes, no one—not even my best friend—would believe such a woman was capable of such an act.

Thirty-five

LARRY LOCKET'S INVITATION-ONLY MEMORIAL service was held at Saint Patrick's Cathedral on a cool, bright June morning. The whole block was cordoned off. Mounted policemen clip-clopped through the milling crowd like centaurs, keeping the crowd at bay. Betty, Gil, and I walked up the front steps of the venerable old church and presented our invitations at the door. Betty's idea of mourning dress was a white pantsuit and a white cap. She looked like the Good Humor Man. When I asked her what prompted her to wear white to a funeral, she said, "It's my new summer suit. Besides, white is the color of mourning in Japan."

I didn't feel it was my place to remind her that we weren't in Japan, so I just let it go. Ushers showed us to the reserved seating section down front and handed each of us a program. We edged our way into the second row of pews.

I sat next to dear old Mrs. Barnes, Larry's house-keeper, who couldn't stop weeping. She was obviously still in shock. I patted her hand and asked her how she was doing, but she was too upset to utter a word. Unfortunately, she seemed to be the only one unable to talk. Everyone else was gabbing away. People craned their necks to say hello to each other or sat engrossed in conversation with the person next to them. It was Memorial-Service-as-Social-Occasion par excellence. The plethora of famous faces in the venerable old cathedral and the hum of excitement was vaguely reminiscent of a Broadway opening night. Taking note of the glittery, twittery crowd, Betty said, "God should play to this packed a house."

"You think they'll serve drinks?" Gil asked.

I could never tell if Gil was serious or not.

Presently, Trish Bromire joined us in our row. Reed thin, wearing large, dark sunglasses, a black suit, and a huge, black hat, Trish said a somber hello to all of us.

"How's Dick?" I asked her.

"I'm on my way to see him this afternoon."

We all knew what that meant, of course. She was on her way to Lexington, Kentucky. The "jail facilitator" had made sure her husband got into a federal medical center prison, which better addressed the needs of those who Betty called "white-collar, black-tie criminals."

Suddenly, there was a flurry of commotion toward the back of the church. I turned around to see what was going on. Walking down the aisle in a solemn procession were the mayor of New York, Justin and Regina Howard, the Norbeaus, and none other than Carla Cole! Everyone turned to ogle them. Whispers echoed through the majestic cathedral. Carla gave me a knowing little smile as she passed. I felt sick to my stomach.

The usher showed the group to the front row. Carla sat

down, flanked by the mayor and Justin Howard. They were soon joined by Miranda Somers, who was obviously covering the event for *Nous* magazine, and by Ethan Monk, both of whom turned around to greet the Watermans and myself the moment they sat down.

Ethan leaned in and whispered to me, "Isn't it a little crepe-hangy of Carla to be here? I thought she loathed Larry."

"It's absolutely diabolical," I said, angrily.

Betty looked at me askance. "Don't exaggerate, Jo. It's not as if she killed him."

"Oh, no?" I said, raising my eyebrows.

Naturally, Betty pooh-poohed the idea because it seemed so preposterous that this woman, at the pinnacle of New York society, could be a murderer. She didn't understand that I was dead serious.

While waiting for the service to begin, I studied Carla's somewhat imperious profile. Her nose sloped down slightly toward lips that seemed in a permanent pout. She looked quite stunning wearing a black suit, black hat, and a strand of cue ball size pearls at her throat. Justin Howard and the mayor were going at her from both sides, doing their level best to keep her amused. I, personally, was filled with a combination of loathing and awe. Let's face it, if there's a perfect defintion of chutzpah, it has to be showing up at the memorial service of a person you've had killed.

Of course, I couldn't say that to Betty. I couldn't say it to anyone. The one person I could have said it to was the deceased himself. Larry was the only one who would have believed me.

The service was relatively brief as Betty and I knew that Larry would have wanted it. Larry loathed pretentiousness and being bored, and he once told me there was nothing more pretentious or more boring than a long and pompous send-off, so we kept the speakers to a minimum. Though many had vied for the honor of speaking at his memorial, we chose only two people.

"Long on music, short on speeches. Leave 'em longing and not longing to leave" is how Betty phrased it. I agreed.

First up was Larry's editor, Dawson Lane, a bright, boyish-looking, unassuming man who gave a heartfelt and often hilarious account of working with Larry over the years. He mentioned the tragedy in Larry's own life and told how it had shaped his psyche and career.

"Larry lost a part of himself when his wife died," Lane said. "But he gave that part back to the world many times over through his work. . . . He was a journalistic Robin Hood, who believed the rich and powerful should not be considered above the law, that they should not be allowed to buy their way out of justice, and that they should be held even more accountable because, as Larry often said to me in that wonderful voice of his, 'they oughta know better.' "

That got a chuckle from the well-heeled audience in the church—all except Carla, who remained stoney-faced.

The second man to speak was a shadow figure in Larry's life, one Father Devlin, a Jesuit priest, who turned out to have been Larry's spiritual guide. Larry had never mentioned him, not even to me. Betty and I learned of him through Larry's will, of which Father Devlin was the executor. After minor bequests to friends including a little landscape painting to me, Larry had divided his fortune between Mrs. Barnes, his housekeeper, and a charitable foundation in his late wife's name to be directed by the old Jesuit priest.

Father Devlin was a short, frail man with wispy, white hair, cornflower blue eyes, and a kindly, wrinkled face that radiated intelligence and compassion. He had severe arthritis and had marked difficulty in walking up to the podium. Once there, however, he took command of his audience with a sprightly charm and a lilting Irish brogue.

We learned that Larry Locket's life had been far more of a spiritual quest than I or anyone ever could have imagined. As Father Devlin spoke, I thought about the day I had confessed my terrible sin to Larry, and I suddenly saw his tolerance toward me in a brand-new light.

"Larry Locket and I first met just after his beloved wife, Helena, died," Devlin said in a lilting Irish brogue. "He told me, with some humor, that he had dived headfirst into the Slough of Despond and that he was wallowing there, not at all sure whether or not he wanted to get out. So I gave him a copy of the *Spiritual Exercises of Saint Ignatius Loyola,* and that, as they say, was the beginning of a beautiful friendship—between Larry and myself and Larry and God. . . . Larry was immediately struck by the sentence, 'Love ought to be put more in deeds than in words.' So he says to me, 'Dev,' he says, 'being a writer, doesn't that put me at a bit of a disadvantage?' "

Mild laughter in the church.

"Well, disadvantage or no," the old priest continued, "Larry Locket spent the rest of his life putting his love into deeds *and* words. His words became deeds of conscience. His words were the love he gave to the world."

The mourners learned that Larry had flirted with the idea of becoming a monk. Father Devlin described how he and Larry had traveled to Italy together on a spiritual mission. I thought of the antique refectory dining table Larry told me he'd salvaged from a monastery in Umbria. Had Father Devlin been with him on that trip? I wondered.

In conclusion, the old Jesuit said, "Finally, I would like to read to you one of Larry's favorite quotes from Saint Ignatius . . ." Father Devlin fumbled for a pair of spectacles in his pocket. The congregation, already enthralled by this gentle man's demeanor, was completely silent. In fact, the silence seemed to echo in the church as he unfolded a piece of paper with his arthritic hands.

He read, " 'In those who go on from good to better, the good Angel touches such a soul sweetly, lightly and gently, like a drop of water which enters into a sponge; and the evil touches it sharply and with noise and disquiet, as when the drop of water falls on the stone.' My dear friend Larry understood that in his life, he had been touched by both angels, the good one and the evil one, and that he had conquered his desire for personal revenge by a desire to *avenge* the less fortunate through his writing. . . . It was my everlasting pleasure to know him. It will be my everlasting penance to mourn him. God bless you, Larry, my dear brother. And Godspeed."

As the old man made a slow and obviously painful descent from the podium, there was only one dry eye in the house, Carla's.

The crowd filed out of the church to the bright strains of a Bach organ fugue. I found myself walking alongside Dawson Lane, whom I'd met several times over the years, usually at Larry's house.

"Dawson, I have to ask you, did Larry show you any of his article on Russell Cole?"

Dawson's soft brown eyes were swollen from crying.

He shook his head sadly. "No, Jo. I wish he had. Larry was secretive about his work. He never showed me anything until he had a solid first draft. Oh, we talked about it and I know he was making a great deal of progress. In fact, he said that you two were going to do some investigatory thing. He wasn't specific. But now it's all been destroyed in the fire. It's just terrible, Jo. Terrible."

In the entryway, I stopped to talk with several people I knew. Gil Waterman was chatting up some famous California collector in one corner. Betty pointed to her husband and paraphrased *The Book of Common Prayer*, saying, "Look at Gil. . . . In the midst of life, we are not in death, but we are in a deal."

As I was getting ready to leave the church, I felt a tap on my shoulder. I turned around. A heavily veiled woman said, "Well, Jo, our knight in shining armor is gone."

The raspy voice was unmistakable. It was Lulu Cole.

Lulu had never forgiven me for the infamous party at my house where she had disgraced herself in front of Max. However, on this sad occasion, she was obviously willing to let bygones be bygones.

"Lulu . . . how are you?"

She lifted her veil. Her eyes were rat red from crying. I felt sorry for her.

"She's won, Jo. She's won it all. I heard what happened to you at the Muni. And I just wanted to say how sorry I am. I'm just so sick about Larry. He was really our last hope to expose this . . . this *creature*." She paused. "Anyway, I know she's here, and certainly I don't want to run into her again. But I just wanted to say good-bye to you, and wish you all the best, Jo."

"Where are you going?"

"I'm taking Courtney to Scandinavia for a few weeks.

I've told my answering service to tell everyone that I'm incommunicado. But I just wanted to say how sorry I am to you. I know how close you and Larry were."

"Thank you, Lulu." I shook her hand and watched her disappear into the crowd.

I saw Carla out on the steps of the cathedral, hobnobbing with the mayor and his entourage. I could hardly contain my rage. Carla Cole was exactly the sort of person Larry Locket spent his life fighting—someone who thinks they are above all rules and all laws because they are so titanically rich. She caught my eye and gave me a curt little nod.

I wanted to march up to her and say, "You murdering bitch. I know you had Larry killed and I know you had June hit and one day I'm going to make you pay for it." But I simply nodded back and moved on.

I nearly choked on my hypocrisy. However, if you can't be hypocritical to those you loathe, whom can you be hypocritical to?

Thirty-six

DEATH IS A GRAND SILENCE. THAT EVENING, I sat alone in my library, paralyzed with despair, dreading the coming weeks and months and years without the company of my dear friend. Even during those periods when I didn't see or speak to Larry very much, there was a great comfort in knowing he was there, and that we would take up exactly where we left off. As one gets older, one's personal landscape vanishes bit by bit. Those people who have been a part of one's landscape for a long time are like those old oak trees that anchor a country scene. When they are cut down, the view changes, becoming sparser and more desolate. No matter what happened now, Carla Cole had won. There was nothing I could do to bring Larry back, and no way I could prove that she had killed him. And yet, I knew she had—knew it in my bones. Larry didn't know how right he'd been about her being one dangerous lady.

I was sitting in a chair, staring out the window, watching the twilight fade when the jangling ring of the phone startled me. I picked it up and said a somber, "Hello."

"Hello, may I speak to Mrs. Jo Slater, please?" said a male voice I didn't recognize.

"Speaking," I replied warily.

The man cleared his throat nervously and said, "Mrs. Slater, my name is Mike Rankin. I'm the captain of *The Lady C*."

In my grief, I'd forgotten all about chartering the yacht. There seemed to be no point in going through with it now. Larry was dead and the boat's deck plans showing the secret room had burned up with him.

"Oh, yes, Captain Rankin," I said, focusing. "Larry Locket spoke very highly of you. I take it you've heard the news."

"Yes, ma'am. We heard. It's terrible. A tragedy."

"I'm glad you called. Obviously, I won't be taking the boat now. I'm sorry. Could you possibly inform the charter company, or I'll call them. . . . I'm sure there'll be a cancellation fee and I—"

He interrupted me. "That's not why I'm calling, Mrs. Slater. Look, uh, Mr. Locket told me that if anything happened to him, I was to get in touch with you right away." His voice was hesitant and he was obviously distraught about something.

"What do you mean?"

"When I spoke to Mr. Locket a couple of weeks ago about the trip, um, he said that I should get in touch with him if I had any more thoughts about what we'd been discussing. But if, for some reason, I couldn't reach him, I was to get in touch with you."

"With me?"

"Yes, ma'am. He gave me your number. He said that if anything happened to him, I was to call you."

"Wait . . . Larry specifically said if anything happened to him?"

"Yes. Those were his words. Quite frankly, he seemed concerned."

I shook my head in dismay, remembering what a brave front he had put up for me.

"Go on," I said.

"Anyway, ma'am, I have some news and I think you should come down here." There was a strange urgency in his voice.

"Where are you?"

"Bridgetown, Barbados, where you and Mr. Locket had planned to pick up the charter."

"You mean, just come down there on my own?"

"Yes, ma'am. If you could. I think you should."

Given my paranoid state, I suddenly wondered if this was a trick by Carla to get me down alone on that boat and dispose of me in some horrible way like she had disposed of Larry, and probably Russell.

"I'm sorry, Captain Rankin, I really don't think I can—not without Larry."

"Mrs. Slater, *please*. Mr. Locket said I was to call *you*—and no one else. *Please trust me*."

"Well, can't you tell me what it is?"

"I don't want to discuss it over the phone. But I have some information. Believe me, I know how upset you must be and I wouldn't be contacting you unless it was urgent."

Something in his voice told me that he was telling the truth. I thought about the secret room and Larry's conviction that some kind of proof still lay on the yacht. I also remembered Larry telling me that Rankin shared our concerns about Carla. I wondered if the captain had found something that incriminated her in some way. I knew Larry trusted Rankin, and I suddenly felt Larry's hand reaching out to me from the grave. I knew I had to take a chance.

"All right," I said tentatively. "I'll come."

I told everyone I was off to Europe for a little rest. They all assumed I was extremely upset about Larry, and most of them kept that decorous distance people do when tragedy strikes. Still, Betty smelled a rat. I usually told her exactly where I was going and in which hotels I was staying so we could keep in touch. This time, I was vague.

"You're up to something, Jo," she said to me on the phone.

"What makes you say that, Betts?"

"What makes me say anything I say? Because I think it, that's why. . . . Is it a man?"

"In a manner of speaking."

"Too bad it's not Max. I just hate to think of Carla becoming the next Lady Vermilion. And it looks like she's headed that way."

"What makes you say that?"

"Oh, it's all over the British press. I just spoke to a pal in London. Let's face it, Jo, Taunton Hall or not, who the hell in their right mind puts up the money for a twenty-million-dollar roof unless they think they're gonna live under it one day? And Trish just told me that Carla is renting their house in Southampton for August for two-hundred-and-fifty thou a week, and that Max is coming to stay!"

"Where's Trish going?"

"Lexington. She's renting an apartment down there to be near Dick. Everyone's going down there to visit him. It'll be Old Kentucky Home week for as long as he's there. . . . But you gotta tell me, Jo . . . who's your new beau?"

"I'll tell you when I get back."

"Oh, come on! You cannot *not* tell me! I'm your best friend, for Chrissakes! You can't keep something like that a secret from me! You know, I figured something was up when I saw how good you looked at Larry's funeral. Screw chemical peels. Sex is what really makes the skin glow."

Or obsession, I thought.

"If it gets serious, I'll call you. Promise."

Betty was miffed, I could tell. I let her hang up still nurturing her illusions.

As I packed for the cruise, I thought to myself: Just as it takes a new romance to cure a broken heart, it takes a new obsession to replace an old one. Not since the planning of Monique's demise had I experienced such a rush of energy. When I looked in the mirror, I saw myself clearly, like I'd come out of a fog into bright sunshine. The path was in front of me and I was ready to follow it.

Thirty-seven

THE FLIGHT TO BRIDGETOWN WAS UNEVENT-
ful. I stepped off the cool airplane into a curtain of heat. After clearing immigration, I
walked into the terminal where Captain Mike Rankin was
waiting for me, ready to escort me to the yacht. Rankin,
wearing his white captain's uniform, was a tall, nice-
looking, middle-aged man, with thick, shiny brown hair,
an even tan, and an affable, if slightly nervous, manner. A
steward from the boat saw to my luggage. As we drove to
the harbor in a spacious black van, Captain Rankin asked
me how my trip was, and once again expressed his condolences to me over Larry's death. He didn't say much
else, and he seemed ill at ease.

We reached the dock and walked down the main pier
to a waiting tender. I sat with the captain in the motor
boat as it skimmed past the muddy harbor water toward
the clear aquamarine sea. Suddenly, there she was, *The
Lady C*, floating on the water, big, white, and placid,
like a great iceberg. There was something sinister about

her, and I suspected that, just like her namesake, this lady, too, had many secrets. The tender headed straight for her and eased its way up alongside the stern. A crew member extended his hand to me and I hopped onto the large platform at the back of the yacht. Captain Rankin jumped out after me, then led the way up the steps to the main deck.

As I climbed those stairs, a vivid picture of Carla Cole flashed through my mind. There she was, standing above me, hand extended, just like she had been the night of the bridal dinner, ablaze in turquoise and diamonds, gracious to a fault, the perfect hostess about to commit the perfect crime. None of her guests could possibly have imagined then what she was planning to do to her husband that night. What was on her mind all the while that party was going on? What did she see when she looked at Russell across the table, knowing she was about to kill him? Or was she so cold-blooded that she was able to relax and enjoy herself and live in the moment? Certainly, it proved my theory that you can never tell what people are truly thinking at parties.

Several members of the crew, wearing their starched, white uniforms, stood at attention in a line on the deck waiting to greet me. The captain introduced me to each one as I shook his or her hand. I knew they were looking me over with perhaps even more scrutiny than usual, as I'm sure it was a rare occurrence to have a single guest charter a yacht that could accommodate at least sixteen guests.

"And this is the purser, who is also my wife, Nancy," the captain said, as we reached the last person in line.

Nancy Rankin was a good ten years younger than her husband, somewhere in her early thirties. She was a lithe, broad-shouldered woman—one of those all-American girls whose tanned good looks and athletic body proclaim a love of the outdoors. Her straight brown hair was pulled back in a ponytail, but wisps of it fell over a pair of blue eyes that crinkled around the edges when she smiled. She, too, seemed oddly ill at ease.

Captain Rankin informed me that my luggage would be taken to my cabin and unpacked for me, if I wished. I accepted the offer, pleased that the old-fashioned standards of service still existed on board this yacht. Then he and Nancy offered to show me around, in part so I could choose which cabin I wanted. Nancy gently reminded me I wouldn't be needing my shoes from now on. Most footwear was forbidden on the sleek decks of the yacht, and was unnecessary on the carpeted interiors. I took off my shoes and placed them in a large wicker basket set aside for that purpose. The weather was wiltingly hot and it was a relief to go inside where air-conditioning kept the temperature comfortably cool.

It was strange being on board again after all this time, and after all that had happened. Viewing her now, I thought *The Lady C* less of a lap of luxury and more of a crime scene. To the best of my recollection, the décor of the rooms was exactly the same as it had been the night of the bridal dinner, yet the ambiance was totally different—more utilitarian somehow. Then I realized that, of course, it was because the great paintings were gone. In their place, mounted in the same frames on the wall, were large color photographs of exotic places from all around the world. Though striking and decorative, they could not re-create the shimmering, jewel-like atmosphere I remembered. How could they? Even an impressive shot of the Lake Palace Hotel in Udaipur hanging above the mantelpiece in the library looked cheap compared to the haunting Gauguin of two Tahitian women bathing in a river that had once hung in its place. Without the great paintings to enhance it, the profound beauty of the interior was gone. No longer a floating museum, it was now just another rich man's boat.

Since I had my pick of the rooms, I chose Carla's old suite, with its faux boiserie and light colors; it was much warmer and cozier than Russell's dark, minimalist abode. Two young stewardesses unpacked my bags for me, leaving me free to relax. Captain Rankin asked if I would mind setting sail right away. I had no objections.

A short time later, we were under way, moving majestically through the water. I lay down and fell asleep, lulled by the rhythms and hums of the boat. When I awoke, we were anchored in a secluded cove. The tropical evening was descending in a pale purple veil.

As I dressed for dinner, I was impressed by all the luxurious touches in Carla's old suite, particularly those in the palatial marble bathroom, with its gold-plated fixtures in the shape of swans. The large room was virtually a miniature spa, with a steam bath, Jacuzzi, bidet, sunken tub, and a separate cabinet for the toilet, which looked amusingly like a tiny throne room, all gilded and hand-painted with heraldic crests. I thought about Carla, in particular what she had said to me the day Russell disappeared, "I always hated that boat." There was such coldness in her voice. But it seemed to me she had a point. Luxurious as it was, there was something claustrophobic about being on a yacht. Though sailing gives the illusion of great freedom because you can go anywhere you want, the fact of the matter is you're still a captive in a confined space—however splendid that space may be. As I soaked in the tub, I thought of how Carla must have languished there herself on many an occasion, fearing she was doomed to spend the rest of her life aboard *The Lady C*, traveling the world with a moody, melancholy man.

The Rankins were waiting for me in the main salon promptly at eight-thirty. They had both dressed for the occasion—he in a blue blazer and white trousers, she in white pants and a pale blue silk blouse. With her hair in a chignon, Nancy Rankin's wholesome beauty seemed more sophisticated, less girlish. They were a handsome couple, demonstrably fond of each other. I felt a twinge of envy. We all had a glass of champagne and talked about the weather and other polite pleasantries. But underneath the banter, I felt a thread of tension, as if they were purposely avoiding what was really on their minds.

It was a balmy night, so we ate outside on deck. The long dining table was elegantly set with crystal candlesticks, white china, and a vivid spray of tropical flowers, a dramatic contrast to the highly polished dark wood. Scattered lights on the distant mainland pricked the deepening twilight. We were served dinner by two stewardesses, whom I encouraged to keep the wine flowing. The conversation was stilted at first, but as the meal progressed we talked more about Russell Cole. The Rankins seemed impressed that I was an old friend of his—someone who had known him before he was married to Carla. Whenever Carla's name came up, they glanced at each other, and I got the distinct feeling that they didn't like her at all. But they were not very forthcoming, and finally, over coffee, unable to contain my curiosity any longer, I said, "Now, Captain Rankin, what was so urgent that you had to get me down here right away?"

Rankin and his wife exchanged looks of concern. He cleared his throat.

"We have a saying on board, Mrs. Slater. What happens on the yacht, *stays* on the yacht."

"What does that mean exactly?"

"Just what it says. Things that are said and done and seen here *remain* here. They go no further."

"Well, if you're worried that I'm going to say anything to anyone about what you have to tell me, I'm not. Believe me. In fact, I was hoping you'd answer a few questions for me in confidence. But you go first."

They glanced at each other again.

"We have something we'd like to show you, Mrs. Slater," Rankin said, rising abruptly from the table.

I followed the couple down two flights of stairs to one of the guest rooms. The captain unlocked the door. It was dark inside. For a moment, I had a terrible feeling that this was all a setup, and that something bad was going to happen to me. Nancy must have sensed my apprehension because she whispered, "Don't be afraid, Mrs. Slater."

Rankin flicked a switch on the wall. A soft glow suffused the large pale room. A man was asleep in the king-size bed. We all quietly drew near and looked down at the sleeping figure. He was an old man with long, matted hair, and a scruffy, brownish beard. His skin was blotched and leathery from the sun. His closed eyes were sunk deep into gaunt cheeks. His mouth was open slightly and his face contorted in bouts of fitful snoring.

I looked at Rankin questioningly. "Who's that?" I whispered.

"Don't you recognize him?" Rankin asked, looking at me with a meaningful gaze.

And, of course, the minute he said this, I understood who was lying there in front of me, unrecognizable as he was. I leaned down and peered at him more closely, unable to believe that the pathetic creature asleep in bed was none other than Russell Cole.

I put my hand to my mouth to stifle a gasp. I stood gazing at him for a long moment. All the life and moisture had been sucked out of him. Even in his sleep, his face seemed coated with suffering. Gone were the boyish looks and the dapper demeanor of the youthful middle-aged man I had once known. In their place was a frail, exhausted soul.

Rankin motioned me to follow him out of the cabin. Nancy stayed behind, adjusting the bedcovers. I followed the captain upstairs to the grand salon, where a steward fixed us both drinks. God knows I needed one. Rankin dismissed the steward so we could talk alone.

"Does the crew know who he is?" I asked.

"I haven't announced it, but I'm sure they've guessed. I don't want it getting out—not yet."

"Tell me the story. What happened? How on earth did he get here?"

"Two days ago, we were refueling in Bridgetown and this dock bum was hanging around, staring at the yacht. He was dressed in rags. He looked like one of those crazy people you see sometimes on these docks. Hapless, hopeless souls. He was working on a trader and I'm always nervous about those guys when they come near the yacht."

"What's a trader?"

"A trader boat is one of those island-hopping rust

buckets. They carry all different kinds of cargo from island to island. A lot of criminals work those boats: drug runners, thieves, ex-cons, fugitives. Probably some terrorists nowadays. The captains don't ask any questions as long as you put in a hard day's work. We always steer clear of 'em. . . . Anyway, he went away, but I remembered him. And then the next thing I know, he sneaked aboard."

"How?"

"Oh, it's not too hard on a yacht this size, believe it or not, particularly if you know the boat. He was wandering around below and the first mate was in the process of throwing him off when I came down. When I saw his eyes, that was when I knew it was Mr. Cole. I didn't let on, though. We took him to a guest suite and tried to give him something to eat, but he was too ill. I told the crew we'd let him stay until he was well enough to leave. But, as I said, I think several of them guessed who it was."

Rankin sipped his drink.

"You think he's been working on one of those boats all this time?"

He shrugged. "Could be . . . sure. And then seeing the yacht again triggered something in him. I tell you, Mrs. Slater, in one of my very first talks with Mr. Cole after he hired me as captain, he told me about his condition. Well, he had to, didn't he? In case he ever disappeared. The fear was always with him, like people who have epilepsy or narcolepsy—they never know when they're going to have a seizure. So they have to prepare the people around them in case it ever happens. I asked him what I should do if, God forbid, he ever did disappear. The one thing he told me definitely *not* to do was to move the boat. I remember he said to me, 'Mike, whatever you do, *don't go*

anywhere. Send out search parties, but don't go anywhere. Just wait for me to come home.' Mr. Cole was always afraid that one day he might get lost for good. He
told me that people afflicted with this condidtion can vanish for weeks, months, even years, if there's nothing to
remind them of who they were or where they came from.
He told me he worked as a bagger in a supermarket during one of these episodes. He was quite funny about it.
He said he felt something was missing, but he didn't
really understand it was his entire life."

"But if something *does* trigger their memory . . . ?"

"Then they can come home," Rankin said. "That's
what happened to Mr. Cole this time. He saw *The Lady
C*, and he came aboard."

"But he has no idea where he's been?"

"He has no idea about anything at the moment. He's
just babbling."

"So I guess this means that he really did have an
episode, after all. Mr. Locket and I were convinced that
Mrs. Cole had somehow done away with him."

Rankin pinned me with a hard gaze. "Don't be so sure
she didn't try."

"What do you mean?"

Rankin put down his drink. "In my last conversation
with Mr. Locket, he mentioned something to me about a
set of plans and a secret room . . . ?"

"Yes! That's why we chartered the boat. Larry wanted
to see if we could find that room and maybe dig up some
evidence of a crime. *Is* there a secret room?"

"There are many," Rankin said with a slight laugh. "A
yacht this size is riddled with 'em. Mr. Cole designed a
lot of storage space for his art and there are hidden passages leading to and from the various rooms. You can

move around on *The Lady* without ever being seen if you want to. But when Mr. Locket told me about the two different sets of plans, I knew exactly what he was talking about. I never thought to look there, but when he mentioned it, I did. And I was surprised at what I found."

"What?"

"Well, come have a look for yourself."

Thirty-eight

FIRST, RANKIN GAVE ME A QUICK TOUR OF ALL the "secret" passages on the boat, a rabbit warren of concealed corridors, rooms, and cupboards. I understood how right Larry had been: the great yacht had a character all her own. This seemingly radiant lady, constructed for pleasure, privilege, and protection, was, in fact, a stealthy creature with twisty insides and a dark personality.

The last stop on my secret passage tour was a "safe room," located off Russell's dressing room behind the long clothes rack in one of the huge walk-in closets. Its entrance was invisible to the naked eye. Rankin pressed a spot in the wall and a panel sprang open, revealing a steel door with a keypad on it. He punched in some numbers and there was a click. He pushed down the handle and the door opened inward. This room was a miniature sitting room, with chairs, a couch, and a desk on which there was a cellular telephone and a shortwave radio. There were books neatly arranged in bracketed shelves, a split-screen television monitor built into the wall that allowed one to see what was going on, not only directly outside in the master cabin, but also on the various decks. There was a stockpile of canned goods and bottled water in a large wooden chest, plus a fire extinguisher, life vests, extra clothing, flares, and an inflatable raft. Rankin pulled open the bottom drawer of the desk. Inside was a twenty-two-caliber pistol and three boxes of ammunition.

"One of Mr. Cole's Renoirs used to hang right up there," Rankin said, pointing to a space on the wall. "He said he wanted something cheerful to look at if he was ever forced to come in here. Mr. Cole's paintings were like his children. He used to put his hand on a painting and close his eyes and just stand there for minutes at a time. He said the thing about great art was that you could physically touch a genius across time."

Rankin pressed the television monitor with his two hands. There was a tiny click, like a latch opening. The monitor and its entire panel sprung forward slightly, revealing another door.

"This is what Mr. Locket was talking about. It's the safe room's safe room," Rankin said. "No one knows it exists except the captain and the owner, of course. It's there for extra protection. It was drafted on the original plans, but it doesn't appear on the engineer's blueprints for obvious reasons. I don't know how Mr. Locket knew about it, unless someone got hold of either the captain's or the owner's copy. I never even thought to look here until I talked to Mr. Locket on the phone."

Rankin opened the door slowly and flicked a switch. A fluorescent light flickered overhead, revealing a small room, like a closet, just big enough for two people to hide in.

"No locks on these safe room doors so you can get out, but the bad guys can't lock you in . . . I haven't moved a thing," he said, pointing down.

There on the gray floor lay a large red plastic cooler, inside of which were two rolls of duct tape, a small hatchet, a box of plastic garbage bags, and an industrial-size container of bleach. I stared down at the grisly cache. I didn't say a word, but to my mind we were looking at Carla's plans for her husband right there in that cooler. This kind of killing was the province of low-life Mafia figures and organized serial killers, not of a rich socialite dancing her way through life on a skein of money and privilege. But then, you just never know . . .

"Did you tell the police about this?" I asked him.

"Look, these things aren't proof of a crime. They're normal to have aboard a boat. I was surprised to see them in here though. But they do kind of point to a theory I have. Come on, I'll tell you about it."

We walked back up to the grand salon. Rankin sat forward on the couch, bristling with intensity.

"These episodes of Mr. Cole's are supposedly triggered by severe emotional distress," he began. "I believe one of the little games the three of them played got out of hand."

"Wait. Slow down. What games? And who are the three of them?"

"Jasper Jenks and Mr. and Mrs. Cole. The three of them had a scene together. The second I heard that Mr. Cole had disappeared, I just figured they'd all been up to their old tricks. I knew Jenks was no good the minute I met him."

"How did he get to be the captain? I remember when Russell disappeared this fellow Jenks didn't really seem to know what he was doing."

Rankin gave a mordant little chuckle. "Oh, he knew what he was doing, all right. But not as a captain. . . . We were in St. Maarten. *The Lady* always draws quite a crowd. Jenks was admiring her and somehow he struck up a conversation with Mr. and Mrs. Cole. Before I knew it, Mr. Cole comes to me and says he wants to hire him. So I interviewed the guy. He'd definitely sailed before, so on Mr. Cole's orders, I brought him on as a mate. Then I lost my bosun and he took the job. But very early on, I sensed there was a whole lot else going on."

"How come?"

"For one thing, I saw Jenks and Mrs. Cole talking when they didn't think anyone was watching. And, believe me when I tell you, Mrs. Slater, they weren't talking to each other like they were strangers. Plus, you get hunches about people—especially in this business because you're very close to people, living with them. Good captains have to be good shrinks, as well. Megayachts like *The Lady C* are basically floating loony bins, you know. You have to be very careful who you let aboard the asylum," he said with a grin.

"So you think Mrs. Cole already knew Jenks? That it was a setup?"

"I'd bet my captain's license on it. The way he and Mr. Cole hit it off right away . . . ? Jenks had to have been coached by someone who knew Mr. Cole very, very well. Right away, he starts talking to Mr. Cole about Mr. Cole's favorite subject: art. Not a usual topic for a seaman, believe me. Mr. Cole's a shy man, and Jenks knew how to get around him, knew just how far to go and when to pull back, you know? Like he'd been coached, as I say. But here's the main thing: Don't you find it strange that two people as paranoid and security-conscious as the Coles would pick some guy up off a dock in St. Maarten and give him a job—just like that?" He snapped his fingers.

"Yes, I do. And Larry thought so, too."

"Particularly with all those pricey paintings around? The rest of the crew and me, we were all checked out within an inch of our lives. It just didn't make sense that they'd just throw caution to the wind like that. But I was ordered to take him on, without the usual vetting . . . Anyway, once Jenks was aboard, the three of them got pretty cozy. I believe that Mr. Cole was a little conflicted about his sexuality," Rankin began matter-of-factly.

"Is that a euphemism for gay?" I asked him.

"No . . . I think that Mrs. Cole prevented him from being actively gay by providing other outlets, shall we say."

"Like what other outlets are you talking about?" I asked him.

"Games," he said, sharply. "Look, to be frank, Mr. Cole sometimes got crushes on crew members. They were harmless, schoolboy kinds of things. But Jenks encouraged Mr. Cole's attentions and flirted with him quite openly. And Mrs. Cole encouraged the two of them. I saw it happening. And I knew it was just a matter of time before the three of them got into a scene," Rankin said.

"A sexual scene?" I said.

"Is there another kind?" Rankin snickered. "Jasper

Jenks is a chameleon. He turns whatever color he has to in order to get the job done."

"That sounds a lot like Carla Cole as well."

"Definitely birds of a feather, those two," Rankin said.

"So what's your theory about what happened?"

Rankin took a deep breath. "Mr. Cole's been raving on about 'the game' and 'the silk,' whatever that is. . . . I'm thinking that maybe they played some kind of sexual game that got out of hand, either accidentally or on purpose, and that it triggered an episode."

"But do you believe they tried to kill him?"

Rankin nodded solemnly. "Well, I can't go that far. But they were definitely up to something."

"Mike, why didn't you tell all this to the police?"

"I *did*. This detective from Interpol came to see me when they found that guy in Castries that they thought was Mr. Cole. I told him all about Jenks and everything. I told him my suspicions—and that was even before I had a look in that little room. You know what he asked me? He asked me if I was just bitter about being fired."

"That's it. That's all he said?"

"Look, Mrs. Cole told everybody that I was pissed at them for canning me and that I couldn't be trusted. I guess they believed her." He shrugged. "But your friend, Mr. Locket, he believed *me*. He was the first one who ever really listened to me."

Before I went to bed that night, I called home on the satellite phone to check my messages. Betty had phoned with a long, gossipy account of what was going on.

"Jo, where the fuck are you?" the message started. "I hurt my knee playing tennis and we've got Missy and Woody staying with us. I'm going nuts. Woody is so boring. Just like his father, only smarter. Well, that wouldn't be hard, let's face it."

I learned that Dick Bromire's pals were all flying down to visit him. It was definitely the thing to do. June was apparently on the mend and more militant than ever, trying to incite a revolution in the building and dethrone Carla. Carla, meanwhile, was holding her own, and was back in New York after a weekend with Max in Saint-Tropez.

"They're very lovey-dovey," Betty said, adding that they were still renting the Bromires' house in Southampton for August, according to Trish.

"We all *miss* you! Me especially. Come home, for Chrissakes! I can't take all the bullshit around here without you! I need someone to talk to aside from Looney Tune June."

There were several other messages from friends, including Ethan, who also wanted to know why he hadn't heard from me. The last message was from Carla Cole.

"Jo . . . Carla," the sultry voice began. "I understand you are having fun in the sun on my old yacht. . . . Do be careful, *cara* Jo. You have such a pale complexion and the sun is so hot in the tropics, especially at this time of year. You could get very badly burned. . . . Oh, by the way, I am reading one of Larry Locket's books. He was a wonderful writer. It is so sad he is no longer with us. . . . *Ciao, bella.*"

I played it back. The obvious threat in her message only strengthened my resolve. I wasn't afraid of her. I just wanted to get her. I turned off the light, but I couldn't sleep. I lay awake in the dark, staring out at the sweep of rectangular portholes, watching shards of distant lightning pierce the night sky. It occurred to me that although

Carla appeared to be holding all the cards, I was now in control of an ace: Russell. He was the one person who could do her some serious damage if my suspicions were right and they really had tried to kill him. I prayed that when he recovered, he would remember exactly what had happened to him.

Thirty-nine

THE NEXT MORNING, I WAS HAVING BREAKFAST
out on the deck when Rankin appeared, looking anxious.

"He's up," he said.

I immediately followed him down to the guest suite.
Russell wasn't in his bed. He was in the bathroom standing in front of the full-length mirror, wearing a terry cloth
robe, rubbing his hands through his hair and up and down
the sides of his face, studying his gaunt reflection in the
glass as if he were looking at an alien being. When he
turned and saw his former captain, his face showed
a glimmer of recognition. Rankin approached him
cautiously.

"Mr. Cole?" Rankin said. "It's Mike, sir. Mike Rankin.
Do you remember me?"

Russell narrowed his eyes. "Mike," he said at last.
"Yes, Mike, of course I remember you." His eyes grew
moist as he stared at his old captain.

"Good to have you aboard again, sir," Rankin said,

moving forward to shake hands. He, too, was teary with emotion.

"What's happened to me?" Russell asked with child-like naïveté.

"You've been away, sir."

"Where?"

"I don't know, sir."

Russell furrowed his brow and nodded his head up and down, beginning to comprehend that he'd endured one of his episodes.

"How long was I gone this time?" he said at last.

"Over six months, sir," Rankin informed him.

He flung Rankin a horrified look, as if the captain had said twenty years.

"My God . . . where's Carla?"

At this point, I stepped forward.

"Russell?"

He stared at me without seeming to recognize me.

"It's Jo, Russell. Jo Slater."

Suddenly, he broke into a smile. "Jo! Of course . . . where's Carla?"

"She's not here," I said.

"Where is she? I need to see her. Would you go get her, please?" he said, growing increasingly agitated.

Rankin and I glanced at each other.

"She's coming," I said. "Don't worry. Russell, do you know that the *whole world* is looking for you?"

He said with tearful petulance, "I want Carla."

Captain Rankin and Nancy spent the day cleaning Russell up and getting him back to a semblance of his old self. He was still very weak. Rankin had to help him shower and shave, then gave him clean clothes—including one of the white T-shirts worn by the crew and given out to guests. The name THE LADY C was stitched discreetly in red thread on the upper left-hand side. When Russell saw the shirt, he said, "Carla designed these, you know. I need to see her. Where is she?"

We all dodged this question again and again, putting him off by telling him we'd explain everything after he'd had a chance to recover. Above all, he had to rest and regain his strength. He accepted our evasions, for the moment at least, like a man in shock accepts whatever he is told. But, also like a man in shock, Russell obsessively returned to the subject of Carla over and over, forgetting what we had said.

After Russell got a haircut, the four of us walked up to the main deck. Rankin took Russell's arm to steady him. As we were proceeding slowly through the yacht, Russell stopped abruptly in front of a dramatic photograph of the Taj Mahal at dawn, hanging in one of the built-in frames. He cried out in a panic, *"My Cézanne! Where's my Cézanne? It should be here!"*

The three of us all glanced at one another. Rankin nodded to me as if to say, "You handle this."

"It's safe, Russell," I assured him. Rankin did likewise.

"But where *is* it?" He looked around and focused in on the other photographs along the corridor. *"They're all gone!* What's *happened* to them? Where *are* they? *Where are my paintings? What are those photographs doing here?"*

He reeled. I helped Rankin steady him. We flanked him and gently urged him to move forward, but it was no use. He refused to budge. Obsessed with the photographs that had replaced his art, he stood his ground, demanding to know where his paintings were and when Carla was coming.

"I'm going to tell you the whole story, Russell," I said in a very calm voice. "But first you need to get some food in you. You need to be strong."

Finally, Rankin and I steered Russell back to his room. We gave him some broth, then Rankin gave him a tranquilizer, hoping that a good night's rest would help him.

Russell was moved to his old stateroom, and over the next few days he gradually regained his strength and some of his equilibrium. He stopped asking about Carla so much. I sensed that he knew the worst was coming and had been trying to prepare himself, difficult as it was. At least now he seemed capable of hearing what I had to say. One rainy evening, Rankin and I sat Russell down in the library for a drink before dinner. Russell and I each had a glass of wine. Rankin abstained.

"Russell," I began hesitantly, "I have some difficult things to tell you."

"I'm ready." He gave me a solemn nod and stared at me intently with his sad, sunken eyes.

I proceeded to tell him everything, starting with the morning he had disappeared. I told him about the worldwide search for him and how there had been several sightings. I told him about the reward Carla had offered, which made him smile. The wine relaxed him, just as I hoped it would. I knew the hardest part was still to come. I then eased into the more personal aspects of the story. He couldn't believe it when I told him that Carla had sold the yacht, which was why Captain Rankin was back in command. The new owner had rehired him. He looked to

Rankin, hoping the captain would refute the fact, but Rankin just nodded, confirming what I'd said.

I told him that Carla had bought the Wilman apartment in New York and that she had spent millions doing it up in grand style.

"But she knows I hated that apartment and I don't want to live in New York," he said, unable to comprehend what she had done. When Russell then absently questioned where she had gotten the money to buy it, I told him that Carla had used the powers of attorney he had given her to transfer the vast portion of his fortune to herself. I told him that in an effort to stop her from plundering his fortune, his own daughter, who I assured him loved him dearly, was trying to get him declared legally dead.

"Courtney's afraid that there won't be anything left in your name by the time Carla's through," I said bluntly.

Russell listened to these things with an intensely perplexed expression on his face, like someone who is looking at a puzzle he cannot begin to solve. I saw that he was trying to figure it out, to take it all in, but that it was too big an effort. He kept shaking his head from side to side, as if to say, "That's not possible . . . Carla wouldn't do that."

I saved what I thought was the worst for last.

"And finally, Russell," I said, pausing to give this bit of news the full weight it deserved, "Carla has donated your collection to the Municipal Museum."

Blanching and no longer able to contain himself, he literally shot up from his chair and started pacing around the room, in complete and utter dismay. Finally he turned and said, "*My* pictures? She donated *my* collection?"

I nodded. "Along with a grant of one hundred million dollars to build the wing that will house it."

Russell sat down again and stared into space for a long time. He took several sips of wine without letting go of the glass. His breathing grew heavier as he seethed under the weight of this news. Neither Rankin nor I said a word. We just stared at him with a combination of pity and morbid fascination, wondering what he would say or do next. I had just described the unraveling of his entire life, an impossible thing to take in all at once.

I failed to notice how tightly he was squeezing his wineglass, so when it shattered in his hand, I let out a startled cry. Russell didn't move, even though his hand was cut and there was blood. Rankin rose from his chair and gently pried open Russell's hand, picking out the fragments of glass from his palm. I dipped my napkin in a glass of water and dotted the tiny wounds. As we ministered to him, Russell just stared at his hand, a blank expression on his face. He didn't seem to feel any pain—or if he did, he didn't care.

Whatever realization Russell had about Carla didn't last long. He went to bed that night bent on exposing her treachery, but the very next morning, he announced that he missed her and that he needed to call her to "straighten things out."

"I have to see her," he said. "I know there's been a terrible misunderstanding. I've had time to think."

I always step back when people say they've had time to think. It usually means they've rationalized themselves into something they want to believe in order to cling to old pathologies. And indeed, Russell's desire to get in touch with Carla had a frantic aspect to it, rather like the desperation of a homesick child. Despite all I had told him, he now refused to believe that his beloved wife had done anything to harm him. On the contrary, he had rationalized everything, convincing himself that she had done it all for his own good. Over breakfast, he insisted to me that there was a perfectly logical explanation for all her actions. He told me I was misinterpreting the facts. He started with the powers of attorney.

"What you don't realize, Jo, is that Carla and I understood something like this might happen one day. I have this condition, you see. I have to have someone with my interests at heart in charge of my business affairs. I don't trust anyone but Carla," he said to me in all earnestness. "I've given it a lot of thought and here's what I think happened. I think the RTC board must have somehow been taking advantage of my absence, doing some things I wouldn't have approved of. And Carla must have found out. I gave her my powers of attorney as a precaution against that very thing happening. She must have been forced to use them. By taking control, she's really looking out for me and my interests. Can't you see that?"

Well, no, in fact I couldn't see that. Russell's naïveté astounded me. It just goes to show that the human mind can rationalize absolutely anything when it wants to.

"Then why is your daughter fighting her?" I asked him.

"I believe you told me last night that Courtney was trying to get me declared dead," he said bitterly. "What does that tell you about *her* motives? She'd inherit everything if I died."

"But *only* because she was trying to stop Carla from putting everything into her own name!" I couldn't believe he had so misinterpreted Courtney's actions.

Russell shook his head. "No, no. You just don't understand the family dynamic. Courtney is under Lulu's thumb and they both hate Carla. You don't see this for what it is, Jo. It's you who are mistaken. Mark my words, Carla is protecting me from those two. She always warned me that Courtney would try and get her hands on my money if I had an episode. When Carla finds out that I'm alive, she'll transfer everything back to me. You just watch. She's only doing things according to my wishes."

"Russell, ask yourself the following things," I began. "Was it your wish to sell the boat? Was it your wish to buy an apartment in New York? Your wish to donate your collection to the Municipal Museum?"

Russell had no answers to these questions and, indeed, they catapulted him into the miasma of confusion in which I had initially found him. The same dull, uncomprehending look came over him as he said, "I know there's a good explanation. There must be. I *know* there is."

I decided to drop the subject, at least for the moment, because one thing was eminently clear to me: Russell Cole was deeply unstable. His ability to sound rational was more frightening, given his sudden retreats into a complete fantasy world. But even his moments of greatest clarity were tainted by a misguided trust in Carla.

A little later on, Russell asked the captain for a portable computer and me for Carla's new phone number in New York. He was very surly with me, and I could tell he was angry. Instead of Carla's number, I gave him the number of my own private line in New York, which I knew would not answer. Rankin and I both agreed we couldn't afford to have Russell contacting Carla just now.

We needed time. First of all, we didn't want anyone to learn just yet that Russell was alive, knowing what a media feeding frenzy the news would touch off. Second, and more importantly, Carla had all the money now. She was in control, whether Russell chose to believe it or not. And as I explained to Rankin, if Russell ever were going to get his money back, he would need to devise a clever plan. In his present frame of mind, however, he would play right into her hands. Indeed, Russell now mistrusted me for having told him so many negative things. Kill the messenger.

Knowing that Carla had disposed of everyone who ever got in her way, I figured she would try to dispose of Russell, too. She must have considered the possibility that he would show up again one day, and, in that event, it seemed to me that her easiest course of action would be to have him committed to an asylum. On the other hand, if she were bent on becoming the next Lady Vermilion, having her husband alive and incarcerated would be terribly inconvenient. What she really needed was to have Russell dead so she could be a widow and free to marry Max.

How well Carla had planned this! I really had to take my hat off to her. She had pulled everyone, even her detractors, into her alternate universe of money and manipulation, where people see only what they want to see.

Russell refused to come to dinner that night. The Rankins and I ate together, spending most of the time discussing how and when we would let the world know Russell Cole was alive. I wanted to postpone the moment for as long as possible, but Captain Rankin felt it was unfair to both Russell and his family not to reveal his whereabouts as soon as possible. I persuaded him to give me one more day and he reluctantly agreed.

Later on, after dinner on the way to my room, I put my ear to the door of Russell's suite and heard the *click-click-click* of typing on the computer, accompanied by a Rachmaninoff piano concerto playing softly in the background. I knocked on the door, but he told me to go away. I went to bed that night feeling disconsolate and helpless. I could just imagine what was going to happen when Russell returned to the States. It would be too late for him then and I would never be able to avenge Larry's death. Carla would continue to reign over New York. She literally would have gotten away with murder. Several times over.

Forty

THE NEXT MORNING I GOT UP VERY EARLY, having passed a relatively sleepless night. As I was walking through the corridor on my way to the upper deck to get some coffee, Russell emerged from his room, haggard and red-eyed. He was still in the clothes he'd been wearing the previous evening. He'd obviously been up all night. His whole manner toward me seemed different, much softer and more solicitous.

"Jo, may I talk to you?"

"Of course, Russell, what is it?"

He led me into his room and sat down at his desk. His face illuminated by the soft light of the monitor, he clicked away at the keyboard, then stopped and looked up at me.

"You didn't tell me about Max Vermilion," he said.

In fact, I had purposely *not* told him about Max, in part to save him from that final humiliation, and also because I didn't think it was particularly relevant, given all the other things that were going on.

"What about him?"

He pointed at the computer. "Read that."

I walked over and looked at the screen. There was an article from a British online newspaper. I read the head-line: "Americans Flock to Taunton Hall Ball." A couple of sentences caught my eye.

> *Lord Max Vermilion escorted Carla Cole, stylish wife of missing billionaire Russell Cole, to the dance. . . . The evening raised more than fourteen million pounds for the Taunton Hall Trust, ten million of which were donated by Mrs. Cole for the much-needed restoration of the famous copper roof . . .*

Russell glared at the screen, seething.

"She knows how much I loathe and despise him," he said.

"Why? Because he went out with Lulu?"

Russell lowered his head and said softly, "This has nothing to do with Lulu. Carla lied to me. She told me she would never see him again."

"What do you mean? They only just met."

"Who told you that? Max?"

"Yes, as a matter of fact, he did," I said.

Russell scoffed. "Figures."

"Russell, what are you talking about?"

Russell got up and closed the door and motioned to me to sit down. He sat behind his desk again. He spoke slowly and hesitantly. I could see how painful this was for him.

"Carla told me everything about her past before we got married. I knew what she'd been. I didn't care. Women like Carla really know how to take care of a man. She didn't compete with me, like Lulu did. She didn't want anything from me except my happiness and my comfort. She always thought of me first. Do you know what a change that was from Lulu, who always thought of herself first and then of her social friends? Never me. Carla loved *me*. Just me. And I loved her. God, how I loved her. . . ." He paused to reflect. "I'd even go so far as to say I was obsessed with her."

He rubbed his temples as he went on. "Everybody thinks I met Carla at a party in New York and that we had this *coup de foudre*, as the French say—this thunderclap of instant attraction. But that's not true . . . Jo." He hesitated. "I've never told this to another soul . . ."

"Go on," I urged him.

"I met Carla long before that night. I met her when I was in a sanatorium in upstate New York."

I purposely didn't let on that I knew all about his stay at Golden Crest. I decided not to say a word until he'd finished.

"I'd had an episode," he went on. "And this place— Golden Crest, it's called—it's one of the only places left in the country where they still give electroshock treatments. I went there more than once. It was a big secret. Lulu said it would be very bad for the family and the business if anyone found out that I was having these problems, not to mention this particularly drastic treatment . . . Lulu was ashamed of me and my condition. She almost never came to visit," he said bitterly. "Lulu wants everything in her life to be perfect, even the people. But people aren't perfect, Jo. Far from it," he said with a mordant little laugh.

He lapsed into one of his trances. Finally, I prodded him gently to keep going.

"I'm sorry," he said, snapping to. "Lulu was ashamed of me and of my condition. Just like she's ashamed of Courtney and her 'condition,' as she calls it. My daughter is . . . well, she has no interest in men, if you get my drift . . . Lulu took it very hard when Courtney told her. She blamed me."

"You? Why?"

"Lulu blamed any 'psychological aberration,' as she called it, on my side of the family—the crazy side, as she always referred to it. So I was at this place—Golden Crest—and so was Antonio Hernandez, Carla's husband at the time. Carla came up there nearly every weekend to visit him. Most times he was too ill to see her."

"Did you know Hernandez?"

He shook his head. "No. I knew who he was, of course. Mexico's pharmaceutical king," he said derisively. "There were a lot of us rich loonies in that place, believe me. Hernandez was just one of many. He stayed in his cabin all the time. I only saw him once, from a distance. He looked like a big bear."

"So how did you run across Carla?"

"It was fate, really," he said, perking up for the first time. "I was walking back to my cabin one Sunday. Sundays were visiting days and there were always more people around. I saw this very striking, elegant woman coming toward me. She was so out of place in that setting—like a rare orchid in a corn field. I loved the way she was dressed—so chicly. We passed each other on the path. She stopped me and asked me if I was visiting and if I knew where the dining room was. She had no idea I was a patient. I offered to show her. We connected immediately. She was so easy to talk to. So lively and so much fun. I'm not usually good at talking to people when

I first meet them—not that I'm much good after I know them, either," he said with touching self-deprecation. "But Carla made me feel so comfortable. As I said, she thought I was a visitor at first."

He smiled at the memory. I couldn't believe anyone was that naïve. It was obvious that Russell was still madly in love with Carla because of how much he relished telling me the true story of their first meeting.

"She told me she came up every Sunday to visit her husband, but that he often couldn't see her, or if he did, it was only for a short time. We went for a long, long walk together on the property. It's a beautiful place. Very rural. Very tranquil. You become intimate quite quickly in a place like that. There's not much small talk. Near the end of the walk, I finally confessed to her that I was a patient there. She stopped dead in her tracks. She couldn't believe it at first. She said I seemed so 'normal.'" He laughed at the memory. I had to stop myself from rolling my eyes in disbelief.

"She asked me what I was there for. I told her a little bit about my condition. She was gentle and sympathetic. Not like Lulu, who was always so denigrating. Eventually I told Carla that I'd had shock treatments, and that I didn't remember long periods of my life. She said she'd like to forget certain periods of her life, and then she confessed to me how difficult her own marriage was. Hernandez was a drug addict and a depressive. He was there to detox, but they just gave him more drugs. It was that sort of a place. You could recuperate if you wanted to, or stay addicted if you wanted to. All they were really interested in was your money. Anyway, she told me her life was difficult, but she was determined to stick with Hernandez because he'd rescued and protected her."

"Protected her from what?"

"From *Max*," he said softly. He paused for a moment, clenching his jaw in a rage. "Max was obsessed with Carla," he went on. "They had a brief affair years ago and Max fell madly in love with her. He wouldn't leave her alone. She told me how Hernandez had helped her get away from him. She made no bones about it. She discussed the whole thing very openly with me. She confided in me, like a friend. She said I was the only one she'd ever been able to talk to about her situation. She said I made her feel comfortable and hopeful and safe. We were friends at first, Jo. Just friends. Nothing more. I promise."

I couldn't believe how clever Carla had been. Like any billionaire, Russell Cole had women flinging themselves at him all the time—all kinds of women, both married and single—all hoping to find a chink in his marriage and take advantage of it. But Russell was a shy, insecure man, clearly frightened by overt sexuality. This was a man who'd married his college sweetheart and who preferred a quiet life. Plus, Russell was no fool. He must have known most of the women who openly pursued him were after him for his money. To approach him first as a damsel in distress rather than a seductress was a stroke of genius. Carla cleverly gambled that her sex appeal and exoticism eventually would speak for themselves. What she needed to gain was his trust. And how better to gain Russell's trust than to make him a friend and confidant? What man doesn't trust a woman he believes he's helping to get through a difficult marriage?

"So Carla and Max have known each other for years. That's fascinating," I said, musing aloud.

I thought back to my conversation with Carla the day

we lunched at The Forum when she asked me if I'd ever been to Taunton Hall. I recalled the dreamy look on her face when she said it was the most beautiful place she'd ever seen and how there was nothing to compare with it. That was the first inkling I got that she may have been interested in Max. Little did I know then how interested she really was. Or he, for that matter.

"Max was mad about her. Obsessed with her. He still is, I'm sure."

"Knowing Carla, I'm surprised she didn't manage to hook him," I said cynically.

"Oh, she wasn't interested in him. In fact, when she heard Max was taking Lulu out, she laughed about it. She said Max was dating Lulu just to get back at her for marrying me."

"Where did they meet?"

"Max leads a double life. Years ago, he took Carla to Hong Kong on a business junket. He often took ladies like Carla on trips like that, when he wasn't likely to run into anyone he knew. He fell head over heels in love with her, and refused to leave her alone."

"Why didn't he marry her?"

"If you know Max, you know what a snob he is. He would never have *married* a woman like Carla. But that didn't stop him from being completely obsessed with her. As I said, he leads a double life. He used to stalk her. Carla and I were both very upset when we found out that Betty had invited him to the bridal dinner. I disinvited him."

"That was the night you disappeared."

He looked at me with a pained expression. "Was it? I don't remember."

"The next night was the wedding. I sat next to Max at

dinner. Carla was there. She acted like she hardly knew him."

"Where was I?"

"I told you. You had disappeared."

He cocked his head to one side with a perplexed expression on his face. "Carla knew I was gone?"

"Yes, of course. There'd been search parties out for you all day."

"And she went to the wedding?" he said in a hurt voice.

"Yes."

"And Max was there?"

"Yes."

I saw where his mind was heading and I did nothing to interrupt that obvious train of thought. Meanwhile, I pondered the grand deception myself: How Max had first pretended not to know Carla when they were introduced in Barbados . . . how he had subsequently been present at nearly every occasion where she was. I thought of the dinner I'd given for Max where he engineered it so Carla and Lulu came face-to-face, knowing that Lulu was bound to make a scene and wind up looking bad . . . I thought about Carla's infamous party, recalling it was Max who had suggested all the women's bags be searched. I suddenly wondered: Was he the one who planted the earring in my bag? He certainly had the opportunity. He all but ruined me that night . . . Was Max trying to get back into Carla's good graces by humiliating her detractors? Was he still obsessed with her, as Russell suspected?

"Russell, let me ask you a question. Why wasn't Carla interested in Max? He's handsome, rich, a lord. Was it just because he wouldn't marry her?"

"No, because he's a complete fraud," Russell said.

"In what way?"

"In every way."

"Give me an example."

"He's broke, for one thing."

I guffawed. "Are you kidding? Max Vermilion? He's rich as Croesus."

Russell shook his head. "Why do you think he only marries rich women? Max was in trouble even before the dot-com downdraft. Carla told me that he'd lost a fortune womanizing and gambling. He's been privately selling off paintings and furniture from his house for years in order to keep up the façade. You ask Gil Waterman. Five years ago Gil offered me two of Max's Canalettos, a portfolio of Rembrandt etchings, and two Dürer drawings from Taunton Hall. I didn't want them. He finally sold them all at auction, as the 'property of an English gentleman.' Gil sent me a copy of the catalog."

As Russell spoke, I recalled the day I'd seen Max lunching with Gil at The Forum, now viewing that seemingly innocuous social encounter in a more sinister light. I wondered if, indeed, Max had been unloading some other precious object or painting from Taunton Hall in order to keep his life afloat.

"Max has closed off rooms on the National Trust tour, saying they're under renovation," Russell went on. "But actually, it's because their treasures are gone. He'll have to sell the whole place soon because he can't afford to keep it up. No one's supposed to know, of course, although some people do. It's a miracle he's kept it quiet for so long. He was only going out with Lulu for her money—and to get back at Carla, of course."

I was utterly dumbfounded. The mighty Vermilion fortune was legendary, and Max certainly lived as if it were still intact. Gil Waterman had never breathed a word of this to me. He certainly had never told Betty because if he had, the world would have known about it in two seconds flat. Gil was much more discreet than I ever imagined. But I guess, given the art trade, with all its wheelings and dealings, he had to be. The idea that Max would have to sell Taunton Hall because he couldn't afford to hang onto it was staggering.

What Russell didn't know, of course, was that while he knew a lot about Max, I knew much more about his wife than he did. Indeed, I was wondering if it was conceivable that Max had told Carla to marry Russell in order to replenish his own fortune. And was that, perhaps, the real reason she had married Hernandez, too—to get money for Max? Was Max somehow behind all this mayhem? Or was Carla merely acting on her own initiative in order to please him?

I decided to spare this pathetic man all the details of his wife's deceptions and my own suspicions about her. His own mind was doing my work for me.

"Well, Russell, all I can say is, now she's put a roof on *his* house with *your* money."

Forty-one

OVER THE COURSE OF THE DAY, RUSSELL worked obsessively on the computer, pulling up all sorts of articles on the Internet that confirmed the things I had told him about the collection and about his fortune. The *Wall Street Journal* had a long piece about the internal fighting in the RTC Corporation. Because it was a privately held company, the exact facts were sketchy, but according to a source "close to the investigation," Carla Cole was now in control of the multibillion-dollar entity. Over objections from the board of directors, she had sold off companies and real estate, using her voting powers to basically line her own pocket. Lulu Cole was suing the board on behalf of her daughter. Courtney was battling Carla and trying to get her father declared legally dead in order to salvage what was left of her birthright. He read and re-read the front-page *New York Times* story about Carla donating the Cole collection to the Municipal Museum. The events I had related gradually took root in his consciousness. I used every opportunity I could to sow more seeds of doubt in his mind.

In Russell's eyes, however, everything paled in comparison to Carla having publicly taken up with Max. This breach of faith trumped all the others combined. Her association with Max was the one thing he couldn't recast in a sympathetic light. He wondered aloud if Carla had ever really loved him, as she professed, or if she saw him, as I now suspected, as a stepping-stone to the position, the house, and the man she had always secretly coveted: Max Vermilion.

I said to him with great seriousness, "Ask yourself this honestly, Russell: Are you sure Carla would have married you if Hernandez *had* left her his fortune . . . ? Or would she have married Max? You know Carla very well by now. Which do you think she'd rather be, Mrs. Cole or Lady Vermilion?"

By posing this question, I knew I was playing on all his insecurities. Russell and I stared at each other for a long moment without saying a word. I could almost see his mottled history with Carla tumbling through his mind as he thought about the answer to that question.

Finally, he said, "Do you think Max put her up to it?"

I could just hear Max telling her in that laid-back way of his, "You get yourself a fortune plus a dash of respectability, dear girl. We'll put a nice new roof over my head, make sure The Hall is secure, and I'll marry you, *what*?"

I figured Max's first allegiance was to his noble heritage. Taunton Hall was the true love of his life. I imagined he would do anything to keep it. He had always married wealthy, well-connected women, but they had been more like stopgaps rather than solutions. Not one of them had the means that Carla now had, nor had they Carla's interest in putting all their money at his disposal. Indeed, he wound up paying two or three of them large settlements. Grand in their own right, they didn't covet Max's title, position, or good opinion the way Carla did.

The idea of the elegant Lord Max Vermilion as a Machiavellian puppet master was suddenly all too plausible.

"Yes, Russell, I think he put her up to it. In fact, I'm sure he did."

Russell was anxious to set sail, so Rankin suggested moving to St. Maarten, which was a good distance away and a leg closer to our ultimate destination: the United States. Russell would have to go home sooner or later. It was just a matter of timing. As things stood now, if he returned, he would not only be powerless but possibly in grave danger. I needed time to work out a plan.

Russell adored sailing. He spent hours at the very front of the yacht, gripping the rail, whipped by the wind, gazing ahead at the open sea. He was so resolute and motionless that he reminded me of a wooden figurehead affixed to the prow of an old-fashioned ship, designed to protect it from bad luck. The journey seemed to do him a world of good. He gained strength every day and with physical strength came mental strength, as well. His mind was gradually opening to the possibility that he had been royally deceived.

Little by little, Russell recalled some of the events leading up to his disappearance. It was an excruciating process for him. Memories seemed to come at him like punches out of the blue. I observed him wince with pain when a certain thought crossed his mind. One by one, he recalled the pieces of a macabre jigsaw puzzle and as they fell into place, a fragmented picture of that ghastly night began to emerge.

Russell said he remembered feeling "strange" at the bridal dinner—"Like I'd been drugged," he told me. He described how, after everyone left, Carla came to his room to play "the game." Though he wouldn't tell me specifically what the game was, I inferred from all he said about it that it was sexual in nature, that it involved other people, and that it was potentially dangerous.

"I told her I was too tired, but she insisted," he went on. "That was part of the game, you see—playing it when you didn't want to, playing it any time someone else wanted to."

Russell described how Carla had led him through the secret passage to her stateroom. Once there, she "dressed for the game," whatever that meant—Russell refused to go into detail. But he did talk about something which he called "the silk," which was apparently the name for the silken ropes they used as props. He described how Carla tied him up in a chair. He remembered her joking that he was "a captive audience."

"Everything was moving in slow motion," he said. "She was laughing and caressing me. Then Jasper came into the room and I knew we were going to begin. I told them I wasn't feeling well enough to play and I didn't want to risk it. But the two of them just laughed and said it was always more fun that way."

Russell then fell silent, absently raising his hand to his throat and rubbing it obsessively, as if it held the key to all his fears.

"I remember Jasper got behind me and put the silk around my neck, like usual," he went on after a few moments. "I told him it was too early. I wasn't ready and I wasn't feeling well. But he just laughed and tightened the silk . . . *oh God!*" he suddenly cried.

"*What?*"

He looked at me with terrified eyes. "I . . . I forget . . ." he said.

"Try to remember, Russell, *try*," I urged him.

Whatever had happened was obviously so painful that it was beyond recollection. Like June's hit-and-run, he had no memory of the traumatic event itself.

"I remember waking up in the dark and feeling very cold," he went on dispassionately. "I was on my side, lying on something very hard, like cement. Every time I took a breath, something stuck to my nostrils and blocked the air . . . I tried to raise my hands, but then I realized they were tied. I felt like I was going to suffocate. I put my head down close to my chest so I could breathe and then I remember trying to work my hands free . . . I worked them free . . . and then . . . then I was in the dark . . ." He paused.

"Was this all part of your game?"

He shook his head. "No . . . no . . . that wasn't the game."

"What happened then?"

His expression grew more intense. He seemed to be reliving the experience almost as if he were hypnotized.

"And *then*—?" I prodded him gently.

He was like a man poised on the edge of a precipice who cannot bring himself to jump. After a time, he deflated, shook his head and said, "I'm sorry. I just can't remember."

We both drew a collective breath. I gave him time to compose himself.

"Russell, what's the very next thing you remember after being in the dark?"

He thought for a moment. "I saw her."

"Who?"

"*The Lady C*. I didn't understand where I was, why I wasn't aboard her. I had a crate of bananas in my hand and there was the smell of garbage. I thought, 'Why am I here and not on the yacht?' I had to get aboard the yacht. They all laughed when I told them I had to get on the yacht."

"Who laughed?"

"The men on the boat."

"The trader boat. But you don't remember how you got on the trader boat, or what you did before you got there?"

He shut his eyes tight as if trying to squeeze the memory out of his brain.

"No . . . I think . . . I remember someone putting something cool on my head . . . I must have had a fever . . . I was so hot . . . oh, I don't know," he said, giving up and shaking his head in exasperation. "I just don't know. I do know that I arrived broken in this world, Jo. And nothing's been able to fix me so far," he said softly. "The pity of it is that I can function quite well up to a certain point. Then some circuit just disconnects . . ." He paused, lost in thought. "I know this has happened several times before, and that the precipitating incident is always something physically traumatic."

"And what do you think the precipitating incident was?"

Russell was silent for a long moment. Then he said, "Maybe they played the game for real this time."

I had a vision of Carla on the day she arrived on our

beach with her accomplice, the egregious Captain Jenks. Had I been gullible in interpreting her distress as profound concern for Russell? Could it really have been profound panic at the thought that he had escaped? Or did she even know he was missing at that point? She may have thought he was dead, having stowed him in that little room, biding her time until it was safe to dispose of his body. Perhaps she and Jenks had put the scull out in the water that morning to make it look like Russell had taken it out and then either run away or drowned.

In any case, I felt it was time for Russell to see what was in the little room. I got Captain Rankin and we both took him there. Russell remained expressionless as he stared down at the plastic cooler and its contents. He walked away in silence, went straight back into his room, asked us to leave, and closed the door behind us.

In the end, I knew that it would be simply Russell's word against Carla's, and she had all the money. In my experience, *people always believe the money*. One could embroider it on a needlepoint pillow. On the other hand, Carla couldn't really afford to have Russell remember what had happened to him that night on the off chance that some people would believe him. She hadn't worked alone. She'd had an accomplice. And who knows what an enterprising detective might find out about Jasper Jenks? A man as evil as Jenks doesn't just materialize out of the blue. The Jenkses of the world have histories. I believed the threat of this was enough to lure her down to the boat where I was prepared to take matters into my own hands, if necessary.

I called Carla on the satellite phone.

"Ah, *cara* Jo . . . How nice to hear from you!" Carla said. "Where *are* you? You got my message?"

"Yes, I got your message, Carla. Loud and clear. I'm on the yacht."

"And how are you enjoying your trip? Have you come across anything interesting on your travels?"

Her taunting voice irked me no end. "In fact, I have, Carla," I said. "Prepare yourself for a shock . . ."

"I am always prepared for everything," she said with confidence.

"Russell is alive."

Apparently she wasn't prepared for that. Several seconds of silence ensued.

"Is he all right?" she said at last.

"Well, that depends on how you look at it," I said.

"What do you mean?" Her voice was icy cold.

"Let me put it this way: He's alive, but not well."

"Is he ill?" she asked, rather hopefully, I thought.

"Not physically. He's just . . . confused."

"Confused? How?"

"Oh, he's rambling on about things."

"What things?" For the first time, there was a note of urgency in her voice.

"I don't want to go into it on the phone. But he's obviously had a very difficult time."

"I want to talk to him," she said.

"I'm afraid you can't. He's resting."

"Wake him up. I want to talk to him."

"You can talk to him later."

"I want to talk to him *now*!"

"I'm sorry, Carla, but I can't disturb him. I'm calling because I thought you might like to come down here and see him before the press gets hold of the story."

"Where are you?"

"St. Maarten. The Dutch side."

"Well, of course I am coming! He's my husband. I must take him home immediately. I must talk to him."

"There'll be plenty of time to talk to him when you get down here," I said. "I think you'll be quite interested in what he has to say."

The implied threat shut her up. She said she would fly down the next day. I called Rankin and had him give her all the pertinent details.

My plan was simple. Carla would sail back to the States with us. I'd have plenty of time to deal with her at sea.

Forty-two

THE NEXT AFTERNOON, CAPTAIN RANKIN AND I went to pick up Carla at the St. Maarten airport. Since she was arriving in a Gulfstream V, Rankin had gotten us permission to meet her on the runway in order to collect her luggage. Rankin and I were sitting in the Jeep when the sleek, white plane landed at four o'clock and taxied into the unloading area. The door opened and Carla emerged, wearing a black linen suit, a large-brimmed, black straw hat, and a solemn expression beneath a pair of sunglasses.

She was not alone. Also emerging from the plane, directly behind her, was a tall, handsome younger man with blond hair and a muscular build. At first I thought he was the pilot. But he wasn't in uniform and, besides, there was something vaguely familiar about him. Rankin bridled when he saw him.

"Jesus, that's *Jenks*," Rankin whispered to me.

Jasper Jenks, Rankin's nemesis and the man I suspected of being a stone-cold killer, was the very last person I expected or wanted to see.

"Did you know he was coming?" Rankin asked me.

"I most certainly did not."

Why did it surprise me that Carla had brought him when I knew her to be a woman who twisted all events to her advantage?

Before Jenks descended the steps, he stood for a moment on the platform, sniffing the air like a wild animal sniffing for game.

"Well, if she thinks they're taking Mr. Cole with them, she's got another think coming," I said to Rankin.

As Rankin and I got out of the car, Carla rushed forward to greet us. Gone was the cool demeanor of the phone conversation. This was hardly surprising. She had an audience now.

"*Cara Jo!*" she cried, flinging her arms around me. "I am a *wreck!* An absolute *wreck!* I did not sleep at all last night, worrying about my darling Russell. Where is he? I cannot wait to see him! Tell me, has he spoken of anything? Does he remember anything?"

"Not much," I said.

Carla tried not to show her relief, but no one is *that* good an actress.

"How terrible!" she said, unconvincingly. "And Captain Rankin, how lovely to see you again."

Carla shook hands with Rankin. "Mrs. Cole," he said coolly.

"And you know Captain Jenks, of course," she said.

The two men gave each other perfunctory nods.

"Jo, do you remember Captain Jenks?" Carla said. "He was with me the morning Russell disappeared. He searched Betty's property."

"Yes, of course, hello," I said, mustering a cordial smile and shaking his hand, despite my deep disgust. I still couldn't be sure if Jenks was the footman who had accused me of taking Carla's earring that night. Rankin was right. Jenks was chameleon-like, ever-changing, a man with no core.

"A pleasure—*playshah*, Mrs. Slater—*Slatah*," he said with the flat A's of a pronounced Australian accent. "I'm flattered you remember me."

"Come on, Jasper, let's go get the luggage," Rankin said.

"There is very little," Carla said.

"Well, come on along anyway," Rankin said to Jenks.

As Rankin and Jenks walked off together, I led Carla to the car.

"Carla, dear, I'm afraid I can't ask Captain Jenks to sail with us back to the States. It would be just too awkward with Captain Rankin. I'm sure you understand."

"Oh, but we are not sailing back. I have decided to take Russell home on the plane."

So that was her plan, was it? Now I understood why she had brought Jenks with her.

"I thought we were going to sail back," I said. "That would give Russell a chance to recover a bit. I don't have to tell you what's going to happen when the press finds out he's alive."

Carla shook her head. "No, no, Jo, dear. Believe me, I have thought a lot about it. He must go to the hospital as soon as possible."

"You're going to have him committed?"

She pulled a long face. "I do *hate* that word—'committed.' But really, Jo, you know yourself, he cannot be allowed to do this again. He has come through it safely this time. But next time, he could kill himself, or *be* killed. Russell must now be in a safe place at all times with professional people looking after him."

We were like two archenemies having a decorous conversation before declaring war. However, I wasn't going to argue with her, fearing I might tip her off as to what I'd planned.

"You could be right," I said. "It's not a bad idea."

When Carla's one suitcase and Jenks's overnight satchel were loaded onto the Jeep, we were off, heading for the docks. Jenks sat up front with Rankin. Carla and I sat in the back. I subtly needed to let Rankin know what Carla was planning.

"Mike," I said, as he drove to the port, "Mrs. Cole is planning to take Mr. Cole back with her tonight on her plane."

Rankin was smart enough to understand he had to play it cool.

"Uh-huh," he said blandly.

Carla wanted to know again exactly how Russell had been found. Rankin told her the story. All the while he was talking, I was thinking of ways to keep Russell on the boat and have Carla sail back with him. Jenks sat silently, staring out the window, a sullen expression on his face.

We reached the port in a little under half an hour. The sun had retreated behind the clouds and Captain Rankin mentioned there might be a bout of bad weather coming. Getting onto the docks where the private boats were moored was not difficult. Captain Rankin inserted his plastic card "key" into a slit and held the gate open for us to pass. *The Lady C* was relatively far away from the main entrance, docked at the end of a concrete pier. The four of us walked in tense silence to the great white yacht, which was by far the largest boat on the dock. I caught Carla stealing a smug glance at Jenks as we boarded.

Rankin trotted on ahead. I knew he was going to tip off Russell and Nancy to the fact that Jenks had come along and that Carla was planning to take Russell back on the plane with her, either that night or the next morning.

"How strange it is being back on the boat," Carla remarked, as we headed toward Russell's stateroom. "And how sad *The Lady* looks without her paintings. . . . The new owner obviously has no taste," she said, glancing with exaggerated disgust at the photographs that had replaced them.

The door of Russell's stateroom was open. Carla, Jenks, and I entered. Russell was propped up in his bed, staring into space. Rankin and Nancy were standing nearby. Nancy stepped forward to greet Carla and Jenks. Carla was less than cordial. Her attention was clearly elsewhere. She couldn't take her eyes off Russell. She whispered, "*Dio mio*, he looks *frightful*."

"I warned you," I whispered back.

Carla walked over to the bed and sat down beside Russell. Her lips quivered dramatically and her eyes brimmed with forced tears as she took one of his limp hands in hers. She held it up to her cheek and said softly, "Russell . . . ? Russell, *mi amore* . . . ? It is Carla . . . your Carla . . . you are safe now, my darling . . . you are going to get all better now. . . ."

Jenks walked up and knelt down beside Carla. He put a sympathetic hand on his old boss's arm.

"Mr. Cole, sir? It's Jasper, sir . . ."

Russell, acting like a prisoner in his own private world, continued staring straight ahead, pretending not to see or hear either of them. Jenks rubbed his hand up and down Russell's arm as Carla held his hand and spoke softly to him, so I could barely hear. After several minutes, Carla rose to her feet and so did Jenks. She addressed Captain Rankin.

"How soon can you get him ready?" she said.

"Ready for what?" Rankin asked.

"I am taking him home on the plane now."

"Mr. Cole is free to go whenever he wants." Rankin shrugged.

Carla stood at the foot of the bed and addressed Russell.

"Russell, my darling, you must get ready now. I am going to take you back home with me where you will be safe," she said sweetly. Then she turned to Jenks and in a harsher voice commanded, "Help him out of the bed, Jasper."

Rankin, Nancy, and I all glanced at each other as Jenks tried without success to get Russell out of bed. Impervious to all cajoling, Russell lurched away every time Jenks touched him. Finally, Carla asked Rankin to help.

"He doesn't seem to want to go," Rankin said.

"But he must come with me. I am his wife," she said.

"Mr. Cole . . . ?" Rankin said. "Do you want to leave the boat and go with your wife?"

Russell shook his head no.

Carla immediately swooped toward him. "Russell, darling! I've come to take you back home with me. You *must* come with me."

"No," he said angrily.

"Russell . . . do you know who I am?" Carla asked him.

"Yes," he replied belligerently.

"Darling, I am your wife. And you must trust me, my darling. You must trust me to take you home and take care of you."

"*No.*" I knew he was seething about Max.

Carla rose to her feet.

"Captain Rankin, please make my husband understand that he must come with me."

"Strickly speaking, Mrs. Cole, if Mr. Cole doesn't want to go with you, he doesn't have to."

"But you can see, he is not in his right mind," Carla whispered.

"He seems to know who you are and where he is. If he doesn't want to go with you, I can't force him. And no one has the authority to order him off this boat but me."

Carla was indignant. "My husband is obviously a very sick man. Any fool can see that. He must go to a hospital back in the United States. He needs treatment. Now, either you help us take him to the plane, or I will hold you personally responsible, Captain. If you do not cooperate, you will lose your license. I promise you!"

"Well, I'll just have to take that chance then, Mrs. Cole, because I'm not going to make Mr. Cole do something against his will."

"He needs help! Can't you see that, you stupid man?"

"He'll get help when we dock in Miami, Mrs. Cole," Rankin said, leaving the room.

"Go talk to him, Jasper," Carla ordered Jenks.

Jenks, a dull but curiously threatening presence, obeyed her and left the room.

"Jo, please help me. You know it is best for Russell if we get him home quickly."

"But doesn't Russell think of this boat as his home?" I asked her disingenuously.

"Home is where his wife is," she retorted. "And *I* am in New York."

"But you're here now, Carla. And short of kidnapping him, I doubt there's much any of us can do if Russell doesn't want to go. The captain's obviously not going to force him."

"I'm not going with you, Carla," Russell said. "I'm staying here."

This was the first sentence that Russell had spoken in her presence, and Carla reacted by again rushing to his side.

"My darling . . . How I have missed you! But I never gave up hope. I always knew that one day you would come back to me."

Nancy, who was standing against the wall with her arms crossed in front of her, looked at me and rolled her eyes heavenward. Jenks popped his bright blond head inside the door.

"Excuse me, Mrs. Cole. May I speak to you for a moment?"

The minute Carla left the room to go talk to Jenks, I sat down next to Russell.

"What's she doing here with Jenks?! I can't bear the sight of them," he said. His hands were shaking with rage.

"You're doing fine," I whispered. "Just hang on."

Carla and Jenks were speaking softly to each other out in the corridor. Their voices grew more animated and Nancy edged closer to the door to try and hear what they were saying. After a moment or two, she shook her head, indicating it was no use. Carla came back into the room. She was clearly perturbed.

"I believe that your husband is making an enormous

mistake by not allowing me to take my husband home on the plane," she said, looking directly at Nancy. "However, my hands seem to be tied. Now I must think of what is best for my husband. So I have decided to accompany him back on the boat. I will sail with him to Miami, if that is all right with you, Jo."

"Of course, Carla. But unfortunately, I can't ask Captain Jenks to join us."

"No, I thought not," Carla said with a knowing little smirk. "Jasper is going back on the plane this evening," she went on. "He informs me that it will take us approximately five days to sail from here to Miami, provided we do not run into bad weather. That includes a stop in Puerto Rico to refuel. Jasper will meet us in Miami and he and I will take Russell back to New York in the plane. That is the current plan."

In reality, the trip needn't have taken more than three days, but Rankin and I had agreed ahead of time it was better to stretch the journey out as long as possible. I should have smelled a rat when neither Jenks nor Carla raised an objection.

Playing the dutiful, concerned wife, Carla sat down beside Russell again, stroked his hair, and talked softly to him, telling him everything was going to be all right. Then she turned to me and said sweetly, "Jo, dear, I know it is a terrible imposition, but would you mind if I had my old room back for the rest of the voyage? I do so want to be near my husband."

I couldn't really deny her request without tipping my hand.

"Of course, Carla. I'll have one of the crew move my things down to a guest cabin."

"I will, of course, compensate you for having interrupted your wonderful vacation," she said.

Rankin drove Jenks back to the airport and waited until he saw the plane take off with Jenks on it. I told him not to take any chances with Jenks, whom I believed to be Carla's creature and a stone-cold killer. The crew were all apprised of our new guest. The cat was now out of the bag and they were all asked not to say anything to anyone about Russell until we landed in Miami. Since Carla had not planned on staying long, she didn't bring along many clothes. I loaned her some of my things.

That evening we set sail for Puerto Rico. Carla and I dined alone together. Russell stayed in his cabin. As the yacht chugged along the dark, open sea, she and I sat inside in the candlelit dining room, eating a gourmet dinner the chef had prepared. Carla began the meal by saying again how odd she felt being back on the boat.

"I never thought I would be sitting here again," she said, arranging her napkin on her lap with exaggerated care. "It is so very strange. But then, life is so very strange, is it not?"

I interpreted this to mean that she never in a million years expected things to go so wrong.

She also said, over and over, how relieved she was to have Russell back and how she prayed he would "be all right." She kept asking me if there had been any "significant change" in him since he first got on the boat, another sign she was worried he might indeed recover. If she had any inkling that Russell had told me everything, she didn't show it. And yet, she was such an intuitive person, she must have sensed I knew more than I was letting on. At dessert, she fired the shot that I figured was designed to derail me.

"And how are you coping with the death of your good friend, Larry Locket, dear Jo?" Carla said, slipping a spoonful of homemade mango ice into her mouth.

I wanted to reach across the table, grab her throat, and yell, "You had him murdered, you bitch!" But instead, I finished chewing the sugar cookie I was eating and said, simply, "I'm doing the best I can. It's very kind of you to ask, Carla. Thank you so much."

We were like two lionesses trapped in the same golden cage, each waiting to make our move. Our conversation was as stilted as it was decorous, a mini version of social life where people so often pretend not to know what other people are really up to. However, our polite banter could not hide the fact that we loathed each other. I said good night to Carla, and before I went downstairs to my cabin, I walked out on deck and stood alone for a long moment in the dark and windy night, wondering when and how I would make my move.

Forty-three

I DOUBT THAT ANY OF US GOT MUCH SLEEP THAT first night, except perhaps the off-duty crew, who were happily tucked into their bunks in their quarters below the foredeck. I, for one, lay awake most of the night, listening to the sound of the engines chugging through the black water, thinking about Carla and Russell in their grand suites on the deck above me. I doubted that either of them had found peace in the lap of luxury. But I was a little worried that Carla might try and influence Russell, working in the territory she knew best—the bedroom. The night finally passed and we sailed into a misty dawn. I dressed for breakfast, and when I went upstairs, I saw Russell standing out on the deck with Carla at his side. They were holding hands and gazing out at the choppy, grey sea.

"Good morning," I said, tentatively.

Carla turned around. "Good morning, Jo!" she replied with ominous buoyancy. "And what a morning it is! *Bellissima!* Not the weather, of course. But I have my darling husband back." She put her head on his shoulder and playfully stroked his arm.

Russell avoided my gaze, which made me suspicious that she had somehow gotten to him in the night. It didn't take a genius to figure out how she might have swayed him over to her side again. The woman was a pro.

"Good morning, Russell," I said purposely.

"Morning," he mumbled.

"We are just taking a little walk before breakfast. Excuse us, won't you, Jo?" Carla said.

I watched them as they strolled up the narrow side deck of the boat. Carla ran her hand along the polished wood railing. Russell turned to her, laughing, and hugged her close. He wasn't acting. On the contrary, he looked relieved and happy, as lovers do when they are reunited with the object of their obsession. Carla was watching over him like a bird of prey and I knew she wasn't going to let him out of her sight from now on. They would always be together and that would make things significantly more difficult for me.

Just as I predicted, Russell and Carla ostentatiously avoided me. They ate by themselves, took long walks together on the deck, holding hands and cuddling like they were on their second honeymoon. Carla read aloud to Russell in the grand salon. They drank white wine constantly—although I noticed that Carla diluted hers with ice cubes. During this period, I got an inkling of just how Carla worked. She was a total geisha, always watching Russell with adoring eyes, laughing at his jokes, agreeing with everything he said, catering to his every whim, and constantly telling him how handsome and brilliant he was. She was the perfect tonic for an insecure man. She was also very seductive and very entertaining, telling funny stories and relating the gossip of social life with the style of a skilled raconteur.

However, the main bond between them was that they had found a common enemy in me. Carla's delight in the surreptitious persecution of me added spice to the saccharine stew of affection she showed Russell. I heard her talking about me, and whenever I came into view, there were whispers and stifled laughter. Nothing bonds people faster than a shared love or a shared hatred. And they both clearly loved each other and clearly hated me.

There seemed to be no hope of separating them. One morning, however, I saw Russell standing alone on deck, leaning against the railing, gazing out at the sea. I grabbed my chance to talk to him, but as I approached him, he said, "I don't want to talk to you, Jo," and turned away. I refused to leave.

"What has she been telling you, Russell?" I asked him. He didn't answer. I went on. "Can't you see how she's manipulating you? She's going to get rid of you, you know. One way or the other. You mark my words. We'll land in Miami and she'll slap you into a hospital so fast you won't know what hit you. You'll see."

He wheeled around and faced me in a rage. "*No!*" he cried. "*She loves me!* She's the only one who's ever *really* loved me. She knew you'd try to turn me against her. You hate her because she knows all about you, Jo. You're being blackmailed for something terrible. Carla told me. She says you're a very bad person and that I can't trust you."

I shook my head in dismay. "Russell, you're forgetting everything we talked about."

"You twisted everything around. The fact is, I don't

really have a good recollection of what happened to me. But Carla does. She told me we were playing the game and I blacked out. I had an episode. She sailed all around searching for me. She was desperate to find me."

"Didn't you once tell Captain Rankin he was not to move the boat if you ever disappeared? Why did she set sail almost immediately and then sell it? Because she didn't want to find you!"

"No! That's not true!"

"Okay, what about the money then? How does she explain that?"

He broke into a gloating smile. "For your information, she intends to give *back* all my money when we get to New York."

"And you believe her?"

"More than *you*. She told me *why* she had to use the powers of attorney . . . because Courtney, my greedy daughter, was trying to get her hands on my fortune— just like I suspected. She was trying to have me declared dead so she could inherit everything. Lulu put her up to it. I knew she would. They're only after my money, those two. Carla always told me that. And I told *you* that. I knew it. Carla was terrified that when I came back there'd be nothing left. That's why she did it."

Russell rambled on, twisting every fact so that Carla looked like a savior.

"What about your collection? Why did she give it away?" I asked him.

"Courtney was trying to get her hands on that, too. Carla donated it to the Municipal Museum because they were powerful enough to fight her. She says they'll give it back to me the minute they know I'm alive. There's no question about that. See, Jo, what you don't understand is that Carla's done all this to protect me from my greedy daughter and my vindictive ex-wife. Carla's the only one who's ever had *my* interests at heart. The only one, *ever*. She says she always knew in her heart I'd come back to her. She is my tigress, protecting me."

"What about Max?" I said, playing my trump card. "Why did she give him millions of dollars to put a roof on his house?"

Russell scoffed at this. "Oh, that's a complete fabrication!"

"You read it yourself in the papers. Why would they make something like that up?"

"Max fed it to them, that's why. Carla told me that when she read it she was outraged. See, it's all part of his obsession with her. She explained the whole thing."

"How did she explain going out with him?"

"She wasn't *with* him. They were just at the party and the press made it look like they were together. She loves me, not Max," Russell said firmly. "You're just trying to confuse me."

"Why, Russell? Why would I want to do that?"

"Because you hate her. And you hate her because she knows all about you. And because you're jealous of her. You tried to have her blocked from going on the board of the Municipal Museum, which she was doing for my benefit."

"For your benefit?" My eyes widened. His naïveté knew no bounds.

"*Yes*. So she'd be sure that they'd give me my collection back when I came home. But they knew what you were up to and they expelled you from the board in a humiliating way. Carla and I read all about it on the Internet."

It was no use. If I hadn't been so outraged, I would have felt sorry for poor old Russell, whose mind was so porous, he was constantly a victim of his last conversation. Carla had managed to twist everything around in that inimitable way of hers. I wouldn't have minded so much, except that Russell's attitude made things much more risky for me and my plan to get rid of her.

Forty-four

I**T WAS RAINING HARD WHEN WE DOCKED IN** San Juan to refuel. The process took several hours. Despite the weather, Carla wanted to go into the city to shop. According to Rankin, shopping was one of the main things she and Russell had always loved to do together. I suddenly had a terrible thought: What if they went into San Juan and Carla persuaded Russell to fly back to the States with her from there, instead of waiting for us to sail to Miami? My fears proved to be unfounded, however. Russell refused to leave the boat. I stayed in my cabin, wondering if I would get the opportunity to expose Carla to Russell before our journey ended. Time was growing short.

When we finished refueling, it was raining harder. Rankin warned us a bad front was moving in and unless we got under way in a hurry, we were liable to be marooned in San Juan for a couple of days. Carla was very anxious to get going. She pushed Rankin to set sail. The sea grew choppier as we headed west, and it was rough sailing. The boat was rocking back and forth and every so often the swells would send it up, then down with a slap. Everything was anchored down or put away so objects wouldn't go careening when we hit a wave. I was too seasick to eat. I went to my cabin to lie down. I must have dozed off because when I awoke, the sea was calm, and we were sailing steadily through the water.

Still vaguely seasick, I changed into a sweat suit and headed up to the main deck to get some fresh air. The storm had passed. Leaning on the railing of the aft deck, taking deep breaths to counter my nausea, I gazed out at the vast darkness all around us. In the distance, a misty moon hung in the sky, casting a pale reflection on the calm, black velvet sea. I remember thinking how small the yacht seemed in that immense setting, how vulnerable. Feeling better, I wandered up to the bridge where Captain Rankin was on duty with the first mate. Rankin was drinking coffee, looking over charts of the area. The glass-enclosed room, surrounded by night, glowed with the lights and sweeping green radar screens of the large control panel.

Rankin was surprised to see me. It was very late. He offered me a cup of coffee and we sat and talked for a while, seated on the long blue leather banquette. We talked about the Coles. I had told him how Carla had manipulated everything to suit her purposes, and how Russell now believed her wholeheartedly. He said it didn't surprise him. "She could always twist him around her little finger," he said.

I stared out at the open water. "God, it's dark out there, even with the moon, it's so enormously black and forbidding."

"I love it," Rankin said. "We're over the deepest part of the Atlantic Ocean right now . . . The Puerto Rican Trench. Ten thousand feet straight down. Sink here and you're really sunk. They'll never find you."

"I find sailing at night a little frightening somehow," I told him.

"Night's my favorite time on a boat. You can really *feel* the sea."

"That's just it. You feel how puny and insignificant you are."

"Don't worry. *The Lady*'s a good old gal. Very seaworthy. Still, I can't say I'll be sad when this trip is over."

Famous last words.

After an hour or so, I grew drowsy and left Rankin and the first mate on the bridge to go back to bed. I went down the two flights of stairs and walked out on deck for one last breath of air before returning to my room. I gripped the railing hard as a strong wind whipped the hair around my face. There were no stars in the sky, just scattered clouds and a hazy ring around the moon. Suddenly, I heard what sounded like a cry above the hum of the engines. I turned toward the sound and listened. After a moment or two, I could have sworn I heard a shot and splash, but it was very difficult to tell. The engines were loud. I walked up to the foredeck to investigate, but there was no one there. I looked out at the sea rushing past. Nothing. Just wavy currents of sparkling, black water lit by the night lights on the lower sides of the boat.

I suddenly had a very bad feeling. My first instinct was to go and check on Russell. I was still out on deck, heading toward my cabin, when I saw Carla, fully dressed in jeans and a windbreaker, coming out of the automatic sliding doors of the grand salon. It was dark and she didn't see me. I followed her as she walked up the narrow side deck toward the outside stairway leading to the bridge.

I heard her calling out softly, "Jasper . . . ? Jasper . . . ? Where are you?"

Jasper Jenks! Was *he* on board?

I kept out of sight, my heart racing.

Was it possible that Jenks hadn't flown to Miami? Had he flown to Puerto Rico instead and slipped on the boat during the refueling in San Juan? Was that what he and Carla had planned before he left the boat in St. Maarten? I recalled the conversation the two of them had in the hall. As Russell himself had proven, it was easy enough to sneak on a vessel of that size, particularly if you knew its workings. As the former captain, Jenks certainly knew the yacht well enough to get himself aboard and then to hide out in the secret passages. It would be relatively easy for him to get rid of Russell and keep out of sight until we reached the shore, where he could sneak off again when we reached port, with no one the wiser.

The thought occurred to me: Was Carla preparing the way for it to look like Russell had committed suicide by throwing himself overboard?

We were in the deepest part of the Atlantic Ocean. The odds were that a body would never be found. I was beginning to think that the cry, shot, and splash I'd heard earlier were not figments of my imagination, but the real end of Russell Cole.

But if Jenks was aboard, that meant I was in danger, too. I knew way too much.

As Carla stood waiting out in the night, I ducked into the grand salon and grabbed one of the perfectly hideous reproduction stone rain god statuettes from its secure niche in the bookshelf. I went back outside where Carla was still standing, softly calling out Jasper's name with more urgency.

After a few moments, a shadowy figure stepped in front of her.

"Jasper!" I heard her say with evident relief.

I gripped the statue harder and backed away instinctively, thinking that if Jenks had killed Russell and they knew I was nearby, I was almost certainly next. But then I heard raised voices. Something was wrong. I drew closer to listen to what they were saying. A shard of light from the interior of the boat hit their faces. The shadowy figure wasn't Jenks. It was *Russell*. He was holding a gun to Carla's head. I assumed it was the .22 from the safe room. He was in a fury, shouting that Carla had sent Jenks to kill him. She denied it, of course, sobbing that she didn't even know Jenks was on board.

"*Well, he's not on board anymore!*" Russell said with a maniacal laugh.

Carla was pleading with Russell not to hurt her when, suddenly, Russell caught sight of me. And there it was: that sharp, murderous sparkle in his eye. His face was a jumble of glee, hurt, and confusion—the very picture of a madman.

"*Jo!*" he called out. "*You were right! You were right!*"

"*Jo! Help! Auitami! He's mad! È pazzo!. . . Don't let him hurt me!*"

"She thought I was Jenks," Russell said. "She called his name. She wanted Jenks to kill me so she can marry Max. . . . Just like you said, Jo . . . . *just like you said . . .*"

He turned back to Carla and raised the gun, pointing it directly at her heart. The roar of the engines muted her cries. Russell's hand was shaking. I was sure he was going to shoot her.

"*Do it!*" I urged him. "*It's your only chance!*"

The night, the wind, and the sound of the engines stopped time. Russell raised the gun higher, pointing it at her face. He winced as if in great pain. His hand was shaking so badly now, I feared he would drop the gun. He either couldn't or wouldn't decide what to do. After a few tense and interminable seconds, he lowered the gun and stalked off. Not everyone is a killer.

Carla turned to me. A sly smile of satisfaction crept over her face. The shadow play made her look demonic. With that, she lunged at me. I was so startled, I dropped the statue I'd been clutching. She was fit and young and strong, and she had me pinned backward over the railing before I could stop her. I managed to grab her by the hair and pull her sideways, but still she had me up against the rail. As we struggled, she must have stepped on the little statue because she suddenly pitched forward with a strangled cry. She was off-balance. A vision of Monique on the balcony flared up in my head.

This has happened to me before.

This is familiar.

I don't want to do this, *but* . . .

As in New York, nothing counts until after the "but."

Larry's face materialized in my mind's eye, egging me on, making me realize that unless I seized the moment, it would never come again. I dropped down, grabbed her knees, and lifted her over the side of the boat, simply helping her complete her forward trajectory. She fell into the sea. I watched her disappear into the churning foam of the hydro engines. When I looked back at the wake, there was no sign of her.

Shaken and exhausted, I just stood there, looking down at the water for God knows how long. Carla was dead. Larry was avenged. Yet, oddly, it didn't feel like a victory. It felt vaguely sickening, and I threw up over the side of the boat. After a time, I started walking back down to my cabin to find Russell. I, too, nearly tripped on the little rain god statue. I picked it up and threw it into the water, feeling sure that the hideous reproduction, along with Carla Cole, would not be missed.

Disasters happen in slow motion, and my recollection of this one is just like the recollection of a dream, filled with disjointed shapes and images. As I wandered around searching for Russell, I noticed that the boat felt different somehow, but I couldn't put my finger on it. Then suddenly all the lights went out. Seconds later, chaos erupted. The first mate, holding a flashlight, hurtled past me on the deck.

"What's happening?!" I cried.

"I think we're sinking," he yelled back. *"Get up to the sun deck!"* He kept running.

Rankin was on the bridge sending out SOS calls and also talking to the first mate with a handheld radio. I heard Rankin say, "Who is it?" to which the mate's staticky voice replied, "The engineer, sir. Jesus, he's been shot . . . he's bleeding . . ."

Rankin wheeled the beam of his flashlight on my face. "Get up to the sun deck, Mrs. Slater," he said. "Nancy's up there."

"Mr. Cole's got a gun," I told him.

Rankin rubbed his forehead. "Listen, Steve, be careful, will you? Mr. Cole's got a gun. If you see him, just get away . . . *Christ* . . . Mrs. Slater, *please* go up top!" he ordered me.

I climbed up to the sun deck, where Nancy was unhooking the lifeboats from their cannisters.

"*Nancy!*" I cried.

She shone her flashlight in my direction. "*Mrs. Slater—thank God!* Grab a life jacket!"

I pulled out a life jacket from the the large chest container and put it on, strapping it tight.

"Are we sinking?" I asked.

"Feels like it. Mike sent the first mate down to the engine room to check it out."

I helped her unhook the lifeboats. We got the first one done. It rolled off the side of the boat and hit the water, inflating into a big, orange raft tethered to the yacht by a cord. We were working on the others when one by one, the crewmembers, startled out of their sleep, made their way up to the sun deck wearing their life jackets and holding flashlights, looking a little dazed and confused.

Nearly the whole crew was up top, including the first mate, who had carried the wounded engineer up on his back. The wounded man told us that he had tried to stop Mr. Cole, but that Russell had shot him in the arm, then disabled the bilge alarm, and opened the sea cocks. The engineer had managed to escape, but Russell was still down there.

"The engine room's completely flooded! We're going down!" he cried.

Nancy ran down to see her husband on the bridge and came back shortly with more news.

"Mike says we're definitely gonna have to abandon ship," she cried out. "We're sinking too fast to go from the main deck, so he says prepare to jump off from up here."

"Oh, wonderful," I said, thinking that I was about to find out just how Monique de Passy and Carla Cole felt hurtling to their deaths. There was such a thing as poetic justice and this was it.

"Don't worry, Mrs. Slater, you'll be fine," Nancy assured me, sensing my anxiety.

"When do we go?" I asked.

"We'll wait for Mike. He's just gone down to see if he can find Mr. Cole."

I was amazed at how calm everyone seemed under the circumstances.

"Nancy, Mr. Cole is insane . . . Mike could be in danger!"

"You don't know my husband," she said. "He's got to try and find him!"

We were listing badly now. All the lifeboats were in the water and there was talk about getting the tenders off when the boat sank as there was no power to launch them from their cranes. Most of the crew was assembled up top. No one said much. We were all too nervous to talk. People held their flashlights and huddled together for warmth and comfort. I could just imagine what we looked like with our pathetic little circles of light pricking the darkness of that vast, watery universe.

Finally, Mike came up on the deck.

"All right, everyone . . . *prepare to abandon ship!*" he

cried. "When you hit water, swim for a lifeboat, and when the boat's loaded, get as far away from the yacht as possible!"

I asked Mike, "Did you find Mr. Cole?"

"No . . . *Go!*" he ordered me.

I held my breath, then jumped into my greatest fear.

Forty-five

IT WAS DAWN WHEN THE COAST GUARD FOUND us drifting in our orange rafts. I now knew how survivors of the *Titanic* must have felt—floating in small lifeboats on a vast sea, trying to comprehend the enormity of what had just taken place. Everyone was silent as we drifted on dark water. We had all retreated into our own little worlds. I replayed the moment on the deck when Carla had lunged for me. If I had not had "prior experience," as they say, perhaps I would have been the one to perish.

For days after that, we were all questioned about what exactly had happened. It was Rankin's theory that the first time Carla and Jenks tried to kill Russell in Barbados, something had gone seriously wrong. He believed that during "the game," they thought they had suffocated him, when, in fact, they had not. Apparently, it's possible to appear dead, like a cataleptic, then come to. Rankin surmised that they put Russell into that little room with intention of "chopping him up for fish food at a later date." But Russell came to and somehow managed to escape. The trauma most likely triggered one of his famous episodes.

Whether Russell got into the scull himself and tried to row ashore, or whether Carla and Jenks launched the scull in order to stage his disappearance, we will never know. In fact, we'll never know if that morning when they both came looking for him at King's Fort they really thought he was missing. It may have all been an act and they may have only discovered he was gone much later, when they went to check on him in the little room. In any case, it must have been quite a shock to Carla when Russell turned up again after so many months. When Russell refused to accompany her back on the plane, she set another plan in motion. Like myself, Rankin was sure that Jenks had sneaked aboard the yacht in San Juan in order to kill Russell Cole—again—and make it look like he'd thrown himself overboard.

But Russell managed to shoot Jenks instead. That became clear when they recovered Jenks's body (he was wearing a life jacket) and found he'd been shot with a .22. Jenks then either fell or was tossed overboard by Russell. Rankin assumed that Russell figured out what Carla had done. Her betrayal was too much for him and, in a mad frenzy, he had killed her, opened the sea cocks, and sunk the yacht.

Parts of this theory were undoubtedly true. Other parts were not. I believed that Carla intended to kill Russell and dispose of his body so he would never be found and so she could be free to steal his fortune. I also believed that when she found out he was alive, she arranged it so Jenks would dispose of him—permanently, this time. I'd heard the shot that either killed or wounded Jenks, and heard the splash when he went overboard. I'd also overheard Russell telling Carla he'd thwarted Jenks's attempt to kill him. However, I kept that to myself, along with so much else. As for the other part of the captain's theory—the part where Russell Cole supposedly killed Carla in a mad frenzy—well, needless to say, I didn't offer an opinion on that, either. I just nodded, agreeing with the explanation Rankin had put forth.

"I guess he just didn't want anyone else to have either of his ladies," Rankin said, referring to both Carla and *The Lady C.*

When questioned by investigators from the Coast Guard who were dissecting the disaster, I said, "Captain Rankin's theory makes perfect sense to me. I heard a shot and then a splash and then I saw Russell Cole running frantically along the deck with a gun in his hand. I didn't see Carla Cole, though, but I assumed he was after her. What a tragedy it all is."

What I didn't tell them was what I really knew: Russell couldn't bring himself to kill Carla face-to-face. But he knew she had to die. And if she died, so would he. That's why he sank the boat. He couldn't live without her and he was just too far gone to care if the rest of us went with them.

Forty-six

I N SOCIAL LIFE, IT'S ALWAYS BEST TO GIVE A
party *for* someone or something. Society loves
a theme. We also love it when one of our own
successfully comes through a terrible ordeal. We want to
be around survivors, especially if they come through it
with their fortune pretty much intact. By that light, Trish
Bromire's dinner dance in honor of Dick's release from
prison was the hottest invitation in town. Dick's reputation had been slightly tarnished by his conviction and in-
carceration, but it was nothing that a couple of billion
dollars couldn't polish up again in fairly short order. Society has a short memory. It has to.

Betty wondered if Trish had meant the hand-delivered,
calligraphed invitation to be intentionally funny, or if she
was oblivious to the meaning of the very English word-
ing, which read,

Trish Bromire

At Home

Taunton Hall

"At home in her dreams," Betty said.

Dick Bromire had rented Taunton Hall to celebrate his release. He was flying friends to London from all around the world. He had booked the whole of Claridge's for the occasion so that all his out-of-town guests could stay there together, ready to board the private buses that would convey them to Oxfordshire, where the magnificent house and grounds stood as a monument to bygone grandeur.

It had been almost a year since that horrific night aboard *The Lady C*. A thousand different versions of the story had circulated a thousand different times at a thousand different luncheon and dinner parties. Frankly, I was weary of the whole subject, juicy as it was, mainly because I could never tell the truth about what I knew. It's tiring telling lies, which is one of the main reasons social life is so exhausting a lot of the time. What really happened on board the yacht that night would die with me. However, there still was one big piece of the puzzle that I was anxious to drop into place. And that big piece resided at Taunton Hall.

In the past year, Max Vermilion had all but disappeared from view. He was rumored to be depressed about Carla Cole's death, as they had been seen in each other's company so much before she died, enough to warrant speculation that he had found true love—again. And as that love had not had time to sour, as all his other loves had done, he was in seclusion, holed up in his beloved house. I figured that a visit to "The Hall" might somehow satisfy my own curiosity on the subject.

"Everyone's going, Jo!" June Kahn chirped to me over the telephone. "It'll be such great fun!"

June was seriously debating whether or not to wear a tiara for the occasion, an idea Betty found endearingly ludicrous.

"Just call her June, Queen of Scots," Betty said.

June had completely recovered from her accident, and was in an especially bubbly mood now that Carla was gone. She and Charlie were talking about buying Carla's apartment, which Courtney Cole had put on the market at a bargain basement price, just to get rid of it and its forty-thousand-dollar-a-month maintenance. Carla had either forgotten or not bothered to change her will, which left everything to Russell. Carla was judged to have died first, which meant that Russell inherited the fortune Carla had stolen from him. His daughter, in turn, inherited her father's fortune. In a byzantine stroke of justice, Courtney Cole had finally received her birthright.

"If June gets her hands on that apartment, take cover," Betty said. "She really will morph into Catherine the Great."

Despite her somewhat jaundiced view of the whole affair, Betty was anxious to go to Trish's "At Home" soiree. She pointed out that since the party wasn't for charity, it would be more interesting, given the fact that events you have to pay for are generally less fun than private functions. Plus, as she also pointed out, it would be a rare chance to see Taunton Hall "in all its glory."

"Trish'll go over the top because this is Dick's coming-out party—literally. This is their bid to start getting invited everywhere again."

Ever the romantic optimist, Betty still had high hopes for me to become Lady Vermilion, despite Max's dicey history with women.

"I know he's had a weird past, Jo, but he's still available. And let's face it, at our old bat ages, every man's gonna have *some* baggage," Betty said with an air of authority. "Any man who tells you he's baggage-free is lying. It's all coming in on the midnight flight. At least with Max, the steamer trunks are Louis Vuitton, not Samsonite. Plus, you'd be getting that spectacular house!"

I held my tongue, of course. I couldn't even tell Betty the truth about Max Vermilion and why there was no future for us as a couple. Still, I wouldn't have missed this party for the world. For one thing, there was Taunton Hall, and for another, we all owed it to Dick to support him, particularly now, after jail, when he was naturally feeling so vulnerable. And I admit I was curious to see Max again, in light of what I now knew about him. I was dying to learn: Was he the puppet master or not? And although the odds were against my ever finding out for sure, I was interested to see if Carla's death had changed him in any way that might give me some insight.

Taunton Hall, an architecturally improbable jewel, was a hodgepodge of styles joined together by unflinching grandeur. Its hundred-odd rooms reflected a minihistory of England. The earliest section was the towering Gothic hall, now home to the famous collection of Chinese bronzes. There were countless other additions, including early-twentieth-century renovations to unify the façade, made by Max's grandfather, the sixth Earl, "the Building Vermilion," as he was known.

Even the people who had been to numerous balls and parties at Taunton Hall said it never looked more magnificent than it did that night. Trish had pulled out all the stops, opening the mammoth eighteenth-century, wrought-iron gates, which were normally never used, so that guests could arrive in horse-drawn carriages through the old entrance. Rows of flaming torches lit the famously long driveway leading up to that grand fairy-tale castle of a house.

Dick and Trish Bromire stood alongside Max at the head of the Great Gallery, on whose carved wooden panels hung huge ancestral portraits dating back to the sixteenth century. The three of them greeted us guests as we filed by. I'd never seen Dick Bromire looking more fit. He'd lost tons of weight, for one thing, and as we waited in line, Betty opined that he could make a fortune if he came out with a book called *The Prison Diet*.

"Think of it," she said. "It's called having your crime and eating it, too."

Trish was all decked out in jewels again. Her inner and outer glow had returned.

"Eat your heart out, Queen Elizabeth," Ethan whispered to me as we neared our sparkling hostess.

Miranda, who was covering the party for *Nous*, said she'd never seen The Hall looking more splendid.

"Max is always too cheap to do anything but hang a ham out the window," Miranda said. "He thinks the honor of being invited here is enough."

Dick was thrilled we'd all come. I confess I was surprised to see people there who had pointedly turned down his lugubrious "going away" party in New York, people he swore he would never see again. But he was in a jolly and forgiving mood, and it was infectious. People who famously loathed each other were kissing each other hello and having long conversations. As dear June always said, it was all just "social life," where the players drift apart and back together again, like flotsam and jetsam on the tide of fortune. Taking it too seriously was always a mistake, from whatever angle one approached it.

Max greeted me with a rueful smile. He looked worn-out. There were dark circles under his eyes and his quirky confidence seemed to have been punctured. Even his "duration" tuxedo appeared moth-eaten and old-fashioned, as opposed to shabbily chic.

"Ah, Jo, how kind of you to come. You're a loyal friend," he said.

"It was kind of Trish to invite me," I said.

"Traveled a long way, *what*?" he said.

"In more ways than one, Max. In more ways than one."

If he noted my insinuating tone, he didn't show it. He moved on to the next guest and I moved on, too, down that celebrated gallery toward the Great Room, as it was called, where so many friends and *amis mondains* had gathered.

Max appeared very morose that night and people were saying it was because he'd lost the love of his life. They were not referring to Carla, but to Taunton Hall. This evening was Max Vermilion's swan song to his famous house. Betty heard the news from some English friends who were there. Having rented it to Dick for some enormous sum for this one evening, Max was leaving it for good in two days' time. He had finally been forced to sell it because he was no longer able to afford the upkeep, and there was no rich Lady Vermilion to help him out this time. A consortium from Ireland had bought it, hoping to make it into even more of a tourist attraction than it now was by restoring the parts that had fallen into neglect over the years, and by refurbishing those rooms that Max had looted of their treasures.

"He's moving to the Turks and Caicos Islands, if you can believe it!" Betty breathlessly informed me. "Jo, think of it, Max Vermilion is going to become a tax exile! Do you know what that means? He won't be able to stay in any place longer than ninety days. The sun will never set on him for *real*!"

After that, Betty cooled on her idea of my becoming the next Lady Vermilion. To her, Max was no longer the grand Lord of the Rings. He was now merely "the Lord of the Fly-by-Nights," as she dubbed him.

During the cocktail hour, Betty, Gil, Ethan, and I took a tour of the house, sneaking into all the roped-off rooms.

"It may be our last chance to see them," Ethan opined, fearing what the new owners might do. "Unrestored antiques are so much better," he said.

Gil, who basically saw every personal misfortune as an investment opportunity, wandered around wondering what paintings might be for sale. While Ethan and Gil investigated the art, Betty and I sneaked into Max's bedroom. Betty was anxious to see the huge, four-poster bed that had once belonged to Henry the Eighth. We came to a roped-off corridor.

"This must be it," Betty said.

Undeterred by the blocked entryway, Betty scooped up the skirt of her green silk ball gown and ducked under the thick, red rope, beckoning me to follow her. I, too, slid under the decorous barrier and walked with her down a long, dark corridor, at the end of which was a massive, old oak door. Betty cracked it open and peered inside.

"This is it," she said, opening the door so we could enter.

Betty flicked on a switch, which illuminated eight ormolu wall sconces with twinkly, candlelight bulbs. The enormous room was littered with suitcases and packing boxes. The walls were covered in dark blue silk damask. Over an intricately carved white marble fireplace hung an Old Master painting depicting the Rape of Lucrece. Two Gobelin tapestries hung on opposite walls, both showing hunting scenes. There were four towering windows. Their elaborate curtains hung on golden curtain rods with arrows at either end. Against the far wall, facing the fireplace, was the royal four-poster bed, whose canopy was a tapestry of heraldic shields.

Betty navigated her way through the boxes and baggage to get a closer look at the bed's carved posters and headboard.

"Jo!" she cried. "Get a load of this!"

I walked over to the bed and looked up to where Betty was pointing. The entire inside of the canopy was covered by a mirror so that Max could watch his every move in bed. While Betty was inspecting the headboard's famous hunting scenes, I walked over and looked out one of the windows. There lay the great estate, with its great gardens and pavilions, lit up and splendid indeed.

Poor old Max, I thought to myself. Having to give up all this for a beach.

After our little tour, we came back to the Great Room,

where Betty pointed to an old lady sitting alone on an ornately carved chair in the far corner.

"See that old lady over there? That's the dowager Countess—Max's mother, Mimsy Vermilion. I don't see her in a bikini, do you, Jo? That's the Vermilion fire opal around her neck. You have to go have a look. It's the most incredible stone you've ever seen."

As I drew near the old woman, I was dazzled by the fiery red jewel, surrounded by diamonds, hanging on a diamond chain. It looked like the inside of a volcano, and its wearer looked like the outside of a volcano, her expression was so angry. The old lady caught me staring at her and immediately turned away with a sort of disgusted grunt. I felt sorry for the poor old soul, and I figured the nice thing to do would be to go over and talk to her, particularly as no one else seemed to be making the effort.

I approached her, fully expecting her to be one of those feeble nonagenarians with whom conversation would be somewhat of a chore. All dressed in black, this diminutive woman had heavy, mannish features. In fact, she looked a little like Max in drag. Her white hair was pulled back into a wispy chignon, and her square face was patchy with peach powder, the kind old ladies use too much of, hoping to give themselves a healthy color. Her eyes were slightly cloudy from cataracts, and in her desiccated hand she held an old-fashioned lorgnette, through which she peered at the assembled company with a markedly censorious air.

"Who are *you*?" she said accusingly, as I sat down.

"My name is Jo Slater, ma'am. I know your son."

"Everybody knows my son," she said, shrugging.

"I was just admiring your beautiful jewel," I said.

"Don't want to buy it, do you? I can give you a good deal, as you Americans say."

She was a feisty old woman, no question about that.

"No, thank you," I said, laughing.

"What about that Christmas tree over there?" she said, pointing with her lorgnette to the heavily bejeweled Trish Bromire. "Think she'd like to buy it? She looks like the type who likes to spend her husband's money."

"I don't know. Why don't you ask her?"

"Never mind. The less one has to do with these people the better."

I was amused by this bitter old bird. She turned and peered at me through her lorgnette.

"So you know my son, do you? You were never married to him, were you?"

"No," I said, laughing again. I couldn't tell if she were serious or not.

"Lucky you. Impossible man, just like his father. Only in my day we didn't believe in divorce. Satanic thing, divorce. My son married rich girls who all wound up costing him a fortune. Four hundred years, we've lived in this house. Now it's gone. And all because of my son's wretched appetite for silly, spoilt girls. Stupid boy."

"Well, the world is very different than it once was, I guess," I said.

She fingered the fire opal. "Tell that to my son. Never worked a day in his life. . . . Just married all these impossible girls. . . . Look at him over there, feeling sorry for himself." She inclined her head toward Max, who was sitting off by himself in a chair, smoking a cigarette, a drink in his hand, looking extremely forlorn indeed. "He should be feeling sorry for *me, what*? At my age, having to pick up stakes and move to some godforsaken place. And he just sits there, pining over that dreadful girl."

I perked up. "What dreadful girl?"

"Oh, you know, the one he married in secret. His father nearly had a heart attack when he found out. Said we couldn't have a girl like that in the family. I said, 'You married her. You should stick with her,' " she said, pointing an accusatory finger at me as a proxy for Max. "His father won out, of course. No one ever listens to me. I don't believe in divorce. It's what's got the world all upset. Makes things too easy . . . and too expensive."

I couldn't imagine who she was talking about. "Which girl was that?"

"I believe she's referred to in gossip circles as 'the Shady Lady Vermilion.' The Shady Lady Vermilion, indeed," she said with evident distaste. "I knew he'd never get rid of her. And then she shows up *again* . . . mutton dressed as lamb, that one. Tries to impress him by putting a roof on this house. Thought he'd marry her again, she did. And this time his father wasn't around to say no . . . ha! Well, now she's gone. And so's the house and so's the roof. . . . Such is life, I s'pose. But I never dreamed that at my age, I'd have to pick up stakes and move to God-knows-where. Stupid boy . . ."

I was on the edge of my chair.

"Lady Vermilion, let me get this straight. Did you say that the woman who put the roof on this house was once *married* to your son?"

She looked at me with exaggerated wide eyes, as though I were an idiot. "What word in the sentence don't you understand, my dear?" she said irritably. "*Yes*, that is precisely what I said. What of it? Couldn't matter less now. That I should live to see this day!"

I was dumbfounded. Carla Cole was the Shady Lady Vermilion. Suddenly, everything made perfect sense. Carla hadn't wanted to get to the top of New York society at all. What she wanted was a fortune and respectability. She needed both to get Max back. Her aspirations were for Max, not money; her crimes were crimes of passion, not possession. I believe she had truly loved him. And from the disconsolate look on Max's face, he may actually have loved her, too.

Forty-seven

A T THE DINNER, I WAS SEATED NEXT TO MAX, who had apparently requested me. Far from being his aloof, laid-back, slightly bemused self, he was now just plain weary. I thought it odd that he had never gotten in touch with me since my now infamous trip aboard the late *Lady C.* As the waiters passed huge roasts on silver trays, Max gingerly introduced the topic.

"So you've really been through it, eh, Jo? Must have been frightening as hell to sink in the middle of the Atlantic Ocean at night, *what*?"

I gave him what was now my standard answer. "In some ways it was the most thrilling night of my life," I said. I then proceeded to elaborate on all sorts of irrelevant details, obviously omitting the salient one: that I had been forced to push Carla overboard.

"Poor Carla," Max said, as if reading my mind. "I rather enjoyed her. She was a game and generous woman."

"But you didn't know each other all that long, did you, Max?" I said, baiting him, wanting to see how he would respond.

He leaned in close to me. "Jo, I'm going to let you in on a little secret. Carla and I were very old friends."

"Were you?"

"Mmm. . . . knew her before Russell. Before Hernandez, even."

"*Did* you?" I said, feigning surprise and not letting on what his mother had told me. "Why did you bother to hide it?"

"Oh, well, you know, Jo . . . women like Carla . . . a fella doesn't like to advertise the fact, *what*?"

We sat in silence for a few seconds. Max stared into space, lost in thought.

"You really loved her, didn't you, Max?"

He winced. "I'm going to miss this old place," he said, avoiding my question.

"Max, I know you were once married to Carla."

He looked at me askance.

"How'd you know that?" he asked, obviously disconcerted.

"Your mother told me you were once married to the woman who put a roof on this house . . . Carla was the Shady Lady Vermilion."

Max shrugged. "Leave it to mother to lose everything but her memory."

"Max, I have to ask you this—not that I expect you to tell me the truth." I paused. "Did you put her up to it?"

"What?" he said softly.

"Marrying Hernandez and Russell?"

Max lowered his head. "That poor friend of yours who was killed, Jo . . ."

"Larry, you mean?"

"No . . . that woman . . . from Las Vegas . . . I believe her name was Ginger somebody." He shot me a glance out of the corner of his eye.

I suddenly felt uncomfortable.

"I don't know what you're talking about, Max."

He stared at me and raised his eyebrows. "No? Really? That's odd. Carla said you did. Told me you and Ginger were quite chummy at one time."

He *knew*. Max knew.

"Well, she was wrong," I told him. "I've never met anyone with that name."

"Oh," he said, nodding. "Well, you can't meet her now. She's dead. Murdered. Ghastly sort of death . . . I must be mistaken, then."

"Yes, you must be."

He paused. I thought that was the end of it, but it wasn't.

"And yet . . ." he went on, "I don't think I am." He smiled. " 'Course, I can't prove it. Very difficult to prove past associations and connections, *what*? And what does it all matter now anyway? Let sleeping dogs lie, that's my motto."

I suddenly understood what was going on. Max *had* put Carla up to it—just as I had suspected. He was the grand puppeteer after all. And this was his way of telling me that he knew all about me, too, and that the two of us had secrets that were better kept to ourselves.

"I think I'm going to enjoy my new life," he said, leaning back in his chair. "As one gets older one prefers warm weather. I'll miss The Hall, of course, but then, all good things must come to an end. No use looking back, *what*?"

Max tilted his head upward toward the vaulted ceiling,

and sat very still for a long moment with a rueful smile on his face. I imagined him basking on a Turks and Caicos beach, gradually tiring of bright, sunny days, thinking about Carla, and longing for his big, old, damp house, now gone, like the love of his life, forever.

Forty-eight

IN ACCORDANCE WITH HER FATHER'S WISHES, Courtney Cole gave the Cole collection to Tulsa, Oklahoma, his hometown. Courtney is building a museum there in her father's memory. Blow as it was to the Muni, Justin Howard didn't protest. The Municipal Museum is above such things. Justin and Edmond took me out to lunch several times, begging me to come back on the board. Eventually, I gave in and said I would. They were thrilled. So was Ethan. There's no point in holding a grudge, although I did mention to Justin my motto: I may not remember, but I never forget.

Charlie persuaded June not to buy the Wilman apartment. He told her it was bad luck since Carla had owned it. June listened to him for once. It's back on the market. The Bromires are back in circulation again, more social than ever. Jail isn't the stigma it once was. In fact, it adds a certain cachet, as well as being an endless source of dinner anecdotes. Betty says that "Prison is the new pink!"

She and Gil are the same, although they do seem a little concerned about Missy's marriage.

"The wedding was enough angst for a lifetime," she told me. "I simply can't take a divorce!"

Miranda continues to chronicle us all in the glossy pages of *Nous*. I miss Larry more than ever. There was just no one like him. Some people really are indispensable.

They never did find Russell Cole. Some say that he's still alive. There are occasional reports of sightings, and he has taken on one of those mythical personas that live forever, like Judge Crater or Elvis. In New York circles, the story of Russell Cole has become a staple of social life, which, like the sea, just goes on and on and on.

Acknowledgments

My thanks again to John Novograd and to the many friends who have cheered me on and up at various times during the writing of this book—especially Kathy Rayner and Lynn de Rothschild.

I am grateful to Captain Rick and Kirsten Morales, Captain Steve Martin, and Dionne Reed, for letting me draw on their nautical expertise and grand imaginations.

My deep thanks to Chuck Adams, a perceptive and patient editor.

And special thanks, as always, to Jonathan Burnham.

Thank you, too, C.L.H.

About the Author

JANE STANTON HITCHCOCK has written three previous novels, the best-selling *Social Crimes, The Witches' Hammer,* and *Trick of the Eye,* which was nominated for both the Edgar Award and the Hammett Prize as the Best First Novel of the Year. She lives in New York and Washington, D.C.